# BLACK AS MIDNIGHT

*An Ariel Kimber Novel*

## MARY MARTEL

Black as Midnight
An Ariel Kimber Novel
By: Mary Martel

❀ Created with Vellum

# DEDICATION

Dedication-
To my girls who are the absolute best thing that ever happened
to me.
Always the bright spots in my life.
Love you. You have no idea how much.

<3

# CHAPTER ONE

The bell over the door jingled and I looked up from the book I had been reading to see who'd entered Fortune's for the Unfortunate. Tyson Alexander, one of my boyfriends, owned the store, and I had a sneaking suspicion that he'd mostly bought it for me. I refused to ask him flat out because I was afraid of the answer I would get in response. Denial and avoidance were my specialties.

From his perch beside me on the counter, Binx hissed at the new arrival.

I knew it wasn't exactly normal to bring your cat to work with you every day, but Binx had insisted and my boss could give a crap less what I did, seeing as he was one of my boyfriends and all, so the little guy came along with me every day. The customers who came in never seemed to mind and thought he was cute... until he hissed at them after they tried to pet him, that is. Then they thought he was a little demon and I always ended up having to apologize for him. That never stopped me from bringing him back with me though.

Binx wouldn't take no for an answer and I knew that sounded insane since we were talking about a cat here, but it was the

1

honest truth. Every time I left to go to work, the damn cat ran out of the cottage door before I could get it closed, and he'd be waiting at my Rover for me to get inside. He'd get in the Rover and ride to work with me without making a peep.

It was weird behavior for a cat, but then Binx was just a weird cat and I'd long since stopped questioning the things he did. Dash always acted like the things his cat did were normal, so I rolled with that and pretended for his sake that this was true.

I was good at pretending most things were normal when they absolutely were not.

"Hi! How can I help you?" I asked, before looking up to see who'd walked through the front door and made the bell jingle.

The smile on my face froze in place and I blinked several times to see if I was really seeing the person who was walking toward the front counter.

"Ariel," Marcus Cole said in a kind, gentle voice. "It's good to see you, sweetheart."

I swallowed painfully past the lump of emotions suddenly lodged in my throat.

Binx hissed angrily and I shooed the damn cat off the counter before he could swipe at Marcus with his claws. I didn't need him drawing blood, not in this shop when bleeding meant more than it normally would, and there were so many things that your blood could be used for.

The cat hopped off the counter and sashayed his way toward the shelves. His tail swished from side to side as he sauntered off, acting like he hadn't just looked feral and like he was almost ready to attack someone.

I sighed as I shook my head.

"Sorry about Binx, Marcus," I apologized quietly for the stupid cat, without looking Marcus in the eyes.

Marcus Cole and I used to have the type of relationship where I looked to him as a father figure, and not just because he'd been sleeping with my fake mother while we'd lived with him. It had

2

more to do with the kind heart he had and the fact he'd been the first adult male in my life to show that he cared about me. Hell, not even the first adult male, but just the first *adult*. Somewhere along the line things had gotten strained between the two of us though, and I wasn't entirely sure why.

I knew he was once again living in the house next door to the Alexander home, the house my mother and I had lived in with him when I'd first moved here. Quinton told me that he'd talked to Marcus about me on several occasions, updating him on what was going on in my life, and he knew pretty much everything about me and all the little things he'd missed when I thought he'd moved away. At first, it had felt nice that Marcus had been checking in on me and Quinton was the perfect person to talk to if you wanted to know anything about me, because Quinton was my ultimate stalker and he worked really hard to be good at it.

Then, after awhile, I had started to feel uncomfortable with it because although he was asking Quinton about me, Marcus never once approached me to see how I was doing or to even talk to me *at all*. I wanted him to check in with me about me. Not go through Quinton. I wanted to have a relationship with Marcus Cole, almost desperately so, and my feelings were getting hurt the more this went on.

And now he was here in front of me, talking to me in his gentle voice that melted my heart immediately and calling me sweetheart. The important question was why? To all of it.

He smiled at me and my chest burned. It had been so long.

"Don't worry about the cat," he said. "I bet he's like that to most men who come around you."

I frowned at him. Umm... say what?

I thought about what he said but shook my head, because I couldn't remember Binx being around another female before so I just assumed that he halfway hated everyone.

"What?" I asked in confusion.

His smile grew bigger. "Never you mind," he rushed to tell me.

3

He hurriedly looked around the empty store before back to me and inquired, "Are you busy?"

I, too, looked around the empty store before smirking at him. "Nope." I shrugged. "Noon time is really slow around here. There's a whole crowd of old ladies who stop in during the mornings for herbs, candles, and a bunch of other weird stuff. Then there's an afternoon crowd of school kids that don't really come here for any reason other than to either make fun of stuff or pretend like witchcraft is the newest trend, and they spend their allowances on things they don't know anything about. The night crowd is where it really gets interesting though, but I don't get to work that shift very much. Julian and Dash or the twins usually work the night shift. Sometimes Ty does."

I slammed my mouth shut as soon as I realized I was rambling away because I was nervous. Another fault I had was diarrhea of the mouth and it got worse whenever I felt nervous or scared... or pretty much anything. Who was I kidding? I always blurted out things I shouldn't.

Ever heard that some things were better left unsaid? Well, I failed at it almost every time.

Marcus cleared his throat and cautiously, quietly, asked, "Can you join me for lunch then, since there are no customers and won't be for a few hours?"

His voice was hopeful but hesitant, almost as if he were scared of what my answer would be. Like he was afraid I would reject him.

"If you have to call someone to come and sit here while you're gone," he continued, "I don't mind waiting for them to get here."

Please. Like they'd leave me here alone and all by myself. That would never happen. I was never alone anymore, even when I woke up in the morning and thought I had the whole house to myself, I was wrong. If Dash needed to go somewhere, then someone else came over and waited for me to get up. I had no idea how I even got to drive myself to the shop alone, but then I guess the stupid cat came with me and I wasn't actually alone.

"Rain's here," I told him cheerfully. "He won't have a problem coming up front and watching over the store for me."

The smile slid right off my face when I watched his mouth tighten in anger and his eyes drop to the floor.

"Marcus," I started hesitantly, "what's wrong?"

"Your father and I don't get along very well," he told me quietly. "I get along with him when I need to and will be nice to him when I'm in his presence, but that doesn't mean I like him. I'm not going to lie to you and pretend otherwise. I have been doing as he asked me to do and giving you space, but I can't wait any longer. I miss you and I am not going to hide from you anymore because of him. I understand why he wanted to keep you to himself for a while, he's your father and you were taken away from him. I get it, if you were my blood and that had been done to us, then I would want to keep you locked up and to myself too. But, as much as I wish it were different, you aren't my blood and you aren't my real daughter. You're his. He has that on me, but that doesn't mean you aren't important to me and I'm not going to treat you like you're my real daughter because I am. I realize that in doing what he's asked me to do, I might have hurt your feelings and made you feel like you don't matter to me when that's not the truth at all. Rain can hate it all he wants but I'm done doing as he says. Done. I'm going to fight for you and if Rain Kimber has a problem with that, then he can just suck it up because there's nothing he can do about it anymore."

I gaped at him.

Was he serious?

When had Rain said something to him, warned him away from me? And, more importantly, why had no one told me about it? I knew for a fact that Quinton and Tyson both knew about this because, oddly enough, Rain seemed to like them both a great deal and the three of them were always talking and acting like they were BFF's. Did this make me uncomfortable, my dad being BFF's with two of my boyfriends? Nope, not in the slightest. If anything, it made me happy to see that they had an older, male role model in their life. They needed to have good people in their lives and, even though Rain was all kinds of scary, he was still good people to me.

The fact that he told Marcus to stay away from me shouldn't really have surprised me, but it had more so caught me off guard than anything else. Marcus would never hurt me and I didn't understand or see the point in warning him off from me.

"I don't understand," I told Marcus seriously, and it was no lie. I couldn't understand why you wouldn't want your child to be surrounded with as many people who loved her and cared about her as possible.

What was Rain trying to do here by alienating Marcus?

"You don't need to worry about that, sweetheart," Marcus growled fiercely. "I'm going to take care of it and I'll make sure it's not your problem to deal with. I can handle Rain Kimber and, I promise you, he'll understand me."

That didn't sound good at all. Was he threatening my father? I hoped not, because Marcus was a really nice man and normally I wouldn't worry about him, but since he no longer practiced his craft and Rain very much did, I felt like I had to worry about him or maybe warn him away from Rain because, like I said earlier, Rain could be very scary.

"Marcus," I hedged, "I don't think—"

He casually waved off my words, as if swatting them right out of the air. Something warm leaked out of him with the wave of his hand and tingles shot down my spine. I looked down at my bare arms to see the tiny hairs on them standing up straight and at attention.

Slowly, I raised my eyes to look at the kind, gentle man standing across the counter from me and my eyes widened as I took him in, really looked him over, for the first time since he walked in here.

Even though it felt kind of gross for me to think it, I wasn't blind, so I couldn't help but notice that Marcus Cole was an incredibly attractive older man. He was in his mid to late fifties, I hadn't ever asked his age before because I felt it rude to do so, but I remember Vivian having said something about him being in his fifties. He didn't look his age though, and if I had to guess I would pinpoint him in his early forties at the oldest. He had light brown hair that when I'd first met him had only had a sprinkling of salt at the temples, but had since spread out through his hair. I hoped I wasn't at fault for his hair turning white, but I felt guilty because I was sure I had a hand in a good deal of it. On a high note for him though, he was going to look like what women called a silver fox, and it was just going to add to his attractiveness. His eyes were a soft brown that were usually filled to the brim with kindness when aimed in my direction but, unfortunately, were lacking their usual depth of kindness at the moment. I assumed this was due to Rain and had absolutely nothing to do with me.

"Go and get Rain, sweetheart," he ordered me.

I snapped my mouth shut as my eyes grew round. Going and getting Rain was the absolute last thing I think I should be doing at this moment in time.

"Uhh," I mumbled under my breath, "maybe that's not such a good idea."

If Rain had warned him against me, then there was no way he'd appreciate him showing up here unannounced, especially since this wasn't just where I worked, but where Rain actually lived too. And, with Marcus clearly being aggressive about the matter and deciding he's done with Rain's shit, this was just a recipe for disaster all around and I didn't want to get hit in the crosshairs.

The look on Marcus's face let me know that arguing with him would be utterly pointless on this subject, so I picked up my cell phone and quickly sent a text off to Rain, letting him know who was here and that I needed him to cover the store for me so I could go out to lunch with my guest.

I set the phone down on the countertop without waiting for a response. Rain rarely texted me back when I was here, instead he always chose to just come to where I was so he could respond face-to-face.

Marcus asked me questions about the store while we waited for Rain to show up. I didn't know if he was genuinely interested or simply asking to be polite, but I answered every question to the best of my ability.

He was smiling down at me with a soft look on his face when Rain walked in from the back entrance.

"What are you doing with *my* daughter, Marcus?" Rain growled menacingly.

I sighed heavily as I looked at my biological dad. He was really going overboard with this whole dad routine. The corner of my mouth tipped up because I couldn't help but love how over-the-top protective he was when it came to me. I'd take all the love I could get, even if it did come from a crazy man.

Rain looked at me and smirked, almost like he knew that no matter what he said or did, it wouldn't mean shit to me because I would love him anyways.

My breath caught in my throat as I stared at him. Rain never smiled unless he was with me. Usually he had a dead, empty look in his eyes that were the same color as my own, and he looked like he could strangle you to death and walk away whistling, without a care in the world.

My dad looked a lot like me, except he was taller and male. I wasn't a short girl though, by any means, and he was still taller than me. We were both on the thin side, but where I was simply thin, Rain was hard and made up entirely of compact muscles. We had the same eyes and ash blond hair. My hair went down past my shoulders and I couldn't remember the last time I'd had it cut.

Rain's hair was shaggy and he too looked like he probably couldn't remember the last time he'd gotten it cut. For once, he was missing his trademark black trench coat that he always wore. He had on a black, long-sleeved thermal shirt, dark blue jeans, and black combat boots.

I looked down at my feet and grinned. We had similar taste in footwear.

I wished he would have pushed his sleeves up his arms because I knew he had a plethora of tattoos on his forearms and other places, and I had yet to see a single one of them. I knew he put magic into them somehow and some of them were for protection. We'd been training for months now, just the two of us, and no matter how many times I asked or how often, he refused to push his sleeves up or tell me anymore about his tattoos. Instead, he always told me that when the time was right he'd share with me.

The smile left my face because I remembered that I was losing patience with Rain, and now he was being an asshole to Marcus who'd done nothing wrong.

"I came to take her to lunch," Marcus answered evenly without missing a beat or returning Rain's hostility.

"Maybe she'd rather have lunch with me," Rain shot back, and I shook my head as I crossed my arms over my chest.

"Really, Rain?" I muttered. "You're going to do this now?"

Rain glared at me and I felt my lips tip up again. That look would have normal people squirming and hoping and praying not to piss themselves. I wasn't normal and I knew I was the only weakness Rain had. He'd never do anything to harm me and that look was all bullshit when directed my way.

"Really, Ariel," he mocked. "You're going to do this now? Here I thought you'd want to spend time with your *real* father and not some pretender who'd chosen your kidnapper over you."

I gaped at him.

"Rain," I hissed angrily.

That was taking things too far, even for him. Marcus had

cared about Vivian and she was dead. I didn't think it was right to hold that against him, no matter what she'd done or what kind of person she'd been when she was alive. There was no reason Marcus needed to be blamed for her mistakes or the fact he'd given a shit about her.

"What?" Rain asked innocently.

I sighed. There was no point arguing with him sometimes. Rain was the single most stubborn person I had ever met in my entire life and once he made up his mind, that was it.

"Are you going to hang out up here while I'm gone or do I need to lock the place up?" I inquired in exasperation.

He glared at me before turning that angry look on Marcus and snarling, "If anything happens to her while she's with you, I'll rip your goddamned heart out of your chest and stomp on it."

With that, he plucked Binx up off the counter and turned away, heading in the direction of the table that the boys used to read cards and tell fortunes.

My mouth hung open as I watched Binx's tail twitch and I heard the little traitor start to purr.

"Well," Marcus drawled, "shall we be on our way now?"

I sighed as I grabbed my phone and hurried after him. I hoped Rain didn't scare off too many customers in my absence. He and Quinton often scared people away.

# CHAPTER TWO

I picked at the corner of the menu nervously. This place
wasn't some fancy-shmancy place that I was expecting
Marcus to take us to when he said he had a restaurant in
mind. This place wasn't a dive either. It was quaint, clean, and
judging by the family filled booths, family friendly.

For the first time since sitting down after the hostess had led
us to the booth, I finally looked across the table at Marcus. I had
never been uncomfortable around the man before and couldn't
exactly pinpoint why I seemed to be nothing but uncomfortable
now.

Marcus didn't seem to be having the same problem as me. In
fact, he looked right at home in his side of the booth. He'd
removed his suit jacket and placed it over the back of his seat
before sliding into the booth, where he'd immediately unbuttoned
his sleeves and rolled his shirt up to his elbows. He'd then sat
back and flipped open his menu. He'd been immersed in it ever
since.

I'd opened my menu but I hadn't actually read a single item on
the stupid thing. This was unbearably awkward for me and I

hated that this was now how I felt around him when I cared so much for him.

"What can I get ya to drink?" a bubbly young woman asked in a chirpy voice.

"I'll have a Diet Coke," Marcus answered without looking up from his menu.

The waitress looked at me expectantly and I muttered that I'd have a Coke. She wrote it down on her little notepad before bouncing off the way she'd come.

"Uh, Marcus," I mumbled.

He peeked at me over the top of his menu. "We can talk after we order," he told me in a gentle voice.

We read over the menus in silence, and it wasn't long before the waitress came back with our drinks and sat them on the table. Marcus carefully placed his menu down and eyed me shrewdly. I got the hint, placed my menu on top of his, and turned to the waitress. After rattling off what I wanted to eat, Marcus ordered for himself. Always the gentleman was Marcus Cole.

I sighed. I hadn't had him in my life for very long, but I sure had missed him when he was gone from it.

The waitress wandered off with our menus in hand after having written down our orders. I stared at Marcus expectantly. I wasn't so sure how much I bought the whole he missed me thing and Rain had been keeping him at bay. I didn't want to think it of Marcus, but most people only came around because they usually wanted something from you. I had taken enough from him already and would give him almost anything he wanted. All he had to do was ask it of me.

He opened his mouth to speak but closed it quickly at the sound of my cell phone ringing.

I pulled it out of my hoodie pocket, looked down at the lit up screen, and sighed heavily. I couldn't do anything these days without Quinton calling me to make sure everything was copacetic with me. Ever since I'd given him his Christmas present he'd been weird with me. Well, weirder than normal, which was off the freaking charts to begin with. He was turning into a stage five clinger and he was driving me absolutely insane.

Unfortunately for me I had to take his phone calls even if I didn't want to, because I didn't like what happened when I didn't pick up the phone. Embarrassingly enough, he would take it upon himself to show up where I was at to check up on me like I was a misbehaving child or something.

I put the phone to my ear and grumbled, "What now?"

He chuckled quietly and I wanted to punch him. Why was he laughing at me? I'd done nothing amusing.

"Always so sweet, baby," he joked.

"Quinton," I groaned. "What do you want? Why are you calling me?"

"Did it not occur to you that I could be calling simply because I missed the sound of your beautiful voice?"

Blushing, I rolled my eyes skyward. He was out of control and I was already done with this phone conversation.

"No," I told him honestly, "that thought had not actually occurred to me because I'm not stupid, and I know you way better than that. I'd be willing to stake my life on the fact Rain called you and tattled about me leaving the shop with Marcus. Rain's a psycho. You're a psycho. And now I'm having to deal with crazy bullshit from the both of you. So, please, do not waste any more of my time and just spit out why you called me. I would like to enjoy my time with Marcus while I have it, and you're messing that up for me."

He was quiet for a minute and I couldn't tell if I'd surprised him, or if he was backpedaling and trying to figure out how to placate me. That was one of his new tactics, trying to placate me. Somewhere along the line he'd stopped trying to rile me up and piss me off, and instead had started working really hard to get on my good side. I didn't know what he was playing at, but I had stopped trying to figure him out a while ago so I just rolled with it. It usually saved me a headache.

"Alright," he sighed into the phone. "I'll give you that one, though, to be fair, you do have a beautiful voice and I miss hearing it when I'm forced to go without it for any given amount of time."

"Quinton," I snapped when he seemed to be done with his explanation that wasn't really one in the slightest bit. He was being ridiculous.

From across the table, Marcus started laughing. I grinned at him, knowing full well why he was laughing. Everyone liked it when I gave Quinton a hard time because he usually deserved it, and nobody else would ever dare poke at him. I got away with it because he liked me.

"Is everything going okay with you and Marcus?" he asked in a tone I had never heard out of him before.

He sounded nervous, which was extremely out of character for him.

The smile slid right off my face. What would make Quinton nervous? I feared I didn't want to know, but I had to ask.

With nothing for it, I blurted out, "What's wrong with you now?"

The boys all were used to me blurting my thoughts out at random and they never seemed to mind. This time was no different because he didn't even comment on it.

"It's just that, ahh..." He muttered and my eyes got bigger and bigger with each word out of his mouth. This wasn't the Uncle Quint I knew and loved speaking. "Rain might have threatened Marcus if anything happens to you while you're with him. And he's, well... I believe he'll do as he says and that worries me. Not that I'm worried about Marcus," he rushed out, "but it's you that I worry about. If Rain did something to harm Marcus, you would never forgive him because you're so attached to the man. I wouldn't put anything past Rain when it comes to you."

His words sent chills down my spine and had me frantically looking around the restaurant for Rain who I feared might now pop out of thin air like the boogeyman.

"What did he threaten?" I whispered, deciding it was best to keep my voice down just in case the boogeyman was invisible and able to hear me. I wasn't willing to chance it.

"That's not important," Quinton stated. "What's important is that you stay safe so I don't have to fight your dad because he unintentionally hurt you."

Fight my...

Fight my *dad?*

I pulled my phone away and stared at it, stupefied. Had he really just said that to me? Now I wanted to punch him more than ever!

"You can't fight Rain," I hissed hysterically after putting the phone back to my ear.

Marcus's eyebrows shot up high on his forehead as his eyes rounded in surprise.

"I'll do whatever the fuck I need to do," Quinton countered with a confidence that had me slumping in my booth. There was the Uncle Quint I knew and loved. Lucky me. "You just make sure nothing happens to you and that you stay safe. I can trust you to take care of yourself for the afternoon, can't I?"

How dare he? Like I couldn't look after myself? Like I got into trouble all the time and needed him to watch out for me?

As if!

I pulled the phone away from my ear and clicked the red button on the screen that ended the call. I wasn't going to argue with him anymore, it was a waste of my time and would only drive me insane. Quinton *always* drove me insane.

I tossed my phone down onto the tabletop and slumped back in the seat. I raised my hands to my face and rubbed my eyes tiredly.

"Did I hear you correctly?" Marcus asked in a voice that shook with laughter. "Did you say that Quinton Alexander wanted to fight your father?"

I squeezed my eyes shut tightly and prayed for either a miracle or a lobotomy. Either would work for me at the moment.

"I don't think we should talk about Quinton anymore," I grumbled, then groaned when I heard Marcus's quiet laughter.

"Would you like to talk about Rain instead?" he inquired and I whimpered.

"Nooooo."

"Everyone in your life seems to be quite the handful," he remarked, and I had the distinct impression he was laughing at me.

He wasn't wrong. Even though my life wasn't hard anymore and I wasn't getting kicked down at every turn, my life was still kind of crazy all the time. It was crazy before Rain came into it and the chaos had doubled since his arrival. As it was turning out, I actually enjoyed chaos in the extreme.

"Are you laughing at me, Marcus?" I asked, as I lowered my hands and peeked at him across the table. He smiled at me and shook his head, but I didn't believe him.

"I happen to like my life as it is at the moment," I informed him snottily. "Thank you very much."

Okay, so that wasn't exactly the entire truth because I could have actually done without the phone call from the psycho boyfriend and the looming threat from my psychotic father. I figured Marcus was aware of that, which is why his smile grew even larger.

As much as I enjoyed seeing him smile and acting like he was happy, I couldn't pretend that things were normal between us when they weren't. I was working really hard to not hide from things anymore and confront them head on. It made my life a whole lot easier if I stopped avoiding things and dealt with them right away. It made me worry less and it actually made it a little easier to just breathe.

"Why are we here, Marcus?" I questioned him plainly. "You avoided me because of Rain, you said, and I can completely understand that. Really, I do. Then you pop up out of the blue to take me to lunch and I would really like to know why. I love that we get to spend time together again, honestly, I do. I missed you so much and I'm glad you told me why you haven't been around. But now I want to know, really know, why you're here now. And don't try to lie to me because I've gotten really good at telling when people are lying to me."

I was also working really hard with Julian to try and come up with some type of spell to ink onto my body that will let me know when someone is lying to me. It had been something I'd been thinking about ever since I found out about Ty's, which let him know when people were trying to use magic on him. I figured I'd start little with the lies and work up to something big like the magic. It wasn't working out very well because Julian excelled at healing people, and I feared he had no idea what he was doing when it came to anything else. I'd never tell him that though.

Marcus sighed heavily and then I watched as he slumped back into the seat.

The waitress showed up with plates of our food and placed them on the table before heading back the way she came.

I watched him while I started eating. Marcus unwrapped his silverware and placed his napkin in his lap.

I tried for patience while I ate, but it was hard. Thankfully, he set his fork down and started talking.

"You're right," he admitted quietly. "I did have something I needed to share with you, which is why I took you out for lunch. I didn't want to discuss it with any of the others around because I'm not ready for this information to get out amongst our community yet."

He paused to take a sip of his Diet Coke and I shoveled another forkful of food into my mouth. I didn't like the way this conversation was starting out. My boys wouldn't run their mouths off to anyone and share his business within the community. They kept to themselves. And Rain... well, he lived on the very, very outskirts of the community and had no intentions of changing that any time soon. In fact, he hid from the Council and they had no idea he'd returned to my life. He didn't want them to know anything about him and I couldn't say that I blamed him in the least, because I, too, wanted absolutely nothing to do with those creepy assholes.

"The Council has asked me if I'd ever take any interest in joining them."

I choked on the food I'd just put into my mouth. I swallowed and quickly chugged some of my pop. I slammed the cup down on the table with more force than necessary and some of the Coke sloshed out.

"You said no?" I croaked out. At least I hoped like hell he'd said no. Anything else would be unacceptable to me.

"I told them I'd think about it."

"No," I whispered. How could he say such a thing to me? Was this some kind of a sick joke? This was Marcus, and after what had happened with his sister I would never have thought I'd hear these words come out of his mouth.

He leaned over the table and I reciprocated the gesture.

"Tell me you said no," I begged. "Those are not good people, Marcus, and you know this. You of all people know this. How could you possibly want that for your life? How could you possibly want *them* in your life?"

I didn't understand any of this and I know it didn't make much sense, but I honestly felt a little betrayed that he would even consider such a thing. And it also scared me on his behalf. If something happened to Marcus, it would rip a hole in my heart that would be irreparable.

Marcus's face took on an ugly look, an angry one I'd never seen on him before.

"I know what Rain is," he whispered in a dark voice, which I wouldn't have recognized as his if he wasn't sitting directly across from me while speaking. "And I know what his family does. I guess I could say what your family does."

I jerked back in the seat and began to shake uncontrollably. The dishes on the table began to rattle along with my body and the lights overhead flickered.

First, Quinton had threatened Rain. Now, Marcus was sitting across from me, and talking about things that he shouldn't have been talking about and they involved Rain.

Rain was mine, all mine, and nobody, absolutely nobody, got to mess with him. Not even Marcus Cole.

I placed my palms flat against the table and leaned forward hostilely. "How dare you," I spat out. "If you think you can sell Rain out to the Council then you've got another thing coming, Marcus. He's my *family*, the only real blood family I have left, and if you cared about me at all, you would shut your damn mouth and never speak of this or him in this way again. You have to know that you mean the world to me and I love you. But this..." I shook my head. "This is what's going to be the death of that love I have for you."

Marcus reached across the table and picked up my hands in his own. He squeezed them gently. The angry look on his face melted away and the kindness he usually radiated when I was around started to shine through.

My shaking slowed down minimally, until only a slight tremor remained. The heat he gave off engulfed my hands and spread up my arms, seeping into my skin and filling my body with warmth.

"I hate the Council," he whispered hoarsely, the emotion thick in his voice. "With every ounce of my soul, I hate every single member of the Council. Most people would be overjoyed by being asked to join their ranks. I am not like most people."

I squeezed his hands in a show of support. I was right there with him in his hatred, only I didn't have a personal reason to hate them the way he did. I disliked them because of their views on women and shady behavior. Plus, it didn't hurt that they terrified me.

"I'm going to take them up on the offer, I think," he divulged, in the same thick voice.

My body twitched and I tried to jerk my hands away from his. He wouldn't let me go.

"They do despicable things, Ariel. Unimaginable things, and they get away with it because there's no one to stand up to them. My poor sister... I want to do this for her. For all the other females out there whose lives are lost to the Council."

My eyes bulged and I hissed, "They're killing girls?"

What the hell? That went against everything I'd heard about them and seen for myself. It made absolutely no sense to me that they would kill them.

"No, sweetheart, that's not what I meant at all," he rushed out to assure me. "I just meant that to end up in their clutches is to lose your life, because it's no longer your own to live. Once the Council has control over you, it's over for you for the rest of your life because you no longer have free will. That's what they did with my sister and she couldn't handle it. It destroyed my family and ruined her. It happens to too many of our females and there's nothing to stop them from doing it."

He drew in a deep, shuddering breath and my heart hurt for him and those girls he was talking about. I was lucky to have been found by my coven when I was, because the Council could no longer get their greedy hands on me. They'd have to go through my entire coven in order to get me.

"The only way I know to be able to help my people is by joining the Council and trying to make some sort of a difference from the inside. In a way, it's the only way I can see to actually make an attempt at a successful stand against them. But, if you can't get on board and be okay with it, then I want you to be honest with me and I won't do it."

I pulled on my hands and this time he let me go. He sat back in his side of the booth and his eyes grew guarded. He was worried I was going to wrongfully judge him and thought this was going to be the turning point in our relationship where things went badly for us. It's what he didn't want me to see behind that guard he'd put up.

I took a drink of my pop and tried to calm myself down while I did it. It hurt me to know that he thought I would ever try to stop him from doing something he felt so strongly about. When he went to move away and I wanted him to stay with me so badly, I never said a word to him about him staying because I knew how important it was to him for him to go at the time. I had my moments like any other teenager out there where I could be selfish, that was just life. But I'd never been selfish where Marcus was concerned and I didn't appreciate that he thought I was capable of being so with him now.

I set my pop down on the table and sat back in my booth. I crossed my arms over my chest and glared at him.

His guard fell away and he grinned at me.

"What do you have to smile about?" I grumbled.

"It's good to see you," he said, "to finally see who you really are when you're not having to hide from everybody around you. You've got quite the personality and, if I must say, attitude. It looks good on you. I wish you had felt safe enough in my home for it to have come out when you lived with me, but I understand why you had to keep yourself hidden away."

I looked down at the tabletop to avoid having to meet his eyes at the moment. There was too much emotion there and it was making me feel uncomfortable.

"Thanks," I muttered ungraciously. Not that what he'd said about having an attitude really warranted receiving a thank you from me. "Of course I'll support you in this. I'd support anything you decided to do because you're a good person, Marcus. I know you're not capable of doing something that would hurt others. I actually think that it's a really good idea, but not something I think I could ever stomach doing myself. I don't think I'd be able to spend that much time around them without my true feelings coming out and ruining the whole thing."

Marcus relaxed, and at seeing it, I knew how much it meant to him to have my support. I knew in that moment I was going to have a seriously uncomfortable conversation with Rain, because I wasn't going to allow him to threaten Marcus in any way anymore, he meant too much to me, and if Rain did anything to him it would ruin our relationship forever. I didn't want to be the person to tell Rain what he could and couldn't do, that didn't sound like it would be fun for me and I knew he wouldn't take it well. Maybe it would be something I could try and pawn off on Quinton.

Yeah. That sounded better to me.

"You have to be careful with the Council, Marcus," I warned him. "You have to promise me you'll be careful. I can't lose you and those assholes are scary, they won't hesitate to do something horrible to you if they find out what you're doing. *And* they are incredibly powerful witches. The most powerful out there, I think."

"I'll be careful," he promised me in a gruff voice.

A thought struck me and I leaned forward over the table again. "What about magic?" I asked him in a hushed voice. His eyebrows rose in question and confusion. "You no longer practice magic, remember? I imagine the Council isn't going to allow you to continue abstaining once you join them."

As far as I knew, Marcus hadn't used his magic in a very, very long time. It was sad really. I couldn't imagine not using my magic now that I knew I had it inside me. It's what made me special and I never wanted to give it up. Now that I thought about it, there were a lot of things about Marcus that made me really sad.

He cleared his throat. "I started practicing again," he quietly admitted. "I had forgotten how much I loved being a witch, how much I loved using my magic. I won't have any problems on that front."

I was happy to hear it.

"The boys, I'm sure, will figure it out on their own once they hear that I've joined ranks with the Council. Still, I would rather we kept this conversation between the two of us, if that's alright with you. I'm not asking you to lie to them, but I would ask—"

I cut him off mid-sentence. "My lips are sealed, Marcus, you can count on me."

He sighed in relief. "Good. I may need your help from time to time as well."

I nodded my head. I could help him, sure. If he wanted Quinton to kick his ass, that is. Rain as well. Maybe even Julian, he seemed like the sweet type but I knew underneath the surface lurked a vindictive psychopath just waiting to come out and play with the rest of us. He only hid it better. Maybe even Dash would get in on kicking his ass as well. Heck, they would all probably want in on it at this point.

"Let's eat our food, sweetheart," he said. "That's enough discussion for today."

I looked down at my plate and sighed. It was probably cold now, but I would eat all of it anyways. I didn't like being wasteful. Not when I knew what it felt like to go hungry.

# CHAPTER THREE

I sat in my Range Rover parked in front of Fortune's for the Unfortunate as I debated whether or not I really wanted to go inside to confront Rain. Marcus had dropped me off and had long since gone, but for whatever reason I couldn't bring myself to go inside yet.

Rain would question me, this I was certain of, and I feared Marcus's secrets would be there in my eyes for him to see and he'd up his game with the questions. Then I'd have to lie to him and he'd know when I was lying. He had the uncanny ability to always tell when I was lying. And I wasn't quite ready to confront him just yet.

So going in there with him wasn't really the best option for me at the moment. The problem was, I didn't see anyone else's cars parked out front and, unless someone had been dropped off while I'd been gone, that meant Rain was the only person available to potential customers. And that could be a truly terrifying thing, because after a certain amount of time running the store, he started to seriously suck at customer service. It's like he had a timer running that only he could see and when the time was up, that was it for him being Mr. Friendly. He'd actually had several people run for the front door in an attempt to get away from him because he'd scared the crap out of them so badly.

Oddly enough, none of the guys seemed to give a crap about this. Half of them found it amusing and I think the other half were too afraid of him to say anything about it.

I worried though, because it was Tyson's business and I didn't want to see it tank because my bio dad scared away all the business, and I was the only reason he had a job there in the first place. I felt responsible for Rain, and even though he was the parent and I was the child in this situation, I took it upon myself to look out for him. But I also needed to look out for my guys too, so I was a little torn here on what to do.

I wanted to leave, but for Tyson's sake and the sake of the shop, I felt like I needed to go inside and finish out what was left of my shift.

My phone inside the front pocket of my hoodie started to vibrate. I pulled it out and read the text message on the screen.

Rain: I can see you, ya know.

I groaned as I dropped my phone into my lap. It landed face up so I was able to read the next text as it came in.

Rain: Get your skinny ass in here. Right now.

I rolled my eyes at the order. He was bossier than Quinton and that was downright scary.

I plucked my phone out of my lap and shot off a quick reply, letting him know I wouldn't be coming inside and was done for the day. Before he had the chance to reply, I pulled up a conversation with someone else and sent off another text message.

Part of my conversation with Marcus at the restaurant was running through my head, and I couldn't seem to forget about it or let it go. It was time and I thought I was ready. I needed to get this over and done with so I could move past my squeamishness and not let anything hold me back anymore.

I put my key in the ignition and fired up my Rover.

I saw Rain as he stepped out of the shop in my rearview mirror as I pulled away from the curb. He had his angry face on that promised a long lecture later on when he finally caught up with me.

I snickered as I pressed the gas pedal to the floor and sped away.

If I were anybody else but his daughter, then I might actually be worried about that look on his face.

---

When I pulled up to the Alexander house, I'm surprised to see the driveway empty except for the silver Escalade that's parked in front of the open garage. An empty garage, I might add. Though I had my very own bedroom here at the big house, I didn't think I had actually been here when someone who lived in the house wasn't home. They were my family, but it still seemed weird to me to be inside their homes when they weren't actually there. Except for Dash's cottage because that was my home too, even though I would, in all likelihood, never refer to it as anything other than Dash's cottage.

At least there was someone here though, so it didn't feel too weird being here.

After my conversation with Quinton, I figured he was either

on his way to the shop so he could yell at me or at Dash's cottage waiting for me to come home after work so he could yell at me. I'd bet money on one or the other. And here I was at his house. Ha ha.

I parked my Rover farther back in the driveway so the guys who actually did live here would be able to get into the garage, and nobody would need to move their car later to let me out when I wanted to go home.

The front door was unsurprisingly unlocked and had me rolling my eyes when I walked in without having to use my key. If I lived here, I knew that it would be stressed that the door remain locked at all times. Jerks.

"Julian," I called out as I shut the door behind me. There was no answer so I moved through the first level, checking in the rooms. I started with the kitchen because that seemed to be where everyone hung out all together when they were here. Probably because the dining room and family room had been opened up to one big room, and instead of having a table of any kind, they had a giant television and comfy leather couches. If you didn't want to eat in front of the television or standing up, then you could sit down on one of the stools pushed up to the breakfast bar at the center island. The room was spotless and didn't look like a place you'd expect four guys to live in. And, much to my delight, someone had put up curtains for the sliding glass doors that took up the whole back wall of the living room area. If I had to guess I'd say it was Damien's handy work. The thought of anyone else picking out curtains and hanging them up in here was laughable.

The rest of the ground level was empty. I'll admit that when I peeked in on Quinton's office, I had a really hard time not opening up drawers and snooping around in there. I did, however, spot a black picture frame on his desk that had a picture of me in it. I was in profile with my face turned to the side and laughing. The picture was black and white, and my hair had been pulled up into a crazy messy bun on top of my head. The good side of my face was on display and from what I could make of the picture, it had been taken at the shop. I couldn't remember Quinton having taken pictures of me while I was working, but I honestly wasn't surprised to see it. It sat beside a framed picture of a man who looked a whole lot like what I imagined Ty would look like if he cut off all of his hair and aged twenty years. It was the first time I'd seen what Tyson's dad and Quinton's older brother had looked like. He'd been handsome and clearly aged well. This probably meant good things for both Ty and Quint.

I got the heck out of there before I started rifling through Quinton's things. The urge was strong, but I fought it like a boss and won because I knew he'd get some kind of sick joy out of knowing I'd gone through his things. He'd get off on it because he was like that.

I yelled for Julian up the stairs and wasn't surprised when I got no response.

I knew what that meant, where he was, and my heart rate sped up.

This hadn't been my idea, but his, and I'd gone along with it because I knew it was well past time for me to suck it up and move past this. I wanted to be able to stay here and not be freaked out that Vivian's dead and rotting body was going to dig itself out of the grave she'd been buried in, in the basement, and climb both sets of stairs so she could rip my flesh apart while I was sleeping.

I shivered as I made my way down the stairs that would take me to the basement.

I had only been down here the one time and I'd been a hysterical mess, but I still knew where I was going. I stopped outside of the door that would open up into the plant room with the dirt floor and sucked in what was supposed to be a calming breath. It came out shaky, so I sucked in another one. And another one. I kept going until my breathing evened out and grew steady.

I might have looked calm on the outside, but I was a jumbled up wreck on the inside. Fake it till you make it, that was my new game plan here, and it was one that would hopefully keep Julian from looking at me with pity in his eyes and worrying needlessly about me.

I opened the door without knocking and stepped inside.

# CHAPTER FOUR

The air in here was cool and I was thankful for having worn my trusty hoodie over my tank top. I thought it was odd that in a room where plants were stored underneath heat lamps that the room would be cool instead of warm, but what did I know? I didn't want to ask why, not with this room, because I feared the answer would more than likely scare the shit right out of me.

Julian had his back to me and was hunched over the big table in the middle of the room.

I walked across the dirt floor on silent feet without him seeming to notice I'd even entered the room. I stopped about a foot behind him and held my breath, waiting for him to realize I was there. When a full minute went by without him acknowledging my presence, I couldn't take it anymore.

I lifted my hand and gently trailed my fingertips down the center of his back, along his spine.

He jumped and whirled around on me with his fist raised as if he was ready to fend off an attacker. I jumped back and held my hands up in surrender. His eyes flashed with heat, and I couldn't help but be mesmerized by the danger in them, almost as if I was drawn to the darkness there.

He dropped his hands as soon as he noticed it was me and the light fled from his eyes. Stupidly, I missed it as soon as it was gone.

He ran his hand through his hair while his shoulders slumped. "Damn it, Ariel, you scared the shit out of me."

"I'm so sorry, Jules," I hurriedly apologized. "I didn't mean to scare you like that. I honestly don't know what the heck I was doing. I knew you didn't know I was in here and should have announced my arrival. I just... I'm sorry."

He smiled at me kindly before lowering his hand and gesturing at the table behind him.

"Not your fault," he assured me. "Sometimes I get so sucked into my work that I often forget where I am and lose myself in what I'm working on. Hours and hours will go by and I won't notice anything that's happening around me, because I'm solely focused on what's in front of me."

I could completely understand that. It happened to me all the time while reading and lately when I was working with Rain, learning to practice my craft.

"You looked like you were about to punch me, maybe I should call you slugger from now on," I joked with him.

He scowled at me as I moved up next to him to stand at his side in front of the table.

"You are not going to call me slugger," he said in a serious voice. "Can you imagine what Quint or Rain would do to me if they heard you were calling me slugger because I looked like I was going to punch you?" He shuddered in horror. "They'd cut off my balls and I'd probably be forced to choke to death on them. Oh, the indignity of it all."

Despite the fact my face heated up in embarrassment at the mention of his private man parts, I couldn't stop the giggle that escaped me at the image his words conjured in my head.

"Rain would make Quinton hold you down so he could do the dirty work himself," I teased, sharing my thoughts with him. "I think he enjoys getting his hands dirty, and he'd also love knowing that Quinton would want to do it himself and it would give him joy to take that away from him. And Quinton will let him, because he loves me and knows that if he tries to boss Rain around it's going to piss him off, and then most likely upset me and we can't have that, now can we?"

Julian's mouth dropped open, and he gaped at me while his eyes widened in shock.

"That's some imagination you've got there," he told me. "Do you often think of people holding me down so that they can torture me?" I opened my mouth to tell him he was crazy, but he shook his head before I could and continued, "You know what, never mind. I don't think that's what's important with what you just said. I think we should focus on the fact that you seem to get some type of sick pleasure out of the fact that your father enjoys playing games with the other members of your coven, and you're totally fine with him doing it. Tsk, tsk, Ariel. I never took you for the naughty type."

The gleam in his eyes told me he was enjoying this, but I was confused. Since when was violence considered *that* kind of naughty? He clearly thought it fit the mark. I realized in that moment that I really didn't know Julian as well as I knew most of the others, and what I did know about him was really confusing because he could be super sweet then seriously scary. He was a bit of a mystery to me and one I was working really hard to figure out by spending more time with him. I hadn't gotten very far as of yet, though.

I cleared my throat before saying, "Those two deserve each other and whatever they dish out amongst themselves. Rain gives Quinton something to focus on and obsess over other than me, and *that* gives me room to breathe and keeps me from mowing him down with my Rover. So that makes it a win-win for me, I think."

Julian chuckled as he picked up a medium sized glass vial from the table. Purple liquid sloshed around inside of it as he shook it in front of my face.

"You're terrible," he said cheerfully, and I shrugged because maybe he wasn't exactly wrong and I couldn't argue with him about it.

I pointed to the vial. "What's with the purple stuff?"

He smirked at me. "I think this just might be what we're looking for. I need you to try it out for me though."

I gulped. I didn't want to try out some purple mystery liquid he'd concocted on his own.

"Uh, Julian..." I mumbled. "What exactly is it supposed to do?"

"You're not very trusting where I'm concerned."

I wasn't very trusting where most people were concerned. He should know that by now and not take it too personally. And this was some magical brew we were talking about, not Grape flavored Kool-Aid for goodness sake.

"What's it supposed to do?" I asked. "I'm not putting it in my mouth until you tell me."

He leered at me and I blushed again.

"Julian," I hissed in embarrassment. First, he wanted to talk about his balls, and now he was daydreaming about me putting certain things in my mouth. This was not how I'd expected this night to go at all.

"Relax," he said. "It's nothing bad, I promise. I wouldn't do that to you. Once ingested, this little baby *should* make it so that I can't tell when you're lying to me. Everything that comes out of your mouth will sound like the utmost truth and I will believe anything you tell me."

Umm...

Say what?

That's not exactly what we agreed on working on here. We were supposed to be coming up with something that would make it so I could tell if someone else was lying to me. This was something I would have no use for... but Marcus, on the other hand... This could come in handy for him now that he was going to be trying to take the Council down from the inside.

"Have you tried it out on anyone else?" I inquired hesitantly, but now just a little excited too. If there was any possibility this could help Marcus, then I was all over giving it a try... but maybe on somebody else first. You know, just to be safe. Maybe Julian should go first. Yeah, that sounded like a good plan to me.

"Nope," he gleefully responded. "I've been saving this moment to share with you."

Geez. I didn't like how excited he sounded about sharing this with me. Why couldn't he be like normal guys and, I don't know, buy me flowers and chocolate or something? That sounded nice right about now, I liked candy bars, and what girl didn't think flowers were pretty?

"Goodie," I replied half heartedly.

He grinned bright and big at me, like a kid who'd just come down on Christmas to find that Santa had stuffed his fat ass down through his chimney some time while you were sleeping and left gifts for you. Personally, I always found Santa creepy, but Jules looked like he would have been into it. Maybe.

He handed me the vial and challenged, "Ladies first."

I sighed heavily as I took the vial out of his hands. I had to trust that Julian knew what he was doing when it came to his magic. If this Grape Kool-Aid was supposed to heal me in some way, then I wouldn't have even questioned it before I emptied it down my throat. Healing was his specialty, yeah, but I'm sure there was more to him than just that. Right?

I put the vial to my lips and asked, "Are we sharing this one or do you have your own?"

His eyes were intent as they roamed over my face. He seemed

far too serious for someone who'd just been joking around and I didn't understand why.

"That's all there is so far," he murmured quietly. "But you've got to take the whole thing in order for it to work."

His eyes dropped down to my mouth and grew heated. The intensity never left but instead grew thicker, heavier, by the second. That look in his eyes told me he wanted to rip the vial out of my hands and replace its spot against my mouth with his lips. Any other time I would have been excited at the thought of Julian wanting to kiss me. He was one of my boys that I hadn't grown close to on any level of physical intimacy, and I was impatiently waiting for our relationship to get there.

At first, it had been me who wanted to take things slow because I had trust issues and a whole slew of other problems, but now it felt like it was because of the guys that things were creeping along at a snail's pace, since they were trying to do what they thought was best for me. They were forcing me to be open about what I wanted with them or run the risk of not getting it at all. It was awesome of them and I respected them for it, but I really didn't enjoy making the first move all the time, so I tended to make no move whatsoever and then end up frustrated in more ways than one.

I wanted to tell Julian to kiss me. But, at the same time, I also wanted to help Marcus out in any way possible with his mission, because I thought what he was doing was more important than my love life. Way more important. My mind flashed back to Annabell on her hands and knees, taking multiple Council cocks at once, and I couldn't help the bile that threatened to climb up my throat at the thought of other girls, innocent ones, being forced into that type of situation. My eyes stung with unshed tears as my imagination ran wild and I forced myself to see things I had no desire to see. Ever.

I parted my lips and tipped the vial back. The liquid was surprisingly warm as it filled my mouth. I didn't waste time and quickly swallowed it in two gulps. It burned going all the way down. I pulled the vial away from my mouth and coughed. The aftertaste was horrible and reminded me of something disgustingly sour.

The corner of Julian's mouth twitched and I knew he was fighting the urge to laugh at me.

"You really did it," he said in awe.

I shrugged. Yeah, I really did it. How stupid was I?

An intense warmth spread through my entire body at an alarming rate. It was there, all throughout my body, and then, in the blink of an eye, it was gone and I felt completely normal once again.

"I don't feel anything now," I told him honestly. "At first it was warm, everything inside me was, but now there's nothing. It's just normal me now."

Normal me was never really normal, that's for sure. Julian looked like he thought the exact opposite.

"Lie to me," he urged, and I blinked stupidly at him. What the hell did he expect me to lie to him about?

"Umm..."

"Come on, Ariel."

"Doesn't it need time to settle into my system before I should lie to you?" Maybe more time would make me feel something different inside. Shouldn't I feel different somehow? I thought so, but Julian didn't seem to agree.

He shook his head and repeated, "Lie to me, Ariel. Give me a good one. Something I will know is a lie so if I feel like I'm believing you, I'll know subconsciously that you're lying to me."

Huh. I could do that.

"I'm a lesbian," I deadpanned.

His eyes widened right before he burst out laughing.

"A lesbian," he hooted. "It feels so real, but I know several of my brothers have had their tongues down your throat and you've enjoyed it. You." He laughed even harder. "A lesbian."

I frowned at him. What a dick. I'd done exactly what he'd asked me to and now he was laughing at me. That wasn't what I'd agreed to.

"It doesn't work," I grumbled under my breath. I didn't know what I'd expected out of him after my announcement, but it hadn't been this.

"No, no, no," he said after getting his laughter under control. "It feels real, that you're into chicks, even though I know it's not. It definitely worked. Try another one. Come on, Ariel, hit me with another doozie."

I did not think so. I wasn't interested in being subjected to more of his laughter at my expense.

"No," I told him snottily. "You want me to lie, then you should ask me questions and then you can tell me whether or not I'm lying. That's the only way this is going to go."

"Okay," he agreed readily, before he took the forgotten vial from my hands and sat it down on the table. "If that's how you want to play it then that works for me."

I frowned, unsure if I liked the way he'd worded that or if he was being sincere.

He turned, facing me, and placed his hands on my cheeks, cupping my face.

"Tell me, sweet Ariel," he murmured, "are you a virgin?"

I tried to jerk back away from him, surprised and thrown off by his question. This was something I'd assumed he already knew the answer to, something all of my guys knew the answer to. Didn't they all get together and talk about these things when I wasn't around?

Lie, that was the point of this. Perhaps he wanted me to lie in answer to questions he already knew the answers to. That way he'd know what he was feeling and could tell whether or not his magical brew was working or not.

"No," I told him in a serious voice. "I'm not a virgin."

Absolute lie, one hundred percent.

His nostrils flared angrily and he hissed, "Who was it? Who did you have sex with? This is absolute bullshit. We all agreed to take things slow with you, and someone went behind our backs and fucked you?"

I reared back at his ugly choice of words and jerked out of his hands. He could not be serious right now.

"Julian," I snapped. "Maybe it would be best if you stopped talking."

Please, pretty, pretty please. Stop talking, I silently urged him. He was going to freak me out if he kept going like this.

"They promised," he whispered in a heated voice.

I shook off my thoughts and stepped into him. I wrapped my arms around his middle and pressed my forehead to his. I scrunched my eyes up tight and hoped what I said next could get him to calm down.

"That was a lie," I rasped out. "I lied to you just like you asked me to. I've never had sex before, but lately I've really wanted to. Nobody will have sex with me though, because apparently you all promised some stupid crap about me that you probably should have asked me about before agreeing to. I really don't like the thought of all of you sitting around and discussing my virginity, and the how's and when's of when it's appropriate or not for me to be rid of it. That's really fucked up if you think about it. I mean, I get that we're all in a relationship together, and we are supposed to work together on everything, but I'm seriously uncomfortable with the rest of you talking about these things without me. Especially because it's *about* me."

I paused to suck in a sharp breath and immediately shut my mouth when it hit me that I was ranting and needed to stop. It wasn't helping the situation at all.

I opened my eyes to find Julian's eyes staring into mine intently. He wasn't blinking either, and for the first time since meeting him, a sliver of fear shot through me. I wasn't afraid for myself, but for the rest of the guys, because I worried he might take his rage out on them in order to figure out who he thought had deflowered me.

"I'm a virgin," I muttered in an attempt to calm him down.

"That could be a lie," he rasped out.

"It's not," I whispered urgently. "I promise."

Honestly, I didn't get what the big deal was here, but apparently it meant something to him.

Because I had to know, I asked, "If this is your reaction now when you just *think* I've had sex, then what are you going to be like when I've really done the deed with one of the guys and it's not you?"

He shook his head and his forehead slid across mine with every move.

"It's nothing you'll have to worry about," he choked out. "It's just the thought of one of them lying to me that has me acting irrational. We went through a lot because of Annabell and I never want to have my brothers, my family, lie to me again because of a female. I don't want to go through that hell again and I don't want them to either. You can have sex with whoever the hell you want to amongst our coven, just don't let anyone lie about it. That's all I ask. That's all any of us should ask."

I dropped my hands from Julian's sides and stepped away from him in frustration. What he was asking was reasonable. Quinton had actually asked me for something similar when it came to honesty, it hadn't been about sex but honesty alone, and I had agreed to be completely honest with him about most things. Though, if you asked him, he'd tell you we agreed to honesty in *all* things, but a girl had to have her secrets every now and then.

It was the mention of Annabell, yet again, that had me frustrated. They had an evil ex who really did a number on several of them and had left her mark. I knew this because I had to put up with the mess she'd left behind and it was starting to piss me off just a little bit. I didn't want to be looked at as untrustworthy because of the actions of another person. That really didn't seem fair to me.

"You're mad," he said quietly.

I shook my head and looked everywhere but at him, and ended up looking at the other end of the room.

The dirt was smooth and a rich, dark brown color.

I stumbled back and connected with a warm body. Julian wrapped his arms around me and held me close to him. His lips brushed my ear as I stared, transfixed, at the dirt where Vivian's body had been buried. My mind flashed back to the bathroom and watching her head bounce off of the countertop before falling to the floor, where blood oozed out of her head. It was an image that would forever be burned into my brain, because it was one of the most horrible things I'd ever seen. I had a whole list of horrible things I'd seen now, and that was only one of them. Like Chuck, another horrible memory I'd never be rid of.

I shuddered violently and Julian held on tighter. His heat surrounded me protectively, but it did nothing to calm down my nerves.

"Did anyone tell you about the dirt?" he asked in a hushed voice.

I shook my head in the negative, too upset to speak. I wasn't surprised to hear something had been kept from me about this room, because the boys avoided saying anything about Vivian's death if possible.

"It's magic," he whispered. "It's been this way for years. It's something Quinton's father and Ty's grandfather taught Quinton. It's considered black magic and is forbidden to be used by the Council. Quinton's father studied everything, no matter it was forbidden or not, he thought he was better than everyone else. He also forced Quinton to learn everything along with him. Sometimes he would even experiment on Quinton to see how well things worked out."

My chest hurt from hearing this news. We were all so

damaged by the people who were supposed to protect and love us the most. It was painful to hear about anyone's past, because I cared so much about them that it almost physically hurt me to know how they'd suffered.

"The bodies act as a fertilizer, enriching the earth," he whispered and I gagged.

Did he say bodies, as in plural? Just how many people had they buried down here? That was a scary thought.

"*Bodies?*" I choked out.

I felt him shrug his shoulders nonchalantly and my body shuddered again for an entirely different reason this time.

"Who else have you buried down here?" I asked in a horrified voice. "How's there... I mean..." I stuttered to a stop, unable to get the words out.

"There are no bodies," he told me. "It's magic. The bodies are swallowed up in the dirt. It's all very complicated. And, as for how many of them there have been, well, that's a question for Quinton, because I think he's the only one who'd know the exact number."

My mind raced over his words.

"Does that mean... So, she's not even down here anymore?" I inquired in small voice. She had to be down here, it was the only thing that made sense to me.

"Nope," he said in a far too happy for my mood voice. "She hasn't actually been here for quite some time. You should feel absolutely safe in staying here from now on, because she's not here to hurt you."

Honestly, that didn't make me feel safe staying here in the slightest bit. I eyed the dirt floor critically. No, that actually made things a whole lot worse for me, in a way.

I took that as my cue to leave and he didn't look surprised when I practically ran from the room after hugging him goodbye. In fact, he almost looked like he was trying not to laugh at me.

I didn't ever want to go back down into that basement again, and I knew I'd have dreams—or more like nightmares—about tripping down there and falling into the dirt. It would suck me under and I'd choke to death on dirt that would somehow magically eat me. I had the worst luck ever sometimes, it could happen. If I had nightmares I was going to blame them entirely on Julian.

On the way home, I picked up a phone call from an apologetic Quinton who felt badly for interrupting my time with Marcus, but still felt the need to ask me what the lunch date had been about.

I lied to him without remorse, and thanks to Julian's magical brew he didn't question me once and bought the whole thing. I hung up feeling smug but worried. I had no idea how long the stuff would stay in my system for and probably should have asked.

I guess there were worse things to worry about than lying to people and getting away with it. I didn't usually make a habit out of lying so I didn't think I really had anything to worry too much about.

# CHAPTER FIVE

I screamed as I dropped down, the air rushing past me. My arms pinwheeled out uselessly at my sides, doing me no good.

The breath left my lungs in a rush as my back slammed into the ground, and for a moment I felt absolutely nothing. There was no pain, nothing but shock.

When I was finally able to suck air into my lungs, the pain hit me full force. I whimpered as I rolled over onto my side and hauled my knees up to my chest. I wrapped my arms around my legs and clutched them tightly.

I squeezed my eyes shut and focused solely on breathing. After a few minutes of just breathing, the pain receded and I could feel something else.

Fear slithered through me as I opened my eyes and took a look around. Immediately, I shut my eyes once again and prayed that when I opened them, I would be somewhere else. Anywhere other than here.

I opened my eyes again and looked around, but unfortunately the scenery remained the same. There was a huge, gaping hole in the earth. Bugs, creepy crawly things that made me gag, were crawling out from it. Crawling out toward me.

Quickly, so as not to let those things touch me, I scrambled to my feet and started scooting backward. From this new angle I was able to see farther down into the hole, which made me wish I had never actually stood up and would have chanced it with the creepy crawlies, because they were less of a threat to me.

Her eyes were what I saw first. They glowed with an unnatural light and were fixated entirely on me. She growled like a wild animal as her broken fingernails clawed at the dirt as she dragged her way up the inside of the hole.

My back connected with something solid, blocking me from moving back any farther as she made it to the top of the hole and her head popped up. It turned to the side at an unnatural angle.

She opened her mouth and a mass of black spiders spewed out. They raced toward me as male shouts rang out through the room.

Her dirty hand raised toward me, and her broken, bleeding finger pointed right at me.

"No," I croaked out. "He said you wouldn't be here anymore. He told me so. You aren't really here. You can't be."

She lowered her hand back down to the dirt floor and climbed her way entirely out of the hole. On her hands and knees, she started to crawl toward me with her mouth hanging open, spiders falling out along the way.

"No," I screamed. "You're not real."


I sat up straight on my loveseat and looked around in terrified confusion.

In my dream there had been angry shouting and I didn't think it had actually been part of my dream, but something I had picked up going on around me in the real world.

My head jerked around the room, looking for the dead, sightless bodies trying to climb out of the earth that I had been dreaming about, but I found nothing. I flopped back onto the pile of pillows I'd propped up behind me last night in a huff. It was only a dream. A horrible, hideous nightmare.

I needed to take a shower because I could feel disgusting things crawling all over me, even though they hadn't touched me once in my dream but, for whatever reason, their phantom touch had followed me back to reality. I knew scrubbing my body thoroughly until my skin was a freakishly pink color would be the only way to get rid of the feeling of those creepy crawlies.

I refused to think about the woman I'd seen crawling out of that hole. She was long since dead and, according to Julian, entirely gone. The ghost of her would not haunt me for forever, or so I hoped.

I looked over at my bed longingly. If I hadn't fallen asleep watching television on the couch last night, I would have slept in bed underneath my dreamcatcher and this garbage wouldn't be happening to me. That sucker wasn't only pretty to look at, but also never once had it let me down, and every single time I'd slept underneath it I never had a bad dream to speak of. Really, it was because of Tyson, who'd never let me down with that one, because he's the one who'd put the whole thing together and even used blood magic to make it safe for me to go to sleep in my bed at night.

I groaned as I tossed the throw blanket that covered me to the side. It was a pretty shade of yellow and was incredibly soft and fuzzy. It had been a Christmas gift from Dash and I absolutely loved it. It was a really sweet gift and I dragged that thing everywhere with me. When we watched television downstairs in the living room it came with me. When I went to watch movies with Damien I brought it along. I fell asleep there once, and he'd carried me to the car and put me in my own bed, and he'd made sure to bring my fuzzy blanket back home with me because he knew how much I loved the thing.

I stood up and moved to the dresser where I always charged my phone every night. I left my phone plugged in as I pulled up my texts. Quickly, I sent off a text to Julian.

. . .

Ariel: I dreamed of dead things, namely people. Thanks. You're a dick.

I frowned down at my phone after hitting send. That wasn't exactly fair of me to send him that, but I did blame him all the same. Which wasn't fair either, because I had agreed to go over there of my own free will and had even thought it was a good idea at the time. I'd thought I needed closure. Instead, I'd gotten nightmares. And I really had no one to blame outside of myself.

Guilt ate at me but I refused to send another text, an apology one. Julian never got to see this side of me, maybe it was his turn, and Uncle Quinton deserved a much needed break for a while.

Nah, maybe they both deserved it for whatever reason. Goodness knows I had enough attitude to throw around at more than just one of them for a while, Marcus hadn't been wrong on that front.

I sat the phone back on the dresser and pulled open my top drawer. I dug around in my dresser until I found some clothes to put on after I got out of the shower.

"What the hell do you think you're doing?" I heard Dash shout angrily from the hallway.

I dropped my clothes to the floor and ran toward the door. Dash never raised his voice, ever, and something seriously had to be wrong in order to have him doing so now.

"She's sleeping," I heard him snarl. "You're not going in there right now and waking her up. Go home and call her later like a normal fucking human being, and get your ass *the fuck* out of my house."

Oh shit. This was so not good. There was only one person I could see Dash talking to like that and it was Rain.

I whipped the door open and stumbled out into the hallway. What greeted me had my breath catching in my throat.

Dash stood tall at the top of the stairs with his arms spread wide, stopping Rain from coming up all the way so he could get to my room.

"Get out of my way, boy," Rain snarled in an ugly voice. "How dare you stand between me and my daughter. That's the stupidest thing you could ever do where I'm concerned and you damn well know it."

Rain put his hands on Dash's shoulders and shoved. Dash stumbled back a step before righting himself and getting back in Rain's face.

Shouting was coming from the bottom of the stairs, but I couldn't make out the words because the world had come to a screeching halt for me the moment Rain put his hands on Dash. Out of all my boys, Dash was the one I had the biggest connection with. He understood me on a different level than everyone else, because of the physical abuse we both suffered as children. We'd bonded over blood and scars, and to see anyone get physical with him with the intent to harm him threw me into a bit of a rage. It didn't matter to me that it was my father who'd touched him.

I lifted my hand and poured my intent and will into my actions as I flicked my fingers in Rain's direction.

His eyes rounded comically as he flew back, slamming into the wall. The shouting at the bottom of the stairs died off as Rain slid down the wall and crashed to the floor in a heap.

Immediately, I felt contrite and wanted to apologize for my actions, but I knew for everyone else's sake that I couldn't tell Rain I was sorry. He was a damn bully and nobody was willing to stand up to him. It was up to me to put him in his place, otherwise he was going to continue to treat the people I cared about like garbage, and I couldn't stand to watch it anymore.

Rain looked up at me with bright eyes that didn't shine with accusation like I'd expect, but with pride instead.

"Don't touch Dash," I ordered in a hollow voice. "He's officially off limits to you and I don't ever want to see you put your hands on him again. I'm not joking, Rain. If you mess with Dash again, I can promise you that you'll live to regret it. Oh, and another thing, this is his house, when you're here you need to treat him with respect or don't come here at all."

I looked at Dash to check on him and see if he was okay, but he wasn't standing where I'd last seen him. He was completely gone.

"Dash," I called out, my voice threaded with fear. Where did he go? He was just here two minutes ago.

"He's in his room," Quinton said quietly from the stairs.

I looked at him and reared back in shock at the look on his face. There was a naked vulnerability there that terrified me.

"What?" I asked in a quiet voice. "What's wrong now?"

"Be careful with him, Ariel," he cautioned me seriously.

I frowned at hearing him use my first name. Something was seriously wrong here and it had nothing to do with Rain's volatile behavior.

"Go," Quinton urged me gently, "but please, Ariel, *please* be careful with him. Remember everything that the women in his life have put him through because he needs you to be different than them."

I started to shake uncontrollably as everything faded away except for the look on Quinton's face as his words and their meaning ran through my mind.

Had I triggered some bad memory for Dash with my violent, rash behavior toward Rain? Tears pricked my eyes at the thought that it could have been my callous actions this time that caused him harm.

I ran to Dash's room and slammed the door shut behind me.

"Did you see her?" Rain asked in awe, the pride ringing clear in his voice. "She used her magic defensively like I've been trying to teach her. I never thought I'd see the day where she actually did it. She was so against harming others that she found even the thought of it repulsive. But she did it. Isn't she incredible?"

"Shut up, Rain," Quinton grumbled, and for once we were on the same page with each other. "What are you even doing here and why in the hell do you have Dash's cat?"

Oh shit. That damn cat! I'd forgotten about him and left him at the store with Rain. Poor little Binx was probably so mad at me right now for leaving him behind.

"Did you know that Marcus joined the Council this morning?" Rain questioned in a haughty voice, which told me he knew Quinton had absolutely no clue about it, and Rain was just taunting him with his superior knowledge.

Oh shit, shit, shit. Quinton was going to lose his damn mind.

I placed both my palms against the door and whispered out a quick spell.

*"Keep out anything with*
  *malicious intent.*
  *Shield this room.*
  *Stand as guard.*
  *Keep him safe.*
  *So mote it be."*

If that didn't keep them out then there was nothing else I could do for it. The door hummed quietly and I knew it was working.

I turned back to face the room and my breath caught in my throat, threatening to choke me as I took in Dash. He was curled up in a ball in the center of his bed, his eyes were staring vacantly up at the ceiling and he wasn't moving. He didn't even look like he was breathing.

It scared the ever loving piss right out of me. This was Dash and he was one of the strongest people I knew, but he didn't look very strong right now. In fact, he looked a lot younger than he really was, like a little boy almost and that broke my heart.

"Dash," I hesitantly said before approaching the bed. He didn't so much as twitch. I climbed into bed with him and pasted my body around his back. I wrapped my arms around him and held on for all I was worth.

I could wait this out with him and be here for however long this took. I'd wait forever for Dash if I had to. He was worth everything to me.

## CHAPTER SIX

It felt like it took hours for him to move, and when he did, it was slow going. My body was stiff from unmoving for so long and my arms hurt from holding onto him so tightly.

Eventually, his body relaxed and his breathing evened out. I still didn't relax behind him. I thought he'd fallen asleep when his hand moved. He placed it over mine and squeezed.

"Ariel," he croaked out in a thick voice.

I buried my face in his neck and prayed the tears that were stinging my eyes didn't spill out. I didn't want him to see how much his pain killed me.

"I'm so sorry," I whispered hoarsely.

Sorry for so many different things. Where to even start?

Dash had grown up with the females in his life being incredibly violent toward him and doing horrible things to him. They'd treated him worse than garbage and he'd never done anything whatsoever to deserve the way he'd been treated outside of being born. The guys all told me that he'd had issues with women because of his past. That's mostly the reason why he had acted like a man-whore before I'd come into his life. He had issues, to be sure, just like all of them had issues, but I knew they revolved around women and violence. I knew better. I shouldn't have acted the way I did in front of him and done that to Rain.

Violence was never the answer. I knew this, dammit. I really did, but I had stupidly acted out anyways and potentially hurt Dash as a result. I would never live this down.

"You'll never know how sorry I am." My voice cracked. "I don't know what happened to me, but I guess seeing Rain shove you like that did something to me and I just snapped. I never, ever should have lashed out and used my magic like that. I never should have used my magic to hurt someone else, especially Rain. And certainly not in front of you."

Dash squeezed my hand before letting go and rolling over to face me. I moved back, away from his neck, and braced for what was to come. He was going to tell me to get out of his bed and get out of his room. Maybe he'd even tell me to pack up my belongings and get out of his house. It would kill me, since this had become my home here with him and Binx. I'd never had a real home before, a place I'd felt safe in, until coming here to live with them. I'd had a home with Marcus but it hadn't been a safe one because I'd shared it with Vivian. It would kill me to leave Dash and Binx, but I would respect his wishes and I would do whatever he wanted me to do.

Dash put his hands up to my face. His thumbs ran over my cheeks, one trailing over my scar in a gentle caress.

His eyes were dark storm clouds and I was caught in the middle of them, sucked in deep.

"Dash," I croaked out. This rejection from him was likely going to be the hardest thing I'd ever gone through in my entire life.

It was in that moment that I realized something important. Something life changing. Something I couldn't ever come back from.

I loved Dash. Like, deep-seated, bottom of my soul, loved him.

I was falling hard here with these people, they were carving their names onto my soul and there would be no scraping them off. Hell, I think part of me even loved Julian already. I was a goner for all of them and that was just that.

"Don't you dare apologize to me," he whispered in a fierce voice that shocked me to my core. "You don't ever apologize for what you did this morning."

My eyes rounded in shock as my body froze solid.

If I hadn't done anything wrong, then why had he run away from me, run out of the hallway, and hidden himself in here curled up into a ball and shut down completely? If I didn't have anything to apologize for, if it hadn't been me who'd triggered him, then what the hell was the matter here? Quinton had seemed like this was important and I had to be careful with Dash.

"I don't understand," I said hesitantly. "I assumed I had triggered something, some type of memory for you because of my violent behavior toward Rain. I never should have done that, it was rash, and I will work really hard to keep myself in check from now on. Not just when you're around either. I pr—"

"Ariel," he murmured as he cupped my face and held on to me. "Stop talking and stop apologizing. You did nothing wrong here. Every single one of us wants to toss Rain into the wall on a daily basis, we just don't do it because we know there'd be horrible consequences if we did."

I sucked in a deep breath. "Then what did I do wrong?" I asked in a quiet voice. I'd done something wrong, I just knew it.

"You've done nothing wrong, sweet girl, I promise you," he gently assured me. "It's just that..." He swallowed painfully before continuing. "But you're right though, in a way. Your actions did trigger a memory for me, but what's more, it's what you did for me that no female in my life has ever done for me before. You stuck up for me, you defended me, and you struck out at someone else who wasn't me. That's never happened before. Not ever. The only people who have ever stuck up for me are the members of our coven. And that's it. But you... what you did... I never expected..."

God, Dash hurt my heart so bad, I felt like I was bleeding on the inside and it wasn't pretty. We'd both suffered, but I felt like Dash had gotten it worse than I had. Not that we were competing here or anything. It would be one of the most messed up competitions ever. Who had the most scars? Dash would win hands down. Most of mine were on the inside. Unless you counted my collarbone and my face, that is. The one on my face would usually mean I would win this game, but Dash's back put my face to shame every time. Which was all kinds of horrifying, considering how he'd come about it.

"Thank you," he whispered hoarsely. "Thank you for standing up for me. You can't ever leave us, Ariel. You prove every single day that you belong here with us, that you're a perfect fit for our coven and it would kill me if you ever left. I need you here with me. And I know I'm not the only one who feels that way."

I sighed in relief. This was familiar territory for me. Most of them had given into their fears at one time or another, and begged me not to leave them no matter what. I had made promises to stay with them and I meant it every time, even though it had scared the crap out of me most of time because it was a heavy thing for me to promise. Especially in the beginning. I was the only one who ever seemed hesitant with promises.

"I'm not going anywhere," I assured Dash. "I'm staying right here with you until you get sick of me and kick me out."

"Never going to happen," he said in a gruff voice. "You will always have a home here with me. Always. And it would be impossible for me to get sick of you when you're the most important person in my life and always will be."

His words filled me with a sweet warmth and left me unable to respond. How did I tell him that he was the most important person in my life too, when it was a lie? He was the most important person in the world to me when it was just the two of us alone together. But the others mattered to me just as much and it changed when I was with someone else. That didn't mean I cared for Dash any less, though. It just meant I had a heart big enough for all of them to have a special piece of. I would worry about this if it hadn't been them who'd encouraged this type of relationship in the first place.

"You're not planning on moving out on me, are you?" he inquired quietly.

I shook my head as his hands slid down my jaw and the pads of his thumbs trailed down the column of my neck. They hit the base of my throat and went wide, tracing my collarbone and, incidentally, the burn marks covering it.

I froze in place, too afraid to move. Like the scar on my face, I never hid these or tried to cover them up. They were a part of me that I wasn't ashamed of or felt the need to hide. The only reason I'd ever cover them up would be because I got sick of people boldly asking me where they'd come from. You'd be surprised how many people actually came right out and asked about my scars. It made things horribly uncomfortable and made me incredibly angry, because I didn't think it was anybody's business but my own.

I had a feeling Dash saw my scars differently than other people did though, since he had so many of his own.

His gaze dropped to his hands, where they were trailing across my skin.

His hands moved back up my neck and he cupped the back of my head, his fingers threading through my hair.

"You're a little warrior," he murmured, as his eyes fixated on my lips. "My girl, my warrior. My savior."

I squirmed, uncomfortable with the words coming out of his mouth. I was no warrior, and I certainly wasn't anybody's savior and never would be. Most days I could barely take care of myself.

"It was hot, you know?" he commented, and my eyes shot to his to see they'd heated with what could only be described as lust.

"I bet I wasn't the only one who thought it was hot too. In fact, I bet the only person who didn't was Rain. Quinton's probably so pissed right now because I get to be in here with you and he's stuck out there doing clean up with Rain."

"I don't think now is a good time to talk about Quinton *or* Rain," I said as my eyes dropped down to his lips.

"Come here," he ordered.

I happily complied, scooting over until I was melded up against his warm body. I wrapped my leg around his hip as his lips brushed softly against mine. My fingers went to his short, red hair at the top of his head and I dug them in. His beard tickled my face as his tongue invaded my mouth, and he kissed me like I was the only thing in his world that mattered at the moment and he'd die if he didn't get to keep kissing me.

He groaned as his free hand slid around my shoulders and down. His grip on my hair tightened and he tilted my head to the side, deepening the kiss.

I moaned into his mouth as his hand slid down my back, underneath my sleep shorts and panties, and he cupped my behind in his palm.

I felt him harden against my inner thigh and fought the urge to rub myself shamelessly against it. Dash had the same thought it seemed, because he squeezed my ass as his arm pressed into me, and he rolled us over so he was on top of me. His knee went into the mattress and he used his thighs to spread my legs apart.

I wrapped my legs around his hips as he ground his hardness against me.

I clung to his hair, holding him tightly against my mouth, tangling my tongue with his in what felt like the best kiss of my whole life.

I cried out in protest when his mouth left mine to trail kisses down my jaw toward my neck. He made his way down my neck, trailing kisses that burned all the way down the column of my throat, and then across my collarbone.

Anybody else kissing me there and it would have been a huge turn off, but things between Dash and me were different, and I completely forgot all about my scars and lost myself in the feel of his lips moving across my skin.

His hand slid up my sides, taking my tank top with them as they moved up my ribs. I shivered as his rough hands roamed over my bare skin, leaving a blaze of heat in their path. I loved that strange heat so much, it was comforting to me, and it immediately felt like it pooled between my legs at my core whenever they touched me and it lingered behind. I didn't think I'd ever be able to be intimate with another person again who didn't have magic, because I craved that heat so much. I didn't know how the guys who'd slept around with normal humans pulled it off. I knew I wouldn't be able to do it.

Maybe it was different for guys. Especially if they were man-whores.

Dash's hands spread out just below my breasts and the tank top went up no farther.

His mouth moved down and he kissed his way across the top of my breasts that were exposed.

"Dash," I panted as his mouth moved down farther and, over my tank top, he sucked one of my nipples into his mouth.

Someone banged on the door and he immediately released my nipple and sat back. He looked down at me with eyes that burned with passion.

He bit his bottom lip as he ground his erection against me again. I sucked in a shuddering breath as pleasure spiked through me and I couldn't stop the whimper that escaped me.

A fist banged against the door again as Quinton yelled, "God-damnit. Open this fucking door right now. Rain is downstairs and he is so pissed he looks like he's going to tear the whole place apart with his bare hands. He's demanding to see Ariel and refusing to leave until he does. Apparently Marcus joined the Council and Rain is freaking out. I need you to open the door,

Dash, and let Ariel out of there. I need her to come downstairs and handle Rain before he loses his shit and we all end up fucked because of it."

Dash immediately backed off of me and flopped down on his back on the bed. His hands went to his face where he pressed his palms into his eyes.

"Shit," he muttered. "This is bad. So, so bad."

"Not really," I told him and he immediately lowered his hands from his face to stare at me.

"What do you mean, not really?"

"I already knew about Marcus," I shared. "He told me. It's really not a big deal."

Dash opened and closed his mouth several times like a fish out of water before shouting, "Are you out of your damn mind? Have you forgotten everything you've learned about the Council? And how could you learn something like this and not tell the rest of us?"

For a second, my insides froze in horror as I waited for betrayal to cross over his face, but it never came. This could have gone so wrong and I hadn't even thought about the repercussions of keeping Marcus's secret from my guys.

"You have to trust me just how I have to trust you," I whispered to Dash. "And I trust Marcus. I would trust him with anything. When he asked me to keep this to myself, I agreed because I didn't think it would hurt any of you. Well, except for maybe Rain's feelings because he's psycho where Marcus is concerned. Otherwise, I knew it wouldn't hurt any of you in a damaging way and it's about time you all trusted me as much as I'm expected to trust you."

I opened my mouth but shut it when Dash's fingers pressed against my lips. "I get it," he told me in a quiet voice. "And you're not wrong. I trust you and, until Rain showed up and things went tits up around here, I would have told you that I trusted Marcus entirely. If you say this isn't going to hurt us and we don't need to freak out about it, then that's good enough for me and it will be good enough for the others."

I worried, though, because even though I knew he'd be right when it came to most of the guys, there was still Quinton and Rain, and they were uber alpha males who would rather gouge out their own eyeballs than see anything hurt me.

"Come on, beautiful." Dash grabbed my hand and dragged me off the bed behind him. "As much as I want to finish what I started and put my mouth all over the rest of that sweet body of yours, now isn't the time. We'll wait until we're home alone and it will only be me who gets to hear the noises you make when I've got my mouth between your legs, and then my cock buried in your tight, wet heat."

Holy shit.

My face flamed as things low in my belly tightened at hearing Dash talk like that. He'd always been very reserved with me, always asked for permission before getting hands-on with me, and was generally very careful with his physical affections where I was concerned—pushing to take things at a snail's pace with me even though we lived together.

It looked like the time for slow was over when it came to Dash, and I could not freaking wait.

Maybe it would be what ultimately pushed the rest of them into being physical with me.

God, I hoped so.

# CHAPTER SEVEN

I wasn't surprised to find Quinton propped up against the wall in the hallway between my bedroom and Dash's. His arms were crossed over his chest and his feet crossed at the ankles.

"Time to face the music," Dash murmured happily.

I didn't think there was much that could deteriorate his good mood. A little bit of snuggling and tonsil hockey apparently did a body good. At least in Dash's case. I was willing to bet Quinton would agree with him.

Quinton studied my face before smirking and stating, "You look flushed, baby. I didn't send you in there so you could get it on with Dash while we all entertained your father down in the dining room."

I couldn't be more embarrassed if I tried.

"Shut up, Quinton," Dash growled in a low, dangerous voice. His good mood suddenly gone.

Ignoring them both, I headed downstairs.

Dash was silent on his way down, but Quinton's cowboy boots clomped loudly the entire way. I had to give it to him, he looked damn good in those cowboy boots.

"You're awfully calm for just having learned this news," Quinton said in an accusatory tone. "It's almost as if you'd learned about Marcus's rash actions before this morning. Like, say, maybe you might have learned of his treachery when he took you out to lunch with him just yesterday. And, perhaps, you'd forgotten about it and that's why you didn't fucking *tell me* what he was doing."

"Hmm..." I muttered noncommittally. He certainly had my number, that's for sure.

I waved to everyone sitting around the dining room table as I headed straight for the kitchen. I had been up for far too long without my caffeine fix, and if I had to go much longer without it, then there was no telling what I might do to someone. They all knew how I felt about my coffee in the morning so it wasn't a surprise when not even Quinton himself followed me into the kitchen.

The first coffee mug I pulled down from the cupboard had a pentagram on it and said something about summoning demons. It went right back into the cupboard and I pulled down a different one that had a pearly set of vampire fangs on it. Much better.

Demons freaked me out. Six months ago I would have sworn that neither demons nor vampires actually existed. Now, I just assumed, like everything else unpleasant in this world, that they were lurking somewhere in the dark just waiting for the opportune moment to strike.

It was disturbing really. All the things you always thought of as merely nightmares, the stuff of horror movies, when you found out they were actually real and all you wished for was for them to once again become the stuff of nightmares and no longer reality.

I poured coffee from the carafe into the mug. Then milk and sugar. I liked it sweet and sometimes I even liked it a whole lot when it tasted nothing like actual coffee.

I took my mug full of steaming goodness into the packed dining room and plopped down in a seat between Damien and

Tyson. The spot between them was the only available seat and I found it odd that I was placed between those two of all the guys. The guys who had previously dated Annabell tended to like Ty a whole lot less than everybody else. To me, it was completely unfair and I wanted to smack some sense into all of them, but was so sick and tired of fighting with Annabell's ghost that every time I even thought of her with one of my guys it turned my stomach.

I didn't want to come off as the jealous girlfriend, so I was trying to keep my mouth shut and my opinions on the matter to myself. It was getting harder by the day though. Sooner rather than later, I was going to explode all over them and tell them just what I thought of their stupidity and inability to move on from the past.

I sat back in my chair and sighed happily as I sipped my coffee.

All around the table males were angrily voicing their opinions as if they had a say in the matter and some of them were even going so far as to tear Marcus's character apart.

I wasn't surprised by any of it, except for the fact they'd found out so soon.

"After everything," Julian snarled, "he went through with his sister. Then having Ariel with us now. This treachery is absolutely unbelievable. To think he would actually join ranks with the very men who were the reason his baby sister ended her life... I cannot fathom it. What a fucking coward. I'll be thanking everything I hold holy that he's no longer responsible for Ariel's well-being because, clearly, he's a traitorous cunt."

That did it for me and pulled me out of my happy *I have coffee* daze.

"Stop it," I hissed angrily. "Just stop talking right this second."

Silence filled the dining room as every single person in the room focused solely on me. Several of them looked angry and they glared at me. The rest of them were giving me looks of calm understanding.

Quinton's gaze was what surprised me the most, because he was of the calm and understanding variety. I had actually expected the exact opposite out of him.

Dash was also one of the calm ones. No surprise there. When he lost his cool we all should really be frightened since he had the most reasonable head on his shoulders.

Tyson was outraged. On my behalf, of course. And I wasn't surprised by this either. He had anger issues and was a bit of a hothead. But he was loyal to a fault. That he would immediately jump to attack something he thought might harm me wasn't a surprise in the slightest. I loved him and he was my BFF for a reason, his outrage on my behalf only being one of many.

Julian, obviously, looked outraged.

Damien appeared haughty but curious.

The twins, however, were my biggest surprise because they both sat back, silently watching what was going on around them. I expected some type of emotion out of them. Be it outrage or sadness or *something*. But no, there was absolutely no emotion on their faces whatsoever.

Rain was angry, practically fuming out of his nostrils. I had no idea where this hatred for Marcus stemmed from, and it seemed to be a whole lot bigger than I had originally thought it to be. I swear, Rain was getting on my last damn nerve. He was lucky he was the only blood relation I had and that I loved him.

"Ariel," Rain started, "I don't think you quite understand what's going on here."

He was wrong. It was him who didn't quite understand what was going on here and it was clearly up to me to set him straight.

"It's you who doesn't understand, Rain," I replied in a calm voice. "You're so blinded by your hatred of the Council and your jealousy of Marcus that you'll believe anything negative about him that you can grasp hold of. Marcus Cole is a damn good person and no amount of slander on your part is going to change that."

That shut everyone up.

I leveled Quinton with a glare. "Yes, Marcus did share with me yesterday at lunch that the Council had asked him to join them and that he was going to say yes. He wanted me to know first, which I appreciate all the more now that you people are acting like this. I'm glad I'm not one of you."

"How can you be okay with this?" Julian ground out between clenched teeth. He was taking this incredibly personal.

"For one, it's his decision to make, not ours. And, for two, he's not joining them because he wants to be a part of their debauchery. He's joining them because he thinks he might actually be able to do some good for our people that way."

Rain slumped back in his chair in defeat. "Goddamn him," he grumbled. "Why am I not surprised that he'd do something for the better of our people, he's a fucking saint."

I was right, Rain was jealous of Marcus and that's why he hated him so much.

"He took care of me," I said as I looked Rain dead in the eyes from across the table. "She had lots of boyfriends, Vivian did, and the majority of them were not nice. Marcus was the first adult in my life to give a crap about me. He means a great deal to me so I'm going to need you to lay off of him. Do I think he's a saint? No, absolutely not. For goodness' sake, Rain, he was sleeping with *Vivian* of all people. That does not say good things about him. It says the opposite in fact."

The guys all looked uncomfortable and were watching Rain carefully since Vivian had been mentioned. My father hated his sister more than I did, and that was saying a lot.

"But what you need to get, Rain, is that none of that matters to me. He might have been with her, but that didn't stop him from taking care of me. I'm not his daughter, but we're family all the same."

"You're *my* daughter," Rain growled in a voice full of gravel.

I threw my arms up in the air in frustration. "I *know* that! Everyone knows that. Nobody's disputing that fact, not even

Marcus. For fuck's sake, Rain, get over yourself already. You're my dad and I love you. You can stop being jealous now and give Marcus a break."

Rain, whose face is usually a mask of emptiness, blinked back tears as he looked down at his hands in his lap.

"You love me?" he rasped.

It was me this time who blinked the emotion back from my eyes.

I cleared my throat, twice, before I could respond. "Of course I love you, you're my dad. I don't think there's any way I could even *not* love you. You're awesome and you're fierce and you teach me things about magic that nobody else will. You gave me pictures of my mother and told me all about her. You told me about my family. You spent years and years looking for me and you *never* once gave up on me. That's crazy beautiful and I would have to be a soulless brat not to love you back. I'd never had someone love me before I moved into Marcus Cole's house and even then, it's not the same as it is with you. I needed someone like you... I... When she left me alone with them..." My voice caught and I choked on the words, not getting anything else out past the lump in my throat.

All around the table the guys were avoiding eye contact and not just with me.

"Fuck," Rain hissed in an ugly voice, before shoving his chair back so hard it tipped over and crashed to the floor. He stormed out of the room in an angry cloud that seemed to suck all of the oxygen out with him.

"He's got that right," Quinton muttered angrily, before standing and storming out of the room after Rain.

I stared after them, where they'd stomped toward the kitchen, in complete and utter shock. "What did I do wrong?" I asked in a quiet voice that shook.

From under the table, both Damien and Tyson reached for my

hands at the same exact time. They eyed each other. Tyson wary. Damien resolved.

Both threaded their fingers through mine and held on tightly.

"You didn't do anything wrong, beautiful girl," Ty told me. "You never do. It's the assholes you grew up with who did something wrong."

"Agreed," Damien muttered angrily.

From down the table someone cleared their throat. I looked up to find the rest of them who'd remained staring at me intently. It had been Julian who'd cleared his throat.

"Since you're feeling so generous with the L word, do you want to toss that sucker my way too?"

I shifted in my seat, uncomfortable with where the conversation was heading.

I wasn't quite ready to go there with Julian just yet, not in front of everyone else. Though, I was sure I did love him, I loved all of them. It's just that some of my connections were deeper than others. We weren't on that level just yet, but given enough time we would definitely get there. Julian was the type of person you bonded with for life, then prayed like hell nobody ever got in your way because he'd destroy them. I was also slightly terrified to bond with him because I knew it would be all consuming and when I was with him, just the two of us, he'd be the only thing that mattered to me. Hell, just thinking this way and knowing what was to come when my relationship with him progressed to that level sent chills down my spine and had me blushing as I looked away from him.

"Leave her alone," Tyson said, coming to my rescue.

I knew I'd chosen wisely when picking out my best friend.

"She hasn't had enough coffee for this conversation yet. Wait until she's nice and caffeinated up, and has been fed properly to spring this type of talk on her. She's a whole lot nicer when she's not operating on an empty stomach."

Okay, so maybe I hadn't chosen wisely and my best friend wasn't just a traitor but an asshole as well.

Good to know.

"We'll make you food," Addison chimed in, sounding far too happy for the situation. "She's already said she loves us. Even if it was throwaway at the time, we're still better off than you are."

The twins bumped fists as they grinned at each other.

"And there are two of us, twin," Abel crowed.

They got up from their seats and practically ran from the room.

I wanted to throw my coffee mug at them but didn't, because it would be a waste of good coffee and, like Abel had so Kindly pointed out, there were two of them—I'd only be able to hit one of them if I threw my mug. Only hitting one of them didn't really seem fair.

Julian's eyes met mine from across the table, fierce and unwavering.

"One day you'll tell me you love me," he proclaimed, "and I swear on my life you'll never forget it."

With that, he stood up and stormed out of the room, muttering something under his breath about having to open the shop today and asshole twins. Poor Jules. I hoped he didn't curse someone in his bad mood.

"Shit," Damien cursed as he let go of my hand and abruptly stood up. "I drove today and I'm supposed to be dropping him off. If I don't get out there he's going to come back in and pulverize one of your Salt and Pepper twins."

I cringed at hearing him call the twins by my nicknames. Did everyone know about that? Geez.

He leaned down and brushed his lips against mine in a barely there, but sweet kiss before turning away and following in Julian's footsteps.

After I heard the front door close behind him I slumped back in my chair and reached for my coffee. If this morning was anything to go by then my day couldn't really get much worse.

Normally, I would say famous last words and all of that, but I was thankfully proven wrong.

After eating breakfast with the twins and everybody who didn't live at the cottage left, I lounged around in my bedroom all day reading the books the guys had given me about tarot cards.

I desperately wanted to sit at the round table in the shop across from a customer and read their cards for them. The guys were all for this but, unfortunately, I actually needed to know what the heck I was doing before I could start. I was a fast learner and if I kept on it, then it wouldn't be long before I was sitting right where I wanted to be.

I had a quiet lunch with Dash before he left to do things unknown to me. He didn't return until the wee hours of the morning, and Binx and I enjoyed a quiet day to ourselves. Something rare I treated like the gift I knew it to be.

I also took advantage of the time alone to get caught up on all of the laundry, something Dash would not have allowed me to do had he been home to stop me. Out of the two of us, he was the domestic one, only because he wanted to be. He got off on taking care of me and I apparently got off on letting him. But, every now and then, when the opportunity arose to be the one to take care of things for the two of us, I took it. I didn't ever want him to think I was a mooch or a horrible roommate.

I called it an early night and crashed on my bed with Binx tucked up beside me, and Coach Taylor bossing boys in football gear around on the TV. It was official, I was gone for Tim Riggins. Taylor Kitsch was a hottie and the long-haired, brooding character he played on one of my favorite shows was exactly the kind of guy I seemed into in real life. Except for, you know, the drinking and being a hot mess part.

After the last dream I had, I wasn't taking any chances of

falling asleep underneath anything that wasn't my beautiful dreamcatcher, so I crashed in bed instead of the loveseat.

I woke up when I heard Dash come home. It might have actually been because Binx got up and left me for his main human, but I couldn't be certain.

I expected them both to join me in my bed, but fell back asleep before they got there.

# CHAPTER EIGHT

The bell over the door rang out, signaling someone entering the store. I looked up expecting it to be one of the guys and immediately looked away when I realized it wasn't.

It wasn't a complete stranger, either, and I very much wished it was. Or that he'd walk right back out the door and disappear into a poof of smoke.

The short, bald, exceptionally round man that resembled a genie and was a big time, hot shot member of the Council of Elders for the American Witches, strolled into the store as if he owned the place. I looked down at his feet, expecting him to have slippers that curled up at the toes with little bells on them. Alas, he wore no such thing. Instead, he wore a three-piece suit that might have looked good on him if it didn't look so out of place with the piercings on his ears and protruding, pregnant belly.

He looked deathly pale underneath the garish lights that ran along the ceiling in here, and the gold hoops in his ears gleamed so brightly they almost blinded me. The same could be said for his bald head. I wondered if he waxed the damn thing, that's how shiny it was.

Unfortunately for me, and it was unfortunate no matter how you looked at it, the door didn't have a chance to close behind the short man. And it didn't because he wasn't alone. This being another unpleasant surprise. Every time he'd come to see me before he'd been alone. But, then again, he'd never come to see me here and had only visited me at the Alexander's big house. As far as I knew he didn't even know this place existed or that it was owned by Tyson Alexander.

It didn't feel good to know that he very much knew of FFTU's existence.

The thought of Rain being in the apartment next door made my stomach churn painfully. He couldn't be found here. Not by these people. It would be bad for all of us.

I plucked my phone up off the counter where, thankfully, Binx was missing from and shot off a quick emergency text.

Ariel: The Council is in the shop. Do not come out here. Text Quinton.

My phone immediately vibrated with a text message, but I put it on mute and tossed it on the shelf below the counter before looking at it.

I hoped to all that was holy that Rain could, for once in his life, follow simple directions. If he came down here and confronted members of the Council, then there was no telling how that would play out and who it would hurt in the end.

I didn't think it boded well for me that the two gentlemen who came through the door behind Adrian weren't people I had ever seen before in my life either.

The heat that blasted off of them and filled the room up with their presence told me all I really needed to know about the two men. They were witches like me and they had a whole lot of magic. I didn't think I'd ever felt something so powerful before. Then again, all the witches in my acquaintance didn't wear their magic on their sleeve for the whole world to check out. They kept a lid on it and made sure they had control over it at all times.

This gross display of magical power was like the witch's version of a pissing contest. I wasn't sure who they thought they were competing with here, but I was sure they both wanted me know that there was no shame in what they were packing.

"Hello, child," Adrian Almatiez purred in his cultured voice, which even put Marcus Cole's to shame. "You are looking lovely and it has been far too long since I've seen your beautiful face."

I wanted to gag but managed to keep my face pleasantly blank. It wouldn't do well to insult the man as soon as he walked through the door, or ever, for that matter.

"It has been a long time, Adrian," I replied in a voice devoid of all emotion. I couldn't quite pull off pleasant so I went for blank with my tone. I was happy to hear I'd succeeded. Even though I didn't want to ask, I did it anyways. "How have you been? I hope well."

Honestly, that last part wasn't exactly a lie because I would never wish ill will on him. He was scary and probably had some magical juju going that would alert him the moment someone had bad thoughts about him, and he probably had a box stuffed full of voodoo dolls poked full of pins because of it.

He walked right up to the counter and held his hands out toward me. Reluctantly, I reached out and took hold of his hands as I leaned down over the front of the countertop. I had to lean down far because I think he was five-foot tall tops, and I wasn't exactly a short girl. Adrian brushed soft, plump lips against my cheek before pulling back and staring into my eyes. He still held on tightly to my hands and I couldn't help it when they started to sweat.

He made me nervous and it was starting to show.

"I must tell you I've been disappointed that you've not kept in touch with me." He squeezed my hands gently before releasing them and stepping back.

I stood up straight and wiped my sweaty palms on my skirt covered thighs, suddenly self-conscious of my attire. I would have dressed differently if I'd known I would be meeting with a Council member today. Instead, I was wearing a blood red tank top with black wording across my breasts that read, *Ask me about my coven.*

I'd skipped the hoodie today and was even more self-conscious that my scars across my collarbone were openly on display for all to see. Strangers seeing them was one thing. This man? Now that was an entirely different thing altogether.

I had opted for a short black leather mini skirt that showed off my long legs, instead of my usual leggings. My feet were slipped into a pair of bloodred flip flops that matched my tank top. I had a black choker around my neck with a silver pentagram hanging from it. It had been a gift from my Salt and Pepper twins for Christmas and I wore it almost every day. It matched the ones they both wore constantly.

My wrists and fingers were bare of jewelry, but the studs in my ears had all been changed out and replaced with bloodred ones that matched my tank top and flip flops. My lip ring was the usual black that I rarely changed out now, because it matched the one Julian wore through the opposite side of his bottom lip from mine. I thought it was cute that we matched so I never changed it out to something different.

My outfit was appropriate for my age *and* my job, but none of it was something you wanted to be wearing when facing off with what was basically one of your race's royalty. Especially not with the word *coven* in all its glory printed across my chest. I didn't think it was smart, nor would he appreciate me drawing attention to the fact I was a witch and a member of an actual coven. Then again, nobody who'd been in the shop today actually took what was printed on my tank top seriously.

I cleared my throat nervously before responding to Adrian. Mostly I was floundering for something to say to him. Did he know I'd been there with Tyson when Chuck, *just call me Chucky*, had fallen to his death? I freaking hoped not because I had no explanation I could give him for that question, not one that wouldn't end horribly for me.

"It's been so long since I've seen you or heard from you that I honestly thought you'd returned to wherever it is you and your people call home."

I held up my hand when he opened his mouth to speak. Not smart, but I felt like I hadn't done myself any good so far while speaking to him and really needed to make up for it before he got the chance to speak. I put my hand to my chest before carrying on, "I had, wrongfully, assumed you would leave the motel and return home after meeting me. I didn't know that I was supposed to be keeping in touch with you because you had never given me your phone number or email or any other means for me to reach out and contact you. If you had left me with your phone number I'm sure I would have contacted you by now, even if it was just to check in with you. You have my sincerest apologies, Adrian. It was never my wish to offend you."

He crossed his arms over his chest as he eyed me shrewdly. "Child," he drawled, "just who in the hell do you think you're talking to here?"

I pursed my lips but shrugged my shoulders innocently. I was caught in my lies and we both knew it.

"For one," he continued, "Quinton Alexander has my phone number and knows how to get ahold of me."

Oh boy. He had me on that one. Not that Quinton would have given me Adrian's number if I'd asked for it. He would have freaked and told me that as the head of my coven, Adrian needed to go through him if he wanted to get ahold of me. It was all bullshit, of course, and part of Quinton's need to protect me from any and every little thing that he could.

"Two," he said and I chewed on my lip ring. There was more? This couldn't be good. "How could you ever think I'd leave without saying farewell to you? There are so few females that the ones we do have are precious to us, the Council especially. You should know this by now, child. You are our future. Young women like you are the future of all witches. Never would I, or my brothers for that matter, leave without the proper goodbyes. That would be far too rude. No, we've been waiting for you to come to us. And now the time for waiting is over."

Shit, shit, *shit.*

He waved his hand around airily. "As, I'm sure, you can see by my arrival at your quaint little shop."

I resented him calling Tyson's store a quaint little shop almost as much as I resented him showing up here out of the blue.

He stared me down as if he expected a response from me, but he wasn't going to get one. I was smart enough to know no good would come out of my mouth.

"Nothing to say, huh?" He smirked at me like he was enjoying this.

I shrugged my shoulders. When he was right, he was right, and that was all there was to it.

"Would you like to meet my companions?" he inquired as he gestured to the two young men standing off behind him, giving us the illusion of privacy even though they could clearly hear every word we were saying.

Though he'd asked a question, I was sure he didn't actually expect an answer out of me this time because I wasn't going to have a choice in the matter. I was meeting his companions because that's what he wanted from me and, I was sensing, the whole reason behind this impromptu visit.

The two men stepped up to the counter, and I finally took them in for the first time since they'd walked through the door.

And wished I hadn't looked at them now because I felt like a traitor to the males in my coven. These guys weren't just pretty to look at, they were *hot*. Smoking hot. Like, take my breath away, make my heart race, freaking *hot*.

Yup, I was a traitor, and if there was a hell I was sure to end up there when my time came.

"Simon." Adrian gestured for the first one to step forward. "I'd like for you to meet the latest female witch to join our ranks, Ariel Kimber. Ariel, this is Simon."

Simon was tall, probably about a whole foot and a half taller than Adrian, putting him around six foot five. His clothing stretched over his muscles, straining against their width. His eyes were silver and his hair was black as midnight. There was something arresting about his looks, ethereal even, and for whatever reason, I found myself immediately drawn to him.

There were black swirls and symbols I couldn't quite make out inked into the skin of his neck, the column of his throat, and they disappeared down into his black, button up dress shirt. When I caught sight of his tattoos, they flashed the same silver of his eyes for a second and I swear I saw them moving around on his skin. I blinked and they were black and unmoving once more, as they should be.

I looked at Adrian quickly, to see if he'd seen it as well. He watched me shrewdly with an assessing look in his eyes that downright frightened me to my very soul. He knew I'd seen the flash of silver, he'd been watching for my reaction. That meant it had really happened and that frightened me even more. I didn't trust the Council for obvious reasons and I didn't want them using any kind of magic to influence me in anyway.

My eyes shot back to Simon's silver ones, and the warmth and concern in them for me wasn't comforting in the slightest.

"Ariel," he murmured in a quiet, husky voice. "It's good to finally meet you."

"And this," Adrian sang happily, sounding far too pleased by the whole thing, "is Trenton."

Trenton wore clothes identical to Simon and that wasn't where the similarities ended. The black hair, silver eyes, and height were the same. Trenton shared the same features as Simon. I might have thought them twins if not for the lines that shot out around Trenton's eyes, marking him as older than what had to be his brother. He'd seen more to life and it had left its mark on him. He also had a jagged scar that started at his mouth and ran down his chin, down his neck, and disappeared into his black button up. He, too, had a neck tattoo that mirrored his brother's and it also flashed the silver of his eyes when I looked at it.

Then *poof*, it was gone in the blink of an eye and back to black again.

Magic, they both had magic inked into their skin and for whatever reason it had flared to life when I looked at it the first time. I didn't think this boded well for me either. So much so, I almost wished Rain would say to hell with it and come out to my rescue anyways.

"Ariel," Trenton said curtly. His voice was the same husky timbre his brother had but rougher, almost like he was a smoker. I didn't smell cigarette smoke coming from either of them. "It's a pleasure to meet you."

I believed he really thought that, it was in his voice.

I looked between the two brothers and almost took a step back at the possessiveness in their eyes. It wasn't normal for having just met someone, and it reminded me of the way Quinton looked at me sometimes. This wasn't right.

"What's going on?" I questioned Adrian in a quiet, but frantic, voice. "Who are these people and why are you really here?"

It was rude to be so blunt with him and went against everything Quinton had coached me when it came to my behavior toward the Council members. But it couldn't be helped because I was freaking out here and there was no stopping it.

I reached under the counter and fumbled for my phone. I clutched it to my chest like a security blanket, or, better yet, a lifeline. I wanted to call Tyson and beg him to get here as fast as he possibly could. He was my partner in crime when it came to the Council. Hell, he was just my partner in crime always. I could really use him right about now.

"Put the phone down, child," Adrian ordered. "I am not here to hurt you. *We* are not here to hurt you. You've got absolutely nothing to fear from us."

I hesitated before putting my phone back under the counter-top. I didn't want to, but I did it all the same. A direct command from Adrian wasn't to be blatantly ignored. That, and it would only get Tyson into trouble if he rushed in here to protect me.

"These two," Adrian continued, "have both taken oaths and sworn themselves into the service of the females of our race. They are protectors, guardians if you will, and have devoted their lives to the safety of our females because there are so few of them these days."

He giggled to himself as he raised a heavily ringed hand to press it against his mouth. It did nothing to stop the giggles and I wasn't fooled in the slightest. He was enjoying my shock and confusion far too much.

"They're here for you, dear," he declared after getting his laughter under control. "They wish to serve you, to protect you. Isn't that just marvelous?"

My mouth dropped open and for once in my life I was at a loss for words.

What did that even mean? I was too afraid to even ask.

The shock wore off as I stared into Adrian's happy face. It was replaced with anger. This man didn't understand that it wasn't okay to give a human being to another as if they were objects.

This wasn't even the first time he'd tried to give me another person.

"Adrian," I drawled slowly, hoping he really took in what I was saying here. "You can't give me another person, and you really can't just assign me what amounts to body guards without my permission. That's just not right. I also don't understand why you think you have any say in what goes on in my life or the people in it. It's weird and it's not right."

I had to snap my mouth shut because I almost said something about him not being my father and that I already had one.

Stupid, stupid girl. I couldn't afford to make mistakes like that.

"You mistake my meaning, dear," Adrian countered in a steady, sure voice. "It's not me who is, as you say, giving them to you. It's their decision to make and it's what they've chosen to do with their lives. The Council would never make those choices for people. We very much believe in free will. We're not here to rule over the witch community. I hate that you would believe that of us. We're here to guide and protect."

Yeah, right. That was a joke if I ever heard one. He thought he was king and wasn't fooling me.

My eyes shot to the brothers, wanting to see what they thought of Adrian's little speech. Neither of them looked like they'd even heard Adrian speak. They were solely focused on me, their eyes gleaming with dark possessiveness that put me on edge.

"You don't even know me," I addressed them, trying to warn them off. "You seriously don't want this. I'm a mess. And, not to be mean here or anything, but I think for the first time my life is actually working for me in a way that I like. If I add anything else to the mix, it's going to rock the boat. I'm really not interested in doing that."

Simon, the younger one, stepped up to the counter and placed his palms on top of it. He leaned toward me, his silver eyes flashing dangerously.

I took a step back without meaning to and Trenton stepped up beside his brother, placing a hand on Simon's shoulder.

"You're it for us," Simon stated in a dark voice.

"What?" I squeaked. "That's crazy. *You're* crazy."

What I really wanted to do was tell them to get the heck out of my store and to take their crazy asses back to the loony bin where they'd clearly escaped from.

"He's not explaining this right," Trenton interjected, his eyes pleading for me to understand.

There would be no understanding on my part. This shit was crazy.

"I'm not sure any explanation would really work for me at this point," I retorted and was horrified when their faces crumbled. They looked crushed.

"We've been searching for you for years," Simon pleaded with me with his eyes. "The magic recognized you. It's destiny."

I shook my head, destiny be damned.

"About that magic..." I began curiously. "I'm assuming you're talking about the silver light your tattoos gave off... What exactly did that mean?"

And did I really, *honestly* want to know?

"It means," Trenton said, "that the magic we had inked into our skin that would allow us to recognize our female has finally done its job. That light was the magic blinking out and leaving our skin for good. You only get one shot at this and it's for life. You're our female, we'd lay down our lives for you, gladly, because to lose you we'd lose ourselves."

I took another involuntary step back, away from them.

"Our kind usually fade not long after our females," Simon shared unhelpfully.

That female business was really starting to bug the crap out of me. I had to put a stop to it.

"Look," I said in my best no-nonsense voice, "I don't know what you think is going on here, but I'm really not looking for another boyfriend or two. My dance card is already full. You're going to want to look for a different female to do, ya know, whatever it is that you do with."

Silence filled the shop as I looked everywhere but at the

people standing before me. I didn't want to see anymore posses-siveness or crushed hopes and dreams.

Out of the front window of the store I saw a big, silver SUV come to a screeching halt in the parking lot.

I sighed in relief, feeling tension leave my shoulders that I hadn't realized had been there since Adrian first walked through the door.

Thank goodness.

My boys were finally here.

# CHAPTER NINE

Adrian stood with his arms crossed over his chest beside Simon, who was standing next to Trenton. They stood like an unmovable wall, facing off against a pissed off looking Damien, Julian, and Quinton.

Rain had come through for me and called Quinton. I needed to give him a hug later for having my back.

"Young Alexander," Adrian drawled in a pleasant voice. "It's so good to see you again."

Adrian was having the time of his life here, it seemed. Good for him, at least somebody was enjoying themselves.

"As head of the—" Quinton started in an angry voice, but stopped when Adrian waved his hand at him.

"Do not even start that with me." Adrian smirked at him. "I came here to see Ariel, not you. She can see whomever she wants and I really don't think you want to tell me I cannot come and visit her. It won't end well for you and we both know it."

It was so ballsy for him to come here and threaten Quinton like that, especially in front of witnesses.

Quinton's face started to turn an alarming shade of red. He looked like he was on the verge of exploding. Not good.

Quickly, I rounded the counter and moved toward him. The overhead lights flickered dangerously and I knew I was running out of time to control this situation.

I stopped in front of Quinton, ready to tell him to calm down, but he didn't let me get a word out. Reaching out, he wrapped his arm around my back and dragged me forward until my front crashed into his. Without looking at me, he gave me a slight squeeze with his arm before turning to the side and gently pushing me behind him. He let me go and turned back to face off against Adrian's crew.

Both Simon and Trenton tensed, their fists clenched tightly at their thighs. Their heated silver eyes were latched onto Quinton, the air around them positively electric.

"You do not get to touch her unless she asks you to," Trenton growled at Quinton.

Quinton stiffened in front of me and I placed my hand on the small of his back, rubbing up and down soothingly. I watched the brothers over Quinton's broad shoulder, hoping they stayed where they were and didn't start a fight here in the middle of the store.

"I don't know who you are," Quinton rumbled in a dangerous voice, "but I want to advise you against concerning yourself with her well-being. She's a member of *my* coven, and I take care of what's mine."

See what I was saying earlier about Quinton's possessiveness? Right there it was in all its glory. And I think only a small part of it had to do with him being one of my boyfriends, and mostly to do with the fact I was a member of his coven and I think he might have been just that possessive of us all.

"She's ours to protect," Simon, very unwisely in my opinion, stated.

"Excuse me?" Damien sneered in all his haughty glory. "She's nothing to you and will remain that way."

Julian and Damien closed ranks, getting closer to Quinton's

sides. They were a formidable wall standing before me and what they thought was a threat to me.

My heart warmed in appreciation at the same time I wanted to tell them to stand down, because I really thought there was nothing to worry about when it came to the brothers. Except for maybe some type of strange worship on their parts.

I put my free hand on the small of Damien's back, along his spine. He shifted to the side, moving into Quinton until their arms brushed up against each other. The move made me invisible from my head down to the people who were facing us.

Quickly, so as to stop this from escalating into a fight, I told them about what had happened before they got here, explaining what the brothers had told me about their magical tattoos and wanting to protect me. I left out Adrian's glee and how happy he seemed by these new developments.

Both Quinton and Damien's bodies tensed tighter and tighter with each word out of my mouth until I feared they might snap apart and break.

"I thought that practice died out over the years when females stopped being born to us with magic," Quinton whispered in a shocked voice. "Why does no one know about them?"

Adrian crossed his arms over his chest as he arrogantly cocked an eyebrow at Quinton. "You just said it yourself, the practice died out over the years when females stopped being born to us with magic. There are all but two left who've devoted their lives to protecting the female race, and they're standing in front of you now. Their magic recognized her, it flared to life before leaving them for good. They are tied to her now in a way that will hurt them if you make them stay away from her. They'll be without a coven and will wither away with no purpose in life. You don't want to be responsible for that being someone's life, do you, young Alexander? You're a great deal softer than your father who wouldn't have hesitated to send them away if it served his purpose."

My stomach dropped at the mention of Quinton's father, and it had already been sinking close to rock bottom as I listened to Adrian talk about what Trenton and Simon's lives would be like without me in it.

"It used to be considered quite the honor to have a guard devote their lives to you," Adrian sneered at Quinton. "What makes you think you're so good, your coven so much better than the rest of us, that you can turn your nose up at not one guard, but *two* of them?"

The thing was, I was incredibly uncomfortable with the thought of having two bodyguards or anyone be so focused on me. It felt like a lot of responsibility and a burden I didn't want placed on my shoulders. Then I felt bad for thinking of them as a burden when they clearly didn't see me that way at all.

"How long have they been with the Council?" Julian asked what I thought was a very good question.

I didn't want them hanging around me, but I *really* didn't want it if they were spies for the Council or had been brainwashed by them.

"They showed up a few months ago," Adrian shared readily. "They claimed to be dreaming about a girl and their father had told them that meant they needed to start looking for her. Apparently, their father died a long time ago and they've been alone in the world since."

Adrian shook his head in what appeared to be genuine sadness. "I don't know when everyone decided the Council was their enemy, but I'll be damned if I'm not going to right that wrong in my lifetime."

I shivered, hoping he was wrong but having a really, really bad feeling that something was coming due to the vow that threaded his tone.

I didn't want him to try and fix anything while I was around, because his version of pretty much everything seemed so very wrong to me.

Adrian locked eyes with me and I felt a shiver for an entirely different reason. The way he looked at me, the heat and lust in his eyes, filled me to the brim with revulsion. He didn't care who I was, what I looked like, or whether or not I was a good person. No, the only thing Adrian really gave a shit about was the fact I had magic and a vagina instead of a dick between my legs. And he wanted me because of it.

Tearing my eyes away from the horrible look in his, I took in Trenton and his younger brother, Simon. Both were older than me and both were strangers to me. There was a naked vulnerability there, and yet a need so strong, it took my breath away. They had no one in this world outside of each other, and they needed me.

I was a sucker for that vulnerability and need. It reminded me a lot of how I had first looked when I had met Tyson for the first time. Man, I'd come a long way since then.

If, as crazy as it sounded, I accepted what they were offering me, by no means did that mean it would have to be anything more than what they had promised. They wanted to guard me, to protect me.

I touched my cheek. My fingertips trailing against my scar. I thought about the cigarettes that one of Vivian's boyfriends put out on my skin like I had been their personal ashtray. The broken bones I'd suffered at Vivian's hands.

All the horrors of my life were suddenly flashing before my eyes in a vibrant display of violence and abuse no one should have been forced to suffer through.

Finding my place in my coven had changed my entire world, for the better, without a doubt.

Could we afford to do the same thing for someone else? We were, after all, a band of abused, messed-up misfits. We fit, we worked, and we loved our family.

Would we, *could* we, still work if we added to that? I didn't know.

But, in that moment, I really wanted to find out.

Out of the corner of my eye, I caught Quinton's attention. Subtly, he nodded to me.

Quinton Alexander, my unwavering hero and the very first love of my life, had not only just placed his trust in me, but the trust of our entire coven, because my response affected them all.

I couldn't love him more in that moment if I tried.

I steeled myself against what I knew was to come and, in a voice full of confidence I didn't really feel, boldly stated, "Simon and Trenton can stay with our coven. They can stay with me."

I could feel both Damien and Julian's eyes burning into me, letting me feel just how displeased the two of them were by my words.

"Excellent." Adrian clapped his hands together excitedly before turning to the two brothers. "Now you may retrieve your luggage from the car and bring it back in here with you."

The finality of that stung through the air like a third degree burn.

"Ariel," Julian hissed under his breath. "I hope like hell you know what you're doing."

That made two of us, because I'd just voluntarily tossed us into the deep end and the chance these were shark infested waters was yet to be determined.

Simon's fists unclenched and he visibly relaxed before my very eyes. Trenton remained stiff and on edge. They both left the shop, to gather their luggage, presumably.

The bell over the door jingled behind them, signaling their departure.

At least they knew how to follow orders.

I moved to the front window. Not so I could spy on them, but instead to flip the *open, come on in sign* over to *closed*.

I had a feeling I wouldn't be getting much more work done today.

"Now that that's settled," Adrian chirped happily, "I must

explain some things about them so you know just what you're getting yourself into."

I groaned as I rubbed my eyes. Of course he would have left some important parts out. I should have expected such behavior out of him.

"You might have thought to do that before," Damien muttered irately under his breath.

"Shut it," Quinton hissed at him.

"You see," Adrian drawled as he crossed the room and pulled out a seat at the velvet covered round table. He sat down heavily in a chair as if suddenly exhausted. "Those boys now belong to you. They're your responsibility. Now, I can see you getting angry and unreasonable again so please, let me explain without interruption. I have other things I need to be doing today and have already wasted enough time on this."

I slid up next to Damien who stood with his arms crossed over his chest, hip resting against the countertop, glowering at Adrian. I wrapped my arms around his waist, resting my head against his shoulder, seeking out the comfort and safety that only my boys could provide for me.

A hand ran up and down my back soothingly. I didn't need to look to know Quinton had come up behind me to offer his support and to touch me, to make sure I was okay.

If I hadn't been draped all over Damien, inhaling his exotic scent into my nose, the urge to turn and wrap myself around Quinton would have been stronger. I was starting to crave them, their touch, their heat. It was exhausting fighting off the need to touch them all the time, and, frankly, a battle I was losing beautifully.

Adrian's sharp, leering gaze drew me out of my thoughts and almost had me pulling away from Damien and shrugging off Quinton's touch. I held steady though, standing firm in my place.

I wasn't about to let the bald version of the boogeyman scare me away from the things I wanted most in my life.

Quinton must have noticed the way Adrian watched me because there was an extra layer of gravel in his voice when he growled for Adrian to get on with it and tell us all what we needed to know about the brothers.

"Well," Adrian trailed his heavily ringed fingers over the deck of tarot cards on the table, "they're fairly destitute. Dirt poor, really. It's a shame. They've never had real jobs and lack any sort of necessary skills that would garner them earning a job on their own. Their whole family has been like that, for generations past. They rely on the female they're sworn to take care of in that regard."

I felt an immediate bond with them because I knew exactly what most of that felt like. Adrian talked like they were beneath him because of it.

"So, what exactly is it that they can do?" Damien snapped.

Adrian smiled indulgently at Damien, seeming amused by his outburst as opposed to upset by it.

"My, my," Adrian purred, "would you look at you. All grown up and no longer your mama's little plaything. Frankly, I'm astounded to have seen the way you are with our sweet Ariel, I'd always assumed you'd bat for the other team. Not, mind you, that there's anything wrong with that."

Quinton and Julian sucked in sharp, painful breaths. Damien's body froze to solid ice. He was so cold I started to shiver just from the amount of contact I had with him. I clutched him even tighter, not about to let my mind go where Adrian had just insinuated.

"You know what?" I asked in a loud, forced voice. "That's okay, I'd rather you not tell me. It will help me get to know them better if they tell me instead of you. I'm sure Simon and Trenton won't mind at all."

The bell jingled over the door again. The brothers walked into the store, both with a backpack on and a duffle bag in their hands.

"Where's the rest of your stuff?" Quinton inquired in a gruff voice. "Do we need to go out to the motel and get it for you?"

Trenton looked at Quinton in confusion. "This is all of our stuff."

Quinton's lips pursed angrily as he looked down at his cowboy boots. I smiled kindly at the two brothers, there was no shame in owning so little. I knew Quinton wasn't trying to make them feel ashamed, he was angry on their behalf. The man was a bear most of the time, but he had a heart of pure gold when it came down to it.

If they stuck around with this crew it wouldn't be long before Damien had his way with them and filled their closets with a brand new wardrobe. That's how it had gone for me.

Realization struck like a bolt of lightning. Where in the heck were they supposed to live? I couldn't just bring them home with me to Dash's house. There was no room. Besides, it would be rude to invite them without making sure it was okay with Dash first. And, this one time, I had a strong feeling it wouldn't be okay with Dash. There was an empty apartment above the store that had been gutted and completely redone, but, again, I couldn't invite them to just move in up there without asking both Tyson and Rain if it was okay with them.

Then I guess I would have to pay their rent for them? I think my paying their way was insinuated by Adrian and I had never been happier in my life to have money. Rain had set up my accounts for me with money that, had I never been kidnapped by my bitch of an aunt and raised by her, would have been rightfully mine. He tried to give me Vivian's money too, but we had donated it all to charity. But the rest of the money Rain wouldn't allow me to give away and had forced me to keep it. I also had a bank account that Marcus had set up for me and still continued to put money in it every month, even though I had asked him to stop.

I could actually afford to support Trenton and Simon easily. A year ago I hadn't had two nickels to rub together. Now I could not only afford to take care of myself, but two more people as well. And wasn't that a weird feeling.

Adrian stood up and headed my way. Everyone, I noticed, and yes, that included the two newcomers, tensed as if ready to take action if he so much as looked at me wrong.

I let go of Damien and held my hands out to him as he came up to me. I only did it out of fear he might actually try to hug me if I were to allow it. I wasn't much of a hugger.

He took my hands in his and pulled gently on them. I took the hint and bent toward him, with my scarred cheek on display. His lips ghosted over my cheek and he let my hands go, stepping back.

"I will see you next week at Marcus's dinner," he told me, before turning to face the rest of the room. "I'm sure I'll see you all there. No need to walk me out, I know the way."

And with that, he turned on his fancy, expensive loafers that didn't suit him in the slightest, and headed for the exit. The bell above the door jingled on his way out.

I wasn't sorry to see the back of him.

"Dinner?" Julian huffed. "What dinner is he talking about?"

"Is there something else you've conveniently forgotten to share with us, Ariel?" Quinton asked in a dry, sarcastic voice.

I shrugged, having no idea what the hell Adrian had been talking about.

"Not this time, Uncle Quinton," I shot back, mimicking the voice he'd used on me. "I'm sure that whatever it is, Marcus will fill me in when the time is right."

"We'll see about that," he muttered irately as he pulled his cell phone out of the back pocket of his jeans. He stormed off toward the back of the shop as he put the phone to his ear. I felt bad for Marcus and if I thought it would make any difference, I would have ran around the counter and shot off a text to him in warning.

Instead of doing what I really wanted to do, which would have been running out the door and far away from my new responsibilities, I turned to face them head on. And I wasn't surprised to see both Damien and Julian with their arms crossed over their chests, watching me with expectation.

Guess I had some explaining to do.

I scratched the back of my neck nervously.

This wasn't exactly how I had expected my day to go.

*Chapter Ten*

# RAIN KIMBER

I sat in the apartment above Fortune's for the Unfortunate and watched every move made on the screens playing out in front of me.

Ariel, my daughter in the flesh, so fucking beautiful she stole my breath away, faced down that atrocious fat man, Adrian, with a bravado and will of steel. It amazed me.

She was everything I had dreamed and hoped for her to be and so much more.

However, it wasn't my beautiful daughter or the obnoxiously bald man who'd belonged to the Council who held my attention. No, that went to the two young men who'd come in behind him. I'd recognize them anywhere, they looked exactly like their father had before he'd been murdered.

They were descendants of the Brothers of the Maidens. Their father had been the last of a very long line of guardians, protectors of the female race of witches. Most of them had died out or gone underground after the witch trials, and with good reason, because they'd failed miserably at their jobs. After that there were so few females that nobody bothered to join ranks with the Brothers of the Maidens and it just sort of fizzled out.

All except for one family. A family shrouded in tragedy and shame.

I couldn't believe the two living members were standing there with my daughter. It had been years since I'd seen them, but I knew they'd remember me. Just like I would never forget them.

*The screams hit me first. Then the smell. Both meant something along the lines of death, carnage, and gore. I felt like I'd been here before.*

*I should have never picked up the phone and instead stayed home with my wife and baby girl.*

*Honor and loyalty were funny things, demanding I come at the desperate calls for help I'd received from a long-lost friend.*

*I regretted my noble actions as soon as I set foot through the door.*

*Hunters had come and they'd done what they did best—slaughtered.*

*All throughout the kitchen, which I'd walked into from the door at the back of the house, were mutilated bodies. Pieces garishly strewn across the room, clashing against the stark white cupboards and marble floor.*

*The smell of copper and raw meat assaulted my nose, almost enough to make me gag. There was no one left breathing in this room and, slumped on the floor against the refrigerator, I found the one who'd called me for help, the one I'd come here for.*

*His right arm had been severed from his body, sliced clean off. It lay in a pool of warm blood on the white marble beside him. His eyes were missing, which was typical. The hunters would take the eyes as some sort of sick trophy. All the bodies on the floor in this room would be forever sightless and not simply because they were dead.*

*A masculine scream of pain and horror rang out from farther in the house, demanding I follow the sound of it, almost like the call of a siren.*

*I left the room, leaving the body of my dead friend behind. I'd come back to it later to take care of his remains, to take care of the remains for all of them. I'd call my father in to help me with that mess, it was too big a job for one man.*

*As I moved through the house on silent feet the tattoos on my arms, the* swirls of magic, breathed to life once again. There was a slight burning before twin, steel blades appeared in my hands. They were hand forged steel, beautifully crafted, and had been in my family for several generations, passed down from father to son. My wife couldn't have any more children so I would be breaking that tradition and one day passing them on to my beautiful daughter.

The door I came up to was partially open, I could see through the crack. A man stood with his back to me, a hood pulled up over his head. I knew from past experiences he'd have a mask on, covering his entire face, except for his eyes, from view. Head to toe, his body was covered in black. I knew from the wide set of the shoulders that it was a male I'd be facing down.

A flick of my wrist had a gentle stream of magic riding through the air, silently opening the door the rest of the way.

The sight before me had my heart lurching in my chest and my stomach dropping horribly.

The walls of the nursery were painted a pale yellow, the wallpaper that ran around the middle safari themed. I couldn't tell if it was meant for a boy or a girl, yellow seemed to be a neutral color when it came to babies.

A female, with a heavily pregnant belly, sat slumped forward in her chair, her throat slashed open, blood still raining down the front of her body.

The body of a young boy lay at her feet, part of his face and throat sliced open. His chest, thankfully, still moved, indicating he wasn't dead. Yet.

Another boy, younger than the one on the floor, let out another ear piercing scream as he launched himself at the hunter. I had missed him when I'd opened the door because he'd been crouched at the feet of the hunter.

That scream, filled with so much agony, a whole world of pain I would one day understand all on my own, would haunt me for many nights to come.

The boy never made it to the hunter because the hunter swiped out *with a vicious looking blade, slicing the boy open from shoulder to elbow. The boy cried out before dropping to the ground, clutching at his arm.*

*I had been too slow to stop the hunter, but I was on him now. With brutal force and skill honed from many years of practice, I palmed my blades so they were angled just right before thrusting them both into the sides of the hunter's neck. They ripped through the fabric of his mask and sunk deep into his flesh. His body jerked violently against mine as his hands went uselessly to his throat.*

*I pulled my blades out in one swift move and stepped back. The hunter dropped to his knees while clutching his throat and making grotesque gurgling noises from underneath his mask.*

*He'd be dead soon enough if I left him like that, but after seeing the carnage in this house, and I hadn't even seen the half of it yet, I wasn't willing to take any chances.*

*I kicked him in the back and sent him sailing forward. His arms left his throat to catch his fall before his face could slam into the carpeted floor.*

*I knelt down beside him, reached around to the front and sunk my blade up through his ribs, piercing his heart.*

*I slid my blade, now covered in slippery, wet, warmth out of his flesh and shoved him face first into the carpet.*

*The threat in this room now eliminated, I left the boys where they were on the floor while I checked the rest of the house to make sure there were no more hunters. I found two of them dead in the basement. The person whom I assumed took them out was a female who lay broken and dead at their feet. One of the few who still had her eyes.*

*The rest of the house was empty, but that didn't put me at ease. There could be more hunters out in the woods surrounding the house, waiting for their friends to join them or ready to come back and lend an ever so helpful hand if need be.*

*I wasn't taking any chances.*

*I slipped my cell phone out of my jacket pocket and made a call to my father. He'd come and help me clean up the mess and he'd know what to do with the boys.*

After ending my call I slid my phone back into my pocket and, with a heavy heart, headed back toward the nursery.

The hunters had evolved over time and, somewhere along the line, they'd gotten their hands on a witch who had no problems betraying their own kind. The hunters now came equipped with their very own magical tattoos that made it impossible to use magic against them. It was the only reason massacres like this were successful. If the people in this house had been able to use their magic to defend themselves, they wouldn't have been slaughtered in such a way. No, it would have been the other way around.

I closed the eyes on the pregnant mother, there was something about the blankness there, the lack of life, that I found disturbing, which was odd, considering I had seen it so many times before. Maybe it was because she was pregnant that it bothered me so much, since my wife had looked that round in the belly not that long ago and it made looking at this dead woman all the harder now, because it wasn't just her light that had been snuffed out. Her round belly had been stabbed multiple times.

Very gently, I closed her eyes and placed her hands over her bloody belly.

I easily scooped up both boys in my arms, the one was a lot younger than he had looked when he'd bravely launched himself at the hunter. All rage and balls and brawn, he'd eventually be just fine if he didn't let his rage at the injustice of it all swallow him whole. The other boy was slightly older and would unfortunately wear the marks of this night forever carved into his face.

I carried them down to the blessedly body free living room and laid them out on the couch.

For the first time in my life, as I looked down at them, I wished I had been born a healer and not a warrior, because it hurt my heart to see them lying there injured and know there wasn't much I could do for them outside of trying to stop the bleeding and hoping like hell they didn't bleed out and die on me.

It was one of the longest nights of my life so far and a part of my heart broke a little when one of my father's associates drove off with the boys, promising them safety.

*My father and I had been left behind to take care of the bodies.*

Eventually, the bald, fat, pompous little prick named Adrian left and the Brothers of the Maidens remained. I couldn't believe what I'd seen going down.

They were here for my Ariel and they were staying with her. This was a miracle, something I could never have planned or hoped for, much like everything that involved my beautiful daughter.

My mouth moved in an unfamiliar, foreign gesture as my lips parted and I smiled at nothing in particular.

Things around here were looking up. I didn't even care that douchebag Marcus was going for sainthood and had done something I would have done if the opportunity had been presented to me. I was all for righting the injustices of our world, or at least I used to be back before my whole entire world had been ripped out from underneath my feet.

The smile slipped from my face and a familiar emptiness sunk in.

I pushed my chair away from the desk in front of me and stood up. The only thing that could possibly fill me with anything outside of misery was downstairs with strangers and people who knew nothing about those strangers outside of the fact they were there for their girl. They were bound to be upset by these strangers and my daughter likely needed me.

Never as much as I needed her.

I headed downstairs toward the only ray of sunshine I had left in my life. Without her, my world was pitch-black and a place no one should ever be forced to live in.

# CHAPTER ELEVEN

"**D**o you both have your driver's licenses?" I asked into the awkward silence.

I crossed my legs at the knee and shifted my weight, my butt already going numb from the hard surface of the countertop I'd hefted myself up on. The room was tense and I was trying to act as normal as I could in hopes my guys might loosen up just a little bit.

No such luck so far.

"We have the papers you ask about," Trenton assured me. "We have fake papers for everything. Our uncle knew someone who took care of all of those things for me."

My mouth flopped open. Well, that wasn't exactly what I meant at all.

"Can you drive?" I questioned curiously.

"Of course," Simon rushed to assure me. "It was part of our training. We both took defensive driving courses that our uncle had set up for us."

"Holy cow," I breathed, finally excited about something. "Do you think he'll let me take this course too? I wanna know defensive driving! I don't even know what it is, but I know I wanna learn."

Simon smiled at me indulgently while Quinton barked out a harassed but firm sounding *no*.

"I'm sure he'd teach you if he wasn't dead," Trenton said in a quiet voice.

I slumped in defeat. "Is everyone you know dead?" I asked, hoping he'd say no, but some form of sixth sense was screaming at me that it would be the exact opposite of what I wanted to hear.

"Yes," Trenton answered in a dead serious voice that made me flinch.

Rain came through the back door and stormed into the place, saving me from having to respond. Not that I would have known what to say to such a thing. Sorry didn't seem to cut it or be even close to sufficient when presented with such an amount of loss.

"Are you for real?" Simon breathed out in a shocked whisper.

"Rain?" Trenton murmured hoarsely. "What are *you* doing here?"

I jumped off the counter, stumbling a little when I landed on my feet.

"You know my dad?" I inquired in shock.

Both sets of silver eyes flashed to me. "Your dad?" Trenton whispered. "Rain Kimber is your father?" He turned on his brother. "Did you know?"

Simon shook his head as he walked straight toward my father. I moved to grab him, to stop him, and arms wrapped around me from behind. Quinton pulled me into his body, his heat immediately surrounding me pleasantly.

His mouth went to my ear and he murmured, "Leave them be. I don't think it's a bad thing that they know Rain."

Simon didn't stop in front of Rain like I thought he would, but instead he got right in his space. He wrapped Rain up in his arms and dragged my father into his body. He whispered words I couldn't hear as he held Rain tightly before letting him go and stepping back abruptly.

Trenton moved right in and, like his younger brother, didn't hesitate to wrap my father up in his arms and hug him firmly.

"Well," Julian muttered irately. "That settles that, I suppose. Looks like we're keeping them. Unfortunately."

I didn't think it was unfortunate at all and wished Julian would give them a chance before judging them so harshly. It was obvious they'd had hard, tragic lives and needed a break here.

I think we all stood there in shock as Rain embraced both brothers back and didn't immediately shake them off and strike them down.

His eyes burned with a horrible light and I swear I saw him blink back tears. One second they were there, then in the blink of an eye it was all wiped away and his cold, dead mask was firmly back in place.

"What happened to your handler that has you up in this place, so far from home?" Rain asked them.

"Dead," they said in unison.

"Killed by hunters," Trenton continued. "The Council had been called in because of the coven the hunters had attacked before attacking us. That's how we ended up with them. After they figured out who we were they decided it was important to take us from coven to coven in search of a female to potentially activate the magic that would let us know when we'd found her. We'd honestly never thought in a million years we'd find her. Even when our father had inked us we knew it was more than a long shot, but tradition is tradition and there was always a small slither of hope. Who knew we'd find her here and with you of all people."

Rain nodded as if this all made perfect sense to him. "My daughter," he said with pride. "The Brothers of the Maidens assigned to my daughter, and two of them at that. Quite the honor you two have bestowed upon my family."

I swallowed nervously as I gripped Quinton's arms. I looked back at him over my shoulder to see him smiling down at me reassuringly.

"He's right, you know?" he spoke quietly. "Now that I know what they are, it absolutely is an honor to have them with you. I, like most everyone, assumed there were no more of them. They're raised to be warriors from birth. It might just be a good thing to have them with you. I know I'll feel a whole lot better about your safety from now on because the only thing they're supposed to focus on is you and your well-being."

I looked at him in horror. This wasn't good. If both Rain and Quinton were on board with this then it was as good as a done deal. I know I had agreed to have them with me, but I had stupidly assumed I could set them up with an apartment somewhere and let them live their lives as comfortably as I could afford to.

Even in my own head that sounded wrong, like they were my secret mistresses that I wanted to lavish money on but hide away from the rest of my life, keeping them separate.

"They can stay at my house," Quinton offered.

Well, at least that settled their living arrangements.

Grateful for his kindness, I leaned in and pressed my lips to his. He made a sound of surprise in his throat before he took advantage and his tongue brushed against my bottom lip.

I pulled away from him before he could get out of control and take things even further. I didn't want to be standing in a magic shop making out with one of my boyfriends in front of my long-lost father.

As if reluctant, Quinton backed off. I turned back to face the rest of them and he buried his face in my hair along my neck.

Of course everyone was staring. I wasn't really big on PDA when we were around everyone. I didn't want to make anyone uncomfortable.

Nobody in here seemed uncomfortable in the slightest.

Rain looked pleased, even slightly amused. Which seemed odd since he was my father.

The brothers looked curious and nothing else.

Damien looked like he was ready for it to be his turn and Julian had a soft, happy smile on his face.

They were all insane.

I looked at my father and asked, "Did you catch all of that on the cameras?" Sometimes I knew he watched in the apartment upstairs but he wasn't up there all the time, which is why I had texted him just to be safe.

"Sure did. Who was that lovely little fat man?"

Quinton's body shook with silent laughter and Julian snorted loudly. Damien looked at his boots but I caught the smirk on his face.

"Adrian Almatiez," I told him. "He's an important member of the Council. When he's not being extremely creepy or an asshole, he's actually kind of nice."

Rain looked at me as if I'd lost my mind.

"That makes no damn sense," Julian commented helpfully.

I shrugged my shoulders. It had made sense to me.

"He gave me a bad vibe," Rain told me seriously. I didn't doubt that he did, Adrian would have probably given Helen Keller a bad vibe just by being in the same room as her.

Quinton gave me a squeeze before letting me go and moving around me. He took control of the situation and started bossing people around, which he was good at.

"Right." He clapped his hands together, getting everyone's attention. "Trenton and Simon, you two are coming home with me. We'll get you moved in, unpacked, and you can meet the rest of the guys. Ariel, baby, go home. You have a training session with Rain in the morning and, honestly, I don't like Dash being home alone right now. Not with the Council showing up out of the blue like this. Damien and Julian can go with you and we'll shut the shop down for the night. Rain, why don't you come back with me since these two already know you, it will smooth things over at my house and might make their moving in go a little bit easier for them."

Sounded like a good plan to me. I'd had enough of the shop and all of the unexpected visitors for awhile. And part of me was right there with Quinton in worrying about Dash. In my mind, I saw him curled up and unresponsive in the middle of his bed and wanted to immediately rush home to check on him. He always went out of his way to take care of me and I wanted to be right there to do the same for him.

The brothers tried to protest this, seeing as they wanted to go with me and thought they should live with me as well. I'm not ashamed to admit that I left Rain and Quinton to deal with them and explain how things were going to go down.

I didn't even bother to lock the door behind me or say good-bye. I just ran.

Damien caught up with me at my Rover.

"Where's Julian?" I asked, as I used the key fob to unlock the locks.

He slid inside the passenger seat beside me and shut the door.

"He drove us here, and he's going to take Quinton and Rain, along with your new bodyguards, back to Quinton's house."

I watched him out of the corner of my eye as I shoved the key in the ignition and turned, bringing my Rover to life.

I was expecting to see some sort of jealousy on his face or even anger. I was surprised to see acceptance and nothing more.

I waited for him to strap on his seatbelt before putting the Rover in drive and pulling away from the curb.

"This was not how I had expected my day to turn out," I grumbled. "A member of the Council walking through the shop door was the last thing I ever expected to happen while I was working. I never wanted to see those creeps again. And now he's talking about some dinner I'm supposed to have with them and Marcus. I don't want to have dinner with those creeps."

I realized I was rambling nervously, but couldn't seem to stop myself. I felt as if I stopped speaking he would bring up the brothers and tell me how messed up it was that I said they could stay with us. Those were decisions we should have made together as a group and I had just said yes on the fly.

"I mean, when I went to the motel with Tyson, I saw them all having sex with that horrible Annabell. Like, all of them at the same time. I've seen Adrian naked and he doesn't even know about it. Doesn't that seem like some sort of extreme violation on my part? I certainly don't want him to see me naked."

I shuddered at the thought of my body replacing Annabell's on that bed and almost threw up all over myself.

Damien's palm landed softly on my thigh and I jumped at the unexpected contact.

"Why are you all of a sudden acting like you're nervous with me?" he questioned in a strained voice.

Damn, they all knew me so well. I couldn't hide anything with them.

Time to put on my big girl panties and be honest with him, lying wasn't something I'd do.

"I didn't ask everybody before I said they could stay. What I did was—"

He squeezed my thigh. "Stop, just stop. Quinton would have told them they could stay had you not done it. He would never leave people like that with the Council and that would have been the case, even before you came along."

"What do you mean, people like that?" I asked curiously.

He sighed as he let go of my thigh and sat back in his seat. "Their tragedy is written all over them. Maybe you didn't notice it since yours is the exact same way and you don't see tragedy the same way the rest of us do because, to you, it just seems normal. Not everybody sees it that way though and those guys had it written all over them. The way they latched onto you like you were their last lifeline spoke volumes about how much they don't have in their lives. They got lucky with you, though, because there are a lot of people out there who would have taken one look at them and used their desperate vulnerability against them and taken advantage of them. You'd never do that. Honestly, them being in the Council's hands is also kind of terrifying. If what Rain says is true and all they've done their whole lives is train to be the ultimate warriors slash bodyguards, then that makes them a serious weapon the Council could have used to their benefit. That they actually brought them out and had them meeting females is a miracle all in itself. They probably thought there was no way they'd connect with someone the way they did with you, and then the Council would get to keep them under the guise of wanting to give them a safe home and a family."

Huh. I really hadn't thought to look at it like that. I was only worried about how much of a burden they were going to be for me if they stayed, not what could have happened to them if they'd had to remain with the Council.

"Quinton has never been like you and worn his tragedy draped all around him like a cloak," he said quietly, hesitantly. It was almost as if he were afraid someone would overhear him and he'd get in trouble for sharing secrets.

"Quinton is a lot stronger than I am," I admitted what I believed as gospel. They all were. Damien too.

"I don't think he'd agree with you on that one. He's just a lot better at hiding it than you are. But, it's still there with him, the pain of his past, and he will carry it everywhere with him until the day he dies. I know he can seem gruff and like an asshole at times, but he's the best of us and has a heart made of pure gold. He's just better at hiding it."

Funny, I was thinking something along those lines about Quinton myself earlier. I was glad to hear I wasn't alone in feeling that way.

"My point is," he continued softly, "they were more than likely coming home with us anyway. Don't worry too much about what the others will think. It's all going to work out just how it should."

As I turned onto the long dirt road that ended in front of Dash's cottage, I hoped like hell he knew what he was talking about.

As it turned out, we had bigger things to worry about than whether or not the guys were upset by our latest additions.

Like, the cottage being on fire.

# CHAPTER TWELVE

"What the..."

I slowed down as I leaned toward the windshield, as if that would help me make sense of what I was actually seeing.

"Is that... smoke?"

"Drop me off here and head to Quinton's, Ariel. Now," Damien ordered.

My heart sunk at his words. It really was smoke billowing up above the trees. If Damien thought everything was fine, he wouldn't have told me to turn around and leave him here.

I pressed my foot down on the gas and sped up.

We drove over a dirt mound that was black and ran all the way across the road and into the trees. It looked charred, burnt, and I assumed went all the way around the house in a large circle. The magical barrier that had been put up around the house for protection hadn't just been broken, but completely shattered.

This was bad, so very bad, and Dash was home all by himself.

"What could break that kind of a magical ward?" I asked in a shaky voice. "We all worked on that thing, even Rain. It should be able to stand against anything. They told me it was safe here."

Damien cursed under his breath, likely calling me a number of bad names for not following his orders, as he pulled his phone out and started tapping away on it.

We skidded around the last bend and I slammed on the brakes, coming to a screeching halt behind Dash's black Camaro.

"Shit," Damien swore. "Get to Dash's now. The cottage is on fire and the barrier is down."

He said something else but I couldn't hear him because I had my seatbelt off in a flash and my door open.

"Fuck," I heard him snarl as I raced toward the cottage. "Ariel, get your ass back here."

"Dash," I screamed as I ran around the Camaro and straight toward the front door.

Smoke was coming from the back of the house in large, black clouds. My guess was that the fire was in the kitchen. Even if it had been in the front of the house, I still would have run in there looking for Dash and Binx.

I ripped open the front door and raced into the mudroom. I tripped over a pair of Dash's boots and went down hard on my knees, my palms slapping against the floor. Pain shot up my arms from where my stinging hands were pressed into the hardwood. Ignoring it, I climbed to my feet.

I opened my mouth to scream for Dash again, but got nothing out because a hand came out of nowhere and wrapped around my mouth. I didn't fight because Damien's heat and scent hit me at the same time, I'd never fight him off.

His mouth came to my ear. "Dash didn't take that barrier down himself, we need to be careful here."

I looked around wild-eyed, expecting someone to pop out and pounce on us at any second. Still, fuck careful, Dash was somewhere in here and we needed to get him out.

Damien slipped something into my palm before removing his hand from my mouth. I looked down at what appeared to be a shiny, silver dagger. What the hell did he expect me to do with this?

He stepped around me, grabbed my hand, and crept toward the living room.

I wanted to scream at him to run, to hurry as fast as he could so we could find Dash sooner, but his warning about someone else possibly being in here stuck with me, and if I wasn't careful I'd be flashing back to a time when Chuck, *just call me Chucky*, had shown up on our doorstep. That had ended up in heartache and bloodshed. I hoped this time would be different.

The living room looked empty but, scarily enough, the couch was turned over onto its side, as if there had been some type of tussle in here. The shelves, with all of Dash's books and movies, had been tipped over onto its side also, the contents strewn all across the floor.

Stupidly, in order to avoid what was really going on before me, I thought about how much Dash would hate to see his things treated in such a way.

Damien tugged on my hand and dragged me forward.

The smoke hit me and I tried to cover my mouth and nose with my free hand. And almost sliced my face open with the dagger I'd forgotten Damien had given me.

I jerked my hand out of his and put my mouth and nose in the crook of my arm. My eyes watered painfully.

The dining room was empty. Nothing out of place in here.

Damien turned on me, put his hand on my chest, and pushed me back up against the nearest wall. Tears trailed out of his eyes, letting me know the smoke was getting to him too.

"I'm going to check in the kitchen," he said in low, gravelly voice. "I want you to stay right here. Do not move away from this spot. I don't want you in the kitchen with me because I don't want you that close to the fire. But I don't want you that far away from me either or off on your own. We stick together and that's all there is to it. So, you stay put."

I nodded my head in agreement. Sure, I'd stay right here where he told me to like a good little girl who couldn't take care of herself.

*Not.*

We were wasting time with this crap and who knew what the hell was going on with Dash. I was done wasting time.

As soon as Damien disappeared into the smoky kitchen, I was off and sprinting two at a time up the stairs. There was still the basement to check, but something told me he'd be upstairs.

It was eerily quiet up here. The whole house seemed to be silent except for the fire roaring in the kitchen, which was mostly a silent killer.

I pressed my back to the wall and slid along quietly. Which was just plain stupid on my part because I had stormed up the stairs and if there was someone up here they already knew I had arrived. I reached Dash's open door and peeked inside. Seemingly empty and thankfully not a mess like the downstairs had been.

I kicked my flip-flops off, something I wished I had done before running up the stairs, and crept inside.

The bed was nicely made, like he took the time to do every morning when he got up at the crack of dawn. The doggie bed on the rug before his bed that Binx liked to snooze on was empty, no Binx to be seen.

I dropped to my knees and checked under the bed. The closet was empty as well. No Dash or Binx in here.

I walked out and headed toward my room, but was brought up short when someone grabbed my bicep and whirled me around.

Without thought, the hand holding the dagger came up and I slashed it toward my would-be attacker's face. Rain would have been proud because we hadn't only been working on defensive magic during our training sessions.

"Jesus, fuck," Damien hissed like an angry cat, before dropping my arm and blocking my attempts to carve him up.

Immediately, I dropped my arm to my side and stepped back.

I put my free hand to my heart that was beating over time, and hissed right back. "You scared the crap out of me."

"Get downstairs, right now," he growled angrily at me. "I told you to stay there."

"You don't get to tell me what to do," I argued. I pointed toward the stairs with my dagger. "You go back downstairs and check out the basement. I'm going to check my room real quick before I go down. If the basement's empty, then we'll *both* head outside together and head around back to search for them. There's also a hose back there we should use on the fire. And there's a fire extinguisher in the closet outside of the mud room. Get that too and I'll meet you downstairs."

Damien eyed me in a way I wasn't quite sure I liked before jerking his chin up in agreement and heading downstairs.

"You better not let anything fucking happen to you, Ariel," he grumbled on his way down. I didn't know if he meant for me to hear him but I did. "It'll kill us all, and then they'll all kill *me* for being whipped and letting you boss me around."

I didn't stick around to watch him disappear down the rest of the stairs. I turned and ran for my room.

My room was how I'd left it when I'd gone to work that morning. My bed made, but somehow looking a lot messier than Dash's did. The top of my dresser had a messy array of nail polish, eyeliner, lips gloss, jewelry—given to me by the guys—and a whole plethora of other girlie things I'd never thought to have in my life.

I turned to leave when something from inside my coffin-sized closet started making an unholy noise and clawing at the door. I raced over to the closet and ripped the door open.

Binx flew out, all puffed up, tail swishing angrily, hissing like the pissed off, angry cat he was.

"Binx," I cried as I bent down to pick the hissing beast up. He didn't mind being picked up by me and I was lucky he didn't try to claw me up.

I cuddled him to my chest with one arm so I could have my dagger hand free in case I needed it.

I sprinted down the stairs two at a time and raced toward the front door. I got there just as Damien was closing the closet door and hefting out a red fire extinguisher.

Binx didn't even hiss at Damien as we ran for the front door. I guess it was okay to hurry now that we knew there was no one inside. It seemed ass backwards to me, but I'd already riled Damien up, a fight right now would take time away from what was important here and that was figuring out what happened to Dash.

The front door was as open as we'd left it. I ran straight to my Rover, which I'd also left the door wide open on. I dropped Binx down onto the driver's seat and quickly closed the door on him. He yowled angrily as he launched his little body at the window.

Binx was having a bad night. First, he was locked in the closet, now my SUV. It was for his own good so he could just get right over it.

Damien was suddenly at my side. "Get in the Rover and go to Quinton's," he urged.

Not this shit again.

I shook my head stubbornly as I ran around him and raced toward the backyard. It was a lot easier to run barefoot than it was to run in flip-flops, I learned as I sprinted across the side yard toward the back of the house.

I skidded around the back of the house and came to an abrupt halt as I stared up at the back of the cottage in horror. Here, the fire could be seen through the sliding glass door and the window above the sink. My heart plummeted down somewhere in my stomach.

I shoved the stupid dagger into the back pocket of my skirt as I raced for the hose that was underneath the back porch. I cranked the water on as I dragged the hose out.

Something moved in the dark out of the corner of my eye and

I dropped the hose. I turned and faced the dark backyard, seeking out what it was I thought I'd seen.

Toward the far corner, where the light from the kitchen didn't reach it, I caught movement.

"Damien," I shouted carelessly as I dropped the hose and ran for the dark corner.

There was a black hooded figure with a creepy black mask covering their face stooped over, with a crumpled body at their feet. They put their hands in Dash's armpits and attempted to heft him up.

The hair around my head started rising with static as I was suddenly filled with a blinding rage. My magic welled up inside of me and this time I felt zero guilt whatsoever for flinging it out at someone else defensively.

I stumbled, tripping over my own feet as the most amount of magic I've ever thrown at anything before felt like it was ripped right out of me. Heat blasted out of my body and raced toward the hooded figure who held Dash aloft.

Dash's hair singed a little on top of his head as my magic hit the hooded figure and blasted *right through him,* leaving him entirely unscathed. It hit the tree line behind them and several of the trees immediately burst into flames.

Oh, shit, shit, *shit.*

My magic hadn't even touched this creep. What was I supposed to do now?

"Let him go!" I screamed as I charged right at him.

The figure dropped Dash to the grass in a heap that had my heart stuttering in my chest as I watched in horror as he face-planted into the grass.

If he'd done any permanent damage to my roomie I was going to do something really unfortunate to that creep, something he'd be sorry for the rest of his miserable days.

"Ariel," Damien screamed from behind me. "Fucking stop right now. Get back here."

I could hear him flat out running from behind me, trying to catch me. I had stumbled when the magic had been ripped out of me but it hadn't slowed me down, and I was once again flat out running.

I crashed into them. They grunted painfully as the air was sucked out of my lungs and we both tumbled into the grass in a heap.

Dash didn't even twitch and it scared the piss out of me.

"Stupid bitch," the figure snarled angrily in a masculine voice, letting me know it was male.

We started to grapple, wrestling around on the grass for the upper hand. He flipped me over onto my back and the air left my lungs again in a rush, my head slamming hard into the ground.

"Get off me," I spat at him, as I clawed at the mask covering his face, trying to rip it off. I don't know why, but it seemed like it would be easier and a lot less terrifying to fend off someone when you could see their face as opposed to a blank mask with holes for eyes.

I ripped away the mask and let out a small cry of victory, which quickly changed to a muffled cry of pain as he reared back and punched me in the face. His fist landed brutally on the side of my cheek right above my scar. Pain exploded in my head and my vision clouded with dark spots. I shook my head, trying to shake the spots out of my vision, and blinked rapidly.

Lucky for me I'd been down this road before and pain and I were old friends.

He sat back on his haunches, looking down at me with the smug face of a handsome devil. He was far too pretty to be such a mega asshole who went around punching girls in the face.

I resisted the urge to punch him back, knowing all I'd do is likely injure my hand. And my goddamn magic didn't work against him.

I did the only thing, the smart thing really, a girl could do in this situation. I shifted my hips beneath him, getting the angle just right so I could reach where I needed to.

He looked down at my wiggling hips, his face a mask of sneered disgust.

"Stop moving, bitch," he hissed at me before reaching for my hips.

With his focus finally lowered, I had the opening I needed to do what I had to do.

I sat forward, cocked my arm back, and punched him right in the crotch.

A man's precious polished jewels. Rain had taught me well, when in doubt, go for the man meat every time.

The pretty creep crouched on top of me, immediately cupped his privates, as his body careened to the side. He dropped to the grass, curling up into a very unmasculine ball, all the while making sad, pathetic little noises in the back of his throat.

I didn't feel sorry for him in the least. For a brief, psychotic moment, I thought about taking out my cell phone and snapping a picture of him real quick for Rain, knowing he'd be super proud of my actions.

Then I came back to reality and realized I was acting like a complete, idiotic moron when Damien dropped down to his knees in the grass beside me, panting heavily.

"You goddamned crazy girl," he huffs out between breaths.

Ignoring both him and the man still curled up in a ball crying about his man parts, I turned and crawled on hands and knees toward Dash's prone figure.

There were loud crashing noises coming from the forest as people came in similar black hoods and masks as the creeps came pouring out of the trees. They were dressed head to toe in black, their faces covered in those ridiculously blank-faced masks. Unlike the one I'd punched in the junk, these bad mothers were holding vicious looking curved swords in their hands.

I whipped around toward Dash again, reaching for his neck. I ran my fingers along, searching for a pulse. His chest moved up and down shallowly but that wasn't good enough for me, I needed more. My fingers tripped over his pulse. It was faint but it was there. That was all that mattered. I sagged against him for one second, allowing myself to feel absolute relief at knowing he was still alive.

A hand fisted in my hair and I was jerked viciously backward. I screamed in pain as part of my hair was ripped out of my scalp as I was dragged farther away. I reached back for the hand in my hair, attempting to pry it off of me as my free hand went around to the back pocket of the skirt that was riding up the tops of my thighs, threatening to expose my panties.

I finally pulled the dagger free as my skirt rode up around my hips.

"You're going to pay for that punch to the balls, bitch," he growled darkly and there was zero doubt in my mind that given the chance, he'd make good on that promise.

I wasn't going to sit here while he dragged me off into the woods to get a chance.

I twisted at the waist while dragging my heels into the slippery grass. I sunk the dagger deep into his thigh, pulled it out quickly, and stuck him again, this time higher up.

I pulled the blade out again after the second time, but didn't get the chance to immediately stick him again because he let go of his hold on my hair, seemingly forgetting about me entirely as he focused on his injured leg.

His leg buckled under his weight, entirely useless now, and he fell back heavily on his butt on the grass.

A grunt had me whipping my head to the side in time to see Damien narrowly avoid missing the swipe of one of those sharp, curved blades.

We were so screwed with it being just the two of us against at least five attackers, each one with blades and the only weapon we had between the two of us was the dagger he'd given me. A dagger that had looked a whole lot bigger earlier before I'd seen those swords being waved around.

None of the other attackers even looked at me as they held their blades high and edged toward Damien. Figured they'd find the male to be a bigger threat than the only female. Dicks. If I thought I had enough energy in me to waste, I would throw some of my magic their way in the form of a fireball to the face or two. Given that it hadn't done jack last time except given Dash a haircut, I figured it wasn't worth it to waste the effort. If I blew out that kind of magic, the chances of passing out and falling flat on my face were high, and who knew what the hell these creeps would do to me if I fell unconscious. I sure didn't want to find out.

Even though my head screamed in agony from being punched in the face and then having chunks of my hair ripped out, I still had it in me to jump to my feet and run toward Damien in order to help him fight off his attackers.

I took two steps toward him before a cold hand wrapped around my ankle. Fingers dug into my flesh, nails breaking the skin. I cried out in pain as I bent over at the waist to peel his hand off my leg. I latched onto his arm just as his free hand grabbed on and squeezed my forearm painfully. With a yank and a startled cry from me, he jerked me forward. I landed ungracefully in the grass at his side, my elbow and chin smacking harshly against the ground.

I groaned, momentarily curling into myself as I clutched my arm to my chest, holding it at the elbow.

He wrapped both hands around my ankle and yanked me back, dragging me along the grass. I'd probably have grass stains in some very unfortunate places after this.

If this creep was smart, he would have grabbed both ankles instead of just the one because it left me free to kick him in the face. Which is exactly what I did. The crunching sound his nose made when my heel connected with it gave me a sick sense of satisfaction.

He grunted in pain as he released my ankle and cupped his nose. I drew back my leg and kicked him again. This time nailing him in the throat.

Two blurs of silver flashed beside me, coming to a dead stop.

"Go," I urged Trenton and Simon. "Help Damien. He needs you more."

Trenton's silver eyes hurriedly trailed over my features before he nodded his head. The tattoos on his arms flared brightly as a black sword appeared in his hands. He ran off toward Damien and I hoped like hell he actually knew how to use that sword of his, and really had been training and fighting his whole life because we needed a skilled fighter right now.

Two of them would be even better though.

"You too," I barked at Simon. "Go with your brother and help Damien."

"No," he protested, disobeying me with a shake of his head. "I stay with you. Besides, the others have it covered."

I finally allowed myself to look in Damien's direction again, not having been able to do so earlier because of the creep who'd attacked me.

Rain was there with him, holding a black sword and fighting off one of the hooded creeps. He wielded his sword like he knew exactly what he was doing with it and I wasn't surprised when he sidestepped a curved sword that was aimed for his head, and thrust his own sword forward into the chest of his opponent.

I looked away when he jerked it out of the creep's chest and he collapsed to the grass.

The twins were there with them, wrestling around on the grass with one of the black clad attackers. I couldn't watch anymore. I didn't want to see them murder someone, even when they probably deserved it. I feared it might change the way I looked at them. It didn't matter with Rain, I knew what kind of man he was and I respected him for it. The twins were different though, they were my safe space and I didn't want anything to tarnish that for me, or for them. They needed that from me just as much as I needed them to give it to me.

Simon pulled the dagger out of my hand and I quickly turned on him, then immediately wished I hadn't when I watched in horror as he lunged forward and dragged the blade across the throat of the creep who'd attacked me, slitting it open.

An unintelligible sound escaped me, sounding far too close to a whimper for my tastes. I had no business being upset about this man's death. He had it coming. I just didn't want to have to see it firsthand.

I rubbed my poor, abused cheek, looking for something, anything, to take my mind off of what was going on around me. Now that I was relatively safe and didn't need to fight for my life anymore, the aches in my head were returning with a vengeance. I felt the back of my head and when it came away wet and sticky, I held it up in front of my face for inspection.

"Shit," I groaned. My fingertips were covered in blood. When had that happened? When that prick had ripped chunks of my hair out? I hadn't noticed it hurting so bad at the time. Even now, that part of my scalp felt numb. I didn't think that was good.

A gentle caress down my arm had me jumping and shaking my head to clear my thoughts. Why was my head so fuzzy?

I blinked stupidly at Simon as he knelt before me. The dagger was nowhere to be seen and I was glad for it.

Simon's hands went to the hem of my skirt that I'd forgotten was now embarrassingly up around my hips, exposing my panties for all to see. His eyes never left mine as he pulled on the hem of my skirt, dragging it back into place and covering up my privates. Simon wrapped his arms around my middle and hefted me up to my feet.

I swayed a little, leaning on him and allowing him to take on most of my weight. I didn't know why I felt so comfortable with him touching me. Normally I wouldn't allow anyone outside of my guys to put their hands on me for any reason. But with Simon touching me right now I felt... absolutely nothing. Almost like I was currently empty on the inside, there was nothing left to me because I'd used up all the emotions I was capable of feeling at the moment, and it had left me empty inside.

Insanely, I wondered if this was how Rain felt most days.

Simon turned me away from the fight and back toward the cottage that was now blazing brightly in the darkness, its loss a devastation so extreme, that even in my empty state of mind tears still trailed silently down my face.

Quinton had the hose on and aimed at the blaze, not looking to be making any progress whatsoever. Tyson stepped beside his uncle with the fire extinguisher in his hands. He was sweeping it from left to right and then back again, all the while spraying out a white cloud toward the fire. I highly doubted one fire extinguisher was going to do much good, and with the fight still raging on around us, I could understand the need for discretion, which meant no fire trucks to put the monster out of its misery.

Julian knelt in the grass beside Dash. He had his big, black bag of tricks open at his side and I knew without a shadow of a doubt that Dash would be perfectly fine, because he was about to get the best medical care a witch could grant him.

Physically, Dash would be fine. Emotionally, I didn't even want to know how he'd feel when he woke up to find his home destroyed.

I shrugged off Simon's support and slowly, weaving around like a drunken fool with the shadow of my new bodyguard, walked back toward the burning cottage. I stopped about fifteen feet behind the Alexander's, not wanting them to realize I was there with them. They'd both frown on what I was about to do and would try and stop me from doing it.

Simon's heat crept up behind me as he moved into my side. The heat was the only thing I felt coming from him, I was still too numb for anything to penetrate my senses except for the destruction of the cottage.

His lips brushed against my ear as he whispered, "Whatever this is that you're thinking of doing, I want you to rethink it. You have this dead look to your eyes that's downright frightening to look at. I've only known you for a day and I know that's not your version of normal. And you can barely stand on your own. I suggest you turn around and walk your pretty ass back to your redheaded friend and stay with him until he heals."

He thought I was pretty and that now was a good time to share that with me? For the life of me I would never understand males.

Blessedly, I didn't let his words penetrate and didn't end up blushing like a fool.

"Aren't bodyguards supposed to be mostly silent?" I asked snottily. I knew as soon as the words left my mouth that I'd regret them later, maybe tomorrow when I felt better, and end up apologizing to him. For now I just didn't have it in me to care.

His face shut down as he stepped back out of my line of sight, giving me my space.

I bowed my head and closed my eyes. Blanking my mind came easier than it ever had before, and I felt like I should have been alarmed at that given what was going on around me, but still, I couldn't find it in me to care.

There was a peacefulness to the emptiness currently inside my head, and it was far easier this way to reach out to the natural magic floating in the air around me. I pulled from the air, from the ground below my bare feet, from my very own body, sucking as much water out as I could get.

Pressure built and built around me, pressing in on me until it was almost too painful to breathe. My skin began to crack and all the hair on my body rose, sticking up straight. I barely opened my eyes to slits, they refused to open any farther.

The world around me seemed frozen in time, all except for

Simon who was no longer the silent bodyguard I'd asked him to be. He stood at the edge of my invisible bubble, banging his fists against the air and screaming my name uselessly over and over again.

I had a feeling he was going to regret ever having met me when this day was all said and done. And we were only on day one of having just met, the poor sucker.

Focusing on the flames licking their way up the outside of the kitchen, I pushed out with everything I had. The bubble I'd created made a loud popping noise as it exploded, rushing toward the cottage.

I blinked and watched as in slow motion Quinton and Tyson dropped to their stomachs on the ground, both wearing identical looks of horror and awe on their faces. They barely missed the storm that blasted into the side of the house.

I missed whether or not all that water did what it was supposed to and put out the fire, because from one slow blink to the next, my body careened to the side and I went down face first toward the grass.

Strong arms caught me before I could bounce my face off the grass. Simon had my back and was looking out for me, even after I had been such an A-hole to him.

My last thought before the darkness swallowed me whole was that he'd make a mighty fine bodyguard if I actually allowed him to do his job instead of taking things into my own hands.

I opened my mouth to tell him as much but my mouth refused to open. My body sagged in exhaustion and I blacked out.

# CHAPTER THIRTEEN

I floated, seemingly weightless, as my body came back online with a vengeance. My skin felt as if it was on fire, the burning an unbearable agony that sent me spiraling back into the nothingness, swallowing me whole. My mind's way of protecting me from the pain my body was in.

The next time I came out of the darkness was different. There was no more pain, but instead some kind of wetness covered my entire body from head to foot. I knew without a doubt that whatever had been spread all over my naked body was the cause for my skin feeling like it was no longer on fire. It was healing me and I knew Julian was behind this.

After taking stock of my body in its healing state, and knowing that at least Julian was with me so I'd be safe, I allowed myself to slip back into the darkness. For whatever reason I didn't want to be alone, even if I wasn't conscious.

Quiet voices are what woke me the final time. I knew they were with me because they were concerned about me, but I remained silent for some reason, not wanting them to know I was awake just yet.

"How did she know how to do that?" one of the twins whispered. I could never tell who was who when they spoke unless I was looking right at them. "With her magic? To my knowledge, no one's taught her anything like that."

"Rain claims it was pure instinct on her part," Quinton whispered back just as quietly. There was a tightness in his voice that I knew I caused and that made me sad. "Says it's in her blood or some other smug shit."

That made me a whole lot less sad. If Rain was feeling proud of me and smug toward my actions, then it couldn't all be that bad.

"Speaking of Rain," Julian muttered quietly. "Shouldn't someone be downstairs keeping an eye on him and those brothers? I heard him say something about wanting to check out the basement where his sister had been buried and Tyson agreed to take him down there. Those damn brothers went along because they are following Rain around like they've been struck with some goddamn hero worship where he's concerned or something. It's all very disgusting really."

I frowned as I shifted restlessly. That sounded absurd to me. Rain didn't like most people, so why would he be okay with my new bodyguards following him around like that? This was way too much crazy for my poor brain to work out at the moment so I shoved the thoughts aside.

"They're fine," Quinton quietly assured him. "I trust Rain and if he trusts those two, then that's good enough for me. At least for now. They're not going to be a problem for today and since we've already got so many of those, I think you shouldn't worry about it for now and focus on the things you can deal with at the moment. Like getting some rest before you collapse. You've damn near drained yourself dry healing Dash, then Damien, and now our girl."

"I know, but I really need—"

Quinton sighed tiredly. "Not buts, Julian. Not right now. I'm barely holding onto my shit and you need to give me this because

I can't handle anything else right now. I don't want anybody going home. I want you to stay here with me, with her, where I know it's safe."

I swallowed thickly, choking down the useless emotions that were threatening to leak out of me in the form of tears. There was so much naked vulnerability in Quinton's voice that it scared me. Had this latest stunt of mine finally broken the formidable man? Lord, I hoped not. I didn't need any more guilt heaped onto my shoulders.

"I don't want to go home anyway," Julian bit out angrily. "I don't want to be alone and Damien isn't going anywhere at the moment."

Quinton let out a shuddering breath before cautiously stating, "You don't need to be alone. You can sleep in my bed with me if you want."

My eyes popped open wide.

"Why would Julian sleep in bed with you?" I asked in a raspy voice. "He has his own bedroom here like everybody else." If they were going to be sleeping in a bed together, I was almost positive it wasn't something I wanted to miss out on. I would need my phone so I could take a picture of it.

Quinton's face came into view as he loomed over me. There were dark rings underneath his eyes and I knew just looking at them that he hadn't slept in days. Again, something I knew to be my fault.

"How long have I been out for?" I rasped.

His knuckles went to the side of my face and he ever so gently ran the back of them down my scarred cheek.

"You scared the shit out of me, baby," he whispered in a shaky voice. "You scared the shit out of all of us. Don't you ever do anything like that again."

The fire. I needed to know if it had been worth it. "Did I at least manage to put out the fire?" I inquired in a voice that trembled. My poor, sweet Dash, that place, the kitchen in particular, had been the only place he'd had any happy memories of his father. And now the kitchen had been entirely destroyed.

"You put out the fire, baby," Quinton gently assured me, as he dropped his hand from my face. "At a great cost to yourself. You drained yourself completely dry. Not only did you exhaust yourself, but the skin covering your entire body cracked and you looked like you had aged twenty years in the span of minutes. Everyone was afraid to even touch you at first because it looked so painful. Rain carried you out of there because nobody else could stomach doing it. We brought everyone back here and you, Dash, and Damien have been in a protective sleep, healing and rebuilding your strength. You had the worst of it, yet here you are, the first to wake up."

Quinton's eyes skirted to the side. My head turned to the side on the pillow that was beneath my head and I realized for the first time that I was lying down in a very large, comfortable bed.

Dash was beside me, tucked underneath the same sheet as me, sound asleep. Damien lay peacefully on the other side of him.

Why was I always waking up from after being injured and finding myself in this bed with multiple males? That wasn't normal, I tell you.

"Why are they in bed with me?" I asked curiously, not really caring because I actually liked that they were with me and I wasn't in bed alone. "And why is Julian going to be sleeping with you?"

I just couldn't let that last part go without getting an answer out of someone.

"Julian has drained most of his energy healing you all," one of the twins said. I turned my head toward the end of the bed to see which one it was.

Abel sat at the foot of the bed, watching me carefully. Oddly enough, Addison was missing from the room and not at his twin's side where I had expected to find him.

"I know," I replied carefully, not understanding where he was going with this. Was he blaming me or accusing me of purposely causing Julian harm? I would never do such a thing.

Then again, to be honest, I hadn't really thought much about anyone but myself and Dash when I did what I did. I hadn't worried about Julian and the limits he would go to in order to put us all back together again.

I sought out Julian, knowing he was in the room with us. I found him sitting in a chair beside the door. He was hunched over, elbows on his knees, chin resting on his fist. There was a grayness to his skin that made him look drawn and sick.

I sat up in bed.

"Julian, I'm so sorry," I said in a rush, my voice trembling. "I never meant to cause you any harm. Please forgive me."

Abel's big hand landed on my foot, staying on top of the sheet. He slid it soothingly up my ankle and back down over my foot. Over and over again.

"That's not what I meant at all by that, pretty girl," Abel murmured quietly, his eyes intense and burning, fixed solely on me. "I don't know what I meant by that, but I do know I didn't mean to upset you. Everyone is on edge and needs to get some sleep."

I nodded absently before turning back to face Julian. "He's right. You should go and get some sleep... in bed with Quinton?" That last part I was still unsure of.

"I just wanted to stay and make sure you all were okay before I rested," Julian explained, before standing and stretching. He yawned so big his jaw made a popping sound. "Wake me up if you need me for anything. I'll be just down the hall."

He headed toward the door but stopped short when I called out his name. He looked at me over his shoulder, his eyebrow arched expectantly.

"Thank you for taking care of me and for taking care of them as well."

"We're family," he stated simply, as if it were obvious. "I'm always going to take care of you. It gives me great pleasure to do so." His eyes cut to Quinton. "Don't do me any favors, asshole. If you're uncomfortable sharing a bed with me then you can sleep on the couch or in my empty one."

Abel snorted before bursting into laughter as Julian strutted out the door as if he wasn't almost drained dry of all his energy.

"Umm..." I stuttered stupidly. "I still don't get it."

Abel laughed harder at my lost expression. "How do you not know?" he crowed. "I thought they all told you everything now. This is awesome."

I scowled at him, not finding anything awesome about this situation, except for maybe the sound of his beautiful laughter which was exactly what I needed to hear. It made my soul feel infinitely lighter than it had in days. I wasn't about to tell him that though.

"Maybe you wanna leave that for Damien and Julian to explain to her when they feel like it?" Quinton suggested dryly.

Abel shook his head and grinned happily at Quinton. "Nope, absolutely not. She has a right to know what goes on with her boyfriends. I thought we were all being honest with each other here, you said it was the only way we would be able to maintain a happy, healthy relationship between all of us. Now you want to hold out on her? I don't think so."

I was so confused and my head was starting to hurt.

"Someone just tell me what's going on here, then get out before you wake the others," I grumbled at them.

I didn't like it at all when people kept secrets from me. Just call me a hypocrite already, I don't even care.

"Julian usually sleeps in bed with Damien when they're home," Abel shared all too happily with me. He gave my foot a gentle squeeze before letting me go and standing up. "Wrap your pretty head around that one."

He sauntered out of the room, putting an extra sway to his hips that had my eyes dropping down to his ass and watching it as he walked away. I had to admit, only to myself of course, that he and Addison both had very round, lush behinds that I admired as often as they were presented to me. Which was basically every time they turned their backs on me.

Quinton laughed openly, and this time I did feel my cheeks heat up in embarrassment. He'd just caught me ogling someone else's ass. And he thought it was funny. No, hilarious by the sounds of it.

Boy, had the times certainly changed. Where had my petty, jealous Uncle Quinton gone and who was this man who'd replaced him? Just how hard had that creep punched me in the face? Was this even real?

Ignoring his hysterical laughter, I asked, "Did he mean like *sleep* or sex?"

The thought of Damien having sex with Julian sent a happy tingle through me, straight down to my core. My nipples hardened as my head filled with images of the two of them doing really dirty things to each other. My imagination knew no bounds —really, since when had I become such a pervert? Hanging around nothing but guys had really changed things for me.

I looked down at my chest and found the sheet had pooled around my waist when I'd sat up and I was completely naked.

"Oh my god," I whispered in horror. How had I not realized I was completely naked and my chest on display for all in the room to see? And how had nobody said anything?

"We've all seen you naked before, baby," Quinton said in a sweet voice.

The bed beside me dipped with his weight as he sat down beside me.

Like the gentleman I knew him not to be, he lifted the sheet up, covering my breasts. My hands followed his and I took the sheet from him, clutching it to my chest.

He smiled sweetly at me. It looked sad on his too tired face.

"I'm sure they didn't point it out because it didn't feel right to check you out after everything you've just gone through and having just woken up from your healing sleep. They were being respectful of your nudity. We all were because you deserve at least that much from us. I know we are a lot for you to handle sometimes, and it's a wonder to me how well you've adjusted to this new life you've been thrust into, but you need to remember that, at the end of the day, you're the most important thing in all of our lives. They'd never treat you like anything other than a princess. And they would never take advantage of you in the state you were in when you first woke up."

He shrugged his shoulders casually, like this was all so normal when it absolutely was not. Maybe I had no idea what normal was anymore.

"And, like I originally said, we've all seen you naked before. Is it a pretty sight? Absolutely. Do we all wanna see more of it? You bet your sweet ass we do. But was now the time for that? Nah, definitely not, so they all ignored it for your sake."

I relaxed. I must have really scared him, because I had never known Quint to not take advantage of a situation where I was concerned.

Then he went and ruined the moment by saying, "Now, if it had been just the two of us I wouldn't have hesitated getting my mouth on those pretty pink nipples of yours. My dick is semi hard just thinking about it."

"Only semi?" I questioned in a mock, outraged voice. "I'm heartbroken." I pulled the sheet back and took a peek down at my bare breasts. "You girls are seriously not working right if we can't even get a full-on chubby out of him. Maybe I should come up with a spell to make you babies a whole cup size bigger."

Quinton's mouth dropped open in shock before throwing his head back and bursting out in laughter. He wrapped his arms around his middle as his entire body shook with laughter.

I smiled proudly at him, ecstatic at being the reason he was laughing so hard. It must have been therapeutic of a sort, because

I could see the stress and worry visibly melt off of him every second his laughter filled the room.

Playfully, I shoved him in the shoulder and must have put more strength behind it than I had planned, because it caught him completely off guard and he fell off the bed. His laughter died a sudden death as he very ungracefully crashed to the floor.

My mouth popped open as my eyes rounded in shock. I covered my mouth with the hand not clutching the sheet to my chest. I didn't want him to see me laughing at him despite the fact he'd just laughed his butt off at me.

Quinton stared up at me from his place on the floor looking as wide-eyed and innocent as I had ever seen him. The look on his face is what did it for me, and my shoulders shook with silent laughter.

"Christ," he muttered under his breath as he ran his hand over his short, brown hair in agitation. "Everything with you is fucking out of control."

I snorted. This couldn't be blamed entirely on me, I wasn't interested in taking all the blame here. If he hadn't laughed at me in the first place he wouldn't be on the floor sulking like a baby right now.

"Don't put this on me," I said through my laughter. "You're the pervert who started this by talking about my boobies."

"Boobies," he repeats on an angry sounding huff. "Fucking unbelievable."

I giggled hysterically into my hand. That word didn't sound right coming out of his mouth. It hadn't even sounded right coming out of my own stupid mouth the first time around.

He pushed himself to his feet, stormed around the bed, and stalked toward the door.

"I'm going to bed," he snapped at me. "I honestly cannot handle anymore of your outrageous bullshit right now. Don't leave the house without someone being with you, eat something, and put on some damn clothes so you aren't tempting everyone who crosses your path that isn't your goddamned father."

I watched his ass in his tight pair of blue jeans as he stomped toward the door. It wasn't nearly as round or plump as the twins, but it wasn't exactly lacking in the handful department either. And it looked firm.

"Stop staring at my ass, baby," he purred without looking back to see if that's what I really was doing or not.

Instead of being embarrassed, I went with amused. This whole episode since waking up had been far, far too weird, even for me.

"Just so you know," I called out in a perky voice as he made it to the door, "it's not going to bother me in the slightest if you have sex with Julian tonight. Next time, though, I want to watch."

His steps faltered. He turned back to glare at me while reaching for the doorknob. He slammed the door shut behind him without a reply.

I didn't need a reply. His reaction alone told me he wasn't having sex with Julian.

I groaned as I flopped back onto the bed. I was still just as confused as ever and didn't understand what the whole thing between Damien and Julian even meant.

"He better not be even thinking about having sex with Julian," Damien grumbled from the opposite side of the bed. "Outside of you and me, Julian's got no business getting physical with anyone else. Not unless he asks for permission first."

Slowly, my head turned in his direction, my eyes felt as wide as saucers.

Dash's eyes were wide open and staring at me. He had a small, secret smile on his lips, like he knew exactly what was going on here and how'd I'd react to it. He was enjoying this far too much for me, just like Quinton had before I'd shoved his ass off the bed.

Dash winked at me and I rolled my eyes at him.

"Uh, Damien," I muttered. "I thought you were a bit of a player. I had assumed that meant you dated a lot of, um, *girls.*"

I scowled at Dash, remembering he used to be more than just a bit of a man-whore himself before I came along. I had no business judging him but, this one time, I'd overheard a conversation between most of them where very unkind things had been said about me and they'd talked about the so called girlfriends they'd once had. I knew there had been others before me, I just didn't want to ever have to hear about them.

"Yeah," Damien immediately shot back. "I am into girls. I thought girls were all there would ever be for me, but then this thing with Jules just sort of happened and now here we are. He's the only male I've ever been attracted to and I know in my heart that there will never be another one for me. But, he's needy, so damn needy. I know, I know, one would think it would be me who was the needy one out of the two of us, but Julian craves that connection between two people who love each other. He needs someone to love him almost as much as he needs air to breathe, and he absolutely *hates* sleeping alone. He's terrified of all the things that could potentially come out at night and eat him."

Lord.

This was all way too much for a girl to handle after just waking up out of a protective, healing sleep. Or coma, or whatever.

"I... had no idea," I mumbled. "Just how long have you two been awake and faking being asleep for?"

They both laughed at me.

Brilliant.

That seemed to be the theme for the night.

# CHAPTER FOURTEEN

The bed shifted and I opened my eyes. Over Dash's shoulder I watched as Damien turned onto his side and propped himself up on his elbow in the mattress.

He wasn't laughing anymore. He looked worried, almost scared even. Scared of... me?

"Does that bother you?" he asked me in a quiet voice. Gone was the haughty brat I'd fallen for. In his place was a very different man. One who'd only opened himself up to me this way a handful of times. I was surprised to see him do so now in front of Dash.

My heart hurt at the thought of Damien thinking I would ever judge him or try to deny him his relationship with Julian. Honestly—also something I wasn't entirely comfortable with him or anyone else knowing—I didn't think there was much I would be able to deny Damien or anyone of them, even if I was against it.

But this? Him having a relationship with someone else that I, too, had a relationship with? How could I ever have a problem with that? I was actually happy for the two of them that they had that between them. Love was love and, so long as it was consensual and both parties were good with it, I was all for it. I also had a really big heart and was capable of being intimate with more than one person, I would never be anything but happy for the both of them. Yeah, I freely admitted to being a hypocrite earlier, but never with something as important as this.

I mimicked Damien's movements and rolled over on my side to face him. I put my elbow in the mattress and propped my head up on my fist.

The fact that Dash was on the bed between the two of us, and now laying on his back with his hands behind his head, didn't seem awkward to me in the slightest. Six months ago I would have found this the most awkward and absurd situation I had ever found myself in, and I would have been blushing like the mostly inexperienced virgin I was. Now, awkward and absurd were my new normal and I just needed to roll with it.

Dash didn't seem to care, so why should I on his behalf?

"No," I answered honestly. "It absolutely doesn't bother me in the slightest. I just wish one of you would have been open with me about it from the start and told me sooner. I feel like I'm always the outsider here with our group, always the one trying to play catch up and, at the same time, working my butt off not to hurt anyone's feelings..."

I trail off when I realize it's my feelings that are hurt this time, because they kept something so vitally important from me. Something I knew every single one of my guys was aware of. They didn't ever keep those kinds of secrets from each other. They only ever kept secrets from me.

The sheets rustled as Dash moved. He slid his hands from out from under his head and turned onto his side, facing me.

"Come here, sweetheart," he said, before reaching for me.

I went to him willingly, and laid my head down on his shoulder after he pulled me into him and wrapped his arms around me. His arms held me tightly as he turned onto his back, dragging me along with him.

I ended up on top of him, naked, and sprawled shamelessly over him with my legs on each side of his. He was just as naked as I was. I sucked in a sharp breath as his erection pressed up against my thigh.

He ran his hands up and down my back soothingly. Ignoring his hardness pressed up against me and the fact my bare breasts were firmly pressed to his chest, I relaxed into him. This was Dash and I could never not feel anything but safe with him.

Dash's hands stilled when Damien used my hair to turn my face toward his. The fear in his eyes had me tensing up again, and Dash's hands picked back up on their soothing movements, up and down my back. He really didn't seem to like the thought of me being uncomfortable with him.

"You hid it from me, the both of you went out of your way to hide it," I whispered to Damien in a voice full of hurt. I closed my eyes tightly. "*All* of you hid it from me."

"Quinton was right," Dash muttered. "Not anybody else's story to tell and not our business. Wasn't my place to tell you, so I kept my mouth shut knowing eventually those two boneheads would get around to sharing with you. Unlike the prick beside us, I knew you'd hold no judgment and wouldn't have a problem with their relationship. Your heart is so big you would never be anything but happy for them. They were stupid for ever even questioning you."

My body completely melted against his. Out of all of them, Dash always understood me the most.

Damien's face took on a pained expression before he scrunched his eyes closed. He opened them and the pleading expression there took my breath away.

"I love you," he disclosed hoarsely. "So does Julian. We all do. But that doesn't mean we know you the same way we know each other. Those bonds can only grow stronger over time. Trust is built over time, and isn't something that can be forced or faked. Julian and myself, we wanted to give you time to settle into your new life and for there to be a great deal of trust in us before we sprang this on you. We never, ever wanted to make things uncomfortable or harder on you. We only wanted to love you. Please don't let me have messed this all up."

I sucked in a shocked breath at hearing him tell me he loved me so openly, and in front of Dash. Then again, he'd just been forced into sharing his deepest, darkest secret with me, it's not like he had anything else to hide here.

I sighed as I melted into Dash's hold, my body going limp against his. His hand moved up my back, up my neck, and his fingers tangled into the messy hair at the back of my head. His other hand dropped to my hip where he squeezed gently, encouraging me.

"It's alright, Damien," I whispered. "I understand why you guys kept it from me and you're right about pretty much everything you said. But that doesn't mean it's okay for you to keep anymore secrets from me from here on out. At least not big ones that are as important as that."

"I promise," he quickly assured me. "No more big secrets. I can't promise no secrets in general because, well, that would make me a liar." I glared at him. "*But* they won't be big ones like that. Not anything that could damage our relationship."

Great. That wasn't exactly what I wanted to hear from him.

He looked at the door, his face scrunched up in concern. I thought I knew what he wanted but didn't want to hurt my feelings by asking.

"Go," I quietly urged. "Go and rescue Quinton from having to share a bed with Julian. We both know he'll do it too, no matter how uncomfortable it makes him because that's what Julian needs and Quinton is all about everyone else's needs above his own. And I can see it in your eyes that you want to go to him. So go. I'm here with Dash and we're doing just fine."

He closed his eyes as if in pain before opening them again. They roamed over Dash and I, not missing anything and seeing things I wasn't sure I was comfortable with others seeing just yet. But I didn't have much of a choice at this point and I really needed to get over my hang-ups.

"I won't leave if you want me to stay," Damien murmured fiercely. "I would never do that to you and Julian wouldn't expect me to. You come first, you'll always come first, it's just the way we're wired."

Instead of filling me up with reassurance, the way I'm sure he'd meant for his words to, they filled me with sadness. They were all about putting me first, every single one of them. That didn't seem fair to me sometimes.

"I think I got this covered, Dame," Dash rumbled in a voice that shook with silent laughter. "You don't have anything to worry about here."

"Yeah," Damien grumbled sarcastically. "You sure look like you have everything covered here."

I closed my eyes as I snuggled deeper into Dash, my face going to his neck, my hands gliding up his sides. His skin was hot to the touch, burning in the most brilliant of ways. It was addictive, the feel of his bare skin against mine, and I couldn't get enough of it.

"Go," I murmured. "Go find Julian before he spoons Quinton in his sleep, not that anybody would blame him for spooning him because it's obvious the guy could use more hugs in his life, but I think it might actually make him grumpier and harder to deal with. And it'll be me who has to deal with it because he's going to blame the entire thing on me."

They both chuckled.

"Well," Damien drawled, "it kinda is your fault. I mean, I did tell you to stay downstairs, then you didn't listen to me. I told you to stay in the Rover. Again, you didn't listen to me. Hell, I tried to get you to leave before we even got to the damn cottage, and did you listen to me then? Absolutely not. If you'd have listened to me like a good girl and done what I'd told you to do instead of taking control of the situation and started bossing me around, then things might have turned out differently."

My body stiffened minutely. I knew he was joking with me, but I didn't like them telling me to be a good girl. The teenage girl in me always felt the need to rebel against it and I ended up doing the opposite of what they wanted me to. And, despite my actions being rash and harmful to myself, I'd done good. I managed to put the fire out and maybe Dash's cottage wasn't entirely unsalvageable now. It was our home and I couldn't just stand by with my thumb up my butt while I watched it being destroyed and do nothing.

Just what did these people think of me? Of course I had to do something, and of course it had to have been the opposite of what some of them would have had me do.

I sighed again. No wonder some of them thought I was a pain in their asses.

Damien leaned down, his face close to mine. His hand came up, his fingers pulling my hair back and out of my face. Something bright and glassy shined in his eyes, looking a lot like unshed tears.

"Thank you, sweet girl," he whispered hoarsely, before his lips brushed against my forehead.

Before I could respond, he was up and out of the bed. The shock of seeing him naked and standing beside the bed didn't hit me as hard as it usually would have. I was getting more comfortable around them and their bodies.

He walked out of the room and closed the door behind him, all without bothering to put on clothes, and I stifled a giggle. Quinton was going to kill him and I *really* hoped he didn't run into Rain while walking around in his birthday suit. My father would be a whole lot less amused than Quinton and I had a feeling he wouldn't hesitate to rip Damien a new one.

"People in this house are crazy," I muttered under my breath when my laughter finally settled down.

Dash's hand fisted in my hair. He used it to turn my head to the side and my eyes snapped open. The move surprised me.

I stared down at him as I chewed on my lip ring nervously.

"You're crazy too," he whispered in a hushed voice that was filled with heat. "You're one of the craziest people I've ever met before."

Huh. That didn't sound good.

"I'm not crazy." At least I thought I wasn't crazy... most of the time.

Using his hold on my hair, he pulled my head down until we were inches apart. He tipped his face up, his lips brushing against mine.

"Crazy beautiful," he muttered distractedly, before his mouth crashed into mine.

I moaned into his mouth as my tongue caressed his, kissing him back feverishly. My hands slid up along his ribs before spanning out, my fingers splayed wide across his chest. I swiped my thumbs across his nipples, causing him to make a pained sound in the back of his throat.

Hmm... I'd have to remember that he liked that. I'd only tried it out because I knew I liked it when it was done to me. I wondered if everything would be that way for him and decided to give it a try.

Turning my head to the side, I broke the kiss. We both panted breathlessly. I kissed along his jaw, moving toward his neck. My teeth grazed his ear lobe, making him groan.

His loosened hand in my hair let go, both his hands now gliding slowly down my back. I kissed my way down his neck as his hands roamed over my hips, only stopping when he cupped the round, fullness of my ass cheeks. His fingers dug into my flesh and he squeezed roughly.

Heat bloomed between my legs, a restless, needy ache that I wanted filled immediately.

"Fuck," Dash hissed, as I ground myself against him. "We

should stop," he groaned, "before things go any further and I hit the point of no return."

I disagreed, stopping sounded like the worst idea I'd ever heard.

"I don't want to stop," I told him honestly, "and neither do you. Unless you're telling me you don't want to have sex with me? Seriously, Dash, we both know that's a lie."

His erection was pressed up hard against me, there was no hiding how much he wanted me. Sitting on top of him with my legs spread, my knees pressed into the bed on each side of him, there was no way for him to mistake just how much I wanted him too, when my wetness was leaking all over him.

Dash sighed heavily, the look on his face full of frustration.

"I do want you, Ariel, more than I've ever wanted anything in my whole fucked up, sorry excuse for a life. But I don't want to rush you into anything, and if you're not ready—"

I was so sick and tired of other people making decisions for me and telling me I wasn't ready when they had no idea. That was a question only I had the answer for.

"I am ready," I stated in a voice laced with steel. "I've been ready for a good, long while but none of you idiots will listen to me."

Dash opened his mouth, likely to protest some more and valiantly protect my virginity, but I'd had more than enough of this ridiculousness. It was time for action, time I take things into my own hands, literally.

In order to quiet his protests, I kissed him. He was hesitant at first, his body tense beneath me. It didn't take long for him to relax again as the kiss grew more heated, frenzied even.

I broke the kiss and went back to trailing kisses along his jawline before moving down to his neck.

"Ariel," he moaned my name as I kissed my way down his body. I flicked my tongue across his nipple, making his entire body jump beneath me.

His hands fisted in the sheets as I continued on my journey, making my way down his body, using my mouth and tongue to taste every available inch of his skin on my descent.

Above his belly button and down to his crotch there was a thick trail of dark, red hair that led the way down to his pubic area.

I had never done this before but I wanted to try. I wanted to make him feel good, and hopefully lower his inhibitions enough for him to give me what I wanted without further protest, because it's what he wanted too.

I dragged my tongue down his stomach, stopping at his hip bone. I looked up at him as I paused for a moment, needing to see he was right there with me and enjoying what I was doing to him.

His eyes were locked on me, hot and burning with desire.

"What do you want, Ariel?" he asked in a thick, husky voice.

"You," I said simply. For me it was that simple. "I just want you."

My thoughts were entirely consumed with Dash. In this moment it was just the two of us and nobody else existed.

"You have me," he whispered.

A surge of victory burned through me. I wouldn't be his first, nowhere near it, but I would have something no one else ever really got from him. He was mine in ways he'd never been anyone else's.

Without breaking eye contact, I palmed his dick in my hand. For something that looked so hard, it was a lot softer than I thought it would be, almost like smooth velvet. And it was burning hot.

I curled my fingers around as much of it as I could and slid my hand up, stopping when my hand bumped up against the tip, and then slowly gliding back down. His hips jerked, coming off the bed. The look on his face turned harsh and he snarled something unintelligible at me.

My eyes widened at the sudden change that had come over him as he sat up and, almost violently, flipped me over onto my back. My hair blew out all around me as I cried out in surprise.

"Dash," I breathed out. "What are you—"

He silenced me with a kiss, his mouth crashing down onto mine, almost much the same as I had done with him earlier.

My hands went to his shoulders and slid around and down his back.

He froze above me for a second, his mouth finally leaving mine and allowing me to breathe. He stared down at me, his eyes full of naked vulnerability as I carefully ran my hands over the scarred up, abrasive layers of skin on his back. He didn't ask me to stop so I kept going, exploring every raised line and hard ridge along the way. There were too many of them to count, from years of torture at his mother and grandmother's hands.

I knew he didn't usually allow people to get this close to him and I reveled in it, taking it as the gift I knew it to be.

"Kiss me," I muttered, not wanting him to get too much into his head, and be here with me in the moment.

His tongue flicked out, tracing my lips before his face disappeared in my neck. He kissed his way down the column of my throat. His hot, wet mouth dropped down to my breasts as he palmed them. One thumb flicked across my nipple, just how I liked it, while his mouth moved to the other one. I moaned as he sucked my nipple into his mouth, his teeth grazing it lightly.

I shifted my hips restlessly as need pooled between my thighs, my core aching. I wrapped my legs around his hips and my breath hissed out of me as his erection pressed up against my center. It felt good, *right,* and I wanted more.

Dash's hand left my breast and slipped down my body. Down past my pubic bone. His fingers glided through my wetness, his thumb going straight to my clit. He circled it in slow motions, causing me to cry out and arch my back off the bed. He kept kissing my breast, playing with my nipple with his tongue, as he slowly slid a finger inside me.

There, right *there.*

That was exactly what I needed, what my body craved. My hips jerked as he slid another finger inside, stretching, but not unpleasantly so. His thumb moved against my clit as his fingers slid outside of me, just to be thrust back in again.

"Okay?" he asked quietly.

I nodded my head frantically. It was more than okay. I might have been a virgin, but I knew how to touch myself and make it feel good. I had been the first person to explore my body this way, but his fingers felt a whole lot better than my own had.

"Ariel?"

"Yeah," I replied huskily. "Everything is okay." My breath hitched as his fingers withdrew just to slide right back into me.

My insides fluttered before clenching around his fingers. Pleasure rocketed through me as I slid my hand around the front of him and down. I grabbed hold of the hand he was touching me with and held on, holding him in place as I rode out my orgasm.

My eyes shut tight as greedy noises left my throat.

I released his hand as my body grew limp and I melted back against the mattress, my legs still wrapped around his hips.

Dash raised his head to look down at me while removing his fingers from where they were inside me. I whimpered as he pulled his fingers free, immediately missing them and wanting them back.

"Christ," Dash murmured. "Please tell me it's true and you're on birth control."

I blinked stupidly at him, coming slightly out of my orgasm induced fog.

"What?" I hissed angrily at him. I *was* on birth control and had been for a long time, I had bad periods and it helped control them and made the pain bearable. The fact that he seemed to know this before I told him shouldn't have surprised me, but it did. They knew almost everything there was to know about me.

I shook my head in exasperation as I muttered, "Yes." I had nothing to be embarrassed about here and should have been glad he thought to ask first.

His lips curled up at the ends as he shrugged his shoulders, boyishly unrepentant.

He palmed his erection and guided it toward my core. He rubbed the head of it up my slit before going back to my opening.

"Kiss me," I commanded, needing his mouth on mine.

He gave me what I wanted and kissed me as he pushed the head of his cock inside my body. He grabbed my hands, pulling them away from his shoulders, and pressed them into the mattress above my head. He held my hands down as he slid slowly inside me, inch by inch, until he filled me up completely. There was a slight stinging and the stretching was almost painful. It was more uncomfortable than painful.

His mouth went to my neck while he otherwise held himself still, giving me a moment to get accustomed to the feel of him inside me.

When I shifted my hips beneath him, restlessly, silently begging him to move, his head came off of my neck and his mouth went back to mine.

He broke the kiss as his hips pulled back before he snapped them forward again, thrusting inside me.

He set a fast pace with his hips while he moved my hands so he could hold both wrists down with one hand. His other hand moved leisurely down my body. His forehead pressed against mine and his eyes, too close for me to fully make out, looked hazy.

Sweat broke out across his face and he pressed his thumb against my clit again, pushing me over the edge.

I clamped down around him, crying out as I came again.

"Fuck," he growled as he let my hands go.

His hands went to my hips where he gripped me tight, lifting my ass off the mattress and holding me in place while he thrust forcefully inside me.

I wrapped my arms around his shoulders, buried my face in his neck, and clung to him as I rode out the aftershocks of my orgasm. It didn't take him long before he found his own. Groaning loudly, he buried himself in deep, his body twitching uncontrollably as he came.

I clutched tightly to him the whole time, unwilling to let him go.

He let my hips go and wound his arms around my back, holding me to him as he fell over to his side and rolled onto his back, taking me with him and staying firmly planted inside me.

The move forced me to let go of him with both my arms and thighs. My legs fell to the bed on either side of his. My forearms went to his chest and I pushed myself up so I could look down at him.

The eyes that met mine were dark and as serious as I had ever seen them before. There was a possessiveness lurking in their depths that stole my breath away.

"Do you know what this means?" he inquired in a guttural voice.

I shook my head, having no idea where he was going with this. I hoped wherever it went ended with more orgasms for me though, I was greedy like that.

"You can never leave now," he continued in that same guttural tone. "I won't let you."

My lips kicked up into a soft smile.

He couldn't get rid of me if he tried, I was going absolutely nowhere.

# CHAPTER FIFTEEN

I hadn't been invited into the sanctuary of Quinton's bedroom before and I hadn't been invited now. I was restless though and the rest of the house was quiet, everyone sleeping because they'd been awake for days waiting for me to wake up and too wired to sleep before that happened.

I couldn't lay there and do nothing anymore, so I showered and explored the closet. Much to my surprise, the entire thing had been changed around and stuffed full of clothes that actually fit me and weren't ridiculously small. Damien had gone shopping, yet again, and I tried not to be disgusted with the excess or worried about what he'd done with the clothes that had originally been in there.

I found a black tank top that had a sliver of a moon on the front of it. I put on black leggings and, underneath it all, matching black bra and panties. I matched all around.

I found my pentagram choker on a shelf in there, my cell phone sitting beside. I put my choker on and held on tightly to my phone. I turned it on and was surprised to find I had a number of missed calls and text messages, which was weird to me because pretty much everyone I knew was here in the house with me.

Marcus had called me several times and finally resorted to texting.

Marcus: Adrian has informed me you've been invited to dinner. I am so sorry, sweetheart. I had no idea he was going to involve you this way.

Shit.

I fumbled, almost dropping the phone. Somehow, with all that was going on, I had completely forgotten Adrian inviting me to some dinner with Marcus. Things really couldn't get much worse around here.

There was another text from Marcus when I never responded to that one.

Marcus: Of course, if you're not up for it, you don't have to attend. I would never force something like that on you. Adrian is playing games and I don't want you to get sucked into the middle of it.

I pursed my lips as I read the next text after that one, shaking my head. It wasn't like Marcus to text so much. He was a lot like Rain in that he'd rather call or just come to where I was to talk. He didn't much care for texting and would rather have an actual conversation with you.

Marcus: Please, don't shut me out now. I need you.

. . .

I closed my eyes tightly as my head fell forward. I clutched my phone tightly in my hand, trying to figure out what in the heck I was supposed to do in this situation.

I sighed before quickly texting back.

Ariel: Sorry, Marcus. Things have been super crazy around here and I haven't checked my phone in a while. When is this dinner? And is it at your place or the motel?

I hated sending him that text because one, I didn't want him to worry, and two, it sounded a lot like I planned on attending this dinner farce when I wanted anything but.

When no reply immediately came, I opened up the other unread texts I had. It was from an unknown number I had never seen before.

Unknown: Hello, Ariel. Dinner will be a formal affair and at the motel we've purchased for our stay here. It's a celebratory dinner to welcome Marcus into the Council. I'm sure you're already aware he's decided to join us.

Unknown: Please, I'd like for you to bring your coven and your new bodyguards with you. We are waiting patiently to see how you all work out together.

I frowned down at the lit up screen in my hand. Adrian had my number and was now text messaging me. How ridiculous and slightly terrifying. I had no idea how he'd gotten ahold of my phone number, but it was obvious he had it now. I wasn't surprised to see he was the opposite of both Rain and Marcus and, given that there were zero missed calls from him, he preferred texting to phoning.

Not only was there that, which I was actually thankful for this time, but the A-hole hadn't bothered to tell me when this dinner was supposed to be happening. It's like he left it out on purpose in order to force me to engage with him.

I would do no such thing. Instead, I'd wait until I talked to Marcus later and I'd ask him, essentially going around Adrian and leaving him out of the whole thing.

Part of me was irrationally angry with the bald man for not texting me before showing up at the store and giving me a heads-up. Why couldn't he have texted me then, huh?

I tossed my phone back onto the shelf where I'd found it and slipped my feet into a pair of obnoxiously pink fuzzy socks.

On the same shelf as my choker and phone was a decorative silver bowl filled with a bunch of pretty colored studs. I dug around in there until I found some that were as obnoxiously pink as my socks. I removed the ones I had in my ears and stuck the pink ones in, dropping the ones I'd taken out into the bowl with the others. I thought it was sweet that they'd gone to so much trouble to make me feel happy and at home here.

I shuffled out of the closet, making sure to close the door quietly behind me. Dash was still in the middle of the bed, his mouth slightly parted, and soft snores were coming out of him. It wasn't an attractive look, probably wasn't for anyone, but still, I thought he was adorable.

I pulled the sheet up around his shoulders, covering all but his neck and head. I tucked the sheet into his sides and he was so out of it that he didn't even twitch.

Binx was tucked up against his hip. His eyes were slanted, his tail twitching angrily. The little beast was not happy with me at the moment. He didn't hiss at me the way he would have one of the guys, but that didn't stop him from giving me his kitty version of a hostile glare. I made no attempts to pet him for fear of my life.

I took one last glance at the redhead in bed with his black cat before slipping out of the door and closing it quietly behind me.

I headed in the direction of the stairs but came up short when a light underneath a door caught my attention. I pressed my palm against the door, listening for any sound or movement on the other side.

Rustling.

Quiet humming.

He was awake in there when the rest of the house was entirely silent.

Figured.

I lowered my palm from the door and headed back down the hallway that would take me to the stairs. The hallways in this house were so confusing sometimes, a person could get lost in here.

The downstairs was deserted and I was thankful for it. I had looked in the mirror for a long time after getting out of the shower, studying my features. I thought that after what had happened between Dash and myself that I would look different in some way, that it would show on my face that I was no longer a virgin.

Yet nothing had changed, and it was the face I'd always seen in the mirror staring back at me. My green eyes were the same as always, wide and filled with pain. Even though I had been happy when looking in the mirror, my eyes still held hints of my past in them and, in all likelihood, probably always would.

That there'd been no sign of a change had really surprised me, because what went down between Dash and I had felt life altering at the time. And I looked the same, but I didn't want to run into anyone. Just because I couldn't see the change didn't mean someone else wouldn't be able to see it. These guys were intuitive.

What if I ran into Rain and he took one look at me and knew

I'd lost my virginity? Good god, that thought was unbearable and not something I thought I'd ever live down.

I made two sandwiches in the kitchen, attempting to be as quiet as possible so as not to draw attention, and I somehow managed to pull it off.

I carried the plate with sandwiches on it back upstairs.

I knocked softly on the door that had the light shining underneath, the plate of sandwiches held aloft in the air between me and the door.

"Come in," Quinton called briskly through the door.

I was suddenly nervous, no longer actually wanting to step foot inside his private sanctuary.

"Get in here, baby."

Shit.

I couldn't simply leave the plate on the floor in front of the door and haul ass back to my bedroom before he could open the door and drag me inside. Now he knew it was me and he'd just chase me down and drag me back.

My hand went to the knob. Before I could bolt like a total coward, I steeled myself. I turned the knob and pushed the door open wide.

I stood in the doorway with my mouth hanging open as my eyes took in his bedroom.

The room was, like every room in the Alexander house, excessively large. That's where the similarities ended.

Unlike the other bedrooms I'd visited here, Quinton's bed was small, twin-sized. There was no headboard or footboard, simply a metal frame underneath it, holding it up. It was up against the wall and between the only two windows in the room. The bed was covered in a plain black comforter with one lone pillow in a white case.

If the walls had been painted any color I couldn't tell because, from floor to ceiling, books were stacked one on top of the other, taking up all the available wall space.

The windows were bare, exposing the entire room to the outside world if they cared enough to look in. I had no idea how he could sleep like that.

Beside his bed there was a black milk crate flipped upside down. On top of it sat his cell phone, wallet, and a black picture frame. I didn't need to see the picture to know it was one of me. There was no one else he'd have a picture of beside his bed, not even his beloved brother. That was a space solely reserved for me.

There were two doors on the opposite side of the room as the bed and I assumed they were for the bathroom and closet. Every bedroom in this house came with a bathroom and closet. Something affordable only due to the sheer size of the house.

Other than that, there wasn't anything else to look at. No dresser. No television. Not even a damn rug on the cold, hardwood floor. The books were all neatly stacked, not a single one out of place.

Just standing in the doorway looking in hurt my heart.

"Uhhh..." I mumbled. "Where's all your stuff?"

Rude, I know, but he would have been the same way with me.

I snapped my mouth shut when I actually paid attention to the man himself instead of inspecting his belongings.

He was sitting on the floor Indian style. There were black candle sticks on the bare floor, their wicks lit and burning bright.

It looked like a goddamned fire hazard to me. Not to mention completely stupid after what had just gone down at the cottage. Quinton didn't seem the least bit concerned.

He had a thick deck of oversized cards in his hands. The side that faced up was entirely black and he was casually shuffling them.

"Are those..."

"Tarot," he said casually. "The boys told me you've never had yours read for you and it's something you've always wanted. They swear it's the reason why you've been putting so much effort in to learn."

It used to irritate me that they'd all talk about me behind my back and with Quinton especially, because he kept such strict tabs on me. That irritation was entirely gone at the moment.

"Really?" I asked in a quiet, hopeful voice. I had waited so long for this moment. Today was turning out to be a serious day of firsts for me.

"Really," he replied seriously. "Been waiting for you, baby. You took long enough to get to me."

Finally, he looked up at me and away from the deck in his hands. His eyes narrowed and I should have known I wouldn't be able to get away with anything where he was concerned.

"Close the door then get your sweet ass over here."

I kicked the door shut behind me with my foot and winced when it slammed closed. I stood frozen for a few seconds, waiting to hear any sound of people moving around throughout the house.

Blessedly, everything remained quiet.

"What kind of sandwich did you make?" he questioned me, as I slowly approached him. "And, most importantly, did you make me one as well?"

I smirked down at him.

"There's cheese, mayo, ham, pickle slices, and tortilla chips on them. Oh, and they're on white bread though because I don't do whole wheat. And yes, I made one for you too."

He stared at me in stupefied silence as I sat down across from him on the floor, mimicking exactly how he was seated. I sat the plate down between us and gestured to it as I picked up half of one of the sandwiches. I'd cut them diagonally instead of straight down the middle. Somewhere in the back of my mind there was a memory floating around, it was foggy at best and I couldn't make out the face of the woman talking to me, but she said to cut it diagonally because that meant it was made with love.

Absolute bullshit, of course, but still, I couldn't dodge the memory no matter how hard I tried and, in the end, I ended up cutting the stupid sandwiches diagonally.

The damn memory had threatened to choke the life right out of me. I didn't remember anything before a certain point in my life. I had always chalked it up to being young and maybe my mind was trying to protect me by shielding me from the bad things that had happened around me that Vivian had brought into our lives, or maybe it was simply because I was too young to remember anything at all. I didn't know, but now I was thinking I had no memories of my early years for a reason. Rain had never specified how old I had been when I'd been abducted and I hadn't had the guts to outright ask him.

"You put chips on your sandwich?" Quinton asked in amusement, snapping me out of my horrible thoughts.

I nodded. "On both of ours. Gives it the perfect crunch. You can't call it a decent sandwich if there's no tortilla chips on it."

He looked at me like I was insane. Which was saying something, coming from him.

I rolled my eyes as I took a huge bite out of the corner of my delicious sandwich. And promptly choked on it when he stated, "You look different. You *feel* different. Something's off with your aura, I can see it."

I coughed around my bite of sandwich. Quinton could see auras? This was news to me. I eyed him skeptically as I quickly swallowed my food. Just what else could he do?

His eyes never left mine as he picked up half of his sandwich, stopping just before it made it to his lips. "Well," he prompted before biting off a huge chunk.

Well, indeed.

Hadn't I just lectured Damien on honesty?

"I had sex with Dash," I stated bluntly, before taking another huge bite from my sandwich.

Quinton choked, coughing.

Yeah, I probably should have handled that better, led into it a bit more, eased him in.

He dropped his sandwich onto the plate and picked up a glass of water that was sitting on the floor beside him. He chugged half the glass before slamming it back down. The clear liquid sloshed around inside the glass, some of it spilling over the side of the rim.

"Excuse me?" he sputtered.

It was almost worth it just to see his reaction and to have him off his game.

"I had sex with Dash," I repeated like it wasn't a big deal. He gaped at me. A sense of victory washed through me. I loved catching him off guard. "It's really not a big deal, you knew it was going to happen eventually."

He snapped his mouth shut and glared at me.

"He didn't hurt you, did he?" he growled.

Oh boy.

Wasn't it supposed to hurt a little bit for all girls the first time? I didn't think it was wise we get into details here. Not about this subject.

I should have kept my stupid mouth shut.

"This is Dash we're talking about," I said in a hushed voice. I wanted him to really think before he opened his mouth again, because it was going to make me incredibly angry if he insulted Dash.

"You do realize there will be no keeping this from the rest of them. Everyone will know eventually."

I shrugged my shoulders, not caring if people knew. I'd done nothing I was ashamed of.

"I hate him," he whispered darkly.

My heart skipped a beat. I'd been afraid of this. He was far too possessive to just let this go without giving me a piece of his mind. At least he wasn't yelling.

"Quinton," I growled quietly. "Does it really matter who I

have sex with first? You knew that eventually it was going to happen. I couldn't remain a virgin forever and, honestly, I've been ready for a while now but none of you would listen to me."

He fisted his hands and looked down at his lap.

"Part of me can't help but being jealous and thinking that maybe if I had been able to talk you into staying here with me, then maybe it would have been me who you'd gone to for that."

I sighed heavily. If I hadn't brought it up like a moron, then I wouldn't be sitting across from him and having this conversation. But I wanted to be open with him, he deserved that much from me. I felt like if he'd found out from anyone but me, then he would have freaked out about it way worse.

"Quinton," I said in a quiet, but serious voice, hoping I only had to say it once. "My having sex with Dash had absolutely not one thing to do with living with him, and everything to do with him and the situation. It just happened and I'm glad that it did. I wouldn't take it back for anything. Dash and I have a very close relationship, it was bound to happen sooner or later. The same thing could be said about you though, too, because we have a very close relationship that grows by the day. Even on the days where I don't like you very much."

"You always like me," he shot back.

He was wrong, I didn't always like him but I did, however, always love him. There was totally a difference.

I waved my hand toward the cards he'd sat down in a neat stack on the floor. "Can we stop talking about sex now and get down to business?"

He leered at me. "Sure thing, baby. We can stop talking about sex and get down to business. In fact, that would make me really fucking happy. By the time I'm done with you, you won't even remember what Dash's cock looked like."

My mouth dropped open.

He was unbelievable.

"Quinton," I hissed in mock outrage. "Stop talking about cocks."

My cheeks heated, likely taking on a very unattractive shade of red that made the rest of me look washed out and overly pale.

"Fine," he grumbled ungraciously, as he picked the deck up off the floor.

My eyebrows shot up in surprise. That was way easier than I had imagined it would be, and he'd handled it very well. I thought he'd get way angrier and have some type of temper tantrum where he threatened Dash's life.

I was proud of him for remaining calm.

He cleared his throat.

"Did you know that the Catholic Church used to say that tarot cards were instruments of the Devil?" he asked me casually as he shuffled the deck, like we hadn't just been having a seriously uncomfortable conversation involving my love life.

"No," I answered, shaking my head. I hadn't known that, but I honestly couldn't say I was surprised.

"It's true, and one of the many asinine things that were made up in order to frighten people away from them."

"I believe you."

He shook his head, as if clearing it. "This deck has been in my family for a very long time. Handmade by one of my great something or another, and spelled to never deteriorate so they'll always remain as they are."

I watched his hands as they carefully shuffled the deck, completely fascinated. This was a new side to Uncle Quint and one I appreciated seeing. He'd rather I be kept in the dark and wrapped up in bubble wrap than to allow me to learn anything really useful. I had been slightly resentful until Rain had come along and pulled the kid gloves off of my training.

It seemed Quinton had decided to follow in dear old dad's footsteps.

Good deal for me.

"They were in the storage unit with the rest of my family's bullshit. I'd honestly forgotten all about them until Ty reminded me they existed a couple weeks ago."

He looked up from his hands and looked me dead in the eyes. Warmth and sadness poured out of him. My face softened at seeing it.

"They're a gift, for you. We both agreed on it."

I broke eye contact, my eyes dropping down to the fingers I was twisting together nervously in my lap. Gifts made me uncomfortable and Quinton kept trying to dump all of his priceless family heirlooms off on me. Tyson went along with it, acting as if the whole thing was remarkably normal. It was getting to be a bit ridiculous if you asked me.

"I cannot accept these," I said in a hushed, controlled voice. "Stop trying to give me your family's antiques."

"You *are* my family," he countered in a smug voice. "Your argument is pointless, they're already yours and I won't hear anything else about it. Now, pay attention."

My head snapped up at the command in his voice and I scowled at him. But I didn't argue, I had since learned when to pick my battles and was smart enough to know when not to push when I knew I was going to lose anyway.

Dropping the subject, probably because he knew he'd won, Quinton held out the tarot deck toward me.

"Shuffle them, please."

I took the deck from his hands and carefully shuffled them. I handed them back to him when I was done.

He laid the cards face down on the floor in front of him and fanned them out, from left to right. Quickly, he picked out three cards, seemingly at random, one right after the other. He placed them face up in a line on the floor between us, again, from left to right.

"Can you tell me what the placement of each card means?" he asked curiously.

This was a basic setup. I nodded my head but refused to look down at the actual cards themselves. I was terrified to see what cards he'd pulled out of that deck and what they might mean for me. I was actually starting to sweat.

"The first card you laid down represents the past."

He arched an arrogant eyebrow, causing me to fidget nervously. I desperately wanted to get this right and not embarrass myself in front of him.

"The recent past," I said more confidently than I actually felt.

He nodded his head in approval. "Go on."

I slumped in relief.

"The second card, the one in the middle, represents the here and now."

"Very good. And the third and final card?"

"What's to come." That was the one that scared me the most.

"You can look at them, baby. They aren't going to bite," he soothed with a soft, sweet voice.

That was easy for him to say when the cards were meant for me and not him.

"I kept things easy, simple even, for your first time. Next time, you'll practice on me. When you have it down, we'll move onto a more complex spread."

Something I had so been looking forward to now filled me with dread. If I messed up I would look like a fool in front of Quinton.

I sucked in a much needed breath before allowing myself to look down at the cards. The moment of truth was upon me and there was no going back now.

The first one he'd laid down was the King of Wands. It depicted a king seated on a throne with a staff in his hand that had blossoms shooting off of it. His cape and throne were covered in lions and salamanders. I remembered from the books I'd read that the lion and salamander were symbols for fire and strength.

I didn't think it boded well that the card was upside down,

facing me instead of Quinton. The meaning changed when the card was flipped upside down like that.

Quinton lightly tapped his finger against the King of Wands card, his face unreadable.

"This," he began quietly, "because it's upside down, represents Rain coming into your life. Arrogant, to the point of being aggressive even. He's ruthless, selfish, and single minded when it comes to the things he wants. You don't want to stand between him and his goals. Yeah, this card is all about Rain coming back into your life. This is not a bad thing."

Nothing about Rain being in my life would I ever consider a bad thing. Even if he was arrogant and everything else Quinton claimed him to be.

"Now, this," Quinton moved on, tapping his finger against the card in the middle, the Strength card, "does not surprise me in the slightest."

The Strength card depicted a woman in a white robe kneeling over a lion with her hands on his head. Supposedly, she's tamed the wild beast, or so I had read about. The infinity symbol floated over her head, representing wisdom.

Honestly, I wondered just how smart she really could be kneeling over a damn lion like that. There were some animals that, no matter how tame they appeared, would forever remain wild and ferocious.

I stared at Quinton sitting across from me looking calm, peaceful even.

Case in point, I thought.

"This is you," Quinton said seriously. "Or, the you that you've recently become."

I frowned at him, not understanding his meaning. I didn't see myself in that card at all. It actually seemed a card better suited for himself than for me.

"You don't believe me?" he asked incredulously. "This is *all* you. You might not be physically strong, I'll admit to that, but you have an inner strength and a resilience that humbles me. It takes courage to have gone through the things you have and still allow yourself to not be beaten down by life and to remain hopeful. You're compassionate and kind, which is another thing that always surprises me about you. This card is *all* about the person you are becoming and I think it says good things about where you're headed as a person."

I swallowed thickly, no longer looking at the cards between us, my focus entirely on the man sitting on the floor across from me.

From the moment he'd laid eyes on me in a dream, he'd been all about me and I'd become the center of his entire universe.

"I don't think you see me the right way," I whispered hoarsely, emotion clogging my throat.

He smiled sadly at me. "It's you who can't see straight. Not where you're concerned."

"Whatever you say, Quinton," I replied in a sarcastic voice. I was almost more uncomfortable having this conversation with him than I had been when we were talking about sex.

He chuckled quietly. "You can never just take a compliment." The thin, white scars covering his finger glinted in the candlelight as he tapped it against the last card. He smirked at me. "And this one?"

I looked down at the last card and gasped.

"Oh, no, no, no," I whispered in horror. "We're all gonna die. Seriously, Quinton, I don't want to do this anymore."

I knew my fear was entirely irrational, but I couldn't seem to make it stop as I stared down at the Death card.

The Death card had a skeleton wearing black armor while riding a white horse. He's carrying a black flag in his hands. A flag that has a flower on it, a rose. The horse and rider are standing over a dead body on the ground while a man, woman, and child stand in front of it.

The picture on the card is fucking terrifying.

"Breathe, baby," Quinton urged in a warm voice. "You're

freaking out about nothing and you need to calm down. It's not actually a bad card and I know you know that because you're smart and you wouldn't have skipped this card in your studies."

My breath evened out as I let his words sink in. He was, of course, right. It's just that word Death is so incredibly final that it was a shock to see.

"Nobody's going to die," I breathed out. "You're right and I'm being irrational. Everything I read about it said it was the death of something, not someone specifically, and the beginning of something."

"That's right, baby," he murmured in approval. "It symbolizes the ending of a phase in your life that's no longer any good for you, and the beginning of something new. Change is coming and it's going to be a good one for you. I'm really digging this card because any change that's good for you is good for the rest of us. Please stop freaking out."

I wasn't freaking out anymore. I was just second-guessing how much I had wanted this in the first place and wishing I could give it back, return it like a bad Christmas present. From now on I really wanted to be on the other side of things, because I didn't think I wanted to know what my future held anymore. Change was on the horizon but I still had no idea what it was.

"Are you tired?" he asked me, changing the subject abruptly.

"Nooooo," I whined. "I could maybe sleep again in like forty-five years." My body felt like it had been asleep for forever.

He laughed at me before climbing to his feet.

"We'll leave your cards in here for now," he told me as he bent over at the waist and blew out each candle.

I stacked the cards in a neat pile as he went around the circle, blowing out the candles. I stood up with the cards clutched in my hand, pressed against my chest. For someone who claimed they didn't want anymore gifts from him, I sure wasn't ready to let the beautiful cards go.

He smiled at me knowingly.

"Come on, baby. Let's go on downstairs. I'm still hungry and could go for something hot to eat this time. Those sandwiches didn't cut it for me."

I placed the neat stack of cards down on his upside down milk crate. It didn't feel right to take them from his room just yet. Maybe it was because I knew I'd have a reason to come back to his bedroom if I left them in here.

He took my hand and pulled me into the hall.

We didn't talk on our way down the stairs, both of us lost in our own heads and not quite interested in waking the others yet.

Because he constantly checked in on me, I felt like we spent more time together than we really did. I planned on taking advantage of the time I had with him now.

# CHAPTER SIXTEEN

"Up," Quinton ordered, as he patted his hand against the countertop.

I slid across the floor on my fuzzy socks until I was right next to him. I smiled up at him, big and carefree.

He stilled, his hand still on the counter. His eyes darkened, his nostrils flared, and the smile slid right off my face.

"Quinton?" I asked cautiously.

"Fuck, but you're so goddamn pretty," he snarled before rushing me. "Always, but it blows me away when you smile."

My eyes grew round. He didn't usually talk to me like this, but it felt good to hear him tell me he thought I was pretty. It wasn't something I usually thought too much about myself. It was something I tried not to think about after getting my face sliced open and permanently marked.

His hands came to my face and he cupped my cheeks in his rough palms. He pressed me back against the counter and my upper body curved backward. He came with me, not giving me an inch of space.

"Smile for me again," he commanded, sounding like he believed it would really be that easy.

I frowned deeper at him instead.

"What's wrong with you?" I inquired in confusion. I often thought he might be possessed. This seemed like one of those times. "Quinton?"

"Even if you were ugly I'd still love you," he growled.

My eyebrows shot up. That wasn't something you said to your girlfriend, at least I didn't think so.

Wait a minute, did he say....

"You love me?" I asked.

He backed up, giving me space, and one of his hands dropped away from my face. He placed his palm over his chest, covering his heart, and slapped it against his chest twice before staying still again, his fingers splayed wide.

"With all my heart and every inch of my fucked-up soul."

The backs of my eyes stung with tears as my heart felt like it seized inside my chest.

"You love me?" I repeated the question, not trusting that I'd heard his answer correctly and needing him to tell me again.

His face softened as he grabbed my hand and placed it on his chest, over his heart. His hand went over top of mine and he slid his fingers in between mine.

"Do you feel that?" he asked me.

I felt all kinds of things when he touched me and looked at me that way.

His heart beat a steady rhythm in his chest. The hard muscle beneath my palm burned through his thin t-shirt as his dark eyes bored into me. There was a different kind of heat in them, one that threatened to catch my skin on fire.

"I feel it," I whispered breathlessly. There was no way I couldn't feel it, not with Quinton.

He dropped his hands to my thighs. They curled around to the backs of my legs and he lifted me up. I let out a shocked, girly squeal as he sat my butt on the countertop.

He pushed his hips into the space between my legs. His hands went to the small of my back where he pushed me forward until my front pressed up tight against his.

His mouth came down on mine as his hand slid up my back. His fingers slid into my hair as his tongue slid into my mouth.

His fingers fisted in my hair. He tilted my head to the side to get a better angle as he quickly took control of the kiss and I let him do it.

My body melted against him as my hands went around his waist. I clung to him as I drank in his kiss. I made a greedy noise in the back of my throat that I was sure I'd be embarrassed about when I thought about it later.

"What, are you trying to eat her?" Rain's low, menacing growl filled the room, bringing me back to reality. "How about you get your hands the fuck off my daughter before I remove them for you."

I shoved on Quinton's chest as I broke our kiss. His mouth went to my neck where he placed a chaste kiss—well, chaste in comparison to the last one. He let me go and, without backing up much, turned around to face down my father. The look on his face was downright frightening, I don't think I'd ever seen him look so mad before.

I grabbed on to the back of this t-shirt as I leaned around him, seeking out Rain. He stood in the doorway to the kitchen, arms crossed over his chest, eyes focused solely on Quinton. Quinton who stood in front of me like a shield.

"Oh my god," I breathed out as I shoved Quinton out of my way. He grunted as I jumped off the countertop and ran toward Rain.

I skidded to a stop in my fuzzy socks in front of him as he continued to send death vibes via his glare in Quinton's direction.

"I can see your tattoos," I cried happily, excited as I reached out to touch his arms.

To my surprise, he didn't jerk away but stood stoically still while I examined the ink covering his forearms. It was like nothing I had ever seen before. Black and white covered almost every inch of skin in designs and markings that I didn't recognize but still found oddly beautiful.

"How old were you when you got your first tattoo?" I asked curiously, probing for any kind of information about himself I could possibly squeeze out of Rain Kimber. My father was still very much a mystery to me, and though he was willing to tell me all about my mother and my grandfather, he kept a lot of things about himself to himself. It was very frustrating and sometimes I wanted to force the answers out of him. He wouldn't let me get away with keeping things from him, he gave me those cold eyes and I couldn't help myself from giving him whatever he wanted in order to make those icy eyes melt back to something closer to human.

"I got my first tattoo when I was five," he shared.

I dropped my hands away from him and stumbled back a step. "Wh-what?" I stuttered. Five? Had I heard that right? That sounded a lot like child abuse if you asked me.

He eyed me warily.

His voice was very careful when he asked, "What is it that bothers you so much about this? If you had stayed with me, then you would have received a tattoo long before now and I assure you, you would wear it with pride."

I had no doubt about what he said, but, the thing was, I *hadn't* grown up with Rain, I'd grown up differently and that led me to seeing things from a different perspective than the people in my life.

"What I don't understand is why you'd get something permanent on your body at such a young age," I told him honestly. "From everything I've heard, tattoos hurt. What type of loving parent is okay with hurting their child in such a way? Wouldn't that make them not really all that loving in the first place?"

What the hell did I know about having a loving parent and how they interacted with their children? I eyed the man in front

176

of me. Too bad I was no longer a child or perhaps I might be able to answer my own question.

"It's a part of our culture that I fear you will never understand until you have children of your own and have lived amongst your own kind for a good, long while," Rain informed me.

My upper lip curled in distaste.

"I never plan on having children," I shared, hoping he never brought up the subject again.

After the things I'd gone through, the things I'd been forced to endure thanks to my Aunt Viv, there was no way in hell I would ever bring another innocent life into this world just so someone could have the opportunity to one day abuse them. Not the most positive outlook, I'll admit that, but it was the only one I was capable of. Maybe things would change with age, but it wasn't something I'd ever hold my breath and hope for.

"What?" Rain asked quietly with a hint of sadness in his voice. "I know you're young—"

"Drop it," Quinton cut in, his voice taking on a hint of defeat. "This is something she refuses to budge on and something I refuse to hear you pressure her over or argue with her about. Maybe in a few years you can approach this subject again but, until then, you leave this be."

"And if I don't?" Rain challenged.

My body stiffened as I took another step back, away from my father, a man I could never be afraid of but, at the moment, I was starting to get angry with. Why the hell he felt the need to fight everyone all the time, I would never understand.

"Then you'll be asked to leave my home and not be invited back."

My eyes rounded in shock at this and had me whipping around toward Quinton.

The look in those dark eyes that were aimed at my father were so far from friendly they were downright hostile, and I had an alarming urge to move to the side, hiding my father from his sight. I would never do that though, never choose between them, and I hoped neither of them ever expected me to. You should never do that to the people you loved and it would be one of the quickest ways to prove they were selfish, narcissistic assholes.

"I don't want to have kids, ever," I told Rain honestly, the words startling me. "As you well know, I didn't have the best upbringing. I'll not risk an innocent child, not ever."

Rain flinched and my heart dropped down to my stomach.

*Fuck.*

That sounded a whole lot worse when I said it aloud to my father than it had sounded in my head.

"Ariel," he whispered my name in a voice that shook.

"That came out sounding wrong," I rushed to assure him, to ease his pain. I hated the thought of hurting him.

He gave a small nod in acknowledgement. "It's okay, baby girl."

It wasn't. His eyes had turned back into cold, dead things that hurt me to my very soul to see.

"I love you," I said honestly, and for the second time.

He froze, all except for his eyes that were so much like my own. They melted immediately, becoming warm pools of green.

"What?" he croaked in a broken voice.

"I love you," I repeated as if it were obvious, and to me it was. "How could I not love you? You're amazing, Rain. I know I've only said it once before now and should have told you a lot sooner, but that has had absolutely not one thing to do with you and everything to do with me. I tend to keep people at arm's length because I'm emotionally stunted and I don't want to put myself out there for fear of getting hurt. But, the thing I'm coming to understand with you, is that you're never going to hurt me, so it's safe to tell you I love you. Honestly, I can't even believe how comfortable I am telling you this now, like I said, I'm messed up."

Rain let out a sound that was filled with so much pain that it had me stumbling back a step away from him and rubbing my hand over my heart. It hurt hearing that noise come from him.

Rain rushed me as I stumbled back. His eyes looked wild, crazed even, as he wrapped his arms around me and picked me up off my feet.

"I love you too, baby girl," he whispered into the top of my head. "So goddamn much, you have no idea. Been waiting to hear those words come out of your mouth for *years*. When you said them the first time I shut down and didn't know how to respond to you without breaking down."

Without hesitation, I wrapped my arms around Rain's middle and held on tightly. This man meant everything to me and hearing him tell me he loved me for the first time made something important settle inside my soul. I hadn't realized I'd needed to hear the words as much as he'd obviously needed to say them to me.

Quinton cleared his throat from behind us. "Are either of you hungry?" he asked cautiously. "I'm going to make spaghetti."

I blinked, coming back to reality as Rain set me down on my feet and stepped back. I'd forgotten entirely why Quinton and I had come down to the kitchen in the first place, that there'd been an actual reason and that had been in order to feed him.

Rain kissed me on the forehead before walking around me, toward Quinton.

"I could go for some spaghetti," he muttered.

I looked around the room as if I'd never seen it before. What the heck had just happened here? Had my long-lost father and I really just had an *I love you* moment for the first time after he'd caught me making out with one of my boyfriends? Just to have him then go off to eat Uncle Quint's spaghetti like nothing had ever happened?

I turned on my heel and watched as Rain pulled out a stool at the island and plopped down across from Quinton. Quinton smirked at me before he moved to the refrigerator and pulled the door open. He came out with a package of hamburger and dropped it down on the counter beside the stovetop.

Rain looked at me over his shoulder and raised a haughty eyebrow.

"Get over here, baby girl, and take a seat," he commanded as he patted the stool beside him. "You're far too skinny and we need to fatten you up a bit so that you look healthy. I hate seeing you so skinny. You can practically see your ribs sticking out through your tank top."

I sighed heavily in defeat as my shoulders slumped forward. Rain didn't see it because he'd already turned back around to face Quinton, expecting me to follow his orders without argument.

I grumbled under my breath about how I needed another male in my life who wanted to shovel food down my throat like I needed a hole drilled into my head.

I had always been skinny because I'd been underfed, and when I did get the chance to eat I'd never eaten anything that was really good for me. That hadn't been my choice though, and if I could have gone back in time and changed things, then I would have and made it so I wouldn't have had to go hungry because my mother spent her money on slutty dresses for herself and alcohol and would have bought food for her child instead. But there was no going back. Vivian hadn't been my mother and now she was dead. I hated to think she got what she deserved, but as I sat down beside Rain the thought certainly did flit across my mind.

I sat there quietly as I watched the two of them interact like they hadn't threatened each other minutes before, like they were somehow friends. It made my heart a little bit lighter to see, which I'm sure they both noticed when my tense body relaxed entirely and I placed my forearms onto the island counter, getting comfortable.

Quinton cooked while keeping up a conversation with Rain about, surprisingly enough, Fortune's for the Unfortunate, of all things. I think he did it just to keep things from getting too heavy again, for my sake.

I thanked him in my own way by eating an overflowing plate of his spaghetti. Neither of them were satisfied with what I'd eaten—even though it had been a lot, more than either of them had piled on their own plates—and tried to shovel more noodles onto my plate.

After rinsing my plate off in the sink and placing it in the dishwasher, I practically ran out of the kitchen and away from the two of them. I didn't even care if they knew I was escaping them.

I needed to get the heck out of here.

# CHAPTER SEVENTEEN

"Give me my goddamn keys," I snarled.

Face completely devoid of emotion, Trenton stared down at me, the keys to my Rover held aloft and out of my reach. He'd easily snatched them out of my hand when I'd walked past him.

"Where do you think you're going?" Simon asked from behind his brother.

My fists clenched at my sides and I had an insane urge to throw my head back and scream at the top of my lungs.

"I don't need a babysitter," I growled, sounding impressively angry, even to my own ears. My angry outburst had taken me by surprise. I didn't make a habit of yelling at people who'd done me no wrong.

"I'm not your babysitter," Trenton replied casually.

A little too casually if you asked me. My hand twitched with the urge to reach out and smack him across his stupid face.

"I don't need a bodyguard either," I snapped, but the heat in my voice was almost gone, the fight going right out of me.

I'd like to think I didn't need a bodyguard, but with masked men with swords running rampant and mother-effers trying to burn down Dash's house, not to mention they'd been happily dragging his unconscious ass off somewhere into the woods... Well, I was seeing why the people who gave a crap about me would think a bodyguard might just be the exact thing I *did* need in my life.

My life was such a mess right now, the whole thing a giant shit show I seemed to have no control over anymore. Not that I really had any control over anything to begin with, that was a lie I'd been telling myself all too often lately.

The cell phone in my hoodie pocket rang and I pulled it out to check the screen. I never used to screen my calls before because I'd never had anyone call me. Now, with Adrian having my phone number and whoever the hell else, I needed to check the caller ID every single time before answering the stupid thing.

I let out a relieved sigh when Marcus Cole's name flashed across the screen. I'd forgotten to give him a return phone call. Too much had happened in such a short span of time that I was still struggling to play catch up, and I'd forgotten something as important as why Marcus had messaged me in the first place. The upcoming dinner I had no desire to attend. The Council I had no desire to entertain, and, make no mistake, that's why they'd invited my coven in the first place.

Ignoring the existence of both Trenton and Simon, I turned my back on them, touched my finger to the screen of my illuminated phone, and put it up to my ear.

"Hello," I answered in a fake, happy voice.

"Sweetheart." Marcus's warm, kind voice came out at me through the speaker on the phone, a welcome distraction from the hulking figures standing behind me. "I see your Range Rover is parked in the Alexander driveway. Can I take that to mean you're next door or has one of the boys borrowed your vehicle?"

My lips tipped up secretively as a plan formed in the back of my mind.

"Are you staying in the old house?" I asked curiously. He'd

been all packed up and ready to go. Then, there'd been a *Sold* sticker slapped across the for sale sign in the front yard. I'd been told he'd moved out but nobody had ever bothered to tell me who'd bought the place.

"My boxes were never unpacked and, before I knew it, they were right back where they belonged—home," he said.

"But, I thought you sold the place," I replied.

"Yes, well," he hedged, "I did. Then I realized the error of my ways and the Alexander boys dealt with that little mess for me. I'd been too out of practice to deal with it myself. At the time. Of course, things are entirely different now."

I didn't know why, but a shiver rent up my spine at hearing his words. I'd yet to experience first hand a Marcus Cole who'd unleashed his magic and used it like a true witch instead of gagging it and pretending it never existed in the first place. He'd had good reason for the things he'd done, that being the family he'd created with the human woman who knew nothing of the world her husband had once lived in. It had been unfortunate for Marcus that his children had been adopted and born entirely human with no magic to speak of. It meant that in order to keep them safe from the Council and their greedy, unethical ways, he kept them away from anything and all things magical. In order to do that, he did the one thing no witch ever dreamed of doing. Marcus Cole had given up his magic, the thing that made him so special, gagging it for years and years inside himself. All for the sake of his family and loved ones, to keep them safe. Now that they were off and living their own lives, his beloved wife long since having passed from this world, he no longer had anyone in his day to day life he needed to hide what he was from.

Marcus was a witch, and it was something I still hadn't yet come to terms with, but I'd get there. Eventually.

"Hmm," I murmured. "You want me to come over?"

*Please say yes*, I thought to myself. This would be the chance I needed to escape my bodyguards I'd stupidly accepted into my life like a fool. It was hard for me to regret the decision too much when they'd been there to assist the night Dash's cottage had been attacked. They'd played an important role that night. Still, I couldn't help but resent their presence in my life at the moment.

I just needed a minute to myself. Or, more like thirty-eight years. You know, whichever helped.

"Would you?" Marcus asked in a sweet voice. "I would really love the company."

I smiled. "I'll be right over."

I pulled the phone away from my ear and touched my finger to the red circle that would end the call. This was exactly the distraction I needed to lose the shadows who'd been following me around since I had left Quinton in the kitchen with Rain, after eating spaghetti for breakfast with them.

They'd been silent until Trenton had plucked my car keys out of my hand like I'd been a toddler he'd easily stolen candy from.

I shoved my cell back into my hoodie pocket before turning around to face them, making sure I wiped the smile from my face and schooled my features.

"Marcus," I told them as I waved my hand in the direction of where I thought the house next door was. "He lives in the house next door, I used to live with him. He... was involved with the woman who had pretended to be my mother and kidnapped me."

Their bodies twitched as they did the opposite of what I had planned and became more alert. Dammit. I should have thought better of what would come out of my mouth before opening it.

"You were kidnapped?" Simon inquired incredulously.

"Rain never mentioned that," Trenton muttered as he eyed me cautiously.

I waved my hand in the air as if trying to sweep the words away, under the proverbial rug, if you will.

"Long time ago," I lied easily. It was much easier to lie to these two brothers than it was to any of my guys. Good to know.

"Anyway," I breezed out, "he was the one on the phone and he wants me to go over there."

I smiled sweetly at them, disarmingly so. Or, at least I hoped. I was better at looking sad than I was happy, so I wasn't sure how well it had worked on them.

"Okay," Trenton drawled slowly, as he shoved my car keys into the front pocket of his dark blue jeans.

I followed the movement of his hands as I fought the urge to scream bloody murder at the unfairness of him stealing my keys from me, and thinking he had the right to pocket them.

I didn't want to hate Trenton or Simon. They'd seemed like decent enough guys when we'd first met in the shop. I'd been stupid enough then to welcome them both naively into my life without thinking about the consequences that would come hand in hand with it. Now I was seeing the error of my ways. They were glaring me right in the face. Freedom be damned and freedom be gone.

I was over this.

"I'm going next door to hang out with Marcus because he wants to spend time with me," I said in a small voice. "My relationship with Marcus is complicated and only just getting back on track. I don't want either of you going over there with me and making the situation more uncomfortable than it's already going to be. I'd like for you both to stay here or whatever it was you were going to do before I tried to bail."

Trenton opened his mouth as if to protest. Or, what I assumed would be a protest. I certainly didn't think he'd be agreeing with me, he'd had yet to do that.

"You can keep my car keys," I blurted hysterically. "I can't go anywhere without those."

Trenton's face softened, making the scar that ran down through his jaw and further down his neck stand out. I turned my eyes away before he could catch me staring. I knew what that felt like, to have people looking at your scars in either perverse curiosity or disgust, and it wasn't a good feeling to be on the other end of it. I might not have wanted them to follow my every move around like shadows, but that didn't mean I would ever be unnecessarily cruel to the brothers.

"We'll wait for you here," Simon replied and finally, and most importantly, very agreeable.

Well, wasn't that a relief to hear. I didn't waste any time getting the heck out of there. I practically sprinted toward the front door.

Thankfully, no one got in my way and tried to stop me. They let me go, but that didn't mean I couldn't feel eyes on me as I crossed the driveway and grass to the front of Marcus's house. They must have watched me from one of the front windows. I seriously thought about flipping them off behind my back, but didn't want to chance Marcus seeing and being disappointed in me.

I raised my hand to knock on the front door but never made contact with it, because it swung open before I could tap my fist against it.

Marcus stood in the doorway, one side of his mouth curved up in a half smile. I smiled back before looking down and froze.

"Are you..." I gaped at him. "Are you wearing *jeans?*"

Marcus laughed quietly.

"I wear pants every day," he pointed out. "I don't understand why you'd find it so strange to see me in jeans. They are quite comfortable. Though... I don't think I've ever actually seen *you* wear jeans either."

"I actually *don't* think they're all that comfortable," I told him.

"To each their own," he remarked, before stepping back and waving me inside. "Come in, come in. If you stand out here any longer, one of the guys from next door will come running and call me an asshole for making you wait on my front step."

Again, I gaped at him.

"First jeans," I said as I stepped inside, "then you're swearing at me. Sheesh, it's like I don't even know who you are right now. What's next? Are you going to offer me a drink, ask me if I want to share a beer with you?"

"Forget the beer," he stated. "We'll just go straight for the scotch."

I laughed with him as he shut the door behind us. I thought he'd been joking, but the serious look on his face told me different. I had never had scotch before, but was more than willing to give it a taste if he offered it up to me. I had a feeling it was something neither Quinton or Rain would approve of and that made me childishly want to do it all the more. I realized with a start that their bonding had kind of bothered me. They could threaten each other one second, then the next act like they were best of friends. There was something about it that was driving me crazy. If someone had threatened me, I didn't think I would be able to just get over it in the blink of an eye and go about my business. I'm a girl, we didn't quite work that way.

I followed behind Marcus as he moved through the house, frowning all the way at what I was seeing. When I'd first moved in here in the beginning of the summer with my... Vivian... this had been a family friendly home, complete with picture covered walls. There'd been photos of all their family get-togethers, holidays, birthdays, and school photos. Vivian had been intimidated and angered by the happy family hanging up all over the walls, smiling down on all of us. She'd tried to convince Marcus to take them down at one point, and he hadn't given into her selfish desires and I couldn't blame him for telling her no. Our family hadn't been happy and there hadn't been pictures to replace them with, not that you could ever replace your loved ones in such a way.

But they were all gone now, the happy family photos having been taken down. The walls were lonely and bare.

"What happened?" I asked curiously, needing to know where his family had gone, where their smiling faces had been taken to, and hoping like hell their absence had absolutely nothing to do with Vivian's death and my moving out of his home.

He looked back over his shoulder at me, an eyebrow arched in question.

I cleared my throat as I threw my hand out and gestured toward the bare walls. "Where have all your photographs gone to?" I looked around the room we were standing in, the living room. There was absolutely no personality in this space either, no personal touches, no knickknacks. Only furniture was housed here and a whole lot of nothing else. "Where is everything?"

Marcus shrugged his shoulders carelessly. "Everything is still packed up in boxes for the moment. I haven't had the time to unpack everything yet and didn't want to have to pay someone else to do it for me."

Hmm...

For some reason that made me incredibly sad. I didn't like thinking about him being here and alone in this house that had once been such a happy place for him and his family before his wife had died, and his children had grown up and moved out to live their own adult lives.

Then Vivian and I had come along, moved in, and turned his whole world upside down after he'd been nothing but kind to us.

And now he was here, all alone, with most of his life packed away in boxes. I wasn't responsible for this change in his life, I knew that. But it was hard not to think about how if Vivian hadn't sunk her claws into him, then maybe he would have found a different woman to invite into his home, a decent one, one deserving of his attention and love. Maybe if we'd never come into his life, then he would have ended up with that kind of woman and wouldn't be  living here all alone now. Or, maybe he actually would have moved on and close to his brother's widow, and eventually gone for what he really wanted out of life.

I knew it was stupid to waste my time thinking about these things when I knew there would never be any way to change them, to make the outcome any different from where we already were now.

"Do you want some help unpacking things?" I asked in a quiet voice, as I followed him into the kitchen. I was glad we weren't heading toward the dining room. I had bad memories in there. Not from actually eating in there at the huge table. Thankfully that hadn't happened, but because I'd once come home from school to hear him having sex with Vivian in there on that very same table. The thought of sitting down in a chair there had my face burning in embarrassment. As far as I knew, Marcus was completely unaware of my having heard him having sex. Vivian, however, had done it on purpose in hopes I'd come home and hear her. She'd been really creative when it came to her many forms of punishment. That particular act on her part had been a punishment for my getting too close to Marcus when she felt he only should have had eyes for her.

Sometimes I forgot just what a bitch she really had been.

"If you want to find a day that works for you and come over and help me unpack some things, sweetheart, I would truly appreciate it and I'm not about to tell you no."

Marcus moved to the coffee pot on the counter. He reached up to the cupboard above and pulled down a black coffee mug. He placed the mug on the counter and pulled out the carafe. He poured coffee in the mug and put the carafe back. He pushed the coffee mug across the countertop and in my direction.

"We'll save the scotch for after you've been decently caffeinated," he teased while smiling softly at me.

I loved that he knew just how much I loved my coffee. It could be the middle of the night and I would still want to brew a pot just for myself.

I picked up the coffee mug happily and moved toward the refrigerator. I set it on the island before opening up the fridge door and reaching in for the milk. Marcus sat a container on the counter next to the milk jug I'd sat there. I thanked him quietly as I put both milk and sugar in my coffee. Heavy on the sugar of course, because that was the best part in my opinion.

I stirred my coffee with the spoon he'd placed beside the sugar container, and then moved to put it in the sink.

I sipped my coffee, humming happily, while he watched me. He stood in front of the counter beside the sink with his arms crossed loosely over his chest, completely at ease in his own kitchen.

"I didn't invite you over here just so I could have coffee with you," he admitted regretfully in a quiet voice. "I've got something I'd like to show you and want your advice on."

I frowned at him in confusion. Marcus needed my advice on something? That seemed unreal to me because he was an incredibly smart man, and I was just a seventeen-year-old girl. What could I possibly give him advice on?

"Marcus?" I asked in confusion. "What do you need from me? Tell me, and if I can help you, you have to know that I will."

Marcus, like Rain, could ask me for almost anything, and if I had it in me to give it to him I would. In that moment realization slammed into me enough that I had to drop my mug down to the counter and take a staggering step back. I slapped my palm down on top of the counter beside my mug as tears stung the backs of my eyes. I had always known Marcus meant a great deal to me, but it wasn't until that moment that I knew, I fucking *knew*, that I loved him just as much as I loved Rain. Marcus was just as important to me, and even though I'd known him for less than a year, I knew there would never come a time in my life where I would be happy to have him not taking an active role in it. It would break my heart into tiny little pieces if he were to walk out of my life and never look back.

All these people in my life now that I loved was really doing a number on me emotionally, because it wasn't something I had ever experienced before and not something I knew what the hell to do with now that I had them. I didn't ever want to disappoint anyone, and I wasn't even sure how to love that many people, even in a strictly platonic way.

I hated Vivian more than I ever had in that moment, because just how much she'd fucked me up in the head was becoming all too real to me and I didn't quite know what to do with that either.

"Are you alright, sweetheart?" he questioned hesitantly.

I nodded, not willing to tell him about what I'd just discovered. I had already told Rain I loved him today, I wasn't ready to tell yet another person the same. Part of me worried I would be giving away too much of myself to people who could potentially destroy me if they ever figured out how undeserving I was of their love and just how lacking I could be.

What if I told Marcus I loved him and he didn't say it back? What's worse, if I told him, he said it back, and then went on to throw it back in my face later on? It would crush me, maybe even kill something vital inside of me, and I just couldn't do it. I couldn't put myself out there that way. Not in a way that would leave me so vulnerable. It was too soon since the last time I'd laid myself bare before someone else.

Thoughts of Dash moving above me, moving inside of me, flashed inappropriately in my mind. Yeah, I really didn't need to think of being vulnerable at the moment, nor did I need to think about the time before last I had put myself out there in such a way. Marcus and I weren't ready for that kind of conversation and I hoped we never would be.

"I'm fine," I croaked out. "Just having a bit of a girly moment. These happen all the time, don't worry about it."

I hoped he believed me, because I absolutely did not want to explain myself.

He eyed me warily. "Okay," he said slowly. "If you're sure."

Boy, was I ever sure. I nodded, almost frantically so, hoping to all that was holy he would drop this subject and we could get back to why he'd really asked me over here. I didn't need to break down and have a moment on him.

"I'm sure," I murmured, hoping like hell he'd leave it alone.

Marcus gave me what he always did, and, that's to say, everything I needed from him, and he let it go. I wasn't stupid enough to think he'd forget about it though, because he wouldn't. He'd keep a closer watch on me from here on out to make sure I really was okay and I didn't have a problem with that. Just so long as I could sweep it under the proverbial rug for now. I was becoming so good at sweeping shit under that rug that it was a miracle the thing still lay flat on the floor.

Marcus sighed as his eyes dropped down to his bare feet. He was letting it go. Yeah, I so totally loved him. Even more so now than I had before because he gave me that, gave me exactly what I needed, and didn't press the issue when it was so obvious he wanted answers.

It made me feel like an asshole for not being honest and baring my soul to him.

"Okay," he breathed out, before straightening his shoulders and dropping his arms down to his sides.

He looked me dead in the eyes and the love he had for me shined bright in them for me to see. The problem I had with this was that I no longer wished to see that emotion coming from him at the moment.

I dropped my gaze from his and glanced back toward the island counter where my coffee mug sat. I picked up the mug and pressed it to my lips. I took a healthy—or not, depending on how you looked at it—gulp of coffee before resting back against the island, my mug held aloft before my chin, and I stared at Marcus.

"What was it you were planning on telling me?" I asked in a quiet but sure voice. The only thing I was sure of was that I didn't want to go back to talking about me. Just so long as he didn't tell me he was getting married or dying I knew I would be okay with this conversation.

Marcus turned away from me and pulled open a drawer. He reached inside and came out with two manila colored folders.

He walked over to where I was standing at the island and set the folders down, one on top of the other. I turned around so my back was facing the wall and I was staring down at the island counter, the folders sitting beside my almost empty coffee mug.

Marcus gestured down with his hands toward the folders. He cleared his throat nervously and the sound of it didn't do anything to put me at ease. What the hell was in those folders?

"I went out to the motel the Council is staying at earlier this week after we had our lunch together," he began. "Adrian had requested my presence there and I didn't think it wise to disobey him just yet."

That 'just yet' part killed me because I could completely understand where he was coming from. This was Adrian we were talking about here and he was a psycho.

"Okay," I said hesitantly. I didn't want to encourage his bad behavior where the Council was concerned, because I didn't think that boded well for anybody and I really did not want this to go badly for Marcus.

"Well," he drawled, "I found some things that were disturbing."

I could understand this, because I, too, had gone out to the motel and found pretty much everything I'd seen there to be disturbing.

"What did you find, Marcus?"

Marcus tapped his finger against the manila files. Once, twice, three times, before looking back at me from beneath his long, dark lashes. It bothered me how attractive I found him, even though he was so much older to me and I saw him as a parental figure. He wasn't my dad, I knew that, but it still bothered me to find the man attractive. I loved him and he'd had sex with Vivian. This was not normal and I hated that.

I was losing my mind, that had to be the only explanation I could think of.

"Open the files," he ordered softly, and I did as he said.

I flipped open the first folder. There was a 4x6 photograph inside of a woman. She looked to be walking down a busy street. Her head was turned to the side and long, straight black hair fanned out around her. There was a look on her face I recognized all too well. She looked scared, haunted even, her eyes were narrowed on something I couldn't see but the look on her face was enough. I was scared for her.

The picture was the only thing in the folder.

"I found the photo on Adrian's desk and made a copy of it. The next folder has a name and a telephone number. I need you to get these to Rain, and I need you to do it soon. I think the phone she uses is a burner phone that she must keep off most of the time, or they would have found her already."

My eyes were glued to the photograph staring up at me, transfixed.

"Why does the Council have a picture of this woman?" I inquired but, in my heart, I already knew. She was like me, but she was hiding from them.

"Rain," I choked out my father's name.

"Yeah," Marcus spoke quietly. "He'll be able to take care of her and keep her safe. But, for me, I can't know anything else about her other than what's in these folders."

I frowned at this as I finally tore my eyes off the picture and looked up at him. "What aren't you telling me?"

He was hiding something, that's for sure. It seemed like everyone was trying to hide something these days. The whole thing was starting to become exhausting.

"The less I know the better," was his cryptic reply.

Fine. Whatever. He could keep his secrets if he really wanted to.

"I'll get these to Rain, but I'm going to leave them in his

apartment for him instead of texting him. Now that I know Adrian has my phone number and knew about the shop, I'm super paranoid about everything." Wasn't that an understatement.

Marcus leaned his hip against the island beside me.

"You're right to be paranoid," he said. "They have secret ways of knowing things and they use magic they forbid others to use."

He reached out and closed the folder, shuffling them into a neat little stack.

"You've been spending an awful lot of time over at the Alexander house this week," he commented casually. A little too casually if you asked me, like he was fishing for information.

"Yeah," I stated. If there was something he wanted to know then he could come right out and ask for it. I was still reeling over the look in the woman's eyes and hoping Rain found her before the Council got their hands on her.

Marcus cleared his throat as he shifted from foot to foot, nervously.

"Is everything okay with you and Dash?"

My cheeks heated in embarrassment as images of Dash on top of me ran through my mind and my skin burned. Was I going to think about having sex with him every time someone brought his name up? I seriously hoped not, because this was really not good. Marcus, like Rain, didn't need to know I'd had sex.

Marcus took one look at my red face and immediately got angry. His fist clenched and he laid them down on the island counter.

"Those idiots better be treating you right," he growled. "If you think they're taking advantage of you in any way, I want you to tell me immediately. In fact, I want you to know that you can move back into your old room any time you'd like. I would love to have the company and you know you're always welcome here. This is your home too."

My shoulders slumped as I placed both my palms on the counter. If only my life were a lot less complicated, and I was in a place where I could move back into my pretty room with the window seat Tyson and I had slept beside each other on the first night he'd introduced me to *Friday Night Lights*. That had been my first *real* bedroom I'd had with anything other than a broken laundry basket on the floor with my used clothes piled in it, and a lumpy mattress that was on the floor as well. Marcus had bought me brand new furniture and all the fixings to go along with my room.

I had loved my bedroom here, it had been the first real thing that was close to a safe space I'd ever had and Marcus had been the one to give it to me. But I could not, under any circumstances, move back in here with him.

Have you ever heard that saying '*don't look back, you're not going that way?*' Well, I already wasted too much time looking back at the past and not enough time reaching for my future. My place was with my coven. My place was at Dash's cottage and now, since I couldn't live there, at the Alexander big house.

"They treat me just fine," I told Marcus honestly, and I realized in that moment that they *actually* did treat me very well, better than I probably deserved most of the time. "But... something happened and I think both Dash and myself will be staying next door at the Alexander house for a while now."

Probably a good long while considering those robed masked people.

He sighed but thankfully let it go.

I drank two cups of coffee with Marcus while I helped him unpack boxes in his office, lining his shelves with books and knickknacks.

After a couple hours of unpacking I asked him if I could borrow a car for a few hours. He said yes, like I knew he would. What surprised me though? He didn't even ask me why I needed to borrow one of his cars when my Range Rover, the one he'd bought for me, was parked in the driveway next door.

Maybe he knew that a girl in a house full of men would sometimes need an escape and a chance to catch her breath every now and then. Then again, maybe he was just being Marcus, the wonderful man that he was, and he was doing what he could to take care of me.

Whatever the case, I didn't care, I was simply thankful for it.

# CHAPTER EIGHTEEN

I shut the door quietly behind me, afraid to make any noise even though I knew nobody would be able to hear me from outside the garage. The walls in here were heavily insulated and with the shade pulled shut on the one door to the outside closed, there was no way someone standing outside would be able to tell there was someone moving around in here.

I pouted as I pressed the button on the key fob, unlocking the car Marcus had given me keys to, and stood still as I watched for lights to flash on the car the fob belonged to. I pouted because his beautiful black Mercedes was parked out in the driveway for once and I knew that whatever set of keys he'd given me did not belong to that car. I wanted to drive that car, badly, with my foot pressed all the way down to the floor as the world blurred past me.

I feared I would now never get the chance to drive it and that made me ridiculously sad.

I shook my head, shaking myself free of my useless thoughts. Envy and greed would get me absolutely nowhere. I thought that had been a lesson I'd learned long ago, but here I was lusting over driving a car I had no business wanting to get behind the wheel of. Couldn't I just be thankful for what I had? Why did I now strive for more?

I shook off my thoughts as I hit the button on the key fob again. This time I paid attention to the vehicles in the garage so I wouldn't have to hit the button a third time.

The tail lights on a black Suburban parked in the farthest corner of the garage that I had never seen before flashed when I hit the button. That was new and I didn't understand why he needed so many different vehicles in the garage when he was the only person who lived here now.

I held the keys in my hand as I headed toward the Suburban, no longer giving a crap what vehicle it was that had bleeped to life for me. It didn't really matter what I drove at this point, just so long as I had a means to escape the madness going on in the house next door. I needed an escape, and Marcus Cole had given me one. Wishing that escape had come in the form of his Mercedes made me an ungrateful brat when the vehicle didn't matter just so long as it got me where I needed to go.

And where exactly was it that I needed to go?

Absolutely nowhere, just so long as I wasn't forced to stay here anymore.

There were too many people in my life these days who wanted to keep tabs on me, keep me in their line of sight at all times. And as much as I loved them for caring, it was beginning to drive me toward the brink of insanity and sometimes made it harder for me to breathe.

I climbed into the Suburban, having had to use the base board to be able to haul my butt on to the driver's seat, and tossed the folders onto the passenger seat. I closed the door and buckled up.

I was sticking the key in the ignition when the front passenger side door swung open, causing me to scream and flinch into my door.

Tyson held the door open as he leaned in, grinning at me.

"Hey, girl," he said cheerfully. "You going somewhere?"

I glared at him as I pressed a palm to my chest, covering my racing heart. It didn't help slow it down in the slightest.

"You scared the shit out of me, Ty," I responded breathlessly. "What the heck are you even doing in here?"

I hadn't heard the door open and I'd heard absolutely nothing coming from the garage. The place had been as quiet as a tomb until I'd pressed on the button on the key fob. How had he even gotten in here?

"You should just be glad your new BFF's aren't here instead of me," he said as he climbed into the big SUV and closed the door behind him, sitting down on top of the folders like he hadn't even noticed them there. "They're restless and going stir crazy over there, now that your dad's shine has seemed to wear off and he seems just like a normal guy to them again."

I frowned at him.

"Rain *is* just a normal guy to them," I commented, as I watched him pull the seat belt down and around his body. He clicked it in and sat back in the seat.

He shook his head as he smirked at me. "I don't think you see your dad the same way the rest of us do."

Maybe he had the right of it on that one. I didn't necessarily have Rain up on a pedestal, but that wasn't saying I didn't see him through rose-tinted glasses, because I often times did.

"I don't want to talk about Rain," I muttered angrily. Suddenly, I was angry again and being angry was really starting to piss me off. "I don't want to talk about Trenton and Simon either. In fact, I don't think I want to talk at all. If that's why you're here then perhaps you should just get right back out again and leave me be."

Okay, so maybe I was being a bitch to Tyson for no reason that had anything to do with him, but I just couldn't seem to shake this bad mood I was in and I needed a target to aim my anger and frustration at. It was unfortunate for Tyson that he'd gotten into this ginormous SUV with me with only the two of us in the vehicle together. There was nowhere else for my anger to go, no other outlet to reach out toward.

"Just get out, Tyson," I ordered in a quiet, controlled voice.

"You know," Tyson began in an oddly somber voice that absolutely did not coincide with the smirk on his face, "those two aren't entirely your responsibility. Uncle Quint would have taken them in if you hadn't. You know that, right?"

He wasn't the first person to tell me that, but, at this point, it wasn't something I needed to hear from anyone. I knew Quinton Alexander and I knew the kind of man he was. He was the kind of man who was worth everything. There was no way he'd turn out Trenton and Simon, no fucking way. They'd have a permanent place in his home and he'd eventually give them as good as he gave the rest of our coven, because we were all a messed up group of people who desperately needed each other. They took me on and it hadn't been easy. They'd take the brothers on the same way, not just Quinton, but all of them. Because their past made it so they fit in perfectly with us.

They were damaged goods and that made them the perfect fit for our coven.

I sighed heavily and repeated, "Just get out, Tyson."

I did not want to talk about the people I'd brought into our lives without asking. I did not want to talk about much of anything.

I wanted to escape. Escape my new version of reality. Escape the people who loved me. Escape my own life. Escape pretty much everything.

"I'm not getting out, Ariel," Tyson countered, sounding tired.

"Fine, whatever," I grumbled under my breath. If he wasn't going to get out then I wasn't going to waste any more time arguing with him about it.

I reached up and pressed the button on the small square device attached to the visor and the garage door opened. I put the Suburban in reverse and backed out. I had never driven a vehicle this big before, so I took extra care to not hit anything on the way down the driveway. At the end of the driveway I hit the button again and watched as the garage door went back down.

I hit the road and cruised past the Alexander house without looking at it. I didn't want to jinx it and with my luck someone would be looking out the window at just that second and see me driving by. Then my phone would blow up and I'd likely go insane.

Tyson moved around in his seat and slipped the manila folders out from underneath him. He held them up and asked, "What are these?"

I sighed.

"There's a picture in one and a phone number in the other one," I said, telling him the bare minimum.

He opened the folder and whistled under his breath. "She's pretty but there's something sad about her. Who is she?"

"Has anybody ever told you before that you're nosy?"

He laughed quietly, his shoulders shaking with it. I noticed he didn't answer my question, though, and that was answer enough for me.

"How has Quinton put up with you all this time?" I inquired jokingly.

Ignoring that, he repeated, "Who is she, Ariel?"

"Marcus thinks she's a witch," I answered him, knowing he wouldn't let it go until I did. "And he thinks she's hiding from the Council. He found this picture and the phone number in Adrian's office."

"A witch?" Tyson echoed in a voice filled with wonder. "There really are more females out there than we thought there were."

Something in his voice bothered me and I hated to think it, but the thought crossed my mind anyways. If there were more female witches out there, then did that mean they'd want to take a good look at them and maybe regret taking me in and inviting me into their coven? Would they want another female if more came to light? Would they want to swap me out for a new, shinier, bright version, one without a fucked up past and scarred up body? Would this change everything for me when I'd just gotten comfortable in my life, was the rug going to be ripped out from underneath me?

And why the fuck had he called her pretty? I know, I know, I'd thought the same thing about her, but had he really needed to say it out loud? Jealousy reared her ugly head and filled me up with her poison. It was a horrible feeling to have and something I wasn't used to feeling.

"Ariel?" Tyson murmured quietly, and I felt his eyes on me but refused to look at him. "Why did he give this to you?"

I hit the button to lower the driver's side window and sucked in a lung full of clean air, hoping it would clear out the bad shit running through my head.

"Rain," I choked out past the jealousy clogging up my insides. "He knows what Rain's family did and wanted me to give it to him to see if there's any chance Rain can find her before the Council does and get her nice and hidden away from them in time."

"Makes sense," he said quietly. "But what I want to know is why you're acting so weird now and why do you look like someone kicked your puppy?"

I shot him a dirty look, not appreciating that last statement at all. I needed to work better at hiding my emotions when it came to my face.

"Can we just not talk?" I asked him, and I think I even meant it too.

"You know you're pretty too, right? You're the only person I want."

I groaned as I hit the button, closing the window, and then I latched on to the steering wheel in a death grip, trying to strangle the life out of it.

"It's okay if you think she's pretty," I said in a quiet, strangled voice. "It's okay for you to be attracted to other people, to want them. I have no room to talk, not when I've got all these boyfriends. I have no right to expect you to only want me."

Tyson's big, warm palm landed on my thigh and he squeezed gently. I was glad for having put on leggings today instead of a skirt because I didn't think I could handle having his hand on my bare skin at the moment.

"I would *never* cheat on you and I fucking hate that you think I would do that."

Shit.

The hurt in his voice killed me. I'd really messed this whole thing up with him and that hadn't been my intention.

"I don't think you'd cheat on me, Tyson," I told him in a small voice. "That's not the problem. I'm the problem here. You say some chick is pretty and I get jealous like an asshole."

He squeezed my thigh. "You don't have anything to be jealous about."

"I know that," I snapped at him. "I'm being irrational and I know that too."

"Okay," he said quietly, sounding confused.

"What happens," I began, "if we find a bunch of women who are all witches and all of sudden you've all got options other than me?"

I said that, me, yeah, that was my voice, my mouth those words had come out of. I'd put it right out there, no bullshit. And I absolutely could not put it back, take it back, and I very much wanted to.

"What the hell are you talking about?" Tyson growled at me. "Why would you ever think we'd want options other than you? That's the stupidest thing I've ever heard come out of your mouth. I'm in love with you. Uncle Quint is in love with you. The twins would rather die than be without you. Goddamn Damien would give up his relationship with Julian if that's what you wanted and Julian would do the same even though it'd kill him to do it. Dash loves you more than life itself, hell, you *just had sex with him.* For fuck's sake, Ariel. What's the matter with you? What's it going to take for you to believe in us, to believe in our relationship? Our love isn't enough for you? I bought you a goddamn building!"

He ended on a shout that had me wincing in my seat, flinching away from him as if he'd struck me.

"Why are you yelling at me?" I snapped back at him. "I tell you how I really feel, give you the truth you're always asking for, and you yell at me in return? What kind of garbage is that?"

Maybe that last bit was unfair, but I didn't give a crap. I'd stopped caring the moment he raised his voice. I'd put myself out there, not for me and certainly not because I'd wanted to. I didn't appreciate having it thrown in my face and being yelled at because of it.

"Why..." He sputtered. "Why am I yelling at you? Are you kidding me right now?"

"You asked and I gave you the truth."

"Well, the truth sucked," he spat.

No kidding, the truth sucked for me too.

"Maybe it's not exactly jealousy taking over me," I mused. "It's probably more like my own self-consciousness coming out. My insecurities taking over. I'm not perfect, far from it, and I'm the first one to admit it. But, most people, if they were to take a look at a photograph of me inside a manila folder just like the one in your hands, they would take one look at me and I can assure you, the word that would come out of their mouths wouldn't be pretty."

I lifted my right hand from the steering wheel, releasing my death grip on the thing to do it, and gestured toward my face.

"I can talk a big game," I continued. "I can even believe it myself, and do. But there's no erasing this shit on my face." I lowered my hand and gestured toward my chest. "There's no erasing the shit on my collarbones. But, the thing is, it's not those scars that are the worst on me, it's the ones I carry on the inside that own that. And I'm okay with that shit too."

"Ariel," he whispered in a pained voice.

I shook my head. "My scars don't bother me and I doubt they ever will. They're a part of me and they aren't a part I'm ashamed of. But, that's me and that's how *I* look at them. That is not, nor will it ever be, the way the rest of the world looks at them or me because I wear them on my skin. It's not me, though, who has to look at me and think *pretty*."

It was my words this time that made me flinch and had absolutely nothing to do with him.

"Shut up," Tyson hissed at me. "Just shut the fuck up. There is nothing, absolutely *nothing* wrong with your face or the rest of your body. You *are* pretty, so fucking pretty, and there's not a person in our entire coven who would say differently, and they would mean that shit from the very bottom of their souls. God, I can't even believe I'm having this conversation with you right now."

I had started this conversation, but I certainly didn't want to finish it.

I pulled up across the street from Fortune's for the Unfortunate and parked alongside the curb. There were two big, black boxy vans parked in front of the store that were out of place and had me not turning the SUV off just yet. Something about those vans was rubbing me the wrong way and putting me on edge.

"There is no other woman for us," Tyson said angrily. "There—"

I cut him off to stupidly say, "There was Annabell once."

He sucked in a sharp breath. I knew that was like a punch to the gut and I'd probably regret saying it later, but my focus had been diverted and I was now no longer paying as much attention as I should to what was going on inside of the vehicle. My eyes were aimed across the street.

"That's not fair," he whispered in a voice full of hurt, and I agreed entirely with him. "You are not Annabell, you're nothing like her. This is different from that and you have to know it. Annabell was never going to be in the place you are right now, and not just because only a handful of us were into her."

Loved her, he meant. Into her is what he'd said.

"Ty," I whispered urgently as I watched a dark figure move behind the glass, inside the store.

He ignored me. "I want to strangle you right now. You are so infuriating that it's hard to handle sometimes. I cannot wait to tell Uncle Quint about this latest shit you've come up with in an effort to distance yourself from us."

"I'm not distancing myself," I argued, as I unfastened my seat belt. I left the SUV running, just in case we needed to make a quick getaway. "I'm just telling you my version of the truth and I'm honestly sorry you're having a hard time dealing with it. Now, love you, babe, and I'm not trying to be mean when I say this, but I'm going to need you to shut up now and pay attention to what's going down across the street."

He sputtered indignantly as I slipped my cell phone out of my hoodie pocket and engaged it. I scrolled down to Quinton's contact and hit go. I put it on speaker and waited while it rang.

"Baby," he answered on the third ring. "Everything okay?"

The sound of his voice washed through me, settling something deep inside me that had been unnerved by my stupid jealousy and insecurities. Quinton was mine, all mine, and he wasn't going anywhere no matter how many female witches were unearthed.

"No," I said honestly. "I am not okay. We have a problem and I think I need you."

I heard things rustling and knew he was on the move. "I'm on my way over now."

I closed my eyes for a second, not allowing myself to take longer than that, not when there were things I needed to be on the lookout for.

"I'm not next door anymore," I told him.

Quinton swore harshly under his breath, impressing me with the creative curse words he'd come up with.

"Of course you're not next door," he growled. "Marcus is smart enough to keep you out of trouble. Where are you?"

"Sitting in a Suburban I had no idea Marcus owned, across the street from the shop. And I'm not alone because Ty came with me. Though," I mused thoughtfully, "I'm betting he's wishing very much right now that he'd stayed home and far, far away from me and I can't even say I blame him."

"Ariel," he groaned. "What have you done now?"

Please, like everything was always my fault? Good grief. This kind of shit never happened to me before I'd met these guys. They were more to blame than I was and that's what I was sticking with.

"I've done nothing," I replied in a snotty voice. "We are parked in front of the shop and I thought things were weird because there's these black vans parked out front. And then I saw someone moving around inside. Normally, I wouldn't freak about that because I would assume it was Rain in there, but Rain is still at the big house with you, right?"

Quinton grunted and I assumed that meant yes.

"Emergency," I heard him bark from a distance and knew he'd moved the phone away from his face and was talking to someone else. "Intruders at the shop. Ariel and Ty are already there and we gotta *go*."

I heard the murmur of male voices on the other end of the phone.

"I want you to stay on the line with me, baby, alright?" he requested in a soft, sweet voice.

I knew he had to be freaking out on the inside but he was keeping it together. For me, he was keeping it together and it just made me love him all the more because if he freaked out then I would freak out and this situation would be made a whole lot worse.

"I'll stay on the line," I murmured quietly as I watched out the window. "Just so you know, you're on speakerphone and Ty can hear you too."

"Good girl," he said in that same voice.

"I didn't see it," Tyson admitted in a small voice. "I didn't even notice there was anything wrong."

I winced at that, knowing it was my fault he felt like crap and was being down on himself. I wanted to look at him but couldn't afford to take my eyes off of the shop for even a second. Instead, I placed the phone on my lap and reached for the hand he still had wrapped around my thigh. I squeezed his hand. He didn't give my thigh a squeeze back.

"Not your fault, Tyson," I said. "I'm an asshole and that conversation didn't go very well because of it."

"Why is she swearing?" Quinton asked, and I knew he was speaking to his nephew and not me. I answered him anyway, before Tyson had the chance to.

"Marcus gave me this picture," I explained, even though I knew I shouldn't be sharing with them when Marcus was even afraid to send a text message to Rain about it, "and a phone number today. It's for a lady he thinks is a witch in hiding. He found it in Adrian's office and made copies. Dangerous, I know, but so damn ballsy. I'm really impressed with the effort he's putting into this farce with the Council. Anyway, he's being extra cautious and careful with everything, so he didn't want to text it to Rain and asked me to give it to him instead."

"Why would he give it to Rain?" Quinton inquired carefully.

"Are you on the road yet?" Ty asked his uncle.

"Yeah," Quinton said, answering his nephew. "We are all on our way. We'll be there in less than ten minutes. You just need to keep her safe until then. You've got this."

I ignored that and shared, "He knows what Rain's family has always done. I don't know how he knows, just that he does. I didn't question it, although I probably should have. I trust him, even with Rain's secrets, and because he's my father, mine. I think he made the right call with asking me to give it to Rain so I headed toward the shop and was going to leave the folders in his apartment."

"Hmmm..." He muttered noncommittally. "And what did you do to Ty?"

I sighed, not wanting to answer him, but knew I had to because he would never drop it if I didn't. Quinton never knew when to leave well enough alone. It used to bother me, but was something I was now accustomed to and didn't fight it often anymore.

"He called the woman in the picture pretty." I gave him the honesty Tyson hadn't seemed to appreciate much. "And I let my insecurities out to play."

"She thinks that because of her scars and shitty past that if more females who have magic are discovered that we won't want her anymore, and will pick another female to either replace her with or add to the mix."

Another figure moved in the shop, another one right behind them. "I just saw two people move inside so we know there's more than one. Not sure how many altogether though. There are three different vans so there's gotta be three different drivers, right? Unless these vans were parked here before now. We have been so busy with the attack at Dash's then resting and healing for days... When was the last time anyone's even been to the shop or checked in?"

"I've got the feeds up now, baby girl," Rain said, and I wasn't surprised to hear his voice. Quinton had put us on speakerphone as well. "From what I've seen so far they've only been there for about a half an hour."

"What are they doing?" I asked.

Rain started to answer but Quinton cut him off. "Are you kidding me with this shit, Ariel?" he interjected in a quiet voice. "Is that something you're seriously worried about happening?"

I watched a black hooded figure step out of the shop carrying a box toward the back of the van while I thought over his question. The hooded figure opened up the back of the last van and tossed the box inside. I didn't even want to know what was inside of that box that he'd stolen from us, but I knew there was no way I could let him actually leave with it.

"With you and with Dash," I addressed Quinton, "the answer is a hard no. You're both mine and you're not going anywhere. I know it's selfish to say, but if you tried to leave me I wouldn't let you go. But sometimes, with the others, I have moments of doubt. Today I had one of those moments with Tyson and I didn't know that he would have had such a hard time with my honesty, because if I had known I might not have been quite so honest with him. Do I know that he loves me? Yes, absolutely. My fear is irrational, I know, but that doesn't mean I can just stop it. I can't."

"We'll work on it, all of us together," Quinton promised in that quiet, sweet voice. I knew why I'd gotten that voice this time, it was because I'd called him mine and he'd liked it. Probably loved it even if I had to guess, and I was guessing because I knew Quinton well. I knew that when we had a private moment later on he would bring it up again and make me say it to him face to face and I was okay with that.

"Can we stop talking about this now?" Tyson grumbled, and if I wasn't focused on the shop I would have turned and laughed in his face. For the first time I was open and willing to discuss my feelings and he was ready to change the subject.

I would never understand boys.

"What are they doing in my building?" Tyson asked loudly, and I snickered.

"How many of them are there, do you know?" I questioned, when I got my amusement on Tyson's behalf under control.

"Six," Rain answered. "And so far, all they're doing is going through everything. They aren't even trashing the place, just looking at shit. It's weird."

"Exactly what shit are they looking through?" I asked curiously. It was killing me to sit in here on my hands waiting, but it would be plain stupid to go in on my own when there were so many of them. "And do you know who they are?"

"I think they're from the same crew that attacked at Dash's place," Rain replied, and I found it funny, not in a ha ha sort of way, that he called it Dash's place just like I did. "There's no way there'd be more than one group of hunters in town. They tend to stick to their little groups because too much fighting happens when there are bigger groups."

Rain sure knew more than anyone else about them, I'd have to take his word for it.

Someone came out of the shop with another box and placed it in the back of a van.

"They're taking things," I shared.

"I can see," Rain said.

What he didn't do was tell me what was inside those boxes and I really wanted to know. In my opinion, if you didn't practice magic or weren't a witch then there wasn't much in the store that should really interest you.

"Shit," Tyson hissed, right before knuckles rapped against the front passenger seat window. I let out a small, embarrassingly girly shriek and whirled toward Tyson.

Blindly, my hand ran over the driver's side door, searching. My fingers glossed over buttons and pressed down on the first one I'd encountered. A distinctive click sounded throughout the SUV and I let out a shaky breath at hearing it. Locked, the doors were locked now, and I told myself we were safe behind those locks. I knew I was lying to myself though.

"What the fuck is going on?" Quinton asked in high, terrified voice.

"Be quiet," Tyson murmured, "or I'll have Ariel hang up on you."

He could threaten his uncle with that, but I didn't think it was a threat that I would actually be able to come through with. Just knowing Quinton was on the other end of the line made me feel a whole lot safer and that small sense of safety wasn't something I was willing to give up.

"But—" Quinton started, trying to argue but was cut off.

"Shut up," Tyson snarled in a quiet, angry voice.

The other end of the phone line went quiet as Quinton took his nephew seriously, finally.

I watched in horror as Tyson hit the button that would lower the passenger side window. It went down several inches and stopped.

The person who had tapped their knuckles against the window stood off to the side, just out of sight from me. I could lean back between the two front seats to check out the back passenger window, but didn't want to draw any more attention to myself and make a target out of me. So, I sat there and I waited and they didn't make me wait long but I knew, if it were the hunters then I was pretty sure Tyson and I were as good as dead.

# CHAPTER NINETEEN

I stood beside Tyson next to the Suburban. We were on the far side of the shop and, hopefully, hidden from view from the people moving around inside. I'd taken the call off of speaker but hadn't ended it before sticking it in one of the front pockets of my hoodie. I still wasn't willing to disconnect from Quinton, even when I knew he'd be here in just a few short minutes. I also didn't hang up because I wanted him to know what was going on and that it wasn't safe for him to bring Rain here with him.

A man I had only seen twice before—the second time he didn't know about—stood before Tyson and I. His arms were crossed over his chest and he was glaring at us like we were his naughty children he'd just caught doing something he'd forbidden us from, multiple times. Now we were in for a lecture and maybe even a time out.

I watched him nervously, warily, as I waited for him to speak. Or yell, I wouldn't be surprised if he yelled instead, he looked about ready to blow.

The reason he made me so nervous was because he was a

member of the Council and I think we all knew by now that they set me on edge.

His name was Daniel. He was either in his early forties or was older and aged well. He had a broad forehead and a wide nose. Not a man I'd ever call attractive in the sense he was beautiful. But there was one thing I had to give him, because *it* actually *was* beautiful and that was his hair. He had dark, thick brown hair that was roped into a heavy braid that fell all the way down to the middle of his back. His hair was a thing to envy, and even if he wasn't a man you'd originally want to take a second look at, that hair would catch you by surprise at the last minute he walked past you and you'd have to take an extra peek over your shoulder at him just to check it out.

Out of the Council members he'd been the one I'd disliked the most. Probably because his eyes weren't mean and cruel like most of the rest of them.

That is to say I'd disliked him the least until I had seen that glorious braid slither around down his back while he and his Council buddies were giving it dirty to Annabell in some weird Council tries to knock up the female witch gang bang that I could have died happy never even knowing about, let alone having seen it.

Odd, I know, because one would think that after all the years I had spent living with Vivian I would have been desensitized to watching other people have sex, but as it turns out that just wasn't the case.

Maybe Quinton *was* right, maybe I was a prude. Please, don't let anyone tell him I said that.

Tyson cleared his throat and bravely looked Daniel in the eyes, and said, "This is private property. What are you doing on it?"

I choked as I turned to gape at him. That's how he wanted to lead into this talk?

"You own the land across the street, Young Alexander," Daniel drawled. "If you want to talk about trespassing on your private property then perhaps we should go across the street and have this conversation."

"I don't think that's a wise idea," I rushed out, and shrunk back when Daniel turned his hostile gaze on me.

"Tell me, Ariel," he started in a casual tone that was at odds with the look on his face. "Why is it you think it's not a wise idea to go across the street to your shop? Why have you two been parked out here for almost ten minutes and not gotten out of your vehicle?"

I scratched at the side of my neck, nervously.

"Well," I said, "technically it's Marcus's vehicle and not ours."

Tyson snickered from beside me and I jerked my elbow toward him, nailing him in the ribs.

Instead of getting angry with me, Daniel glared at Tyson and leaned in to snarl, "You think any of this is funny? You're out here with one of our only females, one that's only recently been brought to our attention, and you want to stand here laughing when there are witch hunters across the street pilfering your store, a store I might add, that she spends most of her time *working* at. Tell me, young Alexander, what part of this scenario here do you find amusing?"

Well, when he put it like that I could understand why he seemed to be so angry and upset with us.

Still...

"How do you know they're witch hunters?" I asked in a quiet voice. He'd sounded so sure of himself. "What are you doing here, Daniel?"

"Girl," Tyson said in a voice full of warning. He wanted me to be careful here while talking to this Council member. He and I both knew what could happen to me for treating them so poorly. However, I was starting to believe, probably foolishly, that the Council wouldn't hurt me for asking questions or even being slightly snotty toward them. Heck, half the time Adrian found it amusing when I talked back to him. The other half he did get angry, though, so I knew not to push my luck too far.

A terrible thought struck me and had me gripping the front of my hoody, my fingers digging into the material to keep myself from reaching out and clutching the front of Daniel's sweater.

"Are you following me?" I whispered in a voice full of horror.

I hadn't noticed anyone following me, but half the time I was too busy rushing from place to place and I didn't always pay enough attention to the world around me.

What if they'd been watching me in the shop and had seen me with Rain? There was no hiding the fact he was my father, we looked too much alike to try and hide it from anyone. What would they do if they found Rain with me? What would happen to him?

I shuddered at the surge of fear that roared through me.

Daniel eyed me warily. "Of course I'm not following you. We would never do such a thing to you. However, that doesn't mean we don't expect reports from Quinton on your progress and welfare because we certainly do. He just doesn't report in as often as he should, and we've been forced to take matters into our own hands if we wanted to know how you've been doing. Today, I came by to check in and make sure you got Adrian's messages about when Marcus's dinner party is, because you haven't responded to him. He might not have gotten so angry if when he tried to get into contact with both your new guards, they had actually gotten back to him. Since they did not, he was going to come out here and see you himself and if you weren't here he was going to stop by the cottage. I didn't think these were wise decisions given his temperament, so I offered to go in his stead. I showed up here and you can imagine my surprise when I see witch hunters pull up and break in. Now, the thing I want to know here, is why don't you seem surprised to see them?"

Ohhhhh boy.

"They attacked Dash's the other night." Quinton's voice came from the front of the Suburban.

I jerked at hearing him, surprised because I hadn't heard him approach or a car pull up. I'd been too engrossed in the conversation with Daniel. We were lucky the hunters hadn't seen us and decided to attack, because we all would have been sitting ducks in our stupidity.

That didn't stop me from running straight for Quinton. I hit him head on, causing him to stagger back a step on his silver cowboy boots. I wrapped my arms around his middle and squeezed. His arms came up around my shoulders and he held me tightly to him. I probably should have been embarrassed by my actions but didn't have it in me. Quinton made me feel safe and I wasn't interested in hiding it from anyone anymore, least of all Quinton.

I shoved my face in his neck, my mouth going to his ear, and I whispered urgently, "Rain?"

He kissed my cheek softly and whispered as his lips ghosted over my skin, "He's fine, baby. Don't worry about him."

I nodded as I tried to step back. I didn't make it anywhere because Quinton refused to let me go. Not that I was complaining, I was just surprised by it because we were in front of a Council member. Then again, he probably had never expected me to literally throw myself at him either, and probably didn't want to let go out of fear it'd never happen again. I wasn't opposed to PDA, I just wasn't usually the person to instigate it.

Quinton's palms glided down my back until his hands were resting on my waist. He picked me up and carried me back over to where his nephew stood with his back against the borrowed SUV. He sat me back down on my feet beside Tyson and squeezed my waist tightly before letting me go. He turned his back on me and stepped over until he stood directly in front of me, blocking me almost entirely from Daniel's sharp gaze.

I almost rolled my eyes at the ridiculous, overprotective move, but didn't because it was pure Quinton and there was a large part of me that loved this about him.

Tyson reached out and laced his fingers through mine. I squeezed his hand in gratitude and directed a small smile, not appropriate for this situation, his way. He missed out on it because his eyes were focused straight ahead and on the Council member.

"I find it odd," Quinton continued in a quiet, but lethal voice, "that it's you who showed up here to visit our girl when it seems to be Adrian who's obsessed with her."

I groaned inwardly. This was not the way things needed to be going down right now. If he wanted to give people a hard time for being obsessed with me, then I thought he should have waited until we sat down for their absurd dinner party. At least then we'd know we had something worth talking about, because Quinton wasn't the only person who had a problem with the Council being obsessed with me or the only person I figured would have something to say on the subject.

I squeezed Ty's hand before letting it go and stepping around Quinton. I didn't get far before an arm covered in bright orange and yellow flames shooting up from its wrist wrapped around my middle and I was pulled backward. My back ended up pressed to his front and he wrapped both his arms around my middle. Normally, I'd get angry at this super alpha male gesture, but I was just going to be thankful today that he didn't shove me back behind him once again in order to keep me out of sight and out of harm's way.

"Can we focus on what's important here?" I asked in a small, tired voice. "And that being what's going on across the street."

"Very reasonable," Daniel said approvingly, and I felt the unfriendly vibes coming off of the two Alexander men standing behind me. "I need both of you Alexanders to take this young female home and keep her safe, at least until it's time for you to bring her to the motel for our dinner party."

I flinched away from him and back into Quinton's warm body. The way he'd worded that hadn't exactly given me the warm fuzzies, but it *had* set off my creeper alarms. After growing up around the men Vivian had liked to fornicate with, my creeper alarm was damn good, there'd been plenty of times and instances to perfect it.

Just what did Daniel think would be happening after this dinner party? I wasn't sure I wanted to know and now I *really* wasn't sure I wanted to go. I mean, I really hadn't before, but now I might actually pretend to have the flu so I could skip out on it for real.

"I'll not be leaving with Ariel," Quinton growled in a dark voice full of gravel. "Though, I do agree with you that I think she should be leaving and nowhere around the hunters."

Even though I was terrified of the hunters, I really didn't want to leave any of my people here with them without me. I was no longer completely useless to them. Hadn't I proved that at Dash's cottage when I put out the fire? I had magic and I now knew how to use it, the thought of them forcing me to sit on the sidelines simply because I was female filled me with resentment.

I jerked out of Quinton's arms and turned to glare at him. He didn't glare angrily back like I would have expected him to. Oh no, instead he had this soft, sweet look on his face while he looked down on me. His eyes were filled with understanding and I had never wanted more to hit him than I did in that moment. He might understand me, but he had no intentions of indulging me. Instead, I'd be sent home like a child he wanted to protect, an innocent who could not defend themselves.

"Get out of my way," I whispered angrily at both Quinton and Tyson.

Neither responded so I shoved them aside and out of my way. I ripped open the passenger side door and climbed up into the passenger seat of the borrowed Suburban. I didn't slam the door shut behind me because even I didn't want to draw attention to our little outside huddle, I wouldn't do that to the ones I loved. The members of the Council could all get fucked because, as far as I was concerned, they were on their own.

The door clicked shut quietly and I slid over the supple leather seats until I was in the driver's seat once again and back behind the wheel. The SUV was still running and it surprised me because I had forgotten in all that had gone on that I had not turned it off, so we would have a quick getaway car if need be.

I hit the button on the door panel that locked all the doors and, without looking, felt the three males standing beside the right side of the vehicle turn and stare at me, assessing my motives.

I pulled my cell phone out of my hoodie pocket and tapped it with a finger until the screen lit up for me. I hit the red circle button that ended the call that had still been engaged to Quinton. I'd honestly forgotten he was still on the line, I'd figured he'd have ended the call when he got here and to me.

I pulled up my contacts and hit go on Rain's name. I knew he liked to coddle me as well, but he'd never lie to me and would tell me what he knew was going on around here.

He answered on the first ring.

"Baby girl," he said. "Tell me you're alright."

His words filled me with warmth. Rain was a damn good father and my happiness and welfare always came before his own or, really, anybody's.

"Where are you?" I barked into the phone.

# CHAPTER TWENTY

Neither Quinton or Tyson had looked impressed when I'd pulled away from the curb and left them there exposed to the street. Guess they should have thought better about things when they had talked about me leaving. I'd given them exactly what they had wanted, just not how they'd wanted it.

Whatever.

You couldn't be a winner when it came to everything.

I met Rain about a block away. He was in my Range Rover and parked in a parking lot in front of a building that looked empty and abandoned. Garbage was liberally strewn throughout the lot, making the place look like a dump even though the building itself sadly looked like a newer build.

I'd honestly never once taken notice of the area around the shop and paid much attention to the neighborhood it was in.

When I parked the black Suburban in the parking spot beside my black Range Rover, I put the SUV in park and shut it down. There was no point in leaving the thing running when we weren't in need of a quick getaway this time, or so I hoped.

I didn't hit the key fob on the ring to lock the doors as I got out. There was no point since I was just going to the vehicle parked in the spot right beside it. If we left I would lock it up, I didn't want anything to happen to Marcus's vehicle he'd so kindly loaned me. Neither did I want anything to happen to the expensive vehicle he'd given me, but I opened the passenger side door and got in all the same.

Rain was seated behind the wheel. Both Simon and Trenton were in the backseat, and I couldn't help but feel sorry for them. I loved my Rover dearly but I wasn't well over six feet tall and forced to stuff all that and my muscles into the backseat. I knew I would like my Rover a whole lot less if it were me stuffed back there with my legs cramped in too small a space for them.

"Where are the others?" I asked, as I closed the passenger side door behind me. "The rest of my coven, I mean."

Rain turned in his seat to look me directly in the eye.

"Dash rode with Damien and Julian in their silver SUV. Your Salt and Pepper twins took their truck. Quinton had driven your Range Rover, but when he realized the Council had arrived on the scene he parked here and ran the rest of the way. Anybody else I'm missing?"

I shook my head, but I was stuck on the fact my father had just told me Quinton had been the one to drive my Range Rover with these three. To the best of my knowledge, none of them had keys to my Rover. Though, I had thought many times about making a set for Rain because I still had no idea how he got around to places and whether or not he had a car. I had never gotten around to it though.

Then it hit me... Trenton had stolen my keys and refused to give them back. That jerk.

"Good," Rain said, and he looked down back at his cell phone in his hands. He held it up for me to see along with the two brothers in the back seat.

There were several tiny squares on the screen, all of them aimed either inside the shop or outside of it.

I spotted the place the SUV had been parked at before I'd driven off and it thankfully was just an empty curb now before an empty lot. The Alexander's and the Council member were nowhere to be seen. Another glance through the squares on Rain's phone told me they weren't *anywhere* to be seen. None of my coven members were, neither were any of the other Council members, if there even were any other Council members on site.

My cell in my hoodie pocket chimed and I pulled it out. I had a text from Quinton and I opened it to read it.

Quinton: The rest of the guys are here as well as several members of the Council.

I frowned down at my phone. Was that supposed to make me feel better? It didn't. It just succeeded in making me feel even more afraid than I already was. Not afraid for myself, but afraid for the people I loved. Like we could trust the Council to help take care of my boys and keep them safe. I would have rolled my eyes if I wasn't so upset about the whole thing. And terrified. It wasn't something I would have admitted in front of the rest of my coven, that I was scared out of my mind for them, to lose them, and maybe I wouldn't have admitted it aloud to anyone.

My phone chimed again and I looked back down at it.

Quinton: Rain should meet you back up at my house. Your new bodyguards will be with him and have guaranteed me they'll take good care of you. Text me when you're home and safe.

This message had me frowning even harder. He expected me to just go to his house, which wasn't my home at all, and relax while

I waited for him to bring the others home safely? Did he not know me at all? There was absolutely nothing in me that gave off the impression that I could be able to do something like that.

Did he think I was that big of a coward or did he think I was just that useless? I understood his need to take care of me, and I even loved him a lot for it because that was how he usually treated the others as well. But this shit was becoming ridiculous. Eventually he'd have to peel back the bubble wrap and let me breathe.

I knew that if it were up to Uncle Quinton that day would never come, and that upset me more than it probably should. Here they were putting themselves in harm's way and I had been forced to the side, to run home and hide with people he thought could keep me safe. All I kept thinking were those people belonged with *my* people, Quinton being one of those, so they could help where it was actually needed.

I didn't text him back, and I think that had more to do with being in a horrible mood because of the way he'd treated me.

I shoved the phone back into my hoodie pocket and turned back to face Rain who was watching me carefully from his seat.

"Was that Quinton?" Rain asked me.

Who else would it be?

"Yeah," I replied quietly in a sad, defeated voice. "He wanted to let me know that the rest of the guys had showed up and more of the Council had as well. He then went on to tell me I needed to go home and meet you, Simon, and Trenton there because you all would keep me safe."

"So what's got you looking so down?" Rain questioned me seriously.

I wanted to tell him how upset I was about being pushed to the sidelines to sit on the bench while the rest of them went off and threw themselves in harm's way, but for whatever reason I couldn't do it.

"Am I a burden to them?" I asked my father without looking

at him. I stared straight ahead through the windshield, not bothering to look at the brothers in the backseat either. "Do they see me as someone less than what they are, just because I am playing catch up with the rest of them? It's not my fault I wasn't raised how they were, surrounded with magic, and the magic I did have had been choked to the point it had been gagged. I get that I'm a female witch and that's a coveted thing. I really do. But now that more are surfacing I'm worried. These other females probably know all about where they've come from and how to use their magic like pros. I'm not like that and always feel like I'm playing catch up here. I did good at Dash's the other night, no matter what anybody else says. I did what I did for Dash, because I know how much his cottage means to him, I wouldn't have done it at such a personal cost to myself if it hadn't been worth it. There isn't a single one of them who would have shied away from it if it had been something they were capable of. I don't want to be wrapped up in bubble wrap for the rest of my life. I want to stand tall with the rest of my coven and actually be something outside of a treasure and something they tried to protect."

I sighed as I slumped back in my seat, my own words washing over me.

"Baby girl," Rain said gently. "They can't help themselves. They've grown up in a world where women like you are a rarity and that's the world they live in now. I can't fault them for this because it's the same world I grew up in, and I can't help but being thankful to the bottom of my blackened soul that I have men like that looking out for my daughter, especially when I wasn't able to. Cut them a break. Not for you, but for them. They'll need it and I'm the last person who wants to say this to you, but I think this is the real deal here for you. They all love you and want what's best for you. It won't matter to these boys that there are other women popping up around the world with magic, because the only woman they see is you."

His words were sweet and what any girl would want to hear

from her long lost father. Rain loved me, there was no doubt about it.

"Wait a second," Rain added thoughtfully. "Did you say that there were other women popping up, women who are witches? What are you talking about, Ariel?"

I raised my hands and I lowered my face into them. I groaned. In my anger I had made a mess of things and stupidly blurted out things I hadn't meant to. I had wanted to give that information to Rain privately and not in front of the two brothers I really knew absolutely nothing about.

I'd spilled the beans about the woman who'd stared back up at me from that photograph Marcus had given me.

Damn.

I hadn't meant to do that.

"Uhh..." I muttered through my hands. "Maybe you could forget about that part?"

Fat chance, I knew.

"What aren't you telling me, daughter?" Rain asked quietly.

I lowered my hands from my face and looked to him in defeat. This wasn't at all how I was supposed to do this. Marcus was going to be so upset with me.

Rain eyed me with hard eyes and a cold look on his face. It wasn't his dead look so I knew I wasn't in trouble just yet and maybe could salvage this situation still.

"I'll be right back," I grumbled under my breath as I jerked the door open and slipped out of the Rover. No one tried to stop me and I wasn't surprised.

I retrieved the manila folders from the passenger seat and brought them back to the Rover. I climbed inside and closed the door behind me. The whole time I wondered why Marcus hadn't just simply put both pieces of paper into one folder. It seemed wasteful to me to use two folders when you really only needed the one. I was tired of everything, though, and not willing to dial Marcus up on the phone and ask him about it.

Rain took the folders from me and opened first one, and then the other, without saying anything to me. Neither of the brothers sitting in the backseat said anything either. And, honestly, I couldn't blame them. They were probably wishing for a different female to guard at the moment.

"Who is this woman?" Rain asked me.

Who indeed? I really had no freaking clue who the woman was.

"Marcus gave those folders to me to give to you," I said in a tired voice. "He stole them from Adrian and thought she was a witch in hiding from the Council."

I stopped there because there was nothing else for me to tell him. I couldn't tell him my theory, and Marcus's, on who she was because there was a chance it might not actually be true and I would never lie to Rain.

"Hmm," Rain muttered noncommittally, as he folded both folders in half and stuffed them inside his black duster.

What the hell did 'hmm' mean?

I eyed him and knew he wouldn't give me an answer if pressed.

"Are we going to take her home and to safety, or are we going to go back and fight the hunters?" One of the brothers asked from the backseat. I didn't know them well enough yet to be able to tell the difference in their voices, but was pretty sure it had been Trenton who'd spoke.

Rain patted his chest, where the folders had been tucked away, and I knew he was done with what was now going on in the shop and ready to move on to what he thought was important. That being the lady in the picture.

"We go home," I said, my voice sounding upset and defeated even to myself. "We go home and we wait for them to come back to us. That's all we can do so that they don't know about Rain."

Both brothers grunted from the backseat like they were angry and upset by my decision. Neither of them argued with it though.

Rain drove us back to the Alexander big house while I watched people die on the video feeds on his phone.

Not a single one of those deaths came from my guys or the Council. Instead, all the hunters died.

And, when we got back to the big house, Rain refused to give me back the folders I'd given him and he'd driven away with my Rover.

Both Simon and Trenton remained my shadows until Quinton got home.

Part of me hated them all.

Poor Marcus probably hated me when I called him later to tell him I'd left his borrowed SUV somewhere and he'd have to find someone to help go and pick it up. Though, he was Marcus, so he didn't act upset in the slightest.

# CHAPTER TWENTY-ONE

I went to bed angry and woke up much the same. I also woke up annoyed because I was all alone in my big bed and the ginormous house was silent. I ran my hand over the middle and empty side of the bed, it was cold to the touch and I knew it had been empty the entire night. I'd slept alone.

I wasn't sure why sleeping alone bothered me so much and tried not to think too much into it. I was already in a horribly bad mood, I didn't want to poke at it and make it even worse.

I got out of bed and dragged my tired body into the bathroom where I showered and blow dried my hair while wrapped up in a plush, white, oversized towel that felt like heaven against my skin.

I padded on bare feet to the closet, still in my towel, and attempted to hunt down something I didn't hate to wear for the day. Later, I planned on driving over to Dash's—if I could locate my Rover and wrestle my keys away from Rain that is—and pack up some of my actual belongings so I could tote them back here with me. I didn't want to pack up all of my things, it would feel too permanent to me and I knew that if I moved in here for good I would never, ever be moving out again.

It seemed like every time I got comfortable in a home, the rug was ripped out from under me, and I was forced to find some place else to live. This time I hadn't been alone though and Dash had been forced to come along with me. We'd both been uprooted together this time and that made the whole thing a lot worse.

I felt like if I moved all of my things out of the cottage, that would be some kind of betrayal toward him on my part. We were a tiny team in the middle of the chaos that was always my life.

I was carefully pulling a pair of panties up my legs while trying to clutch the towel tightly to my chest when I heard the door to my bedroom open and then close. Footsteps padded across the floor.

Quinton stopped in the doorway to the closet. His eyes raked over my bare shoulders and dropped down to where I had my panties at my knees. I straightened quickly, dragging them up the rest of the way. His eyes heated as they followed my movements. A little smile graced his face as he watched me cross my arms over my chest and get ready to do battle with him.

"You're pissed," he observed in an amused voice, which only served to make me angrier than I had been before he'd walked in here.

"No," I said sarcastically. "I'm filled with joy—can't you feel it oozing out of me?"

His lips twitched like I'd amused him even *more* and something terrible came over me. I turned around and plucked the first thing I could reach off of the shelf closest to me. It was a hairbrush I had never seen nor used before. Probably an expensive one too. That pissed me off even more.

I turned and threw the brush across the room, aiming right at his smug face. His arm shot up to protect his face, just in time, and the brush bounced right off his yellow and orange colored forearm. It crashed down to the floor uselessly in a clatter.

Slowly, he lowered his arm and the look in his eyes had me shuffling back a step, away from him, away from that look. It wasn't anger, like I was expecting, that was there just below the surface and starting to leak out of his gaze. It was hunger, and the raw intensity of it aimed in my direction terrified me.

"Get out," I whispered hoarsely.

He shook his head as he stalked toward me. "I don't think so, Ariel. Not this time."

I swallowed thickly. No 'baby' this time, that meant business, and the sweet side to Quinton that was only for me was nowhere to be seen. He was a predator as he prowled toward me, and I was his prey.

This was all a game to him. A delicious game I didn't know the rules to, and I wasn't all that sure if I even wanted to play in the first place.

I let out a startled noise when my back met with the shelves, and various things rattled, but thankfully nothing fell off.

"We should probably talk about why I'm mad at you," I said in a strangled voice.

He shook his head as he got right in my space, in my face. His hands went to my hips and he smoothed his palms up over the towel.

"The time for talking is over," he murmured.

His lips brushed over mine softly in a gentle caress that was hardly there.

"I—" I had no idea why I protested or why I'd been angry with him in the first place. He was fuddling my mind.

Quinton grabbed the edges of the towel and yanked it down. It unraveled from where I had it tucked in the front of my body and dropped to the floor.

"Quinton," I choked out in shock, as I tried to cover the front of my body up with my hands.

It was no use. "What do you think you're doing?"

He pushed up against the front of my body with his and his hands slid down my sides, over my ribs and down. He stopped at my hips but only so he could tug on my panties. My hips jerked as they gave off a tearing sound and were ripped off my body. Quinton tossed them to the side.

"I want to be pissed," he murmured, as he shoved his face in my neck. I shivered as his tongue slid along the underside of my jaw. "That Dash had you first. But I can't do it because that bastard deserves good things in his life more so than the rest of us."

That was sweet, sort of.

"Does it really matter who I had sex with first?" I asked in a quiet voice. It didn't matter to me, but he seemed to care a whole lot about it.

"It doesn't really matter," he said. "But you know by now just how competitive I am and you knew I'd have something to say about this."

He was right, damn it, he was right.

I put my hands on his face and lifted it to mine. I stared into his dark, dark brown eyes that were filled with a fire that set my insides ablaze.

"It's not a competition," I told him in a quiet, but serious voice. "And you damn well know it. If you're upset because I had sex with Dash, then how are you going to feel when I have sex with the others too?"

His lips curved up in a dangerous smirk. "Are you already planning on having sex with the others?" he countered.

Wasn't that obvious?

"I thought that was the plan. Isn't that what you do when you're in a relationship with someone, eventually things get physical?"

"Things are about to get physical right now," he joked. Or, at least I thought he was joking.

I should have known better.

Quinton's hands slid around to my butt and down. He crouched and lifted me up by my thighs, catching me by surprise and making me let out an embarrassingly girly squeal. I wrapped my arms around his neck as I circled his waist with my legs, clinging to him.

He carried me to the fancy two seater couch on the other side of the closet and laid me down on my back on it, while I was still wrapped around him.

His mouth came down on mine in a searing kiss. I cupped the back of his head, cradling him to me, and tangling my fingers in his hair while he continued to kiss me.

He broke the kiss, pulling away from me and sitting up enough to drag his shirt up his chest and over his head. He tossed it to the side and came back to me. The silver from his nipple rings glittered in the light for a moment before he curved his body back over mine. His mouth came back to mine as his hands went to my breasts. He cupped them with both hands, his thumbs immediately moving to my nipples.

I moaned into his mouth as his thumbs ghosted over my nipples in a touch that was barely there and gone before I'd had enough of it. I arched my back into his touch and his lips left mine.

He chuckled as he kissed down the column of my throat.

He sat up and untangled my limbs from around him. My arms fell to my sides and my legs dropped down to the couch on either side of him.

He stood up and kicked off his cowboy boots, one after the other. He used his foot to toe them to the side and out of the way. He watched me with a look of hunger on his face that stole my breath away when his hands dropped down to his belt. He didn't waste time on a slow, seductive show. With deft fingers he unlocked his belt, flicked the button, and unzipped his pants. He shucked them down his legs, taking his boxers, if he was wearing any, with them. He bent over and pulled his pants off from his feet and tossed them behind him.

I had a second to take in his nude body, and the curve of his thick, long cock before he dropped to his knees on the floor before me. It hadn't been nearly enough time for me to look my fill, but it had been enough for me to notice the silver metal balls just below the head of his cock. It looked painful and yet I had the strongest urge to put my mouth near it and flick my tongue against those little silver balls.

He didn't give me a chance to touch him in anyway. Not Quinton, this was his show and he was in charge of how this was going down.

His hands went to my thighs and he dragged me toward the edge of the couch. My butt was right on the edge of the seat. Quinton lifted my feet to the edge of the couch beside my body and spread my thighs wide, leaving me naked and exposed to his scrutiny.

"Quinton," I said in a hushed, embarrassed voice.

"Nope," he replied. "There's no hiding from me, baby. Not anymore."

His words sent a shiver down my spine and I wasn't entirely sure it was a good thing to be so exposed to Quinton, he'd never let me go back on it now.

He shoved his face in my groin and inhaled.

"Jesus, what are you doing?"

"You smell so good," he groaned. "And you give off the most delicious heat I've ever experienced before."

His tongue flicked out and he dragged it through my wetness, making me shiver uncontrollably. My hand went to his hair and I weaved my fingers through it, holding on tight as his tongue flicked against my clit over and over again.

I writhed on the couch and tried to thrust my hips up at his mouth that was driving me wild, but he held my hips in place with his hands, holding me down.

Something inside of me was starting to build, trying to climb its way out, and I began to tremble as he kept at me with his mouth.

"Quinton," I whispered but could say no more.

My back bowed as pleasure surged through me, my orgasm finally set free. My body twitched under his hold as liquid heat pooled in my core and I cried out. I clung to his hair, holding him tightly to me.

His hands left my hips and my body fell limp against the couch. There was no reason to hold me down anymore, I was going nowhere.

He gently untangled my hand from his hair and I watched through half-lidded eyes as he wiped his mouth off with the back of his hand. I felt like I should have been bothered by that, embarrassed even, but I couldn't drum up enough emotion to give a shit. I felt boneless in a way I had only felt when I'd been with Dash before. Self-induced orgasms were alright, but they sucked in comparison to the ones other people could give you.

Quinton trailed a hand down between my breasts, his fingertips brushing over my skin in a gentle caress. It went down the middle of my stomach, past my belly button and stopped at my pubic bone.

"So fucking pretty," he whispered in awe.

I was glad he thought so. Still...

I reached out toward him and murmured, "Come here. You're too far away."

He let me pull him to my body as my legs fell down, my feet coming off of the couch and landing on the floor.

His lips came back to mine and he tasted different now. Sweeter, tangier. It was the taste of myself on his lips and there was a part of me that worried why I wasn't shocked or disgusted by the fact I was tasting myself for the first time, but oddly enough it didn't bother me in the slightest.

His fingers slid through my wetness, gently probing at my entrance. I sucked in a sharp breath as something soft, yet hard and hot brushed against me intimately.

"Does it hurt?" I asked. "Because of the piercing?"

He pressed a kiss to my lips as the head of his cock pushed inside my body.

"No, baby, it won't hurt. I'd never do anything to hurt you. You have to know that by now."

I did. I trusted Quinton completely.

I pulled his head back down to mine, and kissed with all the passion and love I had inside me for him as he slid inside the rest of the way.

Quinton held my face in his hands with his forehead pressed to mine in an incredibly sweet gesture as he moved inside of me. I lifted my thighs around his hips and wrapped my legs around him.

He looked at me with eyes full of love and devotion while he made love to me. Over and over again he moved inside me, just to draw back almost all the way out and thrust his hips back inside again. We were both panting and breathing heavily when my orgasm crashed over me for the second time. I cried out as it moved through me, tearing its way out. Quinton shoved his face in my neck and groaned as his hips stilled in their movements. We both came together and I held him tighter to my body, my nails digging into his back, likely leaving marks behind, maybe even making him bleed.

He nuzzled his face into my neck and sweetly whispered, "Love you, baby. So fucking much it scares the shit out of me."

Every time he said the words I wanted to snatch them out of the air and clutch them to my chest, never letting them go, like they were the most precious thing I had ever heard in my entire life.

"I love you too," I whispered back, and I knew they were words I would never get tired of saying to him, because the look they earned me in return wasn't something I would ever get tired of seeing from him.

# CHAPTER TWENTY-TWO

I raised my hand above the door and knocked softly. It was mid-afternoon and neither of them had yet to make an appearance downstairs. If they were sleeping, I didn't want to wake them up. I knew what it was like to have nightmares chase you all throughout the night, things you just couldn't seem to escape, no matter how hard and fast you ran.

Abel often times slept with the lights on because he couldn't sleep in the dark. Their parents had died in a horrible, terrible accident and both twins had been plagued by sorrow and nightmares ever since. It seemed worse for my Pepper twin.

Abel had horrible nightmares and avoided watching movies about water. He was traumatized by it because their parents had died in a plane crash that had gone down in the water. Lots of people had been eaten by sharks.

The door opened and my Salt twin stood there, half naked, his white hair mussed up and standing in every which way. His face was slightly poofy and I could tell he'd been asleep for a very long time in order for his appearance to be the way it was.

"Hey, pretty girl," he said in a thick voice. "What brings you to our door?"

"Who is it?" Abel called out in a voice very similar to his twin's. "Tell them to go away so we can go back to bed."

I smiled up at Addison. "Is he always this charming when he first wakes up?" I asked in a sweet voice. It must have carried through the room and to the other twin, because the next thing I knew the door was opened the rest of the way and my Pepper twin stood beside my Salt one. He was also shirtless like his brother and I couldn't help but drop my eyes to his chest and drag them down his body.

"I think she's eye fucking you, twin," Addison whispered in a shocked voice.

"Yeah," Abel said in voice full of pride, "she totally is. It's adorable."

My cheeks heated up and I snapped my head up, aiming for direct eye contact instead of looking... other places.

"I wasn't eye fucking you," I lied.

The problem with my lies was that they were never really believable and I always seem to suck at it. At least when it came to lying face to face. I could actually lie fairly well over the phone. Unless I was speaking to either Quinton or Rain, they could always tell the difference.

The twins both laughed at me and my face grew even redder.

"I wasn't," I lied some more.

"Get in here, pretty girl," Abel ordered, as he grabbed my hand and dragged me into their bedroom. The door closed behind me before I could voice a protest.

"Guys," I said as Abel pulled me into his chest, his forehead going to rest against mine. "I didn't come here for this."

Heat hit my back, the delicious kind that always came with the touch of one of them, letting me know Addison was close and closing in by the second.

Arms wrapped around my waist from behind as Addison pressed his front into my body. They were so big that I was entirely cocooned in their embrace, the outside world having fallen away because I couldn't even see it around their big bodies.

Soft lips pressed to mine and I jumped. My eyes flew open and I hadn't even realized I'd closed them until I was met with the shock of Abel's lips on mine.

His tongue swept out, gliding across my bottom lip, and immediately I opened my mouth to him. A little happy moan escaped me as he slid his tongue inside and kissed me for real.

My arms went around his neck as I kissed him back, hungrily, greedily even, trying to drink as much of him in as I could.

Lips grazed the side of my throat, making my nipples immediately harden.

I turned my head to the side, breaking the kiss and breathing hard. Addison continued to trail soft kisses down my throat as Abel's hands came up to my face and he cupped my cheeks.

"Really," I panted. "This is not what I came here for. I had a reason."

I did have a reason, didn't I? I swear there was something I needed to do, but my brain seemed to be in a bit of a fog at the moment, clouded over with lust.

"You didn't come here so we could have our wicked way with you?" Addison asked in a voice full of fake hurt.

I really hadn't, I knew that much for certain. My brain was still trying to play catch up with my body and the fact I'd not only had sex with Dash, but now Quinton as well. Just because I'd had sex with two people absolutely did not mean I was ready to have sex with two people at the same time, because there was no way I was ready for *that*. I wasn't sure I'd *ever* be ready for that. They were a package deal though, so eventually I had to wrap my brain around it. It wasn't likely to happen any time soon, because I had very stupidly Googled some things that had turned out to be slightly scary and I couldn't help but be mad at myself because I had been too stupid to think about how actual sex with them would work out.

I had gone down a very scary, perverted rabbit hole with my good buddy, Google. I had very innocently looked up threesomes and clicked on images. Going to Google for my problems and to absolve my curiosity had been my first mistake. My second mistake had been reading some of the captions from the photos. My *third* and *final* mistake I'd made with my no longer friend, Google, had been looking up images of double penetration. I had been scarred for life and was pretty sure I wasn't ever going back again.

It was one thing if you had a hole for everyone's... cocks. It was an entirely different thing when they stuck both in the same hole. That shit looked *painful* and I was fairly certain that no matter the amount of love I had for them, my Salt and Pepper twins would never ask for and receive that. I knew I needed to talk to them about it eventually so that we could do the adult-like thing and discuss what we were comfortable with and what we weren't. I figured it would be something I really needed to do with them, because there were two of them and our relationship would never be normal. We would need to be open and honest between the three of us for it all to work out peacefully.

I sucked in a sharp breath and blurted out in a rush, "I don't think I'm ready to have sex with the both of you at the same time. It's actually kind of... scary to think about."

I snapped my mouth shut and probably would have run away from the both of them if they hadn't been surrounding me and holding on so tightly. Their arms only got tighter after hearing my confession. They weren't going anywhere and I wasn't either, because they were holding me in place, keeping me from running away screaming.

"You don't have to have sex with us, pretty girl," Addison mumbled against my throat. "If you're not ready then you're not ready and that's okay with us."

"Totally," Abel spoke softly with his face pressed against my neck, the side his brother didn't already have his face in, of course. "We'd never push you and we're willing to wait however long it takes for you to be ready."

Did they not know I had sex with Dash? I wasn't even going to think about Quinton, because nobody knew about that yet and I wanted to keep it that way for at least a few days. Sometimes it sucked that there were never any real secrets between my coven, unless they were secrets the guys were keeping from me, that is. I understood the need for openness but still, sometimes I just needed a little time to process everything before everyone else found out about it.

"What is it that you're so afraid of?" Addison asked in soft voice.

I frowned. Now I'd done it. I was always preaching honesty and absolutely could not lie to either of my twins.

"Well," I drawled, as my wide eyes looked everywhere but at Abel's vibrant green ones that were attempting to pin me to the spot. "Uhh..."

For some dumb reason I couldn't seem to force the words out past my throat.

"It's because there are two of us, isn't it?" Abel concluded, and my eyes shot to his. His green eyes were warm and concerned. "You're afraid of that. Afraid of what it actually means to be with two guys at one time."

The last wasn't a question so much as a statement. He'd figured me out, just like that, and I honestly wasn't surprised by it, because it wasn't normal, wasn't natural. What we had between all of us as a group already wasn't normal or natural. To add the twins in to the mix really made things way out there.

"You're really worried about being with the both of us at the same time?" Addison asked in a hushed voice. "Why ever would you be worried about that, Ariel? You have got to know by now that neither my twin or myself would ever do anything that would hurt you. All you would need to do is say stop and we would. Tell us you're uncomfortable and we'd try something different.

Honestly, we've tried to be with girls separately and it has never worked out for us. We both hated it and missed each other. It's almost painful for us to be separated for any amount of time so it just seems natural that we find the right female to put between us. That doesn't mean we've ever actually found someone to take that spot before, because we haven't. We've fooled around with girls at the same time, but it never actually got to the sex stage before. Yeah, we've had sex before but not together like we want to."

Abel frowned deeply at his twin. "You make it sound dirtier, kinkier than it really is when you say it like that."

He kind of had a point.

Addison sighed before kissing my throat sweetly. He gave my hips a light squeeze before one hand slid up underneath my shirt, gliding across my bare skin, not stopping until he hit just above my belly button. His fingers splayed, his thumb gently caressing directly above my belly button. I fought off the urge to wiggle underneath that touch and was proud when no needy sound escaped past my lips.

"We'll take things slow," Addison whispered gently. "Easy. We will find out what works best between the three of us together. Neither of us are going to force you into anything and we know and hope you would never do the same. We will work it out together, figure it out together. The three of us. There's no pressure here, Ariel, not between us. That's not how we want this to work out."

The weight around my shoulders lifted. His words had set me at ease because I knew he spoke absolute truth, for the both of them.

"What exactly did you look up?" Abel asked me in a curious voice.

I swallowed thickly before admitting to them, "Double penetration. Like the kind where both cocks go in one hole. It was really traumatizing, I tell you."

I snapped my mouth shut, not believing I had actually admitted that out loud to the both of them.

Abel sputtered, his face turning red. My mouth dropped open at seeing his eyes widen in shock. I had never seen him in such a state before. They were both always so self-assured and confident.

"Two cocks in one hole," Addison muttered, sounding intrigued. "I've honestly never thought about that before because there's a hole for each of us. Hmm... the possibilities."

Not happening. At least, not for a while. Not for a good long while.

"I've only had sex twice," I blurted out. "And with a different person each time. I don't think I'm ready for anything quite like that and pretty sure I might never ever be. Maybe I will, I'm not going to rule anything out because that would be stupid, but I need you guys to understand just how inexperienced I am. I need you both to understand that and why I need to take my physical relationship with the two of you slower than the rest of the guys because there are, well, two of you. Together."

"Beautiful girl," Abel muttered. "We love you, we both love you. There's no time limit on our relationship here. It's going to take time for all of us to get there. We're down for taking that time. It will make things more special when we do actually get to the sex."

That sounded nice and was exactly what I wanted to hear from them.

I melted between them, my body going limp. The fight had gone right out of me and I no longer had a reason to tell them no because they'd now made it clear I had absolutely nothing to worry about with them.

If they had dragged me to one of their beds and gotten handsy with me, I would have been more than willing.

They had other ideas though.

"What brought you to our bedroom, pretty girl?" Abel questioned me in a serious voice, his green eyes warm and curious.

The heat was missing from them and I knew the lust had left him entirely.

He was no longer in the mood. My talk and fear of double penetration had taken him right out of it. It was a good thing, too, because I so did not want to be talking about this anymore.

Addison gave my hips a gentle squeeze.

"Pretty girl?" he prompted, having taken the hint his twin was done with the dirty talk and ready to move on with the conversation.

I sighed. "I need to go and get some of my things from Dash's cottage, and I'm not stupid enough to think I can go by myself. I supposedly have bodyguards now, but they are nowhere to be found. I think they've gone off somewhere with Rain and I think I should be upset about that, but I'm not. I have enough guys to keep tabs on that I don't need nor want two more of them to add to the list. Still, part of me is glad Rain has taken them under his wing. That being said, I can't go to the cottage by myself."

"And you chose us?" Addison asked in a quiet, skeptical voice.

I hated that he sounded so unsure that I would choose to spend time with them and pick them to do something like this with me.

"Is that so hard to believe?" I countered in a hard voice. "I would have come in search of the both of you first if I hadn't needed to talk to the bodyguards beforehand. That's not something I even wanted to do, but did because I had to. I actually want you both with me when I go there to pack up some of my belongings. I... you both helped me pack up Vivian's things and I don't think I could have done that without either of you. I know I don't make enough time for you, especially with me working in the shop now, but I hope you both know that I need you in my life and love you both very much."

"We'll go with you," was Abel's immediately reply.

"We need to shower first, if that's okay with you," Addison said, before squeezing me and letting me go. "You can either stay in here to wait for us or we'll meet you downstairs in twenty minutes. We'll be cool with whatever you choose."

"But," Abel added, "we'd really like for you to wait for us in here, in our room, our space. You're on our time now and you need to understand just what that means. We all do."

I thought about all they'd said to me since I'd walked into their bedroom just minutes before. I had come here because I really had wanted to spend time with them and had missed them. But, if I was being honest with myself, I had been slightly nervous because I wasn't entirely ready to have sex with them and didn't want them to expect it from me just because I'd had sex with a few of the others.

"I'll stay in here while I wait," I assured them. They not only deserved that much from me, but they'd well and truly earned it as well.

I kicked off my flip-flops as I shrugged out of their holds. They let me go easily.

I headed toward the bed with the white, messy comforter as I pulled my cell phone out of the back pocket of my skirt. I had texts to respond to and hadn't had the time to do so because I had been too busy having sex with Quinton.

I didn't turn back to watch them, but felt them as they moved toward the other side of the room. I lifted the corner of the comforter and felt them leave the room. They'd not questioned me, but had instead gone to their bathroom. Together.

I knew outsiders would see it as weird that they showered together, but it had never bothered me before and didn't now. They just seemed like they worked so much like a unit that to separate them for any reason was a crying shame.

I laid down underneath the white comforter with my back against the wall. I sat there comfortably while I looked through all of my unread text messages and missed phone calls.

I responded to a lot of them, but I did not return phone calls. It was turning out that I was one of those ridiculous people who didn't enjoy phone calls unless I absolutely had to endure them. I much preferred texts. Unless, of course, you were Quinton or Rain. Or... maybe even Marcus. But definitely *not* Adrian.

I read over his constant stream of text messages, with an ugly feeling filling me more and more with each one I'd read.

He'd given me an actual date and time for his stupid dinner and I'd responded that my coven would be there, but I sent him nothing else and I didn't respond to the immediate text he'd sent me back in response.

We had two days to prepare ourselves for the unfortunate event. Part of me wished it was tomorrow so we could just get it out of the way and done with. Another part of me wished for it to be six months from now and even then, I didn't think we would still be prepared for it.

I sighed as I put my cell phone away. I snuggled under the blanket and closed my eyes. I ended up drifting off to sleep while waiting for my twins to get out of the shower and get ready to go.

They woke me up and dragged my half sleeping self out of the bed. I didn't protest, but I did get angry when my Range Rover was nowhere to be seen and we had to take the twins' truck instead.

I was going to kill Rain when I got my hands on him. It wasn't like he couldn't afford to purchase his own vehicle, instead he had to rob me of mine. Briefly, I wondered if he knew it had been a gift from Marcus and if he'd still want to drive it around once he found out. Some sick and twisted part in me couldn't wait to tell him.

# CHAPTER TWENTY-THREE

From the front, the cottage looked just how it always did, charming and nestled away into its own little world. It looked like a place straight out of a fairy tale, and I half expected birds to start singing and little forest animals to come around the corner, hopping about.

Nothing so pleasant happened and the woods surrounding us remained silent.

Since the twins had already seen the wreckage, they went inside. I went around the side of the cottage and toward the back, so I could inspect the damage.

The sight was a lot worse than what I had been expecting. There were shards of glass scattered all across the grass, making it hard to navigate my way through them. The windows must have exploded from the inside out. Huh. I wondered if that had happened when I'd blasted it with water and hoped not because I didn't want to be responsible for causing any more damage. The back sliding glass door no longer existed and looked like a big, empty hole in the wall. The entire outside of the house was charred and black. Half the porch was missing as well.

I knew that whatever the inside looked like would be a whole lot worse than the outside, and that thought crushed a little piece of my soul.

When I went inside to pack, I knew for certain I wouldn't be venturing into the kitchen to check things out. There were some things a person didn't need to see.

I turned away from the destruction and looked out across the backyard, toward the tree line. Something in the grass glittered, catching the sunlight, and caught my eye.

Carefully, so as not to step on a piece of shattered glass and cut myself, I made my way through the grass toward that thing that glittered. I crouched down in the grass and picked it up.

"Ouch," I hissed in pain and dropped the dagger I'd been given during the fight. It was sharp enough to slice my finger open and now I was bleeding.

I picked the dagger back up and looked at it. I hadn't paid it much attention when Damien had given it to me, I'd been too focused on the horribleness of the situation. Now I looked at it. It was plain, with no markings on it, no nothing. I had no idea where he'd gotten the thing, but it was simple in design.

"Ariel," one of the twins called and I jumped, but thankfully didn't drop the dagger or cut myself again.

I stood up quickly and turned to face the house. I hid the dagger behind my back, keeping it out of sight.

Addison watched me with cool, bright blue eyes. They burned with curiosity but he didn't ask the questions I knew he so badly wanted to. I appreciated it.

I slipped the dagger into my back pocket and hoped to all that was holy that I didn't cut myself again.

"I'm coming," I told Addison, as I made my way back through the glass covered grass.

"It makes me uncomfortable having you out here all by yourself," he muttered uneasily. "Not after what happened back here. Damien told us they were trying to drag Dash off into the woods. We can't have the same thing happening to you."

I understood his reasoning, it was sweet even, but the thought that they'd never leave me alone again certainly didn't fill me with joy.

"I thought you guys got them all at the shop?" I asked.

We walked back around the side of the house shoulder to shoulder. He reached out and took hold of my hand.

"What the—" He started as he dropped my hand and spun to face me. He lifted my hand and glared down at it. "Why are you bleeding, Ariel?"

Huh. I had forgotten I was bleeding.

"I must have nicked it on a piece of glass," I lied, and I didn't even know why it had come out of my mouth. For whatever reason, I didn't want them to know about the dagger. I didn't want them to take it away from me.

"Shit," he said. "We need to get you inside and bandaged up."

"It's fine. Just needs a band aid."

I didn't even really feel it anymore. It had stung at first, but now there was just nothing.

Addison looked at me like I was crazy. He took ahold of my wrist and very gently led me around the house and inside. I followed along behind him without protest. He went up the stairs and into the bathroom, pulling me along behind him.

I had to reach up and cover my nose and my mouth because the smell inside the cottage was so bad it made my eyes sting.

He flipped the lid shut on the toilet and forced me to sit down on it. Again, I went without protest.

He rooted around through the bathroom closet and came out with a medical kit. All this nonsense over just needing a band aid.

Addison carefully cleaned my cut and had to wrap two band aids around it, and I didn't miss the look he gave me when he wrapped that second band aid around my finger.

I looked down at my band aid and giggled. They were black and covered in bright orange pumpkins.

"These are so Dash," I said through my giggles. I sobered

immediately as I looked around the bathroom, suddenly at a loss for words. Little touches of Dash were everywhere. From the orange colored washcloths to the black rug that made some joke about vampires.

Leaving this place sucked so bad, I hated it.

"It's going to be fine," Addison murmured as he crouched down beside me. His finger came to my chin and he used it to tip my face up toward his. "Everything will work out how it's supposed to. You'll see. If this is where you and Dash are really meant to be, then the house will get fixed up just as it was and the both of you will move back in here."

I jerked back away from him. "What do you mean by that? Of course, we're going to move back in here after it's all fixed up again. Why wouldn't we?"

He stood up and backed away with his hands in the air, palms facing me in a gesture that screamed he meant no harm.

"You can live wherever you want to live, pretty girl," he promised as he backed out of the doorway. "My twin and I will be in Dash's room packing up some of his things for him. We put suitcases up on your bed for you. Holler if you need anything."

And then he was gone and I was left alone in the bathroom staring down at the Halloween band aids that covered my hand.

I left the bathroom and moved on sluggish limbs to my bedroom. There were three very large suitcases sitting on my bed waiting for me, just like he'd promised. There was a time when all of my belongings would have fit in less than one of those suitcases. Now, I had too much stuff to fit in all three.

I didn't need to pack my clothes because there was a closet already full for me at the big house, but I did it anyways. First the dresser, then the closet. I packed all of my boots and flip-flops out of the coffin closet and tossed them inside a suitcase as well.

My makeup and all of my girly things went into a big beach bag I had in the closet. I had to make a trip to the bathroom with it and I emptied out the drawers Dash had given me into the bag.

I brought it back into my room and sat it on the floor at the foot of my bed.

The trunk in front of my bed was pulled out. I had to heft the suitcases up and carry them over to the floor beside the door. I pulled my comforter off the bed, folded it and stuffed it inside the trunk. I did the same with my comforter that was folded up and on my wicker love seat. My laptop went inside the trunk next.

I looked around my room, searching for things I wanted to take with me. Some of the books from the bookcase went into the trunk along with empty notebooks the guys had bought for me. I left my band and movie posters on the wall where they belonged, but climbed up on top of my bed and unhooked my beloved dream catcher from its place above my bed. I tucked it carefully away in the trunk and went to close it, but my eyes moved back over the bed.

My black and white ink drawings of the tarot cards that had been in the Alexander family for so long hung over my bed. They'd been a beautiful gift from both Tyson and Quinton. To take them off the wall would feel too much like I was officially moving out. To leave them behind felt like a betrayal.

I said fuck it and yelled out for the guys to help me.

They came running.

And it wasn't lost on me in the slightest that neither of them spoke but kept giving each other secret glances as they took my drawings off the wall. First The Magician came down, then The Moon.

I tried not to cry as they helped me cart my suitcases out to the back of their truck.

It felt like a goodbye and my heart broke a little as we drove away.

# CHAPTER TWENTY-FOUR

"I don't want to wear a dress," I grumbled under my breath. "This whole thing is stupid. Why can't I just wear pants?"

Damien sneered at the black dress pants I held up for inspection. I didn't know what the heck he had to sneer at, they were pants he'd picked out for me and they looked perfectly acceptable to wear to a dinner party, just so long as they were paired with a fancy blouse.

"I will tell you one more time," Damien said in a strained voice. "You absolutely *cannot* wear pants to a dinner party with the Council. They will take it as an insult and we do not need any more problems right now."

I chewed on my lip ring while I folded the pants at the knees and hung them back up on their hanger.

"Can't I just wear a skirt then?" I whined. "Since, you know, you seem so opposed to the pants."

I didn't want to wear a dress to some ridiculous dinner that I'd been forced to attend. I wanted to put on a pretty dress and go on a date with one of my boys. Now that I could get behind.

"You're not wearing a damn skirt," Damien snapped.

I flinched at the tone of voice he'd used because he'd been

keeping it together up until this point. He'd finally snapped because I'd pushed him too far. With good reason. He'd been arguing with me about this for at least an hour now while he'd tried to force me to try on dress after dress. I'd vetoed and argued against every single one and it was a wonder he hadn't snapped on me before now.

"Can I at least pick out my own dress then?" I asked, and actually took a step back when he practically snarled at me like a rabid animal.

"Well, alright then," I mused quietly. "I'll take that as a no."

I swear, I saw steam practically rise from the top of his head before he closed his eyes shut tightly. His lips moved and I watched him count to ten silently. I thought about telling him he should probably count to twenty because he was on the edge of what looked like a complete and total meltdown, but felt it was wise to keep my mouth shut and watch him get himself under control.

"Why the hell do you care so much about what you're wearing?" he inquired in a neutral voice. "Would it really bother you so much to wear a dress I picked out for you? I would never pick something unflattering or that I thought you'd be uncomfortable in, you have to know that by now."

Damien had gotten better about picking out my clothes for me when he went shopping. The thing was though, that when he was left to his own devices and picked out the clothes he actually wanted me to wear they weren't the right size and were bright, perky colors. I was not a bright and perky kind of girl. My breasts were usually the only perky thing about me. If I let him pick out my dress, the chances were high I'd end up in something glaringly pink and covered in sequins.

Pink was okay when it came in the form of underwear and socks, but anything else was a big, fat no for me. I'd take my black, red, and yellow over it any day of the week.

I twisted my fingers together nervously.

"Uhh..." I paused before asking, hoping I didn't set him off again, "Can it at least be a black dress?"

I couldn't do a red one tonight, it would draw too much unwanted attention to me and I already knew I'd be under serious scrutiny as it was. I didn't want to add to it. Yellow would give off a sweet vibe I wasn't willing to sport tonight because I felt anything but sweet lately.

"I can work with black," Damien said softly, and my body relaxed infinitely. "And I'll even let you pick out your own shoes."

I appreciated the last part, even though I knew he'd probably regret it later after seeing my shoe choice.

Damien slid hangers around until stopping on one.

"This is perfect," he murmured, as he pulled the hanger off the rack and turned to me. He held the dress up for my inspection and waited. The look on his face told me that if I didn't approve of the dress he might murder me right here in my ginormous, outrageous closet, consequences be damned.

The dress was far more conservative and plain than I had imagined he'd ever pick for me. It was a long-sleeved black number. The skirt flared out at the hips and stopped mid-thigh, which was my only complaint because it was a little on the short side. There were white cuffs at the sleeves and a white collar at the neck. It was remarkably plain and yet I liked it a whole lot. It looked like something a witch would wear for a night out, and it had the added bonus of covering up the scars along my collar bones. I didn't want them on view tonight for the Council to stare at, that was the last thing I needed right now.

"I like it," I told him honestly, and felt slightly bad for him when his shoulders slumped and he tipped his head back to the ceiling to mutter under his breath, "Thank fuck. She *kills* me with this crap."

I reached out and plucked the dress out of his hands.

He looked me in the eyes and said in a sad voice, "Please, no Chucks tonight."

And with that he stormed out of the closet, the black silk robe he wore billowing out behind him like a cape. I was willing to bet that robe had been a gift from Dash, I had one just like it.

So much for getting to pick out my own shoes tonight. I would have gone with my black and white Chucks if he hadn't said anything. They were comfortable and worked well with pretty much anything. I figured they'd go just fine with the dress, maybe even give the whole look a bit of an edge.

"Oh, and, Ariel," Damien called from the doorway. I turned to look at him, raising an eyebrow in question. "Don't try to cover up your scar." He lifted a hand and waved it gracefully around in front of his cheek. "I've grown rather fond of your face and that includes the scar you wear on it. You try to cover it up and it's going to piss me off."

And with that he really was gone.

Damien could be incredibly sweet at times, he just chose not to show that side of him to many people. I was one of the lucky ones who got to see it.

I wore a small, secret smile on my face as I dropped the towel that I'd wrapped around my body after getting out of the shower. I slipped into a pair of black, lacy panties and matching bra. I pulled the dress over my head and moved to the tall, heavy stand up mirror on the floor in the corner of the closet.

I stared at my reflection in the mirror, tilting my head to the side to study myself.

I had dried my hair in the bathroom because of its length, because I didn't want to get the shoulders on whatever outfit Dame picked out for me wet. The ash blonde locks fell in loose waves around my face, flowing over my shoulders and down to my breasts. My green eyes were beautiful, even I could admit that, but they held a wealth of pain and sadness that I could never seem to get rid of, no matter how much I tried.

As my eyes raked over my figure in the dress Damien had picked out for me, I realized he'd done good, damn good, because

I looked right in that dress. It suited me and was something I wouldn't feel uncomfortable in.

I bypassed my Chucks on the floor and reached for a pair of plain black Mary Jane's and slipped my feet into them. They were soft and comfortable, I'd never worn them before.

Normally, I would not take a purse with me because I'd be able to shove whatever I wanted to carry inside a hoodie pocket. But I needed a purse tonight so I could have a place to keep my cell phone in. I'd leave it home, but needed it with me so I could spam Rain with text messages all night long.

My father was not happy about having to be left at home while we all went off without him, and had made me promise I would text him every half an hour. It seemed a lot like karma if you asked me. Nobody was asking my opinion on anything though.

I found a cute black purse on one of the shelves. I had never seen it before in my life and certainly hadn't bought it for myself, but it's something I would have picked out for myself if I could have afforded it. Now that I had money I never actually needed to spend it on anything except for gas and sometimes food if I was alone when I stopped to get it.

I stuffed my things in the small purse and flung the strap over my shoulder.

I turned the light out in the closet as I walked out, doing the same when I left my bedroom behind.

I weaved my way through the maze of hallways until I hit the stairs and walked down them. I expected to find everyone at the foot of the stairs waiting for me, but the foyer was empty and devoid of human life.

Binx sat at the foot of the steps, watching my descent with wide, green eyes and a swishing tail.

"Hey, fur ball," I greeted as I stepped off the stairs. I bent over and gave him a little scratch on the head. I half expected him to hiss at me because he'd been absent lately and I assumed he was still mad at me for locking him up in my Rover, and was pleasantly surprised when he leaned into my touch. "Miss you too, kitty kitty."

I gave him one last pat on the head before standing up and moving in the direction of the kitchen, in the direction of masculine voices.

Binx followed along beside me, trying to trip me up as he kept rubbing his little head against my ankle.

I found them all in the kitchen, huddled around the island. Some of them were standing and others were seated on the stools. None of them noticed me approaching, their focus firmly fixed on something in the center of the island.

I moved up beside Tyson who stood at the end of the island. I trailed my fingers lightly down his spine and he jumped, whipping around to face me.

"Girl, shit," he said breathlessly. "You scared me."

I grinned at him. They could usually always feel me coming, so it was good to get one up on him for once.

"What are you all doing in here?" I asked.

"Julian brought something for us," Tyson answered as he lifted his hand to reach out to me. His hand paused in the air and a look of pain crossed his face.

Tyson clearly was still upset about what the conversation we'd had the other day while the hunters were running amok.

I, however, had no such qualms.

I swatted his hand out of the air and moved right into him, pressing my front up tightly to his side and wrapping my arms around his middle. I didn't look at him, but I could feel his beautiful brown eyes aimed down on me. I hoped this set things straight between the two of us.

I squeezed his middle and melted into him when his arms came up, circling my shoulders. He pressed his lips into the top of my head in a kiss and I knew it was his way of letting me know we were okay and everything was going to be just fine between the two of us.

I was thankful for it, because he was my best friend in the whole world and it would hurt my heart in ways it had never hurt before if he was truly upset with me.

"Love you, Ty," I murmured quietly, as I rubbed my cheek against the front of his shirt.

Tyson's arms held me even tighter, almost to the point of pain. I didn't complain, though, because I knew it was done out of what he was feeling at hearing my words.

The noise around the room stopped and I looked around the island, taking everyone in. They were all staring at me in Tyson's arms. Some of them had soft looks on their faces. Quinton, oddly enough, being one of them. Others had blank faces. That being Damien and Rain. The rest of them looked at me with heat and tenderness in their eyes.

This is what it felt like to be loved, even those blank faces weren't fooling me.

"What's going on here?" I asked in a timid voice.

"Apparently you and Julian here have been busy behind the rest of our backs," Quinton said. There was no anger or upset in his voice, it had been stated as fact.

My eyes moved to him as a small smile tugged at my lips.

"I want a tattoo," I told him. "A magic infused tattoo. Julian has been helping me and by helping me I mean he's been doing all the work."

I turned to Julian and smiled brightly at him. "Isn't that right, slugger?"

Julian smirked at me. "You know I prefer it when you call me Jules as opposed to slugger, right?"

I did, but slugger had a nice ring to it, and only I knew why I called him that. I had my own private nickname and I wasn't sure I was willing to give it up.

I shrugged noncommittally because I had no intention of

stopping calling him that. He smirked at me, not seeming to be bothered in the least.

"You want a tattoo?" Rain inquired quietly.

I jerked my head in his direction and his face was no longer carefully blank. There was pain and hurt in there now and I didn't understand why.

"Yeah," I said before asking, "Why does that seem like a problem for you?"

"Because," he ground out in that guttural voice of his, "if you wanted a tattoo infused with magic you should have come to me and I would have given it to you."

My mouth popped open as I stared at my father. I couldn't believe that he'd be so upset about this when it wasn't something we'd ever really talked about before. Up until the other day, he'd been completely closed off from me when it came to his tattoos. Heck, I hadn't even seen the ones on his arms until the other day and he'd been in my life for *months* now.

"How was I supposed to know this, Rain?" I challenged in an accusatory voice. "You're so tight lipped when it comes to these things that I never would have even thought to go to you about it. You give me so much, but you've held back on that."

"What do you want to know?" he asked quietly, and I shook my head. It didn't work like that. I didn't want him to tell me these things because I had to force it out of him.

"Just forget about it," I grumbled angrily. "We can argue about it later if you want, but right now we have more important things to discuss."

"If you're getting a tattoo then I'm going to be the one to give it to you," Rain remarked stubbornly.

"Okay," I agreed easily, and his eyes widened in surprise. Really, now, I wasn't *that* difficult to deal with. "But we're not doing that right now so I don't want to talk about it anymore."

I gestured rudely toward the small vials on the island. There was some pretty colored purple concoction swirling around in them. I'd seen this before.

"Tell them what this is," I ordered Julian.

He smirked at me. "I think it's hot when you're bossy. You can boss me around any time."

"You can say that now," Damien muttered irately, "but you didn't have her doing it to you in a house that was on fire. That shit was not hot then, I can assure you of that."

Geez, was he going to hold that against me forever? It was one time.

"Both of you shut the fuck up," Rain snarled.

I sighed. Boys were so overrated sometimes.

"Once you consume the purple stuff," I told them, "it makes it so that people can't tell whether or not you're lying."

"Purple stuff," Julian muttered. There was a smile in his voice and I could tell he found me amusing. "You're adorable."

"How do you know this for sure?" Quinton asked.

"Because she drank some of it and tried it out on me," Julian answered him happily. "I've also been drinking the stuff every day and I can assure you it works. I've been lying to lots of people and nobody has noticed yet."

I snickered. I could only imagine the things he'd been saying to people, the lies he'd been spreading. And no one was the wiser.

"I'm guessing it's here because you want us to take it before we go to the dinner tonight?" I asked.

Julian nodded. "I've also been giving it to Marcus as well. I figured he could use it."

Rain went to snatch a vial off the counter but Julian shoved his hand away.

"I don't think you need anything to help you lie better than you already do," Julian commented in a dark voice.

I couldn't agree with him more.

I plucked a vial up off the counter and pulled the tiny cork free. Before anyone could stop me, I put the vial to my lips and drank it dry. I put the empty vial back on the counter and looked around at all the wide eyes staring back at me.

"Well," I said, "hurry up so we can go and get this over with already."

Everyone except for Rain picked up a vial and drank.

"Don't forget to text me," he barked at me, before skulking out of the kitchen.

"And you think I'm bossy," Quinton grumbled.

They were two of a kind, that's for sure.

# CHAPTER TWENTY-FIVE

I rode in Quinton's sedan with him and Tyson. Dash rode with Julian and Damien, with Julian driving. And the twins rode together in their truck, always separate, but together with each other. This time was different, though, because they'd taken my guards with them. Guards, I might add, who were extremely upset that I had made them ride in a different car than the one I was in.

I didn't care and couldn't get away from them fast enough.

The ride over was so quiet that I imagined if we rolled the windows down we'd hear the distinct sound of crickets chirping and not much else. I almost asked if it was okay to turn the radio on, but the pissed off vibe Quinton was throwing off made me too afraid to ask. I didn't want to talk to him because I knew if he opened his mouth a serious lecture about what I had been doing with Julian would come pouring out and I really didn't need to be verbally sparring with him at the moment. Not when we were walking into would be enemy territory, again.

The motel loomed up ahead, the torches burning bright and falsely giving off a warm welcome. I'd been here twice before and neither time had been pleasant, but the last time I'd witnessed extreme sex with the Council and a psycho falling to his death.

I seriously hoped no one died tonight, because I didn't think I could handle anymore death in my life, even if it was the people I didn't like who were doing the dying.

A woman I had never seen before stood outside at the bottom of the stairs, waiting for us.

"Do you know who this chick is?" I asked my silent companions.

"No," Quinton grunted. Tyson said nothing and I assumed that meant no too.

"Hmm," I murmured.

From a distance she was pretty, and I knew when I got up close to her she'd be a knockout. Her hair was so blonde it was almost white and it hung down in heavy sheets to her wide hips. She was short with voluptuous curves in all the right places. She was dressed in a long, white dress that clung to every curve of her body, hugging her tight. She turned to the side and the light caught her dress just right, making parts of it transparent.

"I can see her nipples from here," I shared with them. "Am I the only one seeing this? That dress is sooo see through. Don't you think you should wear underwear with something that you can see right through? Or a bra or something. Geez. What kind of dinner party is this?"

"Jesus," Tyson muttered under his breath.

"It's the Council, baby," Quinton reminded me. "You never know what to expect from them or what you're gonna get. I'm more concerned with not knowing who this woman is as opposed to the fact I can see how dark her nipples are from here."

He parked the car in front of the motel. The rest of the guys pulled in beside us and parked their vehicles.

"Remember when I told you that we've all met all of the female witches that we're aware of existing?" Quinton asked in a soft voice. I think he worried his voice would somehow travel outside the car and she would hear. "Well, that goes for all the covens, and I've never seen this woman before in my life. But if she's here with the Council then she's a witch. Where did she come from and why is she here with them?"

All good questions that no one had the answers to.

"Let's get this over with," I said, as I unbuckled my seatbelt and reached for my door handle.

"More like, let the games begin," Tyson corrected from the backseat, and I heard his door open.

I laughed humorlessly as I climbed out of the sedan behind him. Let the games begin, indeed. Things were bound to be infinitely interesting with the Council being our hosts tonight. I had to give it to my coven, my life had certainly been interesting since they'd come into my life, that's for sure.

"Don't wander off without one of us by your side," Quinton barked at me, as I got out of the car and slammed the door shut behind me.

Please, like I was stupid enough to wander off on my own or with one of the Council members. That was never going to happen.

Tyson moved up to my side and took my hand in his. The rest of the guys came up beside us.

My eyes moved to the spot on the ground where I'd last seen Chuck lying broken and bleeding as the light faded from his eyes. I couldn't seem to drag my eyes away. He'd pretty much died because of his obsession with me. I wanted to blame Quinton for it, but couldn't when Adrian had told me the Council had gone through his mind, his memories, and he'd been obsessed with me before the love potion, and it hadn't been a pretty, want to love you forever kind of obsession, but one where he'd wanted to do terrible things to me and would have gotten off on it.

I tried to never think of him because those memories only brought on pain and not just because he was dead, but because of what happened to Dash due to Chuck's obsession with me. I would carry the guilt of that with me for the rest of my life.

But standing here, looking at the place where Chuck had died, it did absolutely nothing to me, made me feel absolutely nothing except for sorry Dash had been hurt because of me. But I wasn't sorry Chuck was dead and that worried me, because wasn't I supposed to care? And, what kind of person did it make me because I didn't?

Tyson pulled on my hand as his lips came to my ear. He whispered, "Stop looking. You're not supposed to know someone died there and your staring is going to make it very obvious that's not the case. We don't need the Council asking questions we don't want to answer."

My lips quirked up as I was finally able to look away. I looked up at Tyson with a cruel smile on my face. "Tonight's the perfect night to answer questions we wouldn't normally want to. Jules is my hero."

His eyes widened before he smiled down at me, his white teeth flashing so bright they were almost blinding to look at.

"Greetings," a high, feminine voice called out. "We've been waiting for you."

She made it sound like she'd been standing out here for hours waiting and not only were we late, but we'd inconvenienced her in the extreme. All that accusation and censure wrapped up in a super sweet voice after flashing us all her nipples.

I think I hated her.

"You couldn't have been waiting out here for too long since we're here exactly when Adrian told us to be," Quinton said in a smooth voice.

My smile stretched even wider. Looked like Quinton wasn't too fond of her either. Good to know.

"Of course," she murmured submissively, as she cast her eyes down to the ground.

Her look wasn't fooling me in the slightest. We'd need to take extra care to keep an eye on this one.

I pulled my phone out of my purse and shot off a quick text to Rain, letting him know we were here and giving him a brief description of the woman. I left out some details, like about how she wore a see through dress and the color of her nipples. My father needed to know that even less than my coven did.

I slipped the phone back into my purse and made my way toward her.

Her eyes came up when she met mine, a brilliant blue as pure as the sky on a bright, summer's day. I'd been right, she was definitely a knockout up close. Too bad her eyes took on a malicious glint the longer I stood before her. It kind of dulled the pretty, if you asked me.

I tilted my head to the side as I studied her features, memorizing them.

"And who might you be?" I asked in a falsely sweet voice. Kill them with kindness, it was always the way to go.

Her lip curled in a half smile/half snarl that looked a lot like disgust to me. For whatever reason this woman hated me and she was not doing a good job of hiding it.

"My name is Rachel," she answered in a voice just as falsely sweet as mine. "I've been with the Council now for roughly two months. My home was attacked by hunters and I was the only one to survive. It's a miracle they found me at all. I guess I'm just lucky that way."

If her entire family, or whoever it was that lived with her at the time, were now dead then I didn't think there was any way I would consider her lucky. More like sad and alone.

Quinton stepped up beside me and took hold of my free hand, the one Tyson wasn't already holding on to.

"How is it that we've never seen you before today?" Quinton asked in an empty voice. "We all get to meet the females at one time or another and I've never seen you before in my life. What coven are you from?"

Smart of him to ask.

But I didn't think she was from a coven. Maybe that's what he was trying to force her to say. With Quinton, there was always a motive.

She looked up at Quinton through thick, white eyelashes. "I've never had a coven before. I just lived with my family. We didn't know anything about the Council or anything like that."

The way she looked at him was really starting to bother me and I thought maybe I was just being the jealous, crazy girlfriend when she did something I had not expected. She reached out and ran her finger down the flames that licked their way up his forearms. I watched that finger trail down his arm with a growing sense of unease.

"I'm looking to find a coven to join," she murmured as she continued to watch him through half lowered lids and those stupidly thick lashes.

I swallowed thickly, and went to take a step back so I didn't reach out and snatch that hand away from him when the hand Quinton had ahold of squeezed mine almost to the point of pain. I looked up at him, shocked, and almost took a step away from *him* at what I saw on his face. There was so much rage and hatred in that one look that if it were aimed my way, I would have fled his presence immediately and ran screaming in the opposite direction.

Miss Rachel seemed to be made of thicker stock than me, because she just kept right on trailing her fingertips along his tattoos while she watched him like she wanted to eat him. And he looked back at her like he wanted to rip her throat out and spill her blood right here across the cracked pavement of the sidewalk.

I wanted to tear her fingers away from his smooth, hot skin but was almost afraid to touch her. We were here as guests of the Council and she was much the same. I didn't think getting physical with her would win me any brownie points with them and could probably end up landing me with some severe punishment I wouldn't enjoy. You absolutely did not mess with their females. I knew this because I was considered one of them. I couldn't touch her, not unprovoked. The Council might look the other way if she were male, but not with her being female. I assumed this was why Quinton hadn't removed her touch as well.

It killed me though because he looked upset and she didn't care and kept molesting him anyway.

I was saved from having to get into a verbal tussle with her when Julian strode right up to her and stepped between us. She was forced to take a step back and her hand fell away from him. I wanted to kiss him.

Julian stuck his hand out to Rachel and politeness made it so she was forced to shake his hand or look like the incredibly rude bitch she was.

Quinton pulled on my hand, tugging me into his body. Tyson let me go and I circled my arms around Quinton's waist. He rubbed his arm against mine, rubbing away her touch on his skin.

"Julian," Julian said in greeting. "It's lovely to meet you, Rachel."

He sounded charming, actually happy to be meeting her, and I wanted to laugh. She ate it up like candy.

She, like most others, missed the darkness that lurked underneath the surface with Julian. I wished her all the best of luck with that one.

There was no surge of jealousy this time when she touched one of my guys. Julian held his elbow out to her and she practically preened under his attention.

"Shall we?" he asked her in a sweet, sultry voice.

"Yes," she purred. "They are waiting for you. Let me lead the way." She latched onto his arm like she was afraid he might snatch it away if she took too long.

She turned back to me and gave me a smug look of victory. I almost laughed in her face.

Damien shrugged Tyson aside with a look of apology, but he didn't verbalize it. He pulled me away from Quinton and we held hands as we followed Rachel and Julian around the side of the motel. I'd never been back here before and was somewhat terrified of what we'd walk into.

Damien's mouth came close to my ear while we walked side by side, hand in hand. "You know he doesn't mean anything hurtful by this, right?" he whispered.

I turned, almost bumping noses with him, and he had to jerk his head back. I grinned at him, bright and big, and he stopped walking, pulling me to a stop along with him. He stared at me as if he'd never seen me before.

Quinton put his hands on my back, his heat searing though me as he muttered an irate, "What the fuck?"

I turned my bright, big smile on him and his eyes dropped down to my mouth.

"What's going on?" Tyson asked. There were masculine murmurs from behind him, letting me know the rest of the guys were wondering the same thing.

"Why are you smiling like a crazy person?" one of the twins asked.

I smiled back at Damien as he tugged on my hand. A glance ahead told me Rachel had lead Julian around the side of the building and we needed to hurry to catch up.

"This bitch has no idea what she's getting herself into with him," I said as I snickered.

They all laughed hysterically as we made our way around the building and into the backyard.

None of us were prepared for what greeted us back there.

# CHAPTER TWENTY-SIX

"Ariel," Adrian boomed, as we stood in a huddle at the edge of the yard.

I think we were all worried about what would happen if we stepped forward and we were all far too busy taking in the backyard.

There were fairy lights strung up and hanging all over the place, giving the space a magical feel and illuminating the area brightly against the dark sky above.

An incredibly long table sat in the center of the yard, and I imagined it was several tables pushed together underneath the shiny silver cloth that covered it up. The table was covered with fancy dishes I had no desire to eat off of, and I certainly didn't want to drink out of some fancy teacup that I would be terrified of breaking the entire time.

In the center of the table, all along the entire length, there were black vases filled with bright yellow roses. The color of those roses really bothered me because I knew they were there for me. Not my favorite flower but definitely my favorite color. Now, where had they found that out?

"Where's Julian?" Dash asked in a bored tone. He was right, Julian and the oh so lovely Rachel had disappeared. Perhaps she'd dragged him off to try and molest him.

I wasn't even upset about it because I knew it was something she'd soon come to regret.

"Why," Adrien crowed, "the lovely Rachel has escorted him inside to show him where the restrooms are located. Already she's making friends. Isn't that lovely? Now," he turned his beady, scheming eyes on me, "come here and greet your host, child."

I absolutely did not want to go to him. I let go of Damien's hand and did just that.

Adrian was wearing a long-sleeved, black shirt that flowed around him like something some free loving hippie might wear. It even fanned out at the wrists. The collar was split open down in the front, with dark strings hanging from it that meant he could tie it closed if he wanted to, but clearly chose not to. The front protruded with his pregnant belly. His pants were black dress slacks that were actually the only normal thing about his attire. He was barefoot and I caught several shiny rings glittering on his toes. His hands were laden with rings that sparkled even more than his toes did, and I caught sight of several blinging bracelets on his wrists when he lifted his arms to greet me.

His hands went to my shoulders as I bent down so my face was close to his height. He pressed his chubby cheek to mine and air kissed my face.

When he let me go I didn't hesitate to step back and away from him.

His eyes shone with a weird light that gave me the creeps when he leered at my legs.

"We're so happy you could make it tonight, child. I'm sure you know by now just how pleased Marcus will be that you came. You know, since his brother passed away the rest of his family is entirely oblivious to this part of his life. It's good that he has you now to share in this with. He's a very well suited match to join the ranks of the Council. Very well, indeed."

I nodded because there was nothing I could say to that. Nothing he'd probably like all that much.

"Where is Marcus?" I asked conversationally. I hadn't noticed any of his vehicles parked outside when we'd pulled up.

"Oh," Adrian said as he waved his hand toward the motel behind us. "You know. He's around here somewhere. Several others have arrived recently and they're interested in getting to know him and you both, so don't be surprised when there are people lining up to talk to you tonight. You're a hot commodity you know, child. Everyone is interested in hearing from the girl who didn't even know she was a witch and surprised us all."

I frowned at him, not liking anything he'd said in the slightest.

"There are some people I would like for you to meet tonight as well, Ariel," Daniel said as he strolled up to stand beside Adrian.

Daniel wasn't dressed anything like his Council member buddy. Instead, he wore a black, long-sleeved button down shirt. The collar was pressed and the shirt devoid of anything even closely resembling a wrinkle. His slacks were black—surprise, it seemed to match the entire party tonight in attire—and on his feet he wore brown loafers' sans socks. The sleeves on his dress shirt were rolled up to the elbows, exposing the skin on his forearms, and I caught a hint of ink hiding on the underside of one.

His hair, for once, was unbraided and hung around his body almost like a second person. Long, thick, and beautiful, it hung down past his waist. I didn't like him much, I didn't like any of them much, but that didn't stop my fingers from twitching with the urge to play with his hair.

"You'll get your chance, Daniel," Adrian chided in a very unfriendly voice. "We're all going to get to spend time with our newest female tonight. There's no need to try and insert yourself into our conversation and steal her attention away from me. Come now, brother, we're all here together."

Daniel sneered at Adrian.

"Whatever you say, *Adrian*," Daniel replied in a low, condescending voice.

He turned to walk away, but something prodded me to reach out to him. I grabbed ahold of his arm and his hair flung around him like a curtain as he whipped back around to face me. His eyes widened in shock as he saw my hand attached to his wrist.

"I'd very much like to meet these people you'd like to introduce me to, Daniel," I told him quietly. "Whenever you're ready, you just let me know. Okay?"

His entire demeanor changed, and if I was a different person I would say he melted entirely at my touch and soft spoken words. I wasn't going to say it, though, because that would freak me right the fuck out.

The hand I wasn't holding onto came up to gently caress my hand on his wrist.

"Of course, lovely. I will be back around later to collect you and introduce you to people. You are very kind to me."

I let go of his wrist as if it had stung and he turned away from me and walked away.

What the hell had just happened and why did I now feel like his interest in me had doubled in the last five minutes?

Fuck my life, seriously.

"My, my," Adrian tisked. "It would seem that our Daniel has certainly fallen under your charming spell, Ariel. The rest of them will soon fall as well, I imagine."

Why did that sound so ominous to me?

Ignoring his words, I gestured toward the long table and asked, "Do we have assigned seats tonight or do we sit wherever? And when do you think we'll be eating?"

I swear if he said we had assigned seats and had put me

between people I was uncomfortable with there was a good chance I was going to tell him to get fucked.

Adrian frowned at me as he studied my face far too closely for my liking.

"No, no, child. Nothing like that. You will be able to pick your own seating arrangement just so long as you don't sit at the head of the table. That's a special place reserved for members of the Council. For now, I want you to mingle and get to know the others here. Before dinner there will be a small toast to accept Marcus into our ranks, and then we will have dinner. Afterwards, you're free to go if you so choose, but I want you and your coven to know that we've secured a block of rooms for you all and had them readied in case you'd all like to stay the night here instead of driving all the way back home. We'd be honored to have your coven stay here with us."

That was nice of him but there was no way in hell we'd be staying here. I didn't need to ask the guys to know they'd be in complete agreement with me.

And what was up with him calling it my coven? I know I called them that all the time, but when you got down to the nitty gritty this was Quinton's coven and he ran the show. Rightfully, so.

Quinton stepped up beside me. "That's very kind of you, Adrian. We will take your generosity into consideration when the night draws to an end. I would like to thank you kindly for your invite to the festivities tonight. It is an honor to be included in such Council matters. My coven is most pleased to have been invited and we are all very well aware that we are only here because of Ariel's presence in our lives. We do not mistake where your generosity stems from, and we want you all to know that we are very much grateful for it and give many thanks."

Quinton waved his hand behind him and Dash stepped forward. He held up a big, clear jug that tapered off at the top and had a thick cork stuffed into the opening.

"Alcohol," Dash stated. "Potent and magically induced. Julian made it specifically for this night. We offer it in gift to you and the rest of the Council as thanks for your having invited us to be amongst you and a part of this special night. It is both an honor and a privilege."

Adrian thanked Dash before walking off with the jug held high in his hands, inspecting it.

I did not want to know what the hell was in that jug. I just knew Julian had created it and I would not be ingesting it no matter what. I'd already downed the purple stuff and that was enough for one day.

Dash took my arm and pulled me off toward a corner where there were comfy looking chairs set up in a half circle, a curtain of fairy lights hanging over them and all around them. Right before he pushed me down into a chair he leaned into my ear to whisper, "It's safe to drink the liquor. I promise nothing bad will come to you because of it."

My butt hit the cushion and I sat back, getting comfortable. I was preparing to scope everything out while the others talked around me.

Quinton took the seat beside me. "Yeah, except maybe you'll get drunk off your ass. That shit is potent. If you get drunk just make sure you... You know what, never mind. Someone is going to be glued to your side all night long so you don't even have to worry about that."

I gaped at him. Did he just... encourage me to get drunk, and then tell me I would have someone watching over me if I did so that it was okay?

"Is it just me, uncle, or are you encouraging our girl here to get drunk tonight?" Tyson asked from the other side of the half circle. He was slouched back with one of his arms up and dangling off the back of his chair. He had one leg up, bent at the knee, and his foot resting on his other knee. He looked utterly relaxed and like he didn't have a care in the world. There was a tiny, secretive smirk on his face aimed at his uncle and his eyes were half-lidded.

I could never pull off such a pose. I was far too uptight and anxious.

Quinton shrugged as my Salt and Pepper twins took seats side by side in between us and Tyson. Both Trenton and Simon moved behind me and a quick glance over my shoulder told me they were stationed behind me like sentries, their backs to me, facing off against anything that would come at me from behind. For once, I wasn't annoyed by their presence and thoroughly appreciated having them standing behind me. With this crowd, there was no telling the kind of trouble that could befall me and I definitely needed someone at my back. Dash took the seat between myself and Addison.

Quinton responded to his nephew, but I ignored them. I ignored them all as I looked throughout the space behind the motel.

It was an odd building with the balcony out front facing the parking spaces. But, maybe that was just a thing with old, cheap buildings that were used as motels. The back of the building was lined up with windows on both floors that had air conditioners hanging out of them. Huh, seemed there was no central air here. The heating probably sucked too.

The entire back of the structure looked like it had recently undergone a makeover. The paint looked the purest of white and fresh. There were immaculate brown shutters on each side of every window that did not jive with the front aesthetics of the place. They were brand spanking new and so was the paint job. It made me wonder, though, why change the entire back of the building but leave the front as it was? I was willing to bet they did it so as not to draw further attention to themselves if someone were to stumble upon this place. If you just happened upon it and saw the front state of things, you'd more than likely keep right on driving because you didn't want to end up murdered in your sleep.

They'd taken very good care to make the backyard space a place you'd actually want to spend time in, and it was pretty.

There was a cute, circular table with chairs on a cement patio tucked up close to the motel. A large, black umbrella hung over it. Fairy lights lit up the underside of the umbrella. It was cute because the table had been covered in a black cloth with silver stars etched into it all over the place. On top of the table was another bouquet of yellow roses. There were glass vials of all sizes scattered around the table and they were filled with liquids that came in a plethora of colors. All of them were vibrant, all of them pretty. Beside the vials were dainty teacups that matched the roses in color.

If I hadn't read about Alice going down the rabbit hole when I was a young girl, I might have actually sat down at that table and tried out the different vials, taste testing with the pretty yellow teacups. Now, I was old enough to know better and wouldn't be ingesting anything the guys didn't ingest first.

Farther back and away from the building was a two seater swing under a canopy. It glided back and forth and at first I didn't recognize the person sitting slumped in the corner on it. It was the auburn hair and her incredibly slight frame that let me know it was her.

The dreaded Annabell.

I was stupid for not even thinking I would see her here when she lived with the damn Council.

Annabell didn't even look in our direction. She tipped her head back against the back of the wooden seat, her hair flying out behind her, and stuck her arms up in the air like she was on a roller coaster ride. The swing wasn't even moving faster than a snail's pace so I didn't understand what in the hell she was doing.

"What's wrong with her?" I asked quietly, interrupting the guys' conversations around me and I nodded my head in Annabell's direction. "She looks insane."

Maybe that wasn't a nice thing to say about her, but it was true for the time being.

"She's probably on drugs," Damien replied in a casual tone. "Or, at least that's what it looks like to me." He shrugged like it meant absolutely nothing to him either way.

Tyson watched my face carefully as he gestured over toward the umbrella covered table. "She could have been drinking that shit this whole time as well. With her, you never know. Drunk, high, it's all the same to her. Either way, she's having a good time over there. The only thing that's missing is the male or males who she's currently got wrapped around her greedy fingers."

Tyson's voice was bland, giving nothing away, and I had to wonder what was going on behind that carefully crafted mask. I knew he loved me something fierce, I knew he hated Annabell even. But I often times wondered what he saw when he looked at her. Did he want to go over there and rescue her from her own stupidity? Was he going to watch over her all night long to make sure she didn't get into trouble or, worse, try to interact with one of our other coven members?

I didn't know the answers to my questions and wasn't entirely sure I wanted them.

"Word of advice, baby," Quinton rumbled from beside me. "Don't go drinking shit from that table or anything from a vial that looks like that. In fact, I think you might actually be better off if you stick to Julian's liquor and call it good at that."

It was almost like he *wanted* me to get drunk or something.

I'd been drunk before but it wasn't something I did often. Vivian had a lot of male suitors who'd come over drunk and mean. Vivian herself had been a mean drunk. I wasn't afraid I would follow in her footsteps. That wasn't why I rarely imbibed. No, that had everything to do with the fact I didn't like feeling out of control and getting drunk always made me feel that way. Not that getting drunk had made me feel out of control, just slow, not always myself and, often times, it made me a whole lot louder than was necessary. That was too close to out of control for my tastes.

A man I didn't recognize walked passed me. He had honey colored eyes and hair to match it. He was so thin he bordered on being frail and I had an urge to find something for him to eat. He stumbled a step when he went to walk by me and caught my eye.

His eyes hurriedly raked over me, only taking pause when they hit my cheek, but that didn't stop them from carrying on with their journey and filling with heat.

The look in his eyes had me immediately breaking eye contact and looking away.

Two seconds later, a nasally male voice from in front of my chair asked, "You're Ariel Kimber, aren't you? The new witch. It seems there are a lot of those popping up lately, but not..."

His words trailed off and I finally turned back to look at him.

He trailed his fingers through the air by my face and I swear I think I heard a groan of appreciation come out of him.

"None of them feel anything quite like you do," he purred. "In fact, I don't think I've ever met a female who felt anything quite like you do, witch or not."

It was official, this rail thin man with the honey colored eyes and matching hair creeped me right the fuck out.

"You're very pretty as well," he murmured, while smiling down at me. "Scar and everything. Though, I imagine that a little plastic surgery could fix that right up for you and make you beautiful instead of just simply pretty."

My boys remained deathly quiet, but the tension was starting to build and I knew if I didn't do something soon to shut this shit down there was going to be a fight on my hands.

I stood up quickly and stuck out my hand. "You know my name," I said in a smooth voice, "but I do not have the pleasure of knowing yours."

He took hold of my hand in his. The smooth, softness of his

hand turned me off in a way I had never experienced before. Heat filled my palm and raced up my arm, but it dulled in comparison to when I touched the guys in my coven.

He lifted my hand to his lips and turned it so he could lay a chaste kiss on top. His overly dry lips left a bad feeling on my skin and I quickly yanked my arm out of his greedy grasp.

"I am Aaron Lemond," he said. "And I am the leader of the Lemond coven."

I nodded like I knew what that meant when I absolutely did not.

I fought the widening of my eyes at what he'd said. Adrian had failed to mention there would be head members here from other coven's. He'd just said Council members, Marcus and other people from covens. I felt like there was a distinct difference and it had been kept from me.

"We do not have a female of our own," Aaron divulged, while leering at me with an almost frenzied look to his eyes. He cradled the hand he'd used to shake mine with up against his chest. "Yet."

I had nothing nice to say to that so I very wisely kept my mouth firmly shut.

He bowed to me from the waist. "I look forward to dinner with you, Ariel."

The way he said my name sent a chill up my spine.

He sounded like he was shopping around and I was something that was up for auction, and that's why he was so looking forward to dinner with me. I wanted to slap that insane, heated look right off of his face.

I slumped back in my chair as I watched him walk away and toward a huddle of men I also did not know and never had met toward the far end of the long table.

"This is my worst nightmare," I groaned as I lowered my face into my hands.

Silence rang out from around my half circle of guys, nobody saying anything.

I didn't think that boded well for me and it was made worse by the fact my guards at my back didn't say anything either, but I felt their tension rising even higher. They were on red alert now and just looking for someone to strike out at.

And the night had only just begun.

# CHAPTER TWENTY-SEVEN

An hour later and two other men had stopped by where I'd been sitting with the guys. They wanted to meet the girl witch who'd just recently dropped into their world, coming seemingly right out of thin air. And they eyed me like starving men and I was their last meal.

I had never been more uncomfortable in my whole life. The only thing that saved me from getting out of my seat and running away was the constant stream of incoming text messages of encouragement from Rain. Even when I didn't respond to him he kept them coming. It was almost like he knew I needed to hear from him in any way that I could. I had never loved him more than I did in that moment.

I couldn't even tell you their names because I had been so freaked out by the looks on their faces that I had sat back in my seat after that, and retreated into the safety of my own mind. Quinton had carried on the conversations for me after that, taking the lead like the good leader I knew him to be.

They all walked away looking amused and way too interested for my liking. They wandered around, talking amongst themselves and other men who had yet to make their approach. The Council members that I had actually met before stood amongst them, holding court and eating up the attention they were getting from the men around them.

Julian had yet to return from his venture inside the motel with Rachel and this was actually the only thing I wasn't concerned about at the moment.

Adrian walked out of a door in the back of the motel and raised his hands high. The sleeves of his hippie shirt fell down to around his elbows as his chubby arms waved around in the air.

"Ladies and gentlemen," he yelled, and a hushed murmur went over the crowd of mostly males. "Dinner is ready to be served. If you would be so kind as to take your seats around the table." Male voices rose around the backyard and Adrian stopped speaking. He watched them all as they seemed to argue amongst themselves about something.

That something I thought they were arguing about was me.

And wasn't that just a joyous thought.

The cell phone in my purse vibrated and I wanted so badly to reach in there and read whatever asinine message Rain had sent to make me feel better. I wanted to lose myself in his world and forget the one I currently occupied.

I did no such thing.

It helped me a great deal to know that he was there and knew what was going on here.

I grabbed Quinton's hand that rested on the arm of his chair. I would have grabbed all their hands if I could.

"Let's go sit down at the big table now before everyone sits down and we are forced to be separated," I suggested.

Quinton stood up with me. The arrogant smirk on his face didn't sit well with me. Then again, nothing tonight did.

He gestured toward the big table, "Lead the way, baby."

I wanted to smack him upside the head. This was not the time for his sweet nicknames.

Instead, I smiled painfully at him and walked toward the table. My silent bodyguards moved like a wall behind me.

Nobody actually sat at it yet and I didn't bother to count the seats.

I'd yet to actually see Marcus who this dinner was actually supposed to be about. These people were serious assholes.

Everyone watched as I picked a seat at the middle of the table and sat down. Addison and Abel walked around to the other side of the table and sat down directly across from me. Tyson and Quinton sat on either side of me. Dash sat beside Tyson, and Julian and Damien sat down beside Quinton. Surprisingly, my bodyguards moved over to the other side of the table and sat down next to the Salt and Pepper twins.

Adrian moved to the head of the table and took a seat with flourish. Marcus was suddenly there beside him, sitting in the seat to Adrian's right. He looked down the table at me and winked. Daniel sat beside Adrian. The rest of the seats quickly filled up.

I looked over my shoulder and back toward the swing. My throat closed up with emotion when I saw Annabell slumped over in a heap, the swing no longer moving. Nobody even glanced in her direction.

What happened to females being precious amongst them?

I turned back around in time to see the oh so lovely Rachel sit down beside Marcus. She turned toward him and leaned in intimately. I jerked my gaze away, not needing to see any more of that. Little Miss Rachel seemed desperate for male contact and any male seemed to work just fine for her. Where had she come from, a convent?

Adrian started speaking once the seats were full around the table and young males, looking around twelve or thirteen, started moving around the table with trays held aloft in their hands. They were wearing plain black, long-sleeved button ups and black dress pants. Their feet were oddly bare.

Ignoring Adrian, I leaned into Quinton and asked, "What the

hell? Where did these kids come from? Do you know who they are?"

Rude to ignore your host, I know, but I didn't give a crap at this point. I was done after people started looking at me like they wanted to eat me alive. In my opinion, they were rude first.

"They're orphans," Quinton whispered back. "The Council takes care of them, acting as their parental figures until they come of age. Then they will be given a choice to stay with the Council or petition to join a coven."

"I'd like to raise a toast," Adrian boomed, drawing my attention back to where he stood at the head of the table.

Everyone, myself included, picked up a glass from the table and that jug of Julian's brew was passed around. I filled my glass to the rim and passed it on to Tyson. If Quinton said it was safe for me to drink and not to worry, then I was taking his word for it. I needed something to take the edge off or I was going to start flipping people off for staring at me.

I raised my glass high along with everyone else.

"To Marcus Cole, our brother finally returned to us. We welcome him to the Council."

People cheered, I wasn't one of them, and glasses were tipped back. I put mine to my lips and drank heavily.

And choked on the toxic taste that I had poured down my throat. It left a trail of fire in its wake. The glass was taken out of my hand by a laughing Quinton and placed on the table. My hand went to my throat as my eyes watered.

Nobody else seemed to be bothered by the taste and I ended up scowling, angry at everyone.

"That tasted like shit," I muttered under my breath, as Marcus gracefully thanked people.

"Have you ever drank before?" Tyson asked in an amused voice.

"Not cat piss," I shot back.

The boys across the table openly snickered at me, but I didn't see any of them drinking from their glasses. I picked mine up and chugged some more of it just to prove that I could do it without choking.

A plate was placed in front of me by a teen boy and I murmured my thanks politely. He grinned down at me mischievously before placing a plate in front of Quinton.

I pushed my plate away, not wishing to eat anything from it until after I saw other people eat first. I was paranoid about everything and that kid smiling at me made me want to be extra cautious with the food. I didn't even see what was on the plate.

People around me began eating as they talked amongst themselves. The boys across from me were all digging into their food like all was right in their world. I tell you, I did not understand boys at all.

Quinton nudged me with his elbow and gestured toward my plate with his fork. "Eat," he ordered. "Eat and maybe they will stop staring at you."

I hadn't noticed people were staring at me anymore, I'd chosen to ignore them since the moment I sat down.

I shrugged before chugging back the rest of the vile poison Julian was passing off as magical alcohol. When the cup was empty, I slammed it down on the table and picked up my fork.

Adrian clinked his fork against his wine glass and the conversation abruptly stopped.

"There is one more thing I'd like to discuss." He smirked at me.

Of course there was one more thing he wanted to discuss. I shiver ran down my spine and I knew I wasn't going to like what he had to say next.

"The Council has never had a female grace its ranks before, and we feel the time has come to change that. We would like to offer you, Ariel Kimber, a place amongst us, and we would be honored if you joined our coven."

Oh, hell no.

My eyes widened in shock as my fork clattered to my plate.

"She's already a member of my coven," Quinton said in a harsh voice. "If you were going to try and poach from me and mine, then you should have had the decency to let me know before you tried to fuck me."

"This is not why I'm here," Aaron called out from farther down the table. "You promised us the opportunity to get to meet her and woo her to see if we could coax her away from them. Now you're asking her to join the Council? What game are you playing here, Adrian?"

My stomach churned at hearing his words.

"Woo me," I choked out in a strangled voice. "Nobody is wooing me or getting the chance to. I have a coven that I belong to and I have no plans on switching. I'm not going anywhere."

"It is an honor to be asked to join the Council," Daniel spoke in an annoyed tone. "Especially since you're a woman and aren't accustomed to our ways just yet. We felt that given enough time and training you could be amongst the best of us. You should be careful and reassess your answer before you so quickly dismiss us."

"Are you threatening me?" I asked in a low voice. The lights above the table flickered as my rage mounted. "How dare you invite me here just to threaten me."

The outrage at my words didn't come like I thought it would. Instead, a hush fell over the table as people sat back, either staring up at the lights in awe or staring at me in much the same way.

"You see," Adrian cried with glee, "this is exactly what I'm talking about. There's so much raw power within her. If harnessed correctly, it could be used in so many different ways. It's glorious just to think about. She belongs amongst us, even if we have no idea of her background or what stock she comes from. She's perfect."

What stock I came from? I shouldn't have been surprised but I was, and, oddly enough, I think my feelings were a little hurt.

"Women aren't allowed on the Council for a reason," someone sitting close to Rachel said, and I turned my hostile glare on them.

He was glaringly bald but had a thick, dark goatee that hung down to his chest. His eyes were so dark brown they were almost black. His septum was pierced through with a hoop that had a ball hanging from it. He'd been one of the ones who'd watched me with naked hunger in his eyes. When he wasn't trying to eat me with his eyes, he was scowling at everyone else and, as far as I had noticed, he hadn't come here with a group like the rest of them. He'd been the only one outside of myself earlier who'd looked unhappy to be here.

"I meant not disrespect to you being a female and all," he told me in a soft, kind voice that didn't match the look in his eyes. "You should be treasured, protected, and taken care of the way we always do with our females. There's a reason we do that too and we all know it. Because of our ancestors we're a cursed lot. We need to make up for it by doing right by our females this time around. If you start to allow them positions on the Council, places of power, then you are potentially exposing them to dangerous situations."

He turned his stare onto Adrian and I swear the temperature dropped fifteen degrees when it did. I was learning I was powerful, but I certainly wasn't the only one.

"Especially now with there being hunters around here. Hunters you've allowed to get close enough to her that they tried to burn down where she lived and attempted to kidnap her roommate. Then they went to where she *works*." He said work like it was a dirty word and shook his head ruefully. "Now you want to make her a Council member? I don't think so. Something stinks here and I'm thinking it's you."

"None of this matters," Quinton said. "If Ariel says right here, right now, that she's sticking with my coven, then that's all there is to it and the rest of you can get fucked."

"Young Alexander—" Adrian started in a bored voice.

I cut him off as I pushed my chair back and stood. "His name is Quinton, not young Alexander, and you know that. You only call him that to get under his skin. Frankly, Adrian, it's childish and I would have thought beneath you. That doesn't matter right now though. What matters is he's right. I will not be joining you or anyone else. Not today, not tomorrow, not six years from now."

His face pinched in an angry frown as his eyes grew mean and I knew our welcome here was about to wear out.

"As I'm sure you're aware," I waved my arm out across the table, including the whole lot of them, "*all* of you are aware by now that my mother," I choked over the word, "wasn't a very good person when she was alive and didn't treat me very well. I've never had a real family or even a home before we moved in with Marcus and he made one for me. Then I met the Alexanders and their family, and by some miracle my family grew even larger. If you think I'd ever simply walk away from that because you want me to, then you haven't been paying enough attention to me in the time you've been given to get to know me. I'm loyal and, now that I have a family to call my own, I'll not turn my back on them. Not for anything."

Before I could sit back down again, Adrian, coughed and fell forward, face first. His face landed in his plate of food and he didn't get back up again.

"Oh my god," I cried out. "Somebody help him."

One by one, all around the table, people started coughing and slumping forward in their seats. The only one who remained sitting upright outside of my coven members and Marcus was the man with the goatee.

And I had no idea what was going on.

# CHAPTER TWENTY-EIGHT

"**W**ell, Raven," Julian drawled, "It looks like it's just you and us, tonight."

"Are they..." I sputtered into the now quiet yard, my voice growing louder and more hysterical with each word. "Are they dead?" I ended on an embarrassing shriek.

The bald man with the goatee, whom I was assuming was this Raven person, sat back in his chair and crossed his arms over his chest.

"Calm down, honey," he said to me in a gentle voice. "I'm sure they aren't all dead."

How could he be so blasé about the whole thing was lost on me.

"None of them are dead," Julian said cheerfully. "Tell me, Raven, what do you have against my magical mix of vodka and hocus pocus? Hmm?"

I gaped at him. "What the hell did you put in that drink, Julian?" I ran my hand up and down the column of my throat and had never been more thankful in my life when the urge to cough didn't come over me. "What's going to happen to the rest of us? I drank that crap as well."

"Yeah, baby, you did," Quinton commented in an amused voice. "You drank the whole damn thing. But you also drank that purple shit he forced on us earlier. You're gonna be just fine."

I sat down in my chair, hard, and flopped back. That was a relief, but...

"And they're not dead, you're sure?" I asked cautiously.

"Nobody's dead, yet."

"We have to hurry," Marcus said as he stood up. "There's only so much time and the motel is big enough that it's going to take a while to search."

"Search for what?" I questioned. "And what are you going to do when they wake up angry and upset because they know you drugged them or whatever it was that you did?"

Now that was a terrifying thought, and the relief I had felt just moments before was gone in an instant. This was one of the worst things that could happen. It was very disturbing to be sitting at a table full of people who were face down in their food and looking dead.

"Why are you all standing around here looking like assholes and why is my daughter still here when she should have been taken home by now?" Rain asked from behind me, and I jumped to my feet and whirled around.

There he stood, with his trench coat flaring out behind him, looking dangerous. I wasn't sure what surprised me more, his sudden appearance or the death grip he had on a scared looking Annabell's bicep. Her feet were dangling in the air, her pretty face turned up to him, and she whimpered.

Rain shook Annabell as if she were a rag doll, making her cry out in pain. For the second time tonight I almost felt sorry for her. Almost.

"I caught this little firecracker trying to make a run for it. Boy does she got a mouth on her." He shook her roughly again. "You can't have any witnesses though. Not to tell the tale when your Council wakes up."

"Rain," Quinton hissed as several of the others cursed under their breath. "You cannot be here right now."

Rain's face went cold, dead, and he threw Annabell down at Quinton's feet. "Don't you dare tell me what I can and cannot do. Not while you're off with my daughter. Scratch that, not ever."

"Quinton," Annabell cried in a pathetic voice. "Help me." She grabbed the front of his jeans and clung to him.

Quinton looked down at her in disgust. "Get your filthy hands off me, Annabell," he snarled, "before I'm forced to remove them myself, and we both know you don't want that."

She jerked away from him and landed sprawled out on her back on the grass, her red hair fanned out all around her. The barely there, teal dress she had on rode high up her thighs, exposing things I did not need to see. It was no surprise to me that Annabell had not worn underwear to this event.

A wave of magic flickered over her face, like a cloud before fizzling out. Her scars were exposed to us all.

"Why do you cover your face up and hide your scars?" Quinton asked in a harsh voice. He raised a finger and pointed harshly at me. "You see our beautiful Ariel? She has a scar on her face and she doesn't hide if from the world and she's never tried to. Then again, she didn't earn hers the way you did."

"I bet *Ariel,*" she sneered my name, "didn't get hers by being viciously attacked by a fucking madman."

"Actually," I put in, "I did. But, unlike you, I was physically attacked. Yours was physical in a sense that you were physically harmed, permanently so, but it's not the same thing at all."

She stared up at me with eyes filled with hate.

"Are you really trying to argue with me right now on whose experience was worse?" she asked incredulously.

I shrugged. I really wasn't trying to argue with her at all. Just stating facts. I didn't think she'd care either way, so I kept my mouth shut.

"I think she wears the mask sometimes because it gives off an air of mystery," Tyson said quietly, as he stepped up to my side. "People find her interesting because of it and they want to know what's really beyond the mask. How much damage is there really? And Annabell likes it because it's Annabell, and the only things she loves more than herself are male attention and power."

There was no sadness, no anger, no nothing in his voice. Tyson sounded completely devoid of emotion, as if he were speaking of something that he cared absolutely nothing about and talking about a complete stranger. There was a time where that would worry me and I'd wonder what he was really feeling in there. That time had long since passed and I knew he really did feel nothing for the woman he'd once loved more than anything.

I wasn't sure if I should feel sad or relieved for him.

"We're going to have to do something with her," Dash said, and there was something in his voice that had me turning to him. There was something a lot like glee mixed with malice on his face. He was enjoying this.

"I've already got that covered," Julian added cheerfully, as he rounded the table. An unconscious Rachel was flung over his shoulder and I was happy to see that her dress hadn't ridden up the same way Annabell's had. Then again, hers was see-through, so she didn't really need it going anywhere to show off her merchandise.

Without preamble, Julian shifted forward and dropped Rachel from his shoulder. She landed on top of Annabell with a sickening thud. Annabell shrieked, and none to nicely shoved Rachel's prone body off of hers.

"Well, that wasn't too nice," I said before turning to Julian. "And here I thought the two of you were friends now."

He grinned at me. "Oh, we got friendly earlier, alright. She told me she's been banging Adrian and she promised to hit on all of us tonight to try and get us to turn away from you. Her parents kept her locked up and hidden from people out of fear of what might possibly happen to her. They died when the hunters raided their house, but they missed her because she was hidden away in their little hidey hole. She's been with the Council ever since, and I'm telling you she is loving all of the attention and promises they are handing over to her. But, she's young and doesn't want to spend the rest of her life with a bunch of old dudes. Adrian promised her she could meet some other covens just to see if she liked something else better, you know, like shopping around."

All of that was really disturbing and made me feel sorry for her when I knew I shouldn't, because she was ready to replace me in a heartbeat if my guys had allowed her to.

"Okay," I replied, as I gestured down toward her body. "But that doesn't mean you should go around abusing her. What happened to treating female witches like the precious treasures you all talk about them being?"

Raven and Marcus moved around the table, joining our little group. Marcus was staring down at the two women with a sad look on his face. Raven, however, was looking back and forth between Rain and myself, likely putting two and two together and getting four. This night just kept getting worse and worse by the second.

I shot a panicked look around and noticed something I missed before. We were missing people. Damien, the twins, and both my bodyguards were missing in action. I whirled around, searching for them, but they were no longer in the backyard.

"Where are—"

"We can't have witnesses for this," Rain interjected. He was eyeballing Raven in a way that said he clearly did not trust him and was willing to do whatever it took to keep his, *our*, secrets safe. Rain's scary side was about to come out to play and I really didn't want to see it. Not with so many other people around who seemed to be fighting off the same thing. I'd seen it in Dash's eyes just minutes ago. The difference between Rain and most people was that they actually tried to fight it. Rain did no such thing.

"I'll take care of this one," Julian said, as he gestured down toward a now quietly crying Annabell. The gleeful tone was gone, replaced by a blankness that had matched Tyson's earlier tone. Julian and I weren't as tight as Tyson and I were, but I knew him well enough to know that he no longer had romantic feelings toward the woman anymore. No, his feelings ran a different sort of way now.

Annabell scrambled backward on her hands in some sort of crab walk, but didn't make it far before she crashed into Dash who'd moved behind her. Her arms went out from under her and her back slammed into the grass.

Julian prowled toward her and kneeled down in the grass beside her. She was sobbing now and quietly begging him to get away from her. Any normal girl and I would have been fighting to get them away from her. With this girl I just didn't give a shit.

Dash held her arms as Julian pried open her mouth. She squealed but didn't fight them off. Her body went limp and she just lay there on the grass looking sad and pathetic. Julian put the jug to her mouth and poured it in there. She tried to spit it out, but he set the jug down in the grass and held her mouth shut while he pinned her nose closed. Her body bucked violently but they both held on tight to her. Eventually, she was forced to swallow the bitter liquid and the whole show started all over again when he put the jug back to her lips a second time.

I turned to Tyson and murmured, "This is familiar."

I'd once watched Tyson pour something down Annabell's throat, only she'd put up a better fight that time. I assumed the potion he'd given her had worked wonders because she had never mentioned it to anyone, and her obsession with him and the others had seemed to have faded away entirely.

Tyson wrapped his arm around my shoulders and I leaned my head on his chest as we both watched the show.

"I'm happy that happened before," he told me. "It worked out well for us. Totally worth it."

"We're okay, right?" I asked in a quiet voice. The timing was completely inappropriate and it made me an a-hole for bringing it up right now, but I didn't care.

I had been caring less and less about a lot of things lately and that thought was kind of terrifying. The more I came into my magic and the life I now lived, was I losing pieces of myself? I sure hoped not. I used to be a nice girl, a sweet girl, and I knew I'd lost a little bit of that, but I never wanted to be someone who just didn't give a crap about everything. I actually liked being nice to people. I didn't want the bad shit that had happened to me to ruin any part of my personality or make me some sort of bitter, angry shrew to the rest of the world.

"We're okay, always," Tyson whispered so that none of the others could hear our conversation. "But, are you good? You look sad all of a sudden."

"I don't want to be a bad person," I told him honestly. "I don't want to look at what's going on with Annabell and know that I don't care that it's happening. Shouldn't I care? Shouldn't I want to try and stop it? What kind of person just doesn't care and sits back and watches? This is the second time I've watched something like this happen to her. I shouldn't care that she's a bad person, a horrible person even. I feel like if I want to be a decent human being and someone I can live with, then I feel like I should care and try to do something to stop it. Yet, here I am, standing beside you and watching the show like everyone else."

Someone cleared their throat, closer to our little bubble than I was expecting, and I looked away from Julian to see that Raven had moved into our personal space and now stood close to Tyson's side, so close they were almost touching. He wasn't looking at Ty though, his eyes were only for me.

I was getting real sick and tired of him watching me like that. At least this time he wasn't watching me like I was his prey. Instead, he appeared to be studying me and he looked confused. At least there was that.

"Do you know why I haven't stepped in to stop this?" he asked me in that sweet voice of his, a voice so at odds with his appearance it wasn't even funny. I didn't want to like anything about him and certainly not something like his voice.

I shook my head. "No," I said, shifting uncomfortably. "Was I supposed to?"

My guys hadn't told me much about the other covens except to tell me about some of the women before. I would like to think that they might have told me the key points if they'd known we were going to be ambushed by them tonight. I thought I might be fooling myself with that one though, because they liked to keep me in the dark as much as possible.

Raven looked away from me as he crossed his thick arms over his chest. He watched as Julian dragged a seemingly unconscious Annabell by her ankles off toward the swing she'd been on earlier when I'd first noticed her.

"She came to *visit* my coven before she went to stay with the one you're with now. I didn't fall for her tricks and knew immediately that I didn't want anything to do with her. Some of my guys fell though, and they fell hard. She does good work, I'll give her that much. She only stayed with us for about two months off and on, and my coven wanted to keep her, like, really keep her and have her join our family. I was opposed to it and tried to warn them off from her. They didn't listen and when the time came to ask her to stay she laughed in their faces."

He turned back to me with gleaming eyes and a look so brutal that I almost took a step back, even when I knew that look had absolutely nothing to do with me.

"You see," he rasped out, "my coven isn't abundantly wealthy. We have money because we work hard for it and have a business we run amongst us. That wasn't good enough for her and she called my coven peasants as she laughed at us. She got them to fall in love with her, tried to manipulate them into doing her bidding and, when they didn't, she laughed in their faces as she broke their hearts. They're so closed off now from people that the thought of inviting someone new into our coven would not go over well amongst them."

I could believe that of Annabell.

Unceremoniously, Julian dropped Annabell onto the swing. Her back landed hard and the side of her head smacked against the wooden arm. She was definitely going to have a lump there tomorrow and a wicked headache. Dash was right behind him with Rachel and he tossed her on to the swing beside Annabell. Rachel's head fell into the other woman's lap as her feet landed on the grass.

I turned away from them.

"Then why are you here?" I asked in an accusing voice. "If you know your coven is so against the idea of someone new, then why are you here? You made it sound like earlier that you're here for me. Why? That makes no sense to me."

"Me either," Tyson said under his breath.

"Because you're different."

"How would you know that?" I shot back.

"Everyone is talking about you," he answered. "Didn't you know that? Adrian has been spreading stories about you far and wide to anyone who will listen. We're just the first of the covens who are going to come and see you, who are going to want more than just to take a peek at you. The way Adrian tells it, you're something incredibly special, the likes of which we've never seen before. He claims you're different because of how you were raised and that because you've been forced to suffer so much abuse that you're a survivor now, and stronger than the rest of our females. He says you're sweet too, not a bitch who demands everything be handed to her on a silver platter like that one over there. He says you're like our women of old before we watched them all die, went into hiding, and everything about our culture changed."

My heart rate sped up the more he spoke. He had to be wrong. There was absolutely no way Adrian had been saying those things to people about me. No fucking way.

"You're lying," I croaked out past a suddenly dry throat.

If he wasn't lying then my life would never be the same again. I'd always be on display, and they'd all come to look at me like I was some kind of freak and they'd all want something from me.

Raven turned his big body to face mine as his hands dropped from his chest down to his sides. Tyson's arm lowered from where it'd been wrapped around me and he moved to stand slightly in front of me, between Raven and myself. I was grateful for his presence and that he'd put himself in the middle.

"I'm not a liar," he said softly," and Adrian, as it turns out, wasn't lying about you either. You are different and special. There's something very refreshing about you and I know if the rest of the others of my coven got to meet you, they would see it right away as well. I'll be sticking around for the next few weeks and I'm going to make it a point to visit with you often. I'm just being honest and putting it out there because I'm not an asshole, and I'm not going to hide anything from you or your current coven. I'm telling you right now, I want you to join my coven and I'm going to put in the effort to get to know you and you to know me, so that you can make an informed decision." He shrugged his thick shoulders. "If, in the end, you say no, I will accept that and hope we can part as friends... Good friends, of course."

He grinned at me, big and slightly manic.

This conversation had taken a turn for the worst and I was done with it.

Rain stepped up behind Raven, his dead eyes filled with rage and a nasty snarl on his face. He raised his hand and plunged the needle in it into the side of Raven's neck. He pushed the plunger down, pulled the needle free, and stepped back.

Raven's eyes rolled back into his head and he went down like a sack of potatoes. Neither Tyson or Rain moved to grab him before he hit the ground.

Marcus moved in to our little huddle and bent over to pick Raven up from under his arms. He dragged him around the side of the table and sat him up on the seat he'd occupied during dinner. Marcus took a step back, and we all stood there in silence as we watched Raven tip to the side and fall to the ground.

Marcus shrugged in a gesture that screamed *what can you do* and walked away.

"This is one of the weirdest nights of my whole life," I groaned, and that was saying something, because there had been several doozies in there.

A commotion at the back of the motel had me turning to face the building in time to see everyone else we were missing come running out.

"We got what we were looking for," Damien said, as he came to a stop in front of the table. He held a stack of papers high and waved it at the rest of us. "Everything on the hunters that they had, we made copies of."

My eyes widened. That wasn't what I had expected them to be looking for. I thought it would be about more women.

"I thought you'd find something on them," Marcus murmured thoughtfully. "Hopefully some of it is useful, and you can find out where they are hiding and if they know anything about Ariel."

"That's what this is about?" I asked on a hysterical laugh. "You could have probably asked Adrian about this and he would have told you. I know he's creepy and an a-hole, but I think he actually takes his role as a Council member seriously. He would have given you the information if you'd asked about it. We didn't need to take it to this extreme."

"Doesn't matter," Quinton said briskly. "It's done and over with now. We're going home and they'll be none the wiser. They'll wake up feeling hungover and thinking they had a good time all night long."

Quinton moved into me, grabbed hold of my arm, and dragged me off around the side of the building. I could feel the rest of the others following behind us.

"What about the boys who'd brought out dinner?" I asked

suspiciously. If he'd done something horrible to those young teenage boys, I was going to punch him in the throat and make him cry like a baby.

"Julian took care of them. They'll be sleeping it off as well."

"And they've not been harmed?" I pushed, for some reason needing to know the answer. They weren't mine, but that didn't mean I couldn't look out for them.

Quinton smiled down at me sweetly. "Raven was right," he stated. "You are definitely different than all the rest of them."

I frowned at him as he dragged me to the car.

What the hell was that supposed to mean?

# CHAPTER TWENTY-NINE

Everyone was tucked away in their own beds and fast asleep. I'd chosen to spend the night alone in my big bed that Quinton had given me. When I'd complained before about waking up alone, I knew that tomorrow would be very different and I would welcome the time to myself. I needed it.

I sat the foot of the bed in my pajama shorts, tank top, and pretty silk robe Dash had given me. I was hunched over with my elbows pressed into my knees, and my head in my hands.

I wasn't upset, but I had too much on my mind for me to be able to sleep. It wouldn't shut off no matter what I tried. I'd stared up at my dreamcatcher, counting sheep and trying to relax. Images ran through my mind, interrupting my counting and making it impossible for me to sleep.

I kept going back to those cards Quinton had read for me and kept getting held up on that stupid fucking Death card. He'd said it wasn't a bad thing and it heralded new beginnings, and that was something I could have gotten on board with a couple of days ago. Now, after the epic failure of a dinner party, I couldn't get behind a new beginning. The thought alone terrified me.

It made me think too much about Adrian sitting there and announcing he wanted to invite me to join him and the rest of the Council. All those eyes watching me with hunger and lust. Rachel blatantly hitting on my men. The Council being responsible for young teenage boys who were probably better off at an orphanage than with those creeps.

So much shit swirled around in my head and, what was worse, I was remembering the feeling of that blade sinking into that hunter's flesh when I'd stabbed him. I'd stabbed someone, happily, and hadn't felt bad when he'd been killed afterwards.

That last part ate at me and had been the real reason I'd crawled out of bed and turned the lights back on.

Chucky had stabbed Dash without a second thought and he'd felt zero remorse for doing so. In fact, I think he'd gotten some sort of sick joy out of it. I'd gotten no joy out of stabbing that hunter, but I had felt a sense of satisfaction, just not in a sick way. Still, shouldn't I feel remorseful?

I sighed loudly as I pushed myself up from the bed.

I paced around the room for a good twenty minutes, beating myself up for something I couldn't take back or seem to change my feelings for, and believe me, I'd tried.

When pacing did absolutely nothing to calm me down, and I realized that despite how exhausted I was there would be no sleep for me tonight, I headed downstairs. With the mood I was in, I hoped everyone else was asleep because I didn't think I'd make good company tonight. Nobody else needed to share in my misery.

The foyer and formal living room were empty. The office was the same. There was sound coming from the kitchen area and I knew the television was on in there.

I thought about turning around and heading right back upstairs, but just thinking about sitting in my quiet room all by myself with only my thoughts to keep me company made my skin itch with the need to move.

Maybe I should take up running. Then I could run, pushing myself to the point of exhaustion. I bet I'd sleep well then. It was too bad the thought of wearing running shoes and, you know, actually *running* really did not appeal to me.

The kitchen was empty, the light off.

The living room was not.

Trenton lay on the leather couch with both his hands tucked behind his head. His feet were crossed at the ankles and he was wearing plain black pajama bottoms and a matching short-sleeved t-shirt.

Only his eyes moved as he tracked my movements.

I sat at the end of the couch, next to his bare feet, and curled my legs into my chest. I wrapped my arms around my legs and rested my chin on top of my knee. I didn't look at him, but could feel him staring at me.

"What are you watching?" I asked, as I kept my gaze trained on the ginormous television mounted to the wall. It was the largest TV I had ever seen in someone's home before. Boys were boys, after all, and they liked their toys. Well, except for Quinton it seemed. The only thing he really, really liked seemed to be being an asshole, books, and me. Though, not exactly in that order. I liked to think I came first.

Trenton cleared his throat before mumbling uncomfortably, "*Gossip Girl.*"

I turned to gape at him in surprise before I burst out into laughter.

This scarred up male who had a vibe about him that said he'd kick your ass if you fucked with him, had dedicated his life to being a badass bodyguard, and knew how to wield a sword like he'd been born to it, was sitting here in the dark watching *Gossip Girl.*

When I finally got my laughter under control, I told him, "I think you and Julian have the potential to be great friends. By chance, do you like the *Titanic*?"

"The movie?" he asked quietly, and I nodded my head. "Never seen it before."

"Hmm..." I murmured noncommittally. In my head, though, I was already planning on having a conversation with Julian so I could set up a torture time for him to watch the movie with Trenton. Don't get me wrong, I liked the movie for the most part, but there had been enough room for the both of them on that raft at the end. There was no reason, outside of Rose being a spoiled brat, for Jack to have turned into a popsicle at the end. I would watch horror movies with Damien all night long before I ever watched that movie with Julian. No, thank you.

If Trenton was a willing enough victim then I would happily throw him under that particular bus.

Someone cleared their throat from behind us. Trenton remained still, only his eyes going behind the couch. I, on the other hand, jumped. I flew to my feet as my hand went to my chest and I whirled around.

Rain stood on the other side of the couch, his arms crossed over his chest, and lips that kept twitching in one corner of his mouth.

"Something funny, Rain?" I inquired in an unfriendly voice. I had no idea how long he'd been standing there spying on us. It was a rude thing to do, but I knew I had no right to be upset about it when there were so many people staying in one house at the moment. Privacy was hard won when you lived with a house full of guys.

"Oh, hey," Simon said, as he strolled around Rain and moved to where his brother's head rested against the arm of the couch. "*Gossip Girl*, hell yes, bro. This is my favorite episode. Shove over so there's room for me. If you want to make popcorn too, you won't hear any complaints from me."

Simon tried to sit down, shoving his brother's head over with his hip, and I eyed them both like they were insane. They might as well have been as far as I was concerned.

The brothers argued playfully amongst themselves. I smiled softly at them before looking back to Rain.

"What are you doing down here, Rain?"

Rain gave me a sad smile, this one the furthest thing from amused I had ever seen.

"I was hoping to find you awake," he told me. "I heard someone moving around up here and hoped to find you. If not in here, I was going to go to your bedroom."

That hadn't really answered my question so I asked, "Why?"

He scratched the back of his neck nervously and suddenly he looked uncomfortable.

"Dad," I said in a quiet voice. "What's going on? Is something wrong with you?"

His face immediately softened and his eyes shined brightly. I watched him blink quickly and knew he was trying to get his emotions under control, taking back the control he always held on tightly to with an iron fist.

Rain cleared his throat as he looked away from me.

That soft look on his face was close to my undoing and I almost sat down on the couch, put my face in my hands, and bawled my eyes out like a baby.

My relationship with Rain was so fucked up, there was never going to be anything normal between us and I hoped we weren't always like this. I didn't care to be normal, I never had. How could I when I grew up with the toxic mess that was Vivian? And I had always been okay with that. I did not want the same for my relationship with Rain. He wasn't toxic like his sister had been, and all he really wanted to do was love me and take care of me. He couldn't help it that he'd gone through hell and back, and it had changed him in reprehensible ways. There was no coming back for Rain, but I was okay with that because we were moving forward, not backward, and we would have to learn how we fit, together, and that would take time.

"Nothing's wrong," he responded in a thick voice. "I was going to show you something I drew up for you and wanted to know if you'd like for me to ink it on you. We can add blood magic to it later to give it a purpose, but you need to have the actual tattoo first for it to be long lasting. Eventually, I'll have to touch it up with magic after I add that component, but you will always carry the tattoo on your body."

I stared up at the man who was my father and my heart filled almost to bursting.

I had to clear my throat twice before I could get out words. "What... what did you draw up? Can I see it before you tattoo it on me?"

There was no question that I was going to let him ink me with what he'd drawn up for me, but that didn't mean I did not want to see it first.

Rain held up a sheet of paper and I moved around the couch as if it had a silent pull that I could not resist even if I tried. I didn't try to resist. My feet moved me over until I stood in front of Rain. I took the piece of paper from his hand and stared down at it.

There was no color except for the black ink, the color of the pen he'd used to draw it up with. It strongly reminded me of the ink drawings Quinton and Tyson had given me of the Tarot cards. It was beautiful.

A sliver of a moon that looked like it was dripping, maybe even bleeding, possibly weeping. There were tiny little stars in the distance. It was simple, yes, but the detail that had been drawn into the moon was what made it beautiful.

I loved it.

"I thought we'd start off with something simple for your first tattoo," Rain explained in a quiet voice. He cleared his throat again. "And... there's also something else, something I want to show you."

Rain pulled up the sleeve of his long, black thermal. He flipped his right arm up, baring the inside of his wrist up to me.

"What?" I inquired in confusion. "What is this?"

"This was my first tattoo," Rain said in a thick voice. "It's the one my father gave me when I was a young boy. He got the same one when he was little. My daughter would have received the same thing had she not been taken from me. Mine has had blood magic mixed with ink tattooed into it for years now. It allows me to see auras and things other people cannot see. If you want, when your tattoo has healed and you're ready for it, I will mix the blood magic in with your tattoo as well for you. That will also allow you to see auras and other things. That is... if you want the tattoo."

My eyes stung with tears and I couldn't stop them when they leaked out of the corners of my eyes. I wasn't embarrassed or ashamed to be crying in front of this man. Instead, my heart was breaking in the best kind of way.

"Can we do it now?" I choked out. "I want to do it now. I don't want to go another day without it. That belongs on me just as much as it belongs on you."

A tear escaped out the corner of my father's eye, trailing slowly down his tanned cheek. He raised a hand to my face and, unlike every other male I knew in my life, he ran the backs of his knuckles down my cheek, the unscarred side.

"It would be my honor," he whispered fiercely.

And, in the next blink of an eye, he turned away from me and was gone.

I stood there in confusion, staring toward the empty doorway, crying uselessly.

Someone touched my shoulder, making me jerk, and I turned to glare at them. Simon stood there looking at me with soft wonder on his face.

"You really were lost to him, weren't you?" he murmured in a soft, gentle voice.

I looked up at him with tears pouring down my cheeks and

said the most honest thing I had said in all my life. "Not lost to him. Stolen."

That sent off a whole new round of tears, and, this time, they weren't happy ones.

They were filled with heartbreak and sorrow.

Not just for me, but for Rain as well.

# CHAPTER THIRTY

I excused myself and ran to the downstairs bathroom in the hallway beside Quinton's office. I needed to shut myself away behind a closed, locked door and put myself back together again before I faced the brothers who'd seen me in such a vulnerable state and crying my eyes out.

Hell, I didn't even think I would be comfortable with all my guys seeing me in such a state. I was a hot mess. Less on the hot side and more so on the mess part.

My hands shook as I turned on the sink faucet. Cold water poured out and I shoved my shaking hands underneath the spray. The freezing cold was a shock to my system that served well to drag me out of my sorrow.

I blinked and the tears stopped as if I had willed them to do so.

I turned off the faucet and slapped my cold, wet hands across my cheeks. The slaps stung, but I was so numb it barely even registered, and the part that did made the pain almost pleasant.

God, I was so fucked up that pain didn't hurt, but ended up feeling oddly good to me.

What was the matter with me? Would I always be this way and would it later affect my everyday life?

I didn't want to think about it.

I gripped my hands on the edge of the sink and stared down at the floor, trying to get my shit together so I could go out there and face my father without breaking down and crying in front of him again.

A light knock sounded on the door and I cursed under my breath as I let go of the sink and took a shuddering breath.

Couldn't they just give me a damn minute to myself?

"Ariel," Trenton called through the door. "I'm not trying to bother you, sugar, but your dad is back and setting everything up in the kitchen. I thought you would want to know that you've got about ten minutes to yourself in there before he comes looking for you. If you need more time than that, you should let me know now so I can run interference for you so you get the time you need."

I had thought I'd been alone, but I was wrong. Trenton had followed me to the bathroom to make sure I was okay because he was my bodyguard and that's what bodyguards do.

For the first time since he and his brother had moved in here and disturbed my life by their arrival, I didn't feel resentful toward the brothers.

He was doing what he'd been raised to do and it was the only thing he knew.

I could understand that and, just this one time, not be resentful toward him for it.

I moved to the door and unlocked it. I opened the door and peeked out at him. He looked down at me with a face full of worry as he stuffed his hands into his jeans pockets.

"It's going to be okay, you know," he promised seriously, as his eyes roamed over my face. "Whatever it is that you need from me, I will give it to you. He's your father and was once my savior. Not just mine but my brother's savior as well. We owe him, always will, but he would want us to look after you before that debt was paid, always. Not that any of that matters when it comes to you, you come first for us. You'll always be the priority for the two of us, no matter what. It's part magic, part just who and what we are. If you want me to tell him to postpone this for a night, I will. And, because he's your father, he'll agree with it."

I stared at him blankly, my tears a long gone memory.

His words were welcome but also unwelcome at the same time. I didn't want to be the thing that came between him and my father. Not when he felt like he owed Rain everything. Not when he clearly respected and adored my father.

I reached up and trailed my finger down the wicked looking scar that ran down his chin, past his jaw, and down the column of his throat. He shivered at the touch, but I was aware it wasn't sexual for either of us. It was more of an understanding.

"You can touch mine too, if you want," I said, as I pointed at the scar on my face. I dropped my hand to point toward my collarbones. "Or, if you'd like, you can touch some of the other ones I have also."

I didn't exactly want him touching me, but felt it was only fair to offer it up to him since I had so brazenly touched the scar on his face and throat. And I had only offered it up because the touch hadn't been sexual.

Trenton's eyes grew cold as he stared at my scars. His mouth twitched before his face turned to stone.

"I'm not going to touch your fucking scars," he whispered in a voice filled with rage. I flinched as if he struck me, but he continued as if he didn't see my reaction to his words. "I'm going to be the reason you do not collect any more. Not ever again."

He pressed his fingertips to my lips before placing them over his chest where his heart was.

"This I promise you," he whispered hoarsely.

I wasn't given the time to respond because he turned his back on me and stalked away toward the kitchen.

I shut the bathroom door and slumped against it.

His words hadn't been a promise, but a vow. To me.

And I'd believed him.

Eight minutes later, I walked into the kitchen with my face clear of tears and the ugly red splotches that crying like a baby had given me.

Trenton's words had calmed me down immensely. I would never point that out to anyone ever though.

Rain had a bunch of stuff I did not understand set out on the kitchen island and was setting up a little gun with a needle on the end of it.

I watched him plug something into the wall and place a pedal on the floor by the stool he'd vacated when he'd stood up to plug the thing into the wall.

"Are you ready for me?" I questioned hesitantly, as I stepped into the room.

Rain glanced over his shoulder, his eyes were lit with a fire I had never seen before and it reinforced what I had already been feeling.

I loved the drawing and I loved that it came from my family line. It made it even better that Rain wanted me to have it too.

Still, it was a tattoo. A permanent mark on my body that I could never get rid of. And I wanted it. I had to remember that I wanted it and forget everything else. All the bullshit, all my feelings, they didn't really matter in this moment and I needed to remember this.

I nodded my head. "I'm ready," I said, as I stepped into the room.

Rain smiled at me before turning back to everything he'd set out on the counter.

I ignored the two brothers as they watched me walk toward the island. I pulled out the stool beside Rain's and sat down.

Rain did something with the machine in his hands before setting it down on the island countertop and turning toward me.

He smiled at me, so full and beautiful that my breath caught in my throat at just the sight of it. It was so pure, so full of happiness and pride, that I was forced to smile back at him.

"How do you want me?" I asked, as I placed my right hand on the island, my wrist aimed up.

"That's good," Rain replied, as he turned his stool around to face mine. "Hold still."

I could do that.

For Rain, I had a feeling I could do anything. All he had to do was ask.

"I have a confession to make though," I murmured quietly.

Rain looked up from what he was doing and eyed me questioningly.

"I don't like needles," I confessed.

His mouth twitched and I grinned at him.

"It's okay though," I assured him. "I just won't look. Maybe this will be better..."

I got up and carried my stool around to the other side of the island and sat down across from him. I thrust my right arm across the counter at him, the inside of my wrist up. I laid my cheek against the counter and stared straight ahead at the refrigerator.

"I'm not going to watch," I informed him "and I think I'll be alright."

"You know it's going to hurt, right?" he asked in an amused voice.

"Yeah," I replied.

When I said no more, he chuckled but got down to business. I closed my eyes as a buzz filled the kitchen.

Rain had been wrong. It stung a bit, but it didn't hurt me.

Then again, pain and I were old friends. I had a feeling we always would be.

It took him a little over an hour to finish. He worked without saying a word and the only sounds to fill the room came from the tattoo gun and *Gossip Girl* on the television.

The end result was awesome, and looked like an exact replica of the one Rain had. He did good work.

I looked up from my wrist to see him watching me with a soft look in his eyes.

"I love it," I told him honestly. A thought occurred to me then, and I smiled big and bright at him. "I bet Quinton yells at me when he finds out."

For some reason, that thought made me incredibly happy.

# Chapter Thirty-One

# QUINTON ALEXANDER

I stood back with my shoulder against the doorjamb, watching.

I had never seen Rain Kimber more at ease than he was now, sitting in my living room watching television with Trenton and his daughter, Ariel. There was something about the brothers that made Rain act like almost a normal human being when he was around them.

At first, this had made me incredibly jealous to witness, but that was no longer the case. I couldn't hate them, no matter how hard I tried. They were orphans, like most of the rest of us. And they'd witnessed their entire coven, along with their parents, being slaughtered by hunters when they were just mere children. Rain had been there like some knight in shining armor to save them when no one else had been able to.

What I had originally mistaken for some sort of hero worship was what I was really jealous of, because I realized what it really was. The brothers had been alone for so long, but the moment they laid eyes on Rain again it had been like coming home after years and years of being gone. It was seeing your family again for the first time in forever, and you'd been desperate and missing their presence, their embrace, for so long that coming home finally was the best feeling in the entire world.

The fact that Rain didn't push them away when he did everyone else, except Ariel was where my jealousy stemmed from, because I knew he, too, considered them to be his family.

Rain had been my family, even if I hadn't wanted him to be, from the moment he walked back into Ariel's life. She was my family and always would be the most important person in it besides Tyson. She came with Rain and, for better or worse, that made him my family and important to me as well, because I knew he was now the most important person in Ariel's life and probably always would be.

Ariel's relationship with her father wasn't one I was jealous of. They were both so horribly broken and sad, and they both worked so hard to hide it from the world around them that you couldn't help but be anything besides ecstatic that they'd found each other once again. Being in each other's lives was the only thing that would ever be able to even partially heal those two, but, no matter how much we all loved them, I didn't think they'd ever be whole.

I was okay with that, just so long as I got to be there and beside the both of them for the rest of their journeys in this world to help make it as peaceful and happy as I could. That's what you did for the people you loved.

Rain was my family and I wanted to be the same for him. It hurt me to watch these two brothers waltz into our lives and receive that honor from him immediately when I was really working hard for it and I thought we were maybe getting somewhere.

As I watched their easy going nature between them, I knew I didn't have it in me to begrudge either Rain or Ariel of their easy relationship with the brothers. I'd give them both anything and everything I had to give, and they never even had to ask for it.

Trenton, the bastard, leaned in next to my girl and said something to her that made her smile and her shoulders shake with laughter.

Rain looked up and toward the doorway, catching my eye. His eyes narrowed on mine and I shook my head. I wasn't here to cause problems and I didn't want the rest of them to notice me.

My eyes went back to Ariel and a small smile curved my lips as I watched her laughing at Trenton. She looked carefree and beautiful. Beautiful, as always.

My heart filled at seeing that smile. A smile from Ariel was a rare thing to behold. A carefree one from her was practically unheard of, and there were very few people who'd ever actually witnessed it.

Trenton and Simon were here to keep her safe, to guard her body from harm, and I was okay with that. If they could make her laugh and smile along the way, make her happier than we already did, then I was more than okay with that as well.

My eyes met Rain's again and there was something in his that I had not seen before when directed at me. Something close to respect.

It wasn't the thing I craved from him the most, but I'd take it and hold it dear like the gift I knew it was.

I turned around and walked away before Ariel noticed me and invited me to join them. I didn't want to join them.

But I would not begrudge the brothers because they'd come into my girl's life now, and it wasn't even because I liked them because I was sure I did not.

No, I couldn't begrudge it because I had a really bad feeling that not only Ariel, but all of us, were going to need them with what was to come.


The End.
    For now.

# THANK YOU & WHAT'S NEXT

Dash's Novella will come next. But... I have had something running around through my mind since starting Black as Midnight and you might just get a Rain Kimber novella in there too before the next full-length novel comes out. I just can't let that manila folder he has go.

Thank you so much for reading my book.

Please, if you enjoyed the book I would really appreciate it if you left a review. Reviews mean everything to us Indie authors.

Want to keep in touch with me? Here are all my links.

Newsletter
Facebook Group
Facebook Author Page

What's up next for me? Well, I have a story called Killing Time in an Anthology that releases this summer.

Love, Loyalty and Mayhem
A Motorcycle Club Romance Anthology

Releases: July 16
Pre-Order: https://books2read.com/LLMAnthology

Bad Boy Alpha Alert!

Nineteen of your favorite MC authors come together to bring you brand new, never released stories from some of your favorite motorcycle clubs.

Love-

Life with a biker is an adventure full of twists and turns. When love is involved, MC men never back down from what they want—they fight for it.

Loyalty-

Loyalty is the foundation in any motorcycle club. Break it, they break you. There isn't a line they won't cross to protect who or what they claim as their own.

Mayhem-

These men live a life made by their own set of rules. Chaos tends to always find them. You cross them, the consequences are swift.

Hold on for the ride as this talented group of authors come together to bring you an anthology like no other.

Your favorite clubs, new clubs, and everything in between can be found in this collection filled with suspense, action, adventure, romance and so much more!

**All profits from the Love, Loyalty & Mayhem: A Motorcycle Club Romance Anthology will be donated to Bikers Against Bullies USA.

BAB USA is a national not-for-profit organization created by bikers to raise awareness and empower the community to fight the terrible effects of bullying on young people through education, community outreach and fundraising.

60448098R00180

Made in the USA
Columbia, SC
16 June 2019